KÁRI THE LUCKY

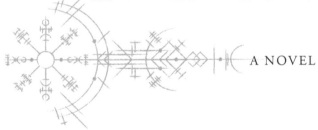

A NOVEL

KNOWLEDGE OF THE TRUTH IS THE FIERCEST REVENGE.

KÁRI THE LUCKY

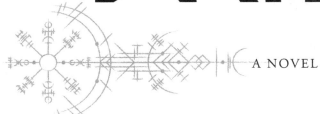

A NOVEL

GORDON BONNET

BESTSELLING AUTHOR OF THE BOUNDARY SOLUTION

TIREE
PRESS

an imprint of
THE OGHMA PRESS

OGHMA

CREATIVE MEDIA

Bentonville, Arkansas • Los Angeles, California
www.oghmacreative.com

Library of Congress Cataloging-in-Publication Data

Names: Bonnet, Gordon, author.

Title: Kári the Lucky/Gordon Bonnet |
Description: First Edition. | Bentonville: Tiree, 2021.
Identifiers: LCCN: | ISBN: 978-1-63373-602-3 (hardcover)
ISBN: 978-1-63373-603-0 (trade paperback) | ISBN: 978-1-63373-604-7 (eBook)
Subjects: | BISAC: FICTION/Historical/Medieval | FICTION/Europe/Scandinavia |
FICTION/Action & Adventure
LC record available at: https://lccn.loc.

Tiree Press hardcover edition October, 2021

Cover & Interior Design by Casey W. Cowan
Editing by Mari Mason & Ginny Turner

Published by Tiree Press, an imprint of The Oghma Press, a subsidiary of The Oghma Book Group.

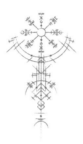

To the memory of the real Kári Solmundarson,
in the hope that he would not be too displeased with the
character he inspired me to create.

ACKNOWLEDGEMENTS

I AM DEEPLY GRATEFUL TO CASEY Cowan of Oghma Creative Media for his continual support and encouragement, and for overseeing the publication of *Kári the Lucky* A sincere thank you as well to my editors, Mari Mason and Virginia Turner, for their sharp eyes and amazing talent at tightening up my writing. I couldn't have done this without both of their support, skill, and expertise.

I would be remiss in not giving my warmest thanks to my inimitable cheerleading squad, who keep me putting words on the page: Andrew Butters, Carla Dugas, K. D. McCrite, Jennifer Gracen, Cly Boehs, and Abby Ives. And last, to my lovely wife, Carol Bloomgarden… thank you for always being there, always believing in me, and always having a hug, a smile, or a glass of red wine ready, and sometimes all three.

The Family of Njál Thorgeirsson

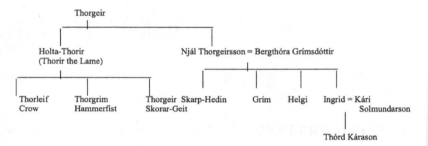

Thorgeir

Holta-Thorir (Thorir the Lame)

Njál Thorgeirsson = Bergthóra Grímsdóttir

Thorleif Crow | Thorgrim Hammerfist | Thorgeir Skorar-Geit | Skarp-Hedin | Grím | Helgi | Ingrid = Kári Solmundarson

Thórd Kárason

The Family of Kári Solmundarson

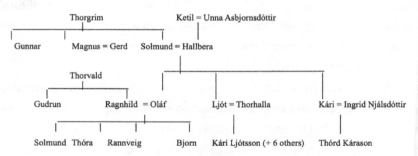

Thorgrim

Ketil = Unna Asbjornsdóttir

Gunnar | Magnus = Gerd | Solmund = Hallbera

Thorvald

Gudrun | Ragnhild = Oláf | Ljót = Thorhalla | Kári = Ingrid Njálsdóttir

Solmund | Thóra | Rannveig | Bjorn | Kári Ljótsson (+ 6 others) | Thórd Kárason

The Family of the Sigfússons

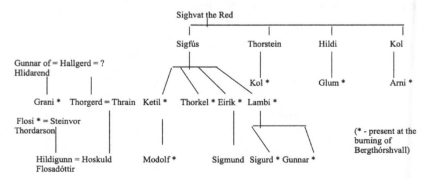

Sighvat the Red

Sigfús | Thorstein | Hildi | Kol

Gunnar of Hlidarend = Hallgerd = ?

Kol * | Glum * | Arni *

Grani * | Thorgerd = Thrain | Ketil * | Thorkel * | Eirík * | Lambi *

Flosi * = Steinvor Thordarson

Hildigunn = Hoskuld Flosadóttir | Modolf * | Sigmund | Sigurd * | Gunnar *

(* - present at the burning of Bergthórshvall)

THE BLOOD-PRICE

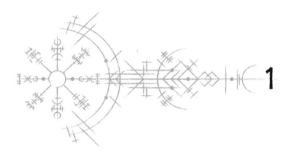

1

IT IS THE END OF AUGUST. I stand on the hilltop looking down at the bay. The wind has freshened and the green sea, which was clear as glass this morning, is now freckled with white. There is a sting in the evening air telling me summer is almost gone. The breeze catches my cloak and makes it curl and snap around my legs. It has a chill to it that was not there even two weeks ago, when I arrived here in Iceland. The frost in the night air has turned the tufts of grass among the rocks to russet and bronze. The gulls are leaving, crying dismally as they dip and sail. They know that the winter storms will not be long. Somehow, they always know.

The ship was being readied and fitted out with supplies. The small figures of the crew moved in the distance, loading up the water and food casks, the sail tightly wrapped. Soon, it will be catching this chill wind and taking me away from Iceland, away from the part of the world I know. Perhaps I will never return, but who knows? Stranger things have happened to me in this life. In truth, the strangest thing of all is that I should be setting sail for Rome with Flosi Thórdarson. The irony is so great that I do not know whether to laugh or to weep. I suppose that it matters little which I do, for either way it will not change the outcome. Everything is nearly ready. Tomorrow, or at the latest the day after, we will set sail—Flosi and I.

My name is Kári Solmundarson. In the past thirty years—ever since

I became entangled with the Njálssons and their troubles—I have found myself pulled from place to place, unable to rest. I look upon the few short years before my wife died as being like a dream, a sweet dream that dissolves upon waking. Afterwards, there is only the wandering, cold and alone, with one purpose in life. Until, at last, the memory of the dream itself begins to fade.

I thought that coming—"home" almost slips from my lips, but Iceland is not my home and never shall be—here, to Iceland, would finally put an end to the knotted skein of death and lies in which I have been caught. Perhaps I felt that coming back here, and finishing what I had started, would give me peace and allow me to relinquish my burdens, but I have found that it was not so. Maybe the old stories about the fates running a man's life are correct after all, and it is my fate to remain snarled until my death.

This afternoon I found a bright lad, living in the care of the priests at Hvitaness, who knows his letters and can commit this story to paper before I am gone, and it is too late. But for what purpose? To ease my troubled conscience, perhaps, so that those who come after may know that I was not wholly responsible for the fate of the Njálssons and Sigfússons. In my heart I know there is another reason, however, and that is my true reason for telling this tale.

I would see this story set down as a warning. There is much evil in this world—some straight and obvious, some covert. I have been responsible for evil deeds, I admit, to my lasting shame, but at least I may say that I have never done evil by stealth and deceit. If I must die for my sins, that shall be my last cry—that there was another, who by cunning and malice began the avalanche that has destroyed us all. It is no excuse for what I have done, but at least it is an explanation. Perhaps I have paid for some of my sins by bringing him to justice. I will let the holy men in Rome decide if I have balanced my accounts.

What terrible deeds have I done that have led me to take such a voyage? More than I wish to recall. For now, it is enough to say that I promised myself never to rest until they were all dead—the ones responsible for taking away the only people whom I ever really loved. I have traveled all over the known world trying to accomplish that one aim—to Scotland, Iceland, Wales, the Orkneys, the Hebrides, Norway. Now I am taking one more voyage. That it will be my last I neither fear nor doubt. I am now fifty-one years, an old man as it is reckoned, and Flosi is even older than I.

So, the ship is being made ready. It is Flosi's ship and has seen many a voyage. Now it will see one more. My friend, Thorfinn Karlsefni, who has traveled widely and is wise in the matters of ships and the sea, has told us that it is not seaworthy. He fears that we will be lost. Flosi just smiled in his melancholy way, and said, "It is good enough to carry a couple of doomed old men."

Karlsefni shook his head, and said, "Well, at least you have Kári Solmundarson with you. He was born lucky. He has escaped fire and swords. Perhaps the sea will have no claim on him as well."

Lucky. I am sick unto death of that word. When I was young, I felt invincible, that death could not touch me, and time and again I came near to dying and have survived. People called me 'Kári the Lucky', and said that God took special care of me. They envied me for it. As I grew older, I continued to outwit death again and again. At first, I too considered myself lucky to have cheated it for so long. But now, as I grow old, I wonder—is it possible to be too lucky? Am I truly lucky to have outlived friend, foe, and family? To have no one, no home to return to, no loving wife to share a bed with, no sons growing to manhood and daughters to womanhood, to take my place when I am gone? Is *that* lucky?

I should not question fate. There is no point in it. I have done what I have done, and I ask for no sympathy. There is no one to give it to me, in any case. No one but Flosi, and, despite the renewal of our friendship, we still worry one another like two tree branches in a windstorm, scraping and creaking against each other until the bark is scraped from the white bones underneath.

Perhaps there is no point in recording this story, either, but I will do it nonetheless. The sun is going down. The days are already getting shorter, the nights cooler. We shall go into Flosi's house, the priest's boy from Hvitaness and I, and he shall record for me what has brought me here to Iceland, at the end of my days, looking out over the seas toward Rome. I shall instruct him to have the priest bind it and keep it in his household. Perhaps there may be someone who shall read this—a year, a hundred years, a thousand years hence? They shall be the judge, those who come after, of whether I was a good man, wise or a fool, a doer of evil or a righter of wrongs. As I stand here, watching the white-flecked sea swinging against the rocks, I myself do not know which of those things I really am. Upon my honor, before the old gods and the new, I swear that I do not know.

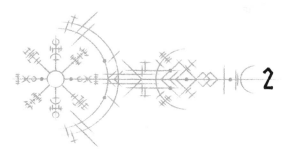

2

I WAS BORN IN THE HEBRIDES, the youngest son of Solmund Thor-grímsson and Hallbera Ketilsdóttir. My father owned much land, where he raised sheep for wool and meat. Although my father was not of high birth, my mother was descended from Jarl Rognvald of Mœr, one of the first Or-kney Jarls. Considering her family lineage, and her beauty and intelligence, many men felt that my mother had made an unfortunate marriage, but I never heard that she was unhappy with her choice.

My father had many men who worked for him. On the whole, he was thought to be a fair man, although a silent one, a shrewd bargainer and a little suspicious of men not known to him. I speak only from what I have heard—for myself, I do not much remember him, as he was frequently gone, bringing cargoes of fine wool and dried meat to other settlements in the Hebrides. When he was gone, he left the care of the farm in the hands of my oldest brother, Oláf. It was Oláf who taught me what I know of fighting, and from him I learned to enjoy physical combat. When my father was at home, and Oláf was freer to enjoy himself, we would race along the seashore, wrestling in the sand, or stage mock sword fights with pieces of driftwood. Oláf was heavier built than I was, and, because of this, he often won in wrestling contests. In sword fights, however, I was far nimbler than he and usually succeeded in jabbing him in the chest with my stick before he could land a single blow.

I recall one time—I was about twelve years old, and Oláf was perhaps seventeen—when a sharp edge of the stick I was holding gave him a great scratch across the chest. He yelped like a kicked dog, and immediately declared himself defeated and killed. He sat down on the rocks, and stripped off his shirt, touching with amazement the long red line across his heart, which ended in a string of tiny beads of scarlet blood.

"If that had been a real sword, I would be lying dead in a pool of my own blood," he told me ruefully.

"I didn't mean to strike so hard."

"It is only a scratch. But truthfully, you could one day make a living swinging a sword."

I stared at him, wide-eyed. "I have no wish to be a Viking."

"There are other uses for swords than in the hands of Vikings. Perhaps, when you are grown, the Jarl of Orkney could use your skills. He is always looking for warriors." Oláf pulled his shirt back over his head and stood up.

"I don't want to go to Orkney either."

Oláf looked at me sidewise. "You can't mean that you wish to stay here." He said the word "here" with a twist of his mouth, as if it tasted bad.

"Why wouldn't I?"

He picked up a rock and threw it out into the sea. It skipped across the water, leaving a string of little marks on the surface, like the line of blood droplets that my stick had drawn across Oláf's chest. Without answering, he started walking back toward our home.

I jogged after him. "Would you leave if you could?"

"It's pointless to talk about it," he said. His voice still sounded bitter, entirely unlike the light, friendly voice to which I was accustomed.

For some reason, I persisted. "Oláf, do you not want to stay here?"

He swung around on me, his eyes blazing. "Does it matter? Father expects me to. When he is gone, I will run the farm. Caring for sheep." He spat out the words. "I have no choice in the matter. You and Ljót may go where you please when you are grown, to live the life you choose. But the farm is to be mine."

I felt sickened, even though I was not the real target of his anger. I had never seen him really angry before, and it frightened me. I tried to protest. "Oláf, you don't..." But that was as far as I got. Without warning he lashed out and struck me in the face with his fist, as hard as he could. The blow knocked me to the ground and stunned me. I remember looking up at the sun, wavering and watery through the tears that came whether I willed them or not. By the time I sat up, he had already gone.

OLÁF NEVER SPOKE TO ME ABOUT what had happened between us. I wore a blackened bruise on my left cheekbone for two weeks, but did not mention it, as I had no wish to be thought a child, whining about every scratch and bump, nor to give my brother trouble over an issue that so obviously caused him pain. As for my parents, my mother surely noticed the bruise, and assumed that I had gotten it playing. My father said nothing and probably did not notice it at all.

It was early winter of that same year that I received a second blow, not from someone's fist, but from fate—perhaps the first tug of that fate which has propelled me ever since. I can recall the day like it was yesterday, even now. I was helping my middle brother, Ljót, with bringing the animals into their pens for the evening. I remember that Ljót was in a lighthearted mood and was singing some ribald song he had learned from the crewmen of one of our father's ships. We were both laughing about it when Oláf came in.

We knew immediately by his appearance that something was wrong. Oláf had long waves of red-brown hair, and although we all tied back our hair when we worked, as was the custom, tonight his fell loose and tangled to his shoulders. He had very fair skin, like my mother, but that day, his face was white, white as chalk, and it seemed to shine like a ghost's face in the dim evening light. His clothes were wet and streaked with mud.

"Ljót," he said, and his voice cracked. "Kári. You must come. Now."

Ljót's laughter died on his lips. He latched the gate and looked up at our brother. "What has happened?"

"Father is dead," he said simply, and then could say no more. He turned and walked back to the house.

Only Ljót wept openly as we approached the door. He was never ashamed to show his feelings, whatever they were, and cared little what others thought of him for that. Oláf, always anxious to be seen as a man, was striving to keep his tears back.

As for me, what did I feel? I hardly knew. I did not feel like crying, that was certain. It was not that I cared if others saw me. My father was dead, and I only twelve. Surely if I wept, it was understandable, and no one could find fault for it. But the truth is, all I felt was confusion. It mystified me that Oláf and Ljót were grieving for our father. Grieve for him? I hardly knew him. I felt I had been told of a stranger's death. I wondered then if they perhaps had known him better than I, but I still do not know if that was so. At the time, the most I felt was pity for my father, and especially for my brothers, who seemed so distraught. I felt no sadness for myself, only a dazed wondering as to how our lives would change now that he was gone.

We entered the house, first Oláf, then Ljót, then myself.

My father was lying on his back on the floor. They had covered him with a fine wool blanket and folded his hands across his chest. His face, always so distant and preoccupied in life, now seemed both pitiable and unreachable. My mother was kneeling next to him, her face in her hands. She was not crying—not yet—simply kneeling, as motionless as if she had been turned to stone. My mother's mother, Unna Asbjornsdóttir, stood behind her, with one brown, gnarled hand on her shoulder.

"Hallbera," said my grandmother quietly. "Your sons."

My mother looked up, and her hands dropped limply to her sides. I think that I have never seen anyone look so stricken. Her beautiful, liquid blue eyes had gone empty and despairing, and she looked from one of us to the other, as if hoping that someone would tell her that this horrible thing had not happened. In that moment, I realized that she had really loved my strange, distant father, and wondered if perhaps I shouldn't have tried to know him better myself.

"Ljót, Kári." She pronounced each of our names carefully. "Your father..." She swallowed, and then continued. "Today, while he was seeing to the loading of a boat at the bay below Kolness, he was taken with a sudden pain, and cried out. Your brother..." All of us looked at Oláf, who was himself staring at the still form of our father, his eyes wide in his pale face. My mother's tears brimmed over, and she could not continue. My grandmother patted her shoulder.

Oláf continued from where she had left off, keeping his voice steady with an effort. "I was next to him when he fell. We were standing in the surf when the fit came on him. He pitched face down into the water. I dragged him out, the other men did not realize what had happened. I think they thought that he had lost his footing and had fallen. I pulled him out and laid him on his back on the beach. The others came crowding around, but it was too late." Oláf turned his gaze on our mother and was silent. Even at my young age, I recognized that at that moment, Oláf had stepped into manhood.

Finally, he said, in a quiet but intense voice, "Mother, what must I do now?"

Our mother looked at him, and seemed to draw herself together, as if she knew that her duties must outweigh her grief. "We must prepare for your father's funeral."

Oláf our mother, and grandmother cleaned my father's body. They dressed him in his finest clothes—a smooth white linen shirt with a carved seal-ivory fastener and embroidered wool leggings. Night though it was, Ljót and I were sent around to tell my father's relatives and workers what had happened.

I almost envied Oláf's job. It seemed the job of a man. What Ljót and I did could easily have been done by a couple of servant boys, but we did it without complaining. My mother was already burdened enough, and our complaints about doing what needed to be done would only have made her lot more difficult. In the end, Ljót went to tell my father's workmen and their families, and I went to tell my father's two brothers.

It was fortunate that the moon was risen, or I would have had to take a lamp with me to see my way. But, it was a clear night, the moon just past full, and it scattered a pale silver light over the hills. It was frosty, and crystals sparkled on every grass stem, reflecting the moon's glow from a thousand brilliant facets. I ran along the path over the ridge of hills which separated my father's land from that of his brothers.

I went first to the house of my father's youngest brother, Magnus Thorgrímsson. My uncle Magnus was always kind to me—kinder, really, than my father was, because he actually took the time to talk to me and listen to what I said in response. What he said today, however, mystified me.

I found him eating his evening meal. His wife, Gerd, and their two daughters were serving him and their son as I entered. "Uncle Magnus," I said, a little breathlessly. "I have ill news from my mother."

Magnus and the others in the room all fell silent and turned their heads as one to look at me. I have always been plain of speech, and I did not know how to say it other than plainly.

"Uncle, my father is dead. He was taken with a fit this afternoon while loading his ship and was gone before anyone could reach him. My mother and grandmother ask that you come as soon as you can." Everyone remained frozen, except for Gerd, whose hand went to her mouth, although she did not utter a word.

I do not know what I expected Magnus to say. Some word about his brother, perhaps, or an exclamation of grief. What he finally said seemed to make no sense at all. He spoke quietly, his eyes focused on mine. "I wonder when the bird will find his wings, now that the cage door has been left open?"

I stood, looking at him in confusion for a moment, but he said nothing further. Gerd and their eldest daughter had begun to weep softly. There seemed nothing more to be said, and I left silently.

From there, I went to the house of my other uncle, Gunnar Thorgrímsson. Just as Oláf, Ljót, and I were all different, my father and his two brothers were different—my father strange and solemn, Magnus kind and generous, and Gunnar hard-handed and swift to anger. I had no real desire to go to Gunnar's house, as all I had ever received there were cuffs and reprimands. However, it was my duty to tell him, and tell him I did.

Gunnar's wife had died young, and he was childless. I always thought that no child would have been welcome in that house in any case and would have had nothing to look forward to but blows and abuse. I found him inside, mending a net, and he glared at me when I entered his door.

I told him why I had come. He looked as if he didn't completely believe me. His face—with its long, thin-lipped mouth that looked to have been cut with a chisel—hardened, and his eyes narrowed as they stared at me. I think he was trying to convince himself that I was lying, and that he should beat the lie out of me.

In the end, he simply said, "Tell Hallbera I shall come," and setting down his net, he stood and left the room.

I returned home. The sky was a smooth black, pierced with thousands of frosty stars, and as I topped the ridge I saw the moon hanging above the horizon, its reflection like a shimmering path on the wavering surface of the sea. The path seemed to call to me. It was a strange thought. I had never seriously considered leaving my home island before. I had pictured myself as an adult, going on shipping voyages, much as my father had done, but always returning to our island afterwards. The thought of actually going to another place and not returning was a wholly new idea.

I wonder when the bird will find his wings, now that the cage door has been left open. What could that possibly mean? The more I thought about it, the more I realized that the bird must be one of my brothers or myself. But which of us, and where did he think we might fly?

By the time I returned, Oláf, my mother, and my grandmother had set up the vigil around my father's body. They had combed his hair and smoothed it down over his shoulders, arraying him with such finery as he had. A silver arm ring that had belonged to his grandfather, who had it of a Viking he had once done a favor for. His knife with the handle of polished deer antler lay on his chest. A simple beaten silver ring was on the index finger of his left hand. Oláf was seated next to him, dressed in his best clothing, his face solemn. My mother and grandmother were on the other side, similarly attired. Ljót had not yet returned, and all three looked up when I entered.

My mother said, in a calm, emotionless voice, "Kári, you must take your place here. Change your clothes and join us."

I went to the place in the house where I slept, stripping off my work clothes. I dressed in my best linen shirt and wool leggings. With my fingers, I clumsily attempted to pull the snarls out of my hair. When I was done, I returned, and joined the others by my father's body.

We spent the night there. My brother joined us, then my uncles. There we sat, in a grim dark circle around my father until morning came. I must have slept, because when I heard my grandmother's voice say, "Hallbera, the morning has come. It is time," I started and looked around me. Everyone there stirred, blinked, and seemed to wake from whatever half-sleep they were in. As remembrance of why we were gathered there flooded back upon us, every face showed grief—except perhaps Gunnar, who was glancing from face to face with his characteristic tight-lipped distaste.

I remember little about the days that followed. My father was laid in the house for three days, during which time no work could be done except what was necessary to feed ourselves and our animals. Even my father's workmen were allowed to be idle, and I was grieved to see that several of them seemed to be glad of it despite the reason. After that time, all of my father's male relatives worked to build his burial mound. It was lined with stone, and my father was laid upon a stone platform in the center, then a stone wall was raised around the sides, and a low roof of flat stones covered it up. I looked down into it, at my father's still face, as Oláf and I placed the last stone onto the roof, closing him in. I knew that it would be the last time I ever saw my father's face. I felt as if I, not him, were being shut into that tiny stone chamber, and a sensation of choking came over me. I almost cried out, "Perhaps he is not dead! Perhaps he is only sleeping! What are we doing to him?" But I thought of all that had happened—Oláf's strange leap into manhood, my mother's silent grief, Gunnar's chilly acquiescence of joining us, the endless vigil in the dark around my father's body, my uncle Magnus's remark about caged birds flying, flying away. The sensation passed, and I remained silent. We began laying strips of turf over the stones, and when we were finished, there was nothing but a gentle mound, a new swell in the ripple of island hills behind our home.

We brushed the dirt from our hands, preparing to return to the house for the funeral feast, which my mother, my grandmother, and Aunt Gerd and her daughters had made. I watched Oláf, leading the way, and I realized that in three short days, he had gone from being a seventeen-year-old child to being a seventeen-year-old man. Something in his bearing was different—a heaviness in his step, as if he were only now recognizing the burden of duty, but along with it, a determination to live up to his own expectations. I watched him with some degree of astonishment, wondering that someone I had known so well could change so quickly. Then, without warning, my uncle Magnus clapped me on the shoulder.

"It won't be long for you, Kári Fairhair." He often called me this, as I alone in my family have very light-colored hair, and Magnus liked to tease me for it.

"What won't, Uncle?"

He nodded toward Oláf. "You will be a man soon, too. It won't happen for you like it did for your brother. But because of that, you will be freer. Don't waste it."

I still didn't completely understand, but I looked at him, nodded, and didn't reply.

"Youngest brothers, like you and I, are usually thought unfortunate," he went on, after a time. "The best share of the money and land and family name doesn't go to them. At the funeral feast, Oláf will be asked if he is willing to accept you and Ljót into his household."

I was surprised, as I had never heard of this tradition. "What if he refuses?"

Magnus smiled. His was the first smile I'd seen since my father died. "Do you really fear that Oláf would do that? I have never heard of a brother who refused, regardless of any bad feelings in the family. Such a man would find himself alone. No one would help out someone who had refused his own kin. So, don't fear the outcome. But it does make your position plain as the younger brothers."

"What do you mean?"

"You were all part of your father's household, all equal. Now you and Ljót are members of your brother's household, and he is above you." He thought for a moment, and I realized much the same thing must have happened to him when my grandfather died. After a moment, he added, "That all sounds unfortunate, does it not? But there are advantages."

"What kind of advantages?" I was beginning to feel that my lot was to be dismal and was eager to hear anything encouraging he might have to say.

"I said that the best share of the land and money would not come to you. But neither will the best share of the responsibility and duty. The farm will be Oláf's to run, not yours."

"What will I do then, when I become a man?"

He shrugged. "That is it exactly. You are free to do what you wish. If you wish to stay here in the Hebrides, you certainly should do so. There is good blood between you and Oláf, and that is not always so between brothers." He cast a wry glance at Gunnar, who was ahead of us, staring straight ahead with his narrow gaze. "Oláf would welcome your help to run the farm, I think, should you choose to stay. But I think you will not. There is too much of the adventurer in you, Kári. Ljót is different. He needs no excitement. He may still leave, but it would be for different reasons. Knowing him, a handsome woman on another island, most likely. As for you, you have a wandering heart. I have watched you—one youngest brother looking after the welfare of another, you might say—and I have known that for a long time. As long as your father was alive, you would not have left, but now? I feel sure that the first adventure that comes your way will sweep you from your feet and carry you far away."

"You were a youngest brother, yet you stayed here," I pointed out.

"Yes." He gave a little laugh. "But I am not the adventurer you are."

"I've never thought about adventure," I said truthfully.

"Your body has. I've watched you and Oláf with your mock sword fights. Your hands and feet know what to do. Your body knows better than your mind sometimes. Listen to it." He smiled. "I've heard it said that you were born lucky. Remember that. Grab your luck with both hands and fly with it."

I looked up at the cloudless blue sky, heard the gulls' piercing cries as they soared over the sea, unseen in the distance. "I don't feel lucky today. I feel confused."

"That's because you're trying to think too much. Thinking has never been your best ability. Your skills lie elsewhere—fighting, running, wrestling. Your skills are in your body. In a few years, you may find that your body has a couple of other skills you've only dreamed about." He made an obscene gesture and laughed.

My cheeks went scarlet, and Magnus laughed louder. Gunnar turned a quick, disapproving glare at us, and then seeing it was his brother who had laughed, just as quickly faced forward again.

"Save your blushes for the young women," Magnus said, still chuckling. He clapped me on the back again. "There will be plenty of them."

———

THE FUNERAL FEAST WAS LAVISH, WITH roast mutton, fresh fish, stew made with dried fish, onions, and wild herbs, and loaves of oat bread. There were bottles of mead, which my father had saved for special feast days. I wondered if it had ever occurred to him he might be hoarding them away for his own funeral feast.

Oláf performed the ritual flawlessly, draining a wooden cup filled with mead, breaking the cup and tossing the broken pieces into the fire, and then moving to our father's seat. His face was solemn and determined. As the oldest man of the household, the duty of overseeing it now fell onto his shoulders, and it was clear he intended to fill our father's shoes to the best of his ability.

Our mother now deferred to him—it was strange to see it done so, as if their roles in one fleeting moment had been turned on their heads. The feast had nearly been concluded when my grandmother nodded toward Ljót and I, and asked Oláf what he "meant to do" about us.

I immediately pricked up my ears. Magnus had said this would happen. However, the question seemed to puzzle Oláf, and Ljót seemed alarmed. I wondered if I might be the only one of the three who knew what was happening. "Do about them? What do you mean, Grandmother?"

She looked at our mother and smiled a little. "You are now the master of this household, and it is your place to ask them to stay if you desire it."

"Of course, I desire it," said Oláf, as if the thought had never occurred to him. It probably hadn't. "Where else would they go?"

"Your father's brothers might take them. It is for you to decide."

Gunnar and Magnus exchanged glances. Magnus seemed pleased, I think, but Gunnar's face was pinched and sour.

Ljót and I also looked at each other. I could tell that he was thinking, not Gunnar, no, please, not Gunnar, with his evil countenance and hard fists. I wanted to reassure him that he need not fear our being put out, but I knew I must remain silent.

Then Oláf said, "I need their help, and all of your help. I have no wish to break with my brothers."

A wave of relief went around the room, although not unexpected, I would guess.

"Although you won't have their help long, Oláf," said my grandmother. "There's Viking blood in us. In Viking families, younger brothers have a way of going a-wandering."

"Not I, Grandmother," said Ljót quickly. "I have no wish to leave."

Several glances turned in my direction, to see if I would add my agreement to what Ljót had said or not. I simply looked back at them without answering. Indeed, what could I, a boy of twelve, say with assurance? I was too young to know my own heart. But truly, I wondered—if my grandmother had said that four days ago, before my father's death and that odd, strangely exciting conversation with Magnus, would I have spoken the same as Ljót had, and as quickly? Undoubtedly so. But now, I was not sure. In the end, I said nothing, and eventually the conversation began again. Only Magnus gave me a small, secret smile before returning to speaking to my mother about the management of the household.

I spent the remainder of the feast in silence, thinking.

I began to see a cage where I had seen none before. And I, too, wondered when the bird would find his wings, now that the door was opened.

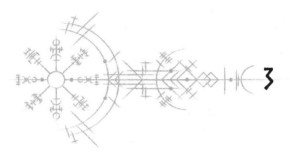

IT WAS SHORTLY AFTER MY FATHER'S death that my brothers and I were looking through some of my father's possessions. He had been a man of few needs, and luxurious clothing and jewelry were something he neither wanted nor could afford. Other than his tools and various pieces of plain clothing, all he had was a wooden chest.

This chest was kept in a corner of the house. It was usually buried beneath piles of woolen cloth, skins, and other oddments, and to my knowledge my father never opened it. We were forbidden to touch it, and none of us knew anything more than that it contained various possessions of my father's which were seldom needed but were too precious to discard.

Now that my father was dead, Oláf decided the time had come to go through the contents of the chest. We gathered in the dimly lit corner, pulled the metal hasp, and lifted the lid.

I do not know what I thought would be within. Surely not gold or jewelry, knowing my father's simple ways. As we peered down into it, a smell of dust and long-trapped air struck me, and I wondered how many long years it had been since it had been opened.

The chest was less than half full. In fact, upon looking more closely, we saw that it contained only three things. One of them was a neatly-folded stack of finely embroidered clothing. On top was a shirt that was so ornate

I could not imagine my father wearing it. The second was a heavy silver torque, a beautiful piece of work, but once again so elegant that my father surely never wore it.

The third was a sword.

To my astonishment, I reached past Oláf and Ljót and lifted it out. As the youngest brother, it was not my place to do so, but I could not stop myself. I drew it from its sheath. It was tarnished, but was a fine weapon, light and well-balanced. Even in my inexperience I recognized that much. How my father had come by it, I didn't know and still don't know. I doubt my father ever had occasion to use it. While on his ship-voyages, he carried with him a long knife, which had many uses and was not as cumbersome as a sword, but I never heard that he had occasion to use a sword for fighting. Frankly, it was hard to picture him doing so.

Oláf and Ljót watched me, kneeling on the floor with the sword in my hand, my eyes traveling eagerly up and down the long, slender blade. I looked up, as if noticing them for the first time, and the impropriety of my having taken it before Oláf washed over me. I expected him to reproach me, but his face was rather sad.

"It sits well in your hand, Kári. I don't know if that is good or bad fortune for you. Of the three of us, you are the one who will need the use of it, I think."

So, my father's sword became mine. That day, I cleaned and polished it carefully until it shone, and then returned it to my father's wooden chest. Afterwards, I used it daily, although in practice rather than in combat, fighting imagined foes and wondering what it would be like if they were real men. Still, over the next few years I grew to know its feel and its balance as if it were part of my own body. And, as Magnus had predicted, my desire to leave our island and go to a place where I might put the sword to use grew daily as well.

FOR SEVEN YEARS I REMAINED IN my brother's household, helping in any way I could. Now that Oláf had taken our father's place, he was frequently gone as our father had been, seeing to the transporting and sale of wool and meat to the neighboring islands. When I was sixteen,

Oláf married Ragnhild Thorvaldsdóttir, the daughter of a local family with whom my mother was friendly. Ragnhild was a sweet girl, rather shy and quiet, but she suited Oláf well.

During those years, Oláf was happy for my help, and I for my part seemed blessed with an inordinate good fortune. When I was seventeen, there was a winter storm that washed away the base of one of the low cliffs on the south side of the island. I was overseeing the gathering together of a part of our flock that had strayed into that area with some animals from a neighboring farm. I was urging the shepherd boys to move the animals along quickly when part of the cliffside collapsed. Two shepherds and twelve sheep were killed—none of them ours. Our shepherd boys passed the story that I had foreseen the collapse of the cliff and had saved their lives and the lives of our animals. In honesty, I was simply trying to get a dull job over with quickly. This event reinforced my nickname of 'Kári the Lucky', and at the time, I relished the idea that the gods might be smiling on me. It boded well for my future—the thought of which was never far from my mind.

As for Ljót, he and I worked side by side happily until one day Ljót accompanied Oláf on board ship, to bring a cargo of wool to the island of Saudey, which lies to the south of our home island. They were gone for twelve days—much longer than usual for such a voyage—and Oláf came back without Ljót.

Oláf was clearly furious with our brother when he returned. This was so unlike his usually calm disposition that I was not inclined to question him about it until the fires had died down somewhat. I gathered that Ljót would not be coming back, but whether because he and Oláf had quarreled, or for some other reason, I could not fathom.

It was some days before I finally got the answer out of Oláf, and it turned out that my uncle Magnus had foreseen it with a seer's accuracy when he spoke to me after my father's burial. Ljót had fallen headlong in love with the daughter of the chieftain on Saudey, and apparently the young woman felt the same way about him. The chieftain, however, did not fancy his daughter married to the middle son of a dead sheep farmer from another island, with no name or money or land to his credit, and refused to allow Ljót to see her.

I knew my brother Ljót's buoyant personality. By this point in the story, I could predict what happened next well enough.

"Ljót found a way to stay behind, thinking that given enough time, he could win her father's approval."

"You've said it, Kári." Oláf's face was still flushed with anger. "I tried to talk sense into him, but he can be as stubborn as an overworked cart horse when he has the mind to. I would have had to force him onto the ship, and what would have been the point of that?"

"No point," I said. "Although I hope for his sake that he is not foolish enough to ignore her father's wishes and have her to bed in any case."

"It would not surprise me," said Oláf darkly. "He thinks he can do as he pleases, and that there will be no consequences." He became thoughtful for a moment. "Odd how you were born lucky and seem not to know it, and he was born unlucky and seems not to know it."

"And what about you, Oláf?" I asked. "How were you born?"

He raised an eyebrow and looked at me wryly. "I was born unlucky," he said. "But I know it."

LJÓT NEVER DID COME BACK. HE was still on Saudey when I left the Hebrides, waiting patiently for his chieftain's daughter. It was not until I returned many years later that I learned of the outcome.

The following year, Oláf and Ragnhild had their first child, a son, whom they named Solmund Oláfsson. It pleased my vanity that Solmund was born with the same flaxen hair as me, and people immediately said how the child was "handsome like his Uncle Kári." He showed every sign of being a strong, healthy child, and my brother was obviously delighted with him.

In some subtle way, however, Solmund's birth made my position in the household even more awkward. With every step, Oláf was moving away from me. First as the head of the household, then as a married man, and now as a father with a son to take his place after him. He was growing to be less and less like the amiable older brother I had known as a child. Each time, I felt more uncomfortable staying in his house, which was steadily seeming less like my childhood home and more like the home of friendly strangers.

***

When I was nineteen years old, there came word that Jarl Sigurd Hlodvisson of the Orkneys was sending his men around the islands to collect tribute. The Jarl of the Hebrides, Gilli Klapa, had been late in sending the tribute due. Sigurd, never a man to forget about the payment of a debt, decided to see to it that it was paid and paid quickly.

Jarl Sigurd and Jarl Gilli were on friendly terms, although each regarded the other with a fair amount of suspicion. Gilli was a fat man with a loud voice and bad stomach, frequently imagining plots on his wealth, jarldom, and life.

Since Sigurd was more powerful than Gilli, there was a rivalry between them which concerned Gilli much more than it did Sigurd. Jarl Gilli was suspicious of everyone, even his own family, but he looked upon anyone with ties to the Orkneys with double suspicion. Now, a number of Hebridean families have Orkney blood. In fact, we ourselves are cousins of Jarl Sigurd himself through my mother's family. So, when Sigurd's men showed up on Gilli's doorstep looking for the missing tribute, Gilli sent them to us, and to other families with Orkney ties. Better to bleed dry his rival's allies than his own.

Oláf welcomed Jarl Sigurd's men into our home with courtesy, but the talk quickly came down to how much we were to give over in wool, meat, and so on. From what was said, my brother clearly thought—and I agreed—that Jarl Sigurd simply wanted what was due him and did not wish to leave hardship and hard feelings behind. My brother and the Jarl's men dickered for a time, but finally came to an agreement regarding what was fair. Afterwards, there was eating and drinking, as it was mid-day, and everyone was hungry. Ragnhild and my mother served the men with the best we could provide.

I, for my part, remained silent, looking at these men who came from so far away. My heart stirred at the thought of following them. Magnus always said I was waiting for an adventure to carry me away—I felt it then, that something in me yearned to cross the seas and find whatever awaited me. But it was not my part to speak up, nor, I thought, would the Jarl's men take an unknown boy with them for no reason other than his desire.

Once again, my luck was with me, although at first it seemed the opposite.

One of the Jarl's men had indulged in one too many cups of strong mead, and was growing loud and boastful, taunting and needling Oláf and the rest of us.

"Seeing this desolate sheepfold makes me double glad I don't live here," he said, refilling his cup.

"Be silent, Asbjorn," said the leader, a man named Egil Skaptason, who seemed to me to be a good man—intelligent, direct, and quick of speech. "You do a discourtesy to folk who have treated us with nothing but honor."

Asbjorn laughed contemptuously. "Honor out of fear, perhaps. Had we treated them less courteously, what would they do? Get their sheep to attack us?"

One or two of the other men laughed, and my face flushed with anger at the treatment of my household. Yet I knew it was not my place to speak if Oláf did not, so I restrained myself.

Egil glared at Asbjorn. "I ask your forgiveness," Egil said to Oláf, who sat stiffly but silent at the head of the table. "It is the mead which speaks for him. You need not trouble yourself for your honor's sake."

Again, Asbjorn laughed. "Trouble himself? Neither his troubles nor his honor would last long. A shepherd's crook against a sword. Which will win?"

At this, my wrath boiled over, and I could no longer remain silent. "You are not the only one who can handle a sword," I shouted, leaping to my feet, "and with your leader's permission, I will prove it to you."

Asbjorn turned, as if noticing me for the first time, and gave me an ugly grin. "I need no permission to teach a churl a lesson. Although it may be your last."

Oláf went white, but he did not dare interfere. Asbjorn was clearly a dangerous man, and I was furious. I am certain he also felt the disdainful sting of the other man's words, and perhaps he was glad that I had spoken.

I strode to the wooden chest that had belonged to my father, opened it, and withdrew the sword. With the care I had given it, it shone as if new. It was truly a beautiful thing. Egil's eyebrows went up slightly, but he said nothing.

"I would not stain my brother's house with your blood," I said to Asbjorn, trying to give my voice a confidence I was not sure I felt. "Let us go outside, and we will see who will learn a lesson."

Egil seemed angered, although whether at myself or at Asbjorn, or both,

I did not know. Still, such disputes are not uncommon, and he did nothing to stand in our way. Oláf followed us, but Ragnhild stayed inside with little Solmund, weeping with fear of seeing me killed.

Asbjorn was a big man, heavier and stronger than I. His long sandy hair was plaited on both sides of his head, and he wore a heavy leather vest that would protect his upper body. I knew that my hope lay in speed and accuracy. With his strength, he would need no more than one stroke to land. We faced each other for a moment on the rocky ground in front of my brother's house. All was silent but the wind, which lifted my hair and sighed in my ears. I had only time to think that it might well be my last time to hear it when Asbjorn attacked.

Gripping his heavy sword with both hands, he came towards me, bellowing with rage. He swung with all his strength at my head, trying to cleave my skull in two. I could not hope to parry such a blow. I stepped sideways, and his swing went wild. At the same time, I turned and swung my sword in a backhanded arc, upwards and out. The point of my blade caught him along the back of his right arm, but it merely grazed the skin.

Insignificant though it was, the cut infuriated Asbjorn, and he rounded on me, quicker than I thought he was capable of with his extra weight and the extra mead he had drunk. He swung at my legs, hoping to sweep them out from under my body. I leapt up over the blade's pass, and it whistled harmlessly beneath me. I heard his comrades laughing.

Asbjorn looked at me with some amazement, but it was clear that he was also ready to be done with this.

"Fine dancing," he snarled at me. "Try dancing the same step over your own guts." And, for a third time, he swung his blade at me, trying to slice across my midsection.

I stepped back to avoid the blow, which would certainly have killed me, but I caught my heel on a stone, and fell over onto my back. I heard Oláf cry out in dismay, but then Asbjorn was upon me, grinning hideously and swinging downward with a blow that would have split my head in two. At the last moment, I rolled aside, and his sword point drove into the ground. As he was pulling it out, I rolled over and slashed upward at the inside of his leg.

The blow landed, and my blade bit deeply. Within a second his leg was drenched with blood. Asbjorn howled and went down onto one knee, catching at his wounded leg with one hand. His sword dropped onto the ground. I bounced to my feet, standing behind him, my sword still in my hand, stained scarlet all along one edge.

Asbjorn was clearly seriously wounded. He was white in the face and panting. He turned his head to look at me, and the contempt was still clear in his face, but he couldn't stand up. I looked around at the men who were watching, uncertain of what I should do. Oláf was pale and tense. Egil's face was taut, one eyebrow raised slightly, and the other men's expressions varied from interest to approval to boredom. Asbjorn himself was glaring at me, his teeth drawn back into a snarl of disdain. Then Egil's gray eyes met mine.

"Finish him off," Egil said dispassionately.

Asbjorn turned and looked with dawning amazement at his superior. "He dares not," he said, his voice strained.

I lifted my sword and struck off his head.

The circle of men erupted in shouts. Oláf came quickly forward, clapping me on the back. I feared at first that Jarl Sigurd's men were angry at the death of their comrade, but they seemed, on the whole, to approve of what had happened. I had killed one of them, but they apparently considered that it was with ample provocation.

I stood, looking at Asbjorn's body. I felt no remorse at having killed him, only a kind of hot glee that set fire to my veins. I stooped and wiped the blood off of my sword on the hem of Asbjorn's cloak.

Egil came up to me, looking at me appraisingly with his clear gray eyes.

"You have deprived me of one of my men," he said, his voice stern.

I bristled. "He insulted the honor of my family. I could do no different."

"Perhaps it was your brother's place to settle questions of honor." Egil's voice was steady, without the disdain of Asbjorn's taunts, but I felt that I was once again on the defense.

"My brother is responsible for his family and for the rest of this household. Had I been killed, it would have been less of a hardship."

"That may be. But nonetheless, it was not your place to defend the family's honor, but your brother's."

I looked at Oláf, who was standing aside, watching us intently. "I have no wish to brag," I said quietly. "But he lacks the skill."

One of Egil's eyebrows went up, and he smiled slightly. "You handle a sword well for your age, to have come through such a fight without losing any blood. But do not deny that luck served you well." He paused. "I do not yet know your name."

I glanced around me. All of those present were once again watching me intently, their expressions much as they had been before, during the sword fight. I suddenly realized that this was a battle, as much as my fight with Asbjorn had been, but a battle fought with words instead of swords. Egil, however, was a far worthier adversary, and more dangerous as well.

"My name is Kári Solmundarson."

"Well, Kári Solmundarson, however the matter of honor stands, you have deprived me of one of my men, as I said before. Asbjorn was a loudmouth and a braggart, but he was a good swordsman and knew much about sailing. His loss will be heavy on us. How do you intend to repay me that?"

Oláf stepped forward. "We can pay his blood price..." he began, but Egil cut him off with an impatient gesture of his hand.

"With your permission, I am speaking to Kári now," he said to Oláf. "It was your place to defend your family's honor, but your brother has taken that place from you. Now that he has killed a man, it is for him to answer for the loss."

I looked around at them all—first at Egil's men, then at Egil himself, watching me with no discernible emotion on his clean-cut, handsome face. I then looked at Oláf, and at Ragnhild, who was watching from the doorstep, with little flaxen-haired Solmund in her arms. Suddenly my heart blazed within me, spilling fire into my blood, and my words came out before I had even thought about them.

"Take me with you in his place."

Egil frowned. "A callow boy, to replace a seasoned sailor and swordsman?"

I met his level gaze, and suddenly, strangely, I felt like laughing aloud. "I can learn sailing. As for sword fighting, was Asbjorn not killed by the edge of my own blade?"

Egil's frown vanished, and he once again gave me his little smile. "It is well spoken. I will speak to your brother about it, if that is your desire."

"It is."

"A trade of one man for another. An interesting idea. Jarl Sigurd will be pleased, I think." He then directed his men to see to Asbjorn's burial. He and Oláf went together back into the house.

MY BROTHER AND EGIL SKAPTASON MADE arrangements for my departure. It was agreed that if I were to give good service to Jarl Sigurd for two years, and Oláf would contribute two extra bales of raw wool above the tribute due both this year and next year, the blood price for Asbjorn's death would be considered paid. Asbjorn had no near kin in the Hebrides or Orkneys, and therefore there was no blood feud to be resolved. Egil was eager to do his job and be gone. He had no wish to place the matter before the Jarl Gilli and the Assembly, waiting for a decision to be made. In any case, Gilli would likely not take great interest in an affair that was between our family, for whom he had little love, and the Jarl of Orkney.

That evening, my brother and I sat together in the house talking. Seeing that our house was too small to comfortably house them all, Egil and his men had courteously chosen to make camp on the beach. Oláf and I bade them good night and made our way back to the house. Once inside, we lit oil lamps and stayed up long past the time everyone else had retired. We both realized it might be the last time we would have a chance to speak together alone.

"Are you truly resolved to go to Orkney with these men and serve Jarl Sigurd?" asked Oláf.

"I am."

There was a pause, and there were no sounds except the tiny snores of Solmund, asleep under a soft woolen blanket. Finally, Oláf spoke. "Your challenge of Asbjorn. It was bravely done."

"I did not think about being brave. I acted purely out of anger."

Oláf gave me a thoughtful look. "You may wish to keep your anger under closer control with these Orkney men. You have killed one of them and have come off well enough. Should it happen again, I wonder if you will be so lucky."

I shrugged. "Egil Skaptason seems a fair man."

"So he seems to me," answered Oláf. "But his fairness may end if he loses another man. Simply be careful, brother."

"I will."

Again, there was a pause. The flame of the oil lamps flickered in the draft, and made strange, misshapen shadows dance and leer across the ceiling.

"Will you not change your mind?" Oláf said, with sudden vehemence. He spoke louder than perhaps he had intended. Solmund stirred, moaned softly, and then resumed snoring.

"Do you wish me to stay here so much?"

He sighed, and his voice became quiet once more. "I only wish you to stay if it is your wish as well. I knew we would part one day, but I did not realize it would be so soon. I have a feeling that I shall never see you again, Kári." He stared into the flames of the lamp. "I am no seer, but I am as certain of it as I am that you and I are here together."

"If what you say is so, can we change our fates?"

He looked up. "No, I suppose not. The gods know I would change mine if I could, despite all I have to be thankful for."

I was touched by the intense sadness in his voice. "What is it you wish for, Oláf?"

"I wish I was free, as you and Ljót are. I was angry with Ljót for chasing after his chieftain's daughter, but half of my anger was because he was free to do it and I was not. He has no responsibility, no farm to come back and manage. If he wants to do something—even if it is something foolish—he can simply do it. And you are the same, Kári, following your heart wherever it takes you."

"You are not happy here?" I wondered if he would rage at me even for asking the question, as he had when we were children, but all he did was smile sadly.

"In truth, I don't know. I have everything that a man should need to make him happy, and yet it seems that it is not enough." He looked up at me, and his face was all quiet resignation. That in itself seemed sadder to me than if he had shouted out his anger. "It is my fate to be what I am, and it is yours to be what you are. If I seem to envy you, it is not because I am angry at you, but because I grieve for my own lot."

———

THAT NIGHT, OLÁF ASKED IF I wished to change my mind, but in the end, I was not given time to do so, even had that been my intent. Egil and his men intended to leave at daybreak the following morning, and I had only enough time to gather together my few meager possessions. I bundled together my clothes and strapped my sword to my belt. I would have to count on any other needs being provided by my new lord, Jarl Sigurd Hlodvisson.

That morning, I stood on the beach, watching Egil and his men prepare to row out to where the ship was anchored. Oláf, Ragnhild, and Solmund came out to see me go, and also my uncle Magnus. Uncle Gunnar was absent, which I both expected and felt grateful for.

Ragnhild was weeping, and I thought that Oláf was near tears himself. It was a bright, cool morning, with the wind in the west. Everywhere one looked there was green and blue and white, such a brilliance of color that it dazzled the eye. I felt I should be sad for leaving, but my excitement overtopped any fear or regret at my decision. It seemed that my life was opening up before me.

Uncle Magnus seemed almost as excited as I was. "Grab your luck, and fly, fledgling!" He gave me a grin. "Fly where you will."

I embraced him, and then Ragnhild. I tousled Solmund's fine flaxen hair and was rewarded with a toothless smile. Last, I embraced Oláf.

"You are doing what you wanted," he said. "Don't ever forget what a gift that is."

One of Egil's men called to me from where he stood in the prow of the skiff, beckoning with his hand. I clasped Oláf's arm. "Farewell, brother," I said, and then turned, wading through the calf-deep surf to where the skiff was waiting.

Two oarsmen rowed the skiff out to the waiting ship, and we all clambered aboard, drawing the skiff up behind us. I turned and looked back at the beach, already grown to no more than a narrow tan border between the green hills and the blue surf. My family were tiny figures which raised their hands in a final farewell. Then the ship's anchor was drawn up, the sail billowed out, and within minutes we had rounded the headland at Kolness.

It took no more than fifteen minutes to leave behind everything I had ever known.

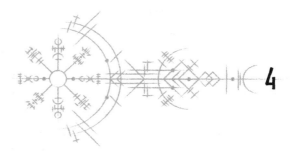

I HAD BEEN ABOARD SOME OF the flat-bottomed ships my father
and brother had used for transporting wool and meat among the neighboring islands, but until this time I had never before been on a real longship,
such as were used by the Vikings in their raids, wars, and explorations. The
smell of the sea was intoxicating as we threaded our way among the countless little islands of the Hebrides, stopping every so often to collect more
tribute for Jarl Sigurd. The coast of Scotland was green and misty to our
right, and we stayed well away from it. The Scots were unpredictable, hostile
one moment and friendly the next. At one point, however, we had no choice
but to come nearer to the coast. We were passing through a narrow strait,
with a Hebridean island shore on our left side and Scotland on our right,
only a little farther than a long bowshot away. Egil had us take in the sail and
row, hugging the shore of the island, where there lived many men who owed
allegiance to Jarl Gilli Klapa, and who were friendly to Jarl Sigurd. Warriors
or no, we did not trust the Scots and had no wish to find ourselves in a battle
of one ship against many.

Soon, however, we came into open waters, with nothing but sea as far
as my eyes could reach. We hoisted the sail once again, and the wind carried
us, our prow slicing through the water. I, for one, was happy about this. I
had thought that farm work was hard, and considered myself strong and fit,

but navigating the strait had seemed to last a lifetime. Rowing for hours was exhausting, leaving my hands blistered and my arms as weak as wet thread. I watched the other men around me, rowing tirelessly and singing all the while, and marveled at their strength.

I was concerned at first that the fact that I had killed one of their comrades, and then had been welcomed aboard the ship by their leader, would cause bad feelings towards me. I wished to be accepted as part of the crew, as one of Jarl Sigurd's men, as quickly as possible. As it fell out, I had nothing to worry about. I soon discovered that Asbjorn had been roundly disliked. Even among these tough, hard-fisted and battle-scarred men, Asbjorn had been considered a boor and a lout, given to sounding his own virtues and scorning all others. The general feeling was that if I hadn't killed him, someone else soon would have, and there was much admiration for the skill I had shown in the fight. As a result, I was welcomed as a comrade sooner than I had expected, and without any struggle at all. Once more, my luck had blessed me.

Within three days we came once more in sight of land—a distant, rocky headland, very far to our right, almost lost in the mist. Egil told me this was the north coast of Scotland, and we were about halfway to Orkney. I felt as if the world was expanding as I moved. I had never dreamed it was so large, I, for whom a two-day voyage to one of our neighboring islands had seemed long. We were covering vast distances, and yet, to hear the men talk, it was only a tiny fraction of the whole world. There were men here who had been to Iceland, Norway, Denmark, Wales, Greenland. One man, a one-eyed veteran over twice my age, even spoke of having led Viking raids in Normandy, which he claimed—and at the time I hardly believed him—was a land that lay on the other side of Scotland, Wales, and England, and across more sea to the south. My imagination was overtopped with the size of a world grander than anything I could have conceived.

That day, it began to rain—a steady, hissing drizzle that soaked us all to the skin. It was midsummer and still reasonably warm, but with the wind, and being burdened with several pounds of sodden, dripping clothing, it was still uncomfortable and unpleasant. The rain lasted for almost a day and a half without letting up. By the time a weak, watery sun broke out at noon of the following day, we were all chilled and cheerless despite the double ration of mead that Egil had seen fit to dispense.

"Better than the storms you'll see in winter," said a tall man named Eyjolf, who had bright copper-colored hair unlike anything I'd seen before. Eyjolf had been one of the first to welcome me, and in the days that followed, we had become friends. "Wind that can flip a vessel and sink it and black waves taller than the mast."

"Do you venture overseas in such weather?" I hoped that my voice simply sounded curious, rather than apprehensive.

"If Jarl Sigurd wants us to go, we go," Eyjolf answered with a shrug.

By the morning of the next day, we began to encounter small islands, which I was told were the outlying islands of the Orkney chain. Most of these were only inhabited in summer, when men would bring over flocks of sheep for the good pasturage, but the sweep of the winter storms made them inhospitable places at any other time. The water became shallower, with dangerous shoals just below the water's surface. I began to be able to recognize these from a distance by the way the waves broke over them. Egil soon discovered that my eyesight was far better than that of most of his men.

We came into the harbor of Orkney under full sail the afternoon of the following day and anchored some way out. Men were left behind to unload the ship, but Egil, I, and a few others of higher rank left the ship immediately to meet with Jarl Sigurd.

"I must tell him of the successful completion of our voyage, and you must be presented to him," Egil said. "It would be better if you did not speak unless he speaks to you. Jarl Sigurd is a hard man, but a fair one. He has little tolerance for garrulousness. Also, if he asks you a question, answer him honestly, and do not evade or lie. Of course, I do not think that is your way in any case."

Clustered along the shore of the harbor were a number of buildings, of finer construction than any I had ever seen. Men and women were at work among the buildings and on the shore—some cleaning and salting fish and hanging them to dry, others mending nets, and a group of men repairing the bottom of a damaged boat. We passed all of this activity without stopping, heading for the largest building in the group.

A tall man, finely dressed, stood outside of the door, holding a long spear. Egil approached him.

"We have returned, Thormod," Egil said. "Is Jarl Sigurd within?"

Thormod stepped aside. "He is."

Egil and the others led the way into the dim interior of the house. As the lowest both in age and rank, I entered last, but Egil motioned me forward to stand nearer to him. I looked around the room. It was plain and dimly lit, with a table, several benches, and various assorted oddments as you would find in such a hall—plates with the remains of the midday meal, a cloak that someone had left behind, a short knife, a tool for mending nets.

Other than ourselves, there was only one other person in the room. Sitting in an elegantly carved wooden chair against the far wall was Jarl Sigurd Hlodvisson.

He must have heard of our arrival and come inside to wait. I could not imagine this man sitting inside a dark house out of sheer idleness. Every part of him radiated an intense energy that seemed to fill the room. I have never seen a man who was so obviously accustomed to action than Sigurd was. He was taller than myself by several inches—and I am judged tall—and far broader of shoulder. Even through his shirt, his powerful musculature was obvious. His fingers were constantly in motion, flexing and drumming against his leg, as if anxious to pull an oar or swing a sword. He had straight sandy hair that fell to his shoulders, and a short-cropped mustache and beard. His skin was weathered by the salt air, but his eyes were a bright blue and glittered with a restless intelligence that I would soon find was, like his body, seldom at rest.

I could hardly imagine anyone more different from the fat, dyspeptic Jarl Gilli Klapa of the Hebrides.

At first, I thought that Jarl Sigurd did not recognize that there was a newcomer among his men. Had I known him better, I would have realized that little escaped his notice.

Initially, the talk was of the voyage and its purpose, as well as about plans for the future, of which I understood little at that time.

"You have collected all of the tribute due us from the Hebrides?"

"I have," answered Egil. "And met with no trouble."

"Did Gilli Klapa send his greetings?"

Egil smiled slightly. "Only with grunts and groans and sly words about selecting which of his people should provide the greatest share of the tribute. He thought to tax most heavily those he likes the least, but fortunately he left the collecting up to us. We saw to it that it was done fairly."

"That is good. I am glad you have returned quickly. It is in my mind that there may be trouble elsewhere before the year is up. My steward in the east of Scotland, Havard Arnljótsson, has sent word that the Scots are beginning to show signs of massing men near his settlements, and he fears an attack before this year is out. I wish to pull together as many men as we can spare to drive the Scots back, and teach their King Kenneth a lesson, before the winter storms set in. I will lead, but I want you in charge of assembling our men."

"I can have them outfitted and ready to sail within a week."

"Excellent."

"Now, Egil, tell me—who is this young colt who is pawing the ground behind you? I don't recognize him."

I had been fidgeting slightly as we stood there, out of a combination of boredom and nervousness, and had thought that I had gone unmarked. Now I froze, looking into Jarl Sigurd's bright blue eyes, which seemed to bore into me, reading my thoughts.

Egil motioned me forward. "He is Kári Solmundarson, a man from the southern Hebrides, the brother of a landholder from whom we were collecting tribute. One of our men, Asbjorn Kolbeinsson, gave the family brag and insult—" here Sigurd snorted, and his mouth grew wry "—and Kári challenged him to back his words with his sword. They fought, and Asbjorn was killed."

Jarl Sigurd regarded me in an amused way. "And so, Egil, instead of running the young fool through then and there, you have brought him back here for me to do it myself?"

I do not know if I truly believed that he was going to kill me, but my body stiffened, and I held my head up proudly. "I am indeed part of Asbjorn's blood price, Jarl. If you have no better use for me than to dull your sword edge against, then I must be content."

Egil gave me a sidewise glare, and I fell silent.

"I decided, Jarl, that this young man might well do to replace Asbjorn, when he has learned something of sailing, and something of following the advice of those who know more than he does—" he gave me another quick frown "—and so I took him as part of the blood-price for Asbjorn's death, along with a double payment of wool for the next two years from his brother's household. Kári has agreed to serve you well for two years, and I have given him my word that at that time, the blood-price will be considered as paid. I need only your agreement, and we can look upon the matter as finished."

Again, Sigurd gave me an appraising look, and then turned his gaze back on Egil. "I would not have you go back on your word. He may stay. Let him prove himself when we go to Scotland."

After this, the talk was all of the upcoming voyage to Scotland, and the plans for the attack. I understood little of it, having no knowledge either of tactics nor of the places and people who were mentioned. Still, I tried to remain attentive, knowing that even though Jarl Sigurd seemed to take no notice of me, he was aware of everything that went on in the room.

The following week was a strange mixture of excitement and boredom. I attempted to help out with whatever I could—fitting out ships with supplies, sharpening swords, running messages—but in truth, there was little enough to fill the long summer days, and my skills in most of what needed to be done were meager. As a result, much of my time was spent in idleness. I found that Eyjolf, my copper-haired companion of the previous voyage, was to be coming along, which cheered me.

Also, to come along were three brothers from Iceland, who were guests at Jarl Sigurd's court—Skarp-Hedin, Grím, and Helgi Njálsson. The three Njálssons had gone abroad seeking adventure, and had found favor with Jarl Sigurd, as they had great courage and prowess. I was impressed with them at once, both for their confidence and forthrightness, and also for the great devotion they had for each other. I was told that they had each sworn to never accept a favor that was denied to one of them, and to defend each other to the death. In the week before we sailed, I spent much time with them, and found that I was very quickly looked upon as a friend.

Skarp-Hedin, the oldest of them, was also the biggest, almost as powerfully built as Jarl Sigurd, but a little shorter. He had curling chestnut-brown hair and sharp blue eyes. His appearance was marred by crooked teeth and a long, jagged scar that ran from the corner of his mouth to the angle of his jaw on the left side, but he was nevertheless every inch the warrior. Grím, the middle brother, was the smallest, with dark hair and eyes. He seldom spoke, but when he did it was worth listening. He was intelligent and capable, and the best swordsman of the three. Helgi, the youngest, had a curling mane of sandy hair, and was quick to laugh and quick to anger. He seemed the most excited about the upcoming fight and talked about nothing but sailing and Scotland and sword fights.

Twelve ships sailed on the expedition a week after my arrival in Orkney, and Skarp-Hedin saw to it that I was on the same one as the Njálssons. By chance, Eyjolf was also aboard the same vessel. The voyage seemed to me shorter than the first one had been. Only a little over two weeks had passed since I had left the Hebrides, but already I was in the company of men who knew me and recognized my value. The fact that I was given tasks to do, and treated as one of Sigurd's men, made the time pass quickly. I was posted as lookout, and twice sighted ships before anyone else had seen them, even though our vessel was third back from the lead. Each time, the strange ships vanished into coves and inlets on the coast of Scotland before we could pursue them.

Within a few days, we had reached the mouth of a great river, and into this we sailed. Great rocky, treeless hills rose on either side of the river. Even in my inexperience, I realized immediately that there were any number of places where an enemy could hide undetected in this land. I was determined to watch carefully for any sign of movement on the shore. As if to support my hunch, shortly after entering the river, the commander of our ship, a tough, scarred veteran named Kolbein Arnason, ordered us to keep to the center, and doubled the lookouts posted.

The fortified settlement where Jarl Sigurd's steward lived was not far upstream, on the north side of the river. As I scanned the shores, I wondered how anyone could live in this barren land. The Hebrides, where I had grown up, were for the most part rocky and treeless, but we had lush green grass, and rich pasturage for our flocks of sheep. Here, it was hard to imagine how anyone could scrape a living from these desolate hills, where only bracken and heather seemed to grow. As far as I could see, there were nothing but undulating, folded dales and valleys, and in many places the dark bones of the earth jutted through the thin skin of soil and vegetation. I wondered why Jarl Sigurd was so desperate to hold onto this place, and why the Scots seemed so determined to defend it. It seemed as thoroughly unlovable a place as I had ever seen.

Nevertheless, I held my tongue, as I had sworn to serve Sigurd faithfully in all respects, and his causes must then be mine, whether or not I saw the sense in them. The river up which we sailed was gradually narrowing, and I had the impression that the banks of the river were slowly closing in on us. A feeling of dread began to pervade us all, from what source we could not guess.

We had only gone a few miles upstream when I cried out and pointed. Lookouts on the other boats heard me shout, and everyone turned to look where I was pointing. Soon, all of us were staring.

In the distance was a column of black smoke, rising straight up into the overcast sky. It was perhaps five miles away, and must have resulted from a great burning, but the likeliest explanation did not occur to me until Eyjolf, who happened to be near me, said grimly, "They have burned the settlement. Jarl Sigurd will be overwrought."

"Would they dare to do so?"

Eyjolf shrugged. "We shall see if they did. They would not have dared had they known we were so near, but surely that was not known."

We did not have long to wait. We were sailing up river on a strong east wind and reached the settlement in less than an hour. Our ship's commander, Kolbein Arnason, directed us to follow the lead ships in taking in the sail, and rowing to the side where the current was the slowest. There we anchored, scarcely a quarter-mile downstream from the settlement, along with the rest of our ships.

I looked out toward the place where the settlement had lain. Eyjolf had been correct. The buildings were burned, and recently. The flames were only just dying down, and the smoke still rose acrid and black into the gray sky. Jarl Sigurd had already cast off in a skiff with only a handful of his men, leaving the rest to follow as they would.

"He must be in a fury," said Grím Njálsson. "Sigurd is too much of a tactician to strike off like this unless he is out of his mind with rage."

Skarp-Hedin, Grím's older brother, said, "We should follow him immediately. The Scots may still be lurking nearby."

This seemed like excellent advice, and Kolbein, our commander, wisely decided to take it. We immediately began to cast off for shore, leaving only enough men behind to tend to the ship.

The Njálssons, Eyjolf, and I were on the first skiff from our ship to strike shore. We waded onto land and drew the skiffs up out of the water. I saw that the other men were silently drawing their swords, and I did the same, and we walked up into the ruined settlement without speaking.

There was no building untouched. All were razed, burned black. Everywhere there were dead bodies of men, women, and children, struck down by arrows for the most part, but some hacked to death with swords. We came upon Jarl Sigurd, standing by the body of a man wearing a once-fine cloak, now rent and bloodstained. He had a long, feathered arrow through his throat, and lay crumpled, staring unendingly and unseeingly at the empty sky. Sigurd had gone white, but two spots of hot color stood out on his cheeks. I remember thinking that I had never in my life seen a man so angry.

He only stood there for a few moments, and then wheeled around, calling out for Kolbein and the other ships' commanders to meet him on the shore. Egil Skaptason, the commander of the ship that had taken me from the Hebrides to Orkney, was one of them. The Njálssons, Eyjolf, I, and a few others remained in what was left of the settlement, looking around us.

The scene was horrifying. It was not the sight of blood and death that appalled me. After all, only a little more than two weeks ago, I had killed a man. That, however, had been in a fair fight. Here were women and children, cut down as they fled, with no mercy shown. Not one of the inhabitants of the settlement had been spared.

Eyjolf gestured toward the dead man with the fine cloak, the sight of whom had so enraged Jarl Sigurd. "Havard Arnljótsson. The steward of east Scotland, and the Jarl's brother-in-law."

Skarp-Hedin and I exchanged glances, and then we all went down to the shore, where Jarl Sigurd was meeting with his commanders.

"We shall follow them," the Jarl said. "The path they have taken is easy to discern. We have four hundred men here, and I cannot imagine that the Scots have more or better men than we have."

In less than an hour we assembled, each under the leadership of our ship's commander, and set off inland in pursuit of the marauders. I immediately saw what the Jarl had meant about their path being obvious. They had trampled the bracken down in their retreat, and it would be easy to follow them, as long as the land did not become bare rock.

We set off at a jog, and I once again realized that I had only thought I was fit. These men kept up an amazing pace, hardly even breaking a sweat or becoming winded. I heard several men behind me singing a song as they ran, a song of blood and war and revenge. I was able to keep up, but before long, my lungs were burning within me, and my legs ached.

It is fortunate for us that the Scots did not realize that they were being pursued, for they went slowly and unwarily. Within three hours, we had caught sight of them, cresting a hill on the further side of a broad, shallow valley. Sigurd ordered us to halt and remain motionless until the last of them were out of sight, to make it less likely that we would be seen, and then to redouble our speed in pursuit. I groaned inwardly, massaging my aching thighs, and wondered if I would have strength enough to fight, if we caught up with them.

It took us another half hour to reach the top of the hill where we had first seen them. I expected them to be once again nearly out of sight, but as I said, they were not yet aware of our presence. They had descended into another, deeper valley, perhaps two hundred men all told, and were scarcely a quarter-mile away. Jarl Sigurd gave a fierce smile, and said, in a quiet but intense voice, "After them. Today, we take no prisoners."

We immediately pelted off down the hill toward them, fanning out as we came nearer. My fatigue evaporated as if it had never been. I saw before my mind's eye those women and children, struck down as they fled. I found I was shouting, sword upraised.

The Scots turned, and we heard echoing shouts of alarm and dismay. There was a ringing of drawn swords, and then we were upon them.

I do not know how many men I struck down that day. I was on fire, and no one could stand before me. I saw Skarp-Hedin near me, shouting out a battle cry as he ran a Scottish warrior through with his sword. He showed his crooked teeth in a frightful grin, and turned to defend his brother Helgi, who was being attacked from two sides at once.

The battle had raged about me for some time, when I suddenly found myself in a temporary calm. I looked about me. In places to my left and right, the Scots were still fighting fiercely, but our numbers were overwhelming, and our victory was assured. Near me, I saw Jarl Sigurd himself crossing swords with a huge Scottish chieftain. I took a step toward them, to add my sword to the Jarl's, when I saw that from behind him, a Scottish spearman was stealthily approaching.

The spearman crept forward, his narrowed eyes focused on the Jarl. He did not seem to see me. I watched, spellbound, not wanting to shout out, for fear that the Jarl would turn, and the swordsman would kill him. But a spear in the back would have been just as deadly. I did not know if I could reach the spearman in time, but I had just decided to rush at him when, with a swift movement, he reared back, and hurled his spear.

I cried out and leapt forward. I do not think I have ever put such strength into a leap. One-handed, I caught the spear as it flew, and in a single motion, I turned and slung it back at the man who had thrown it. His eyes widened, but he was frozen to the spot, and the spear struck him full in the chest. He was dead before he hit the ground.

I then turned to the Jarl's defense, but as I did, his sword point grazed his opponent's forehead. Blood spilled into the warrior's eyes, blinding him. The man howled and reached up to wipe his face. Jarl Sigurd let out a shout and struck off the warrior's head.

The Scots were broken and defeated within an hour. Some of them had no doubt fled, but most were killed on the battlefield. We had lost only twenty-three men, and about twice that many were wounded. Of my friends, only Helgi Njálsson had more than a minor injury. Helgi had suffered a long but shallow cut on his left forearm. As we bound it, he gave his ringing laugh and said that the Scottish warrior who had given it to him had gotten much worse in return.

I was unscathed, not so much as a drop of blood shed. Eyjolf shook his head, and clapped me on the back, saying that the gods looked after me. He had heard about how I had saved the Jarl's life and saw to it that everyone found out what I had done.

The Jarl was safe as well, with only a few minor cuts to show for his afternoon's work. I found him standing near the point where we had first encountered the Scots, watching dispassionately as they executed the few prisoners who were left alive. "We will show them as much mercy as they showed Havard and his family," he said grimly.

One by one, the Scottish prisoners were sent to the sword. Some of them said nothing, others begged for mercy in their language, but found none. Then one, a lanky man with reddish hair like Eyjolf's, cried out, "I beg you, show me mercy!" in our language.

Jarl Sigurd shouted, "Stop!" The swordsmen halted their bloody work.

"Bring him to me," Jarl Sigurd said.

The man was pushed roughly until he stood in front of the Jarl. His eyes were round with fear, but he held himself as proudly as he could manage.

"You speak our language?" the Jarl asked.

"A little," the man stammered.

"How do you come to speak it?"

"I was with the king's party who went to a parley between the Scots and the Norsemen in Caithness, and I stayed behind for six months as a guarantee for the agreement that was reached. I learned some of your speech there."

The Jarl nodded. "I remember that agreement. Your king agreed that his people would not molest our settlements in eastern Scotland, as I recall. An agreement he seems to have broken today. Who commanded you here?"

"Diarmaid MacEowain. He is dead, killed in the battle."

"And he ordered the destruction of our peoples' settlement?"

"No. It was ordered by King Kenneth himself."

Jarl Sigurd nodded. "I see." He regarded the man, his eyes narrowed. "What is your name?"

"Ciaran," the man said. "Ciaran MacLochlainn."

Jarl Sigurd nodded. "Very well." He motioned to the guard who was holding the man, and said, "Remove his shirt."

The man's shirt was pulled none too gently over his head, and the guard held him, stripped to the waist, his arms pinned behind him. Then Jarl Sigurd drew his sword and brought the point near the middle of the man's chest. Everything was silent, everyone watching, wondering what the Jarl would do, and wondering why he had singled out the one Scottish warrior who spoke our language. Then I remembered his anger when he had seen his brother-in-law lying dead, and I felt sure that he was going to kill the man slowly and painfully. I wondered if I had the stomach to continue watching but knew that I would be looked upon as weak if I turned away.

Ciaran himself clearly expected the worst, and he stiffened in the grip of the man who held him.

The Jarl advanced, and the tip of the sword touched the man's skin above his left nipple. Ciaran winced, and closed his eyes.

Jarl Sigurd drew the sword point down at an angle, then across the man's breastbone, and then down at an angle again toward his navel. It was only a shallow cut, but the man shrieked and writhed, and a ribbon of scarlet blood trickled down his chest. Then the Jarl stopped and wiped the tip of the sword on the bracken.

"There," he said, and Ciaran opened his eyes. "That is an S-rune. 'S' for Sigurd Hlodvisson. Tell your King Kenneth that I was here and show him what I have written on your body. Let him think twice before he attacks one of my settlements again." The Jarl gestured toward the men who held him. "Let him go."

The guards released him, and he stood for a moment, panting and trembling, then he picked up his shirt from where it had been tossed aside, and took off at a run.

The Jarl then ordered some of his men to see to the execution of the remaining Scottish prisoners and called his commanders to come speak with him. To my amazement, he spoke my name, and motioned for me to join them.

When we had gathered around him, he spoke to us. "Though I am grieved at the death of my brother-in-law and the destruction of the settlement here, I am pleased that their deaths were properly avenged. I ask you to see to it that your men receive double rations tonight. You may tell them after we have seen to the proper burial of our dead, we will return to Orkney." Jarl Sigurd then turned his clear blue eyes on me, and said, "And you, Kári Solmundarson—none could have proven himself better than you have. At first, I questioned Egil Skaptason's judgment, taking you in the place of Asbjorn, whom you fought and killed. But today I have seen your ability with my own eyes, and I owe you my life. Were you to leave us today, I would consider Asbjorn's blood-price more than paid."

He reached out and clasped my forearm. I could find no words to say.

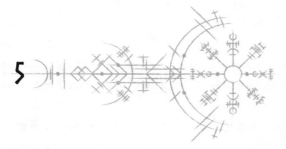

5

WE RETURNED TO ORKNEY IN HIGH spirits. Jarl Sigurd, despite the loss of his brother-in-law, was pleased with the exploit, and commended all of us on our courage in defeating the Scots. It was clear we were in high favor.

The Njálssons did not return to their home in Iceland for some time and accompanied the Jarl's men—I now include myself in that designation, as it was clear the Jarl so accepted me—on a number of different expeditions. We went as far south as the city of Jorvík in England. Until that time, I had never seen such a huge settlement. I fought not to reveal my ignorance of the world by gawking, openmouthed. We also traveled frequently to the other settlements in eastern Scotland.

Only once was I not allowed to go. This was when the Jarl's men were sent to deal with a further reluctance to pay tribute on the part of Jarl Gilli Klapa in the Hebrides. I think that Jarl Sigurd may have thought that because of my birthplace, my allegiance would be divided. Should it come to fighting—which in the end, it did not—I could not be counted upon to support the Orkney men against men who were Hebrideans like myself. I did not argue with his judgment, but in all honesty, I felt great devotion to Sigurd. He was a man who inspired either that or fear in all who met him. I also had little enough love for Gilli Klapa, who was no friend of myself or my family. I would not have hesitated to bear sword against Gilli and his men, had Sigurd commanded me to do so.

It was almost two years since I had left the Hebrides, and the time of my indenture was almost over, when a newcomer arrived in Orkney. He was an Icelander named Thrain Sigfússon, and he was known to the Njálssons, although I thought that they treated him with the forced courtesy usually reserved for those whom a man dislikes but has no real reason to take action against.

I soon discovered why. Thrain was a boastful and arrogant man. Not boorish and loud like Asbjorn had been, but sly, smug, and self-congratulatory. He was handsome, insolently so. Lean and lithe like a fox, with light, fine-textured hair which he wore very long, and proud, flashing blue eyes. Every move he made seemed calculated to make the greatest impact on those around him. When he entered a room, he always looked around it as he strode in, as if to watch who marked his entrance. Women especially seemed overwhelmed by him. I once heard him say that no woman he wanted had ever refused to share his bed. As unpleasant as I found him, I did not find that difficult to believe.

Jarl Sigurd, whose judgment of others I had seldom had reason to question, seemed to recognize immediately what kind of man Thrain was, but chose to treat him deferentially because he was known to the Njálssons.

"Why Thrain has come here I cannot imagine," Helgi Njálsson said one day. It was a warm day in late spring, and we were working together on the shore of the harbor. A ship containing bales of wool, casks of dried meat, and stacks of skins had been unloaded, and the goods stacked on the beach. The Jarl wished us to see to their safe storage.

"He has done nothing here thus far," said Skarp-Hedin, "except brag about himself and find a way to get between the legs of every handsome woman on the island."

"I wonder if he thinks to capture glory for himself somehow, by some connection with the Jarl."

"Little enough chance for that without the kind of hard work and risk that Thrain prefers to avoid," growled Skarp-Hedin. "Don't worry. The Jarl recognizes Thrain for what he is."

At this point, my curiosity got the better of me. "Is it just his superior manner that you dislike, or do you know something ill of Thrain Sigfússon? I thought that you behaved coldly toward him from the first."

Grím and Helgi exchanged glances, and Skarp-Hedin said, "Thrain Sigfússon slew our foster father."

I was speechless for a moment, and then I cried, rather louder than I had intended, "Then why do you not kill him?"

Grím deftly caught a bundle of fox-skins tossed to him by Helgi. "It is not that simple," he said quietly.

I looked from brother to brother, waiting for further explanation. All three looked serious, even Helgi.

Finally, Skarp-Hedin continued. "There has been a blood feud for many years between our family and Thrain's. Perhaps this evening we can tell you the story. I warn you, it is an ugly one. All the more ugly because my heart says that it is not over yet."

THE NJÁLSSONS WERE STAYING IN A small house on the edge of the settlement, and that evening, after our meal, I went back with them there. Dark clouds showed on the horizon, and the wind was rising. It looked likely to rain by midnight. We went inside. No one made a move to light an oil lamp. As we talked, the darkness grew, until finally the three of them faded first into obscure shapes in the gathering gloom, and then into voices without any source.

It seemed that the three had decided to let Grím do the speaking, and he began without any preamble.

"The quarrel between our family and Thrain's family began because of a trifle. There is a woman named Hallgerd, who has a double connection to Thrain. By her first husband, she had a daughter, who is Thrain's wife. Also, Hallgerd's second husband was Gunnar of Hlidarend, who is Thrain's cousin. Now, our mother quarreled with Hallgerd over who should have the higher seat at a feast, and my mother was given the place of honor."

"That should be the host's decision," I said.

"It was, and the host's decision was so made. But Hallgerd is a haughty, proud woman who does not accept slights meekly, and my mother is no less proud. Now, my mother had a servant man named Svart whom she liked, and who had worked for her family for many years. Hallgerd decided to repay my mother for the insult that she felt she had received, and she had one of her own servants kill Svart."

"That was unkindly done."

"It was. My mother demanded his blood-price be paid. Gunnar, who was a fair man, willingly did so, although he was displeased with what his wife had done. There the matter should have ended. But my mother was still angry and had one of her servants kill Hallgerd's servant man who had done the first slaying.

"Gunnar and our father, Njál Thorgeirsson, did not wish the feud to continue, but you know how difficult that can be once one begins. In the end, after the fighting had gone back and forth more times than I wish to recount, and several more had died because of this women's quarrel, some men of our father's family ambushed and killed Gunnar of Hlidarend himself."

"Why? Were Gunnar's hands not innocent of the blood that was shed?"

"Entirely," replied Grím. "Hallgerd was far guiltier than he was, but no one would mete out revenge upon a woman. The men who killed Gunnar thought, I believe, that it would end the feud. And one of the killers was our foster father, Thórd Freedmansson, whom our father had taken in as a brother despite his low birth, and who had treated us like his own children."

I nodded, remembering what Skarp-Hedin had said that afternoon. "And Thrain Sigfússon slew him."

"Yes." Grím fell silent. I waited for him to continue, but evidently the story was finished.

I felt I had to point out the obvious but was reluctant to do so. "Surely, he had reason, in revenge for the killing of Gunnar..."

Skarp-Hedin interrupted. "We do not dispute Thrain's right to Thórd's life. We do not seek revenge. Indeed, if we sought it we should already have it, as we are four against one and in high favor with Jarl Sigurd. But our father desired an end to the feud, and thus asked us to swear not to harm Thrain, and to help him if he needed help, as if he were one of us. We have so sworn. Nevertheless, he did not ask us to love Thrain Sigfússon."

"And we do not," added Helgi. "I am sure enough that we shall regret swearing to help him before this affair is finished."

AT THE END OF THAT SUMMER, the Njálssons decided that they would return to Iceland before the winter storms began and acquired a ship from Jarl Sigurd that would carry them there. Whether their desire to remain in Orkney was soured by Thrain's swaggering presence, or because they simply wished to return to their homeland, they did not say. For myself, I was grieved for the loss of my comrades. In the two years I was on Orkney, we had become fast friends.

"Come back to Iceland with us," urged Helgi, as I was helping him load water and food casks onto his ship, which lay at anchor, from a skiff we had rowed out into the harbor. "Surely your heart aches to see new lands."

I grinned. "Enough chance of that working for Jarl Sigurd."

"Yes, but with us you won't have to risk your skin every time you touch dry land. Not that that's a problem for you. You haven't lost a drop of blood in any battle you've been in. Skill, luck, whatever it is. You have your share of it."

"My grandmother always said I was born lucky."

"That seems likely enough."

We finished unloading the casks. Helgi jumped down from the ship into the skiff, and we rowed back to shore.

"In any case," I said, "I am happy here working for the Jarl, whatever the danger. Although I am grieved to see you go. There will be less cheer here without you."

We had left Skarp-Hedin and Grím on the shore, dickering with a merchant for lengths of rope and sail cloth. However, when we returned, the harbor shore was empty, except for a few men working on repairing a boat. Neither the brothers nor the merchant was to be seen. Helgi frowned. "I thought they would have waited for us. I wonder if the Jarl could have called for them."

"It could be," I replied. We walked up the shore towards the men working on the boat.

"Have you seen my brothers, speaking with a merchant?" Helgi asked one of the workers. "A big man with curling brown hair, and a smaller one with dark hair. They were here less than an hour since."

The man shrugged. "I saw them, but they left some time ago with another."

"Who?" asked Helgi.

"A newcomer. I have only seen him this summer. A tall blond sneering fellow." The man pointed up toward the settlement, in the direction of the house where the Njálssons were staying.

Helgi's jaw tightened, but he did not respond. I knew of only one "tall blond sneering fellow" in the settlement, and it was clear that Helgi thought the same as I did. He and I walked up toward the house.

As we approached, we heard voices—angry voices—within. Helgi opened the door and strode in. Three faces turned toward us as we entered. Grím was, as always, somber and unreadable. Skarp-Hedin was angry. The tension was clear in his face. I thought that he looked as if he was ready to fight but dared not. I had no doubt that his had been the angry voice we had heard as we approached. The third man in the room was Thrain Sigfússon. He sat at their table, his long legs stretched out, seemingly at his ease. But his face, too, showed anxiety, though he strove to hide it.

"I am glad you have returned, Helgi, and you also, Kári," said Skarp-Hedin. "Perhaps you can help us decide what to do with this woman-chaser."

Thrain gave his insolent grin, but it looked a little strained.

"What has he done?" The contempt in Helgi's voice was obvious. "And what does he want of us?"

Skarp-Hedin made an angry gesture toward Thrain. "He wasn't content with fucking every unmarried woman in Orkney, and most of the married ones as well. Now he's bedded the Jarl's daughter, and Sigurd is out for his blood."

"Let him have it," said Helgi scornfully.

"He begs our help in his escape." Skarp-Hedin laid emphasis on the word begs.

"Why us?" asked Helgi. "If Thrain can't keep his pants on, what business is it of ours? And what business is it of ours if the Jarl hangs him up by the part of him that did the damage?" He gave Thrain a wicked smirk. "Which is what the Jarl will do if he catches you."

"*If,*" said Thrain, but I noticed he had gone several shades paler than before.

"It is our business because of the oath we swore to our father," said Skarp-Hedin.

"We promised not to harm him," argued Helgi, "we did not promise to get him out of problems of his own making."

"We promised," replied Skarp-Hedin, "to help him if he needed it."

"But why us? Why not some other fools who don't know him any better?"

Thrain gave Helgi a malicious grin. "Because no other fools have a ship at hand."

Helgi took a step forward, fists clenched, but Skarp-Hedin came between them. "Nothing is being accomplished by this. Helgi, have I ever stepped back from a fight before? If we had not sworn to our father, I would first help you thrash him, and then the four of us could bring him to the Jarl ourselves. As it is, we need to decide what to do before Jarl Sigurd finds him here, as he is certain to do so if we stay here much longer." He turned to Grím, who had not yet spoken. "What say you, Grím?"

Grím shrugged. "That we cannot do any different but what we have sworn."

"Helgi?"

Helgi looked at Thrain, still sitting there with his arms folded and his long, sleek hair falling down across his shoulders. Helgi's fists clenched and unclenched once or twice. "I agree. But when we return to Iceland, I will ask father to release us from this oath, which I feel will cause trouble before this is over."

Thrain was visibly relieved, but still managed to maintain his superior air, as if he were the one doing us a favor. "When do you sail?"

"Tomorrow or the next day," said Skarp-Hedin.

"Make it tomorrow. Hide me on your ship. I will pay you richly when we reach Iceland."

"What will you pay us to redeem our honor at having betrayed Jarl Sigurd, who has himself shown us nothing but honor?" snapped Helgi.

"Ask your father, to whom you swore this oath, that question," shot back Thrain.

Skarp-Hedin turned to me. "And what does Kári think of this?"

I looked from face to face—quiet, somber Grím, Helgi barely containing his fury, Skarp-Hedin, steadfastly doing what he saw as his duty by what they had sworn, and Thrain Sigfússon, still arrogant and swaggering even in the face of mortal danger.

"I think you do right, based on your oath to your father. I will help you if I can. Not for your sake," I said, glaring at Thrain. "I would as soon see the Jarl give you what you deserve. But for the sake of my friendship with the

Njálssons, I will give what help I can, and only hope that it does not turn to ill fortune for all of us."

SKARP-HEDIN HAD BEEN RIGHT WHEN he said that the Jarl's men would not be far behind Thrain. We heard a commotion outside, and looking out, I saw several of the Jarl's guards striding toward the house. The Njálssons helped Thrain, who had turned a little pale at the sound, to hide beneath a pile of skin coverlets in the corner of the house.

Within less than a minute after we first heard their approach, the guards walked into the house without so much as a knock on the door.

"Jarl Sigurd is searching for Thrain Sigfússon, who I think is known to you," said the leader, without any preamble. "Do you know where he is?"

"I do not," said Skarp-Hedin without hesitation. "I saw him earlier, but he went away, up toward the settlement, and I do not know where he is now."

I thought of the man who was working on the boat and was glad that Skarp-Hedin admitted having seen Thrain. Had he denied it, and it come out later that Skarp-Hedin and Grím had been seen talking to Thrain on the beach, it would have looked ill.

The guard did not seem satisfied. "And the rest of you?" he asked, looking from one of us to the other.

Deception does not come easy to me, nor, I think, did it to the Njálssons. But all of us denied knowing where Thrain was.

"Should we see him, what are the Jarl's wishes?" asked Helgi. It seemed to me that he was enjoying the knowledge that Thrain could hear every word being spoken.

"Disarm and hold him," said the guard, "but do not kill him unless it is unavoidable. The Jarl wishes to deal with this man himself."

Helgi nodded to the guard and gave me a furtive little smile.

After they had gone, Skarp-Hedin went over to the pile of skins. "Get up." He nudged the pile with his foot. "They are gone."

Thrain uncovered himself and sat up, seeming embarrassed at having had to hide. "Now what?" he asked, using an irritable tone to cover his shame.

"Tonight, we will row you out to our ship, and you will hide there. We have some empty casks that you could hide in should the ship be searched. Then, tomorrow we will sail for Iceland."

Thrain seemed satisfied and reclined against the skins. His superior grin flashed out. "Let me know when all is ready." He sounded for all the world like a powerful Jarl commanding his lackeys. I looked at Helgi, who again looked as if he wanted to strike him, and the thought crossed my mind that the Njálssons' oath was forcing them into an alliance with a scoundrel.

I SLEPT IN THE NJÁLSSONS' HOUSE that night, hoping that my absence from my usual sleeping quarters would not be noticed. It was almost midnight when Skarp-Hedin woke me. I got up, dressed, and quietly followed as we led Thrain down to the harbor shore, where Helgi was waiting with the skiff to row him out to the waiting ship. Thrain seemed almost subdued. I believe it was fear. Knowing the Jarl as I did, I knew that he was right to be afraid. He had heard the guard say that the Jarl wanted him captured, not killed. Thrain had had several hours to imagine the reasons for which the Jarl might want him taken alive.

Skarp-Hedin and I stood watch on the shore while Helgi rowed Thrain out to the ship. Grím, who was already on board, and Helgi were to hide him safely away. It seemed to take forever, standing there in the dark. The moon was a waning crescent and hardly lit the sky at all, and the familiar shapes of rocks, trees, and boats were only ghostly shadows, dark against darker.

I do not know how long it took them to return, but finally we heard the muffled strike of oar on water, the splashing of legs in the shallows, and a grating sound as the skiff was beached. Soon Helgi and Grím were at our sides, speaking in whispers.

"The fugitive is safely stowed in a cask for the evening," said Helgi. "But I was sorely tempted to affix the cover and throw it overboard."

"A cask is not the most comfortable of beds." Skarp-Hedin gave a grim laugh. "I wonder if the pleasure he got from Sigurd's daughter was worth it."

We all laughed, as quietly as possible, and then bid each other farewell. I returned to my quarters and the Njálssons to theirs. I was relieved when I found that the five comrades with whom I shared living quarters seemed to be sound asleep as I entered. I undressed as quietly as possible, stretched out on the mat on which I slept, and was asleep within minutes.

I woke to find that it was already day. The sun was streaming in through the small openings in the side wall, and two of my comrades had already dressed and gone. I stretched like a cat, and then sat up, yawning and blinking. Kol Skagason, who shares my quarters, was pulling on his shirt as I sat up. When he noticed that I had awakened, he gave me a wry look.

"You were out late last night."

My heart skipped a beat. The penalty of the conspirator, the fear of every action giving one away. "I was," I said, trying to make it sound like a challenge. It's not your concern.

Then Kol grinned. "Is she pretty?"

I stared at him dumbly for a moment, not comprehending, but then realization dawned. He thought I had been with a woman. So, I grinned back and said, "Prettier than you are, anyway," and Kol laughed heartily, picked up his cloak, and strode out.

I stood up, stretched again, and began to dress, wondering who else had noticed my absence—and worse, who might have seen us ferrying Thrain over to the Njálssons' ship.

After eating, I went up to the Jarl's house to ask the commander of Sigurd's men what was expected of me that day. But the commander was gone, and so was Jarl Sigurd. I asked the guard at the door, a huge bear of a man named Bjorn, where they had gone.

"They are up in the Assembly Field. They have gone to arrange for three executions." Bjorn spoke flatly, as if there were nothing unusual in what he was saying. "Jarl Sigurd believes that the Njálsson brothers know where that fellow Thrain Sigfússon is. He has given them until tomorrow morning to tell him, and if they refuse he will have all three of them killed."

I gaped at him as if I had been punched in the belly. Bjorn knew of my friendship with the Njálssons and seemed to believe it was only that which prompted my reaction. "Don't try to talk him out of it, Kári," he said, not unkindly. "Once the Jarl decides that someone will die, there's nothing that can be done. The Jarl thinks highly of you, and it would not do to change that by interfering in this matter."

"Until this morning, the Jarl thought highly of the Njálssons, too," I replied. Without waiting for an answer, I went around the house, and up toward the top of the hill to the field where the annual Assembly was held.

There, I saw Jarl Sigurd with several of his high-ranking men, standing before the Njálssons. They were bound hand and foot and were sitting on the ground with their backs together. None looked afraid, but Helgi especially looked furious at his treatment.

The Jarl was speaking, his voice filled with rage. "I will either have Thrain Sigfússon's head, or I will have yours. You were seen talking to him yesterday, and I believe you know where he is. I have been a judge of men for many years, and I know when a man is lying. I believe you are doing so now. Is the life of this boaster worth yours?"

"I cannot answer that," said Skarp-Hedin. "I do not weigh one man's life against another."

"I have sent men out to search your ship," said Sigurd. "I was certain we would find him there. Yet they found nothing. Do you find that strange?"

Helgi looked up, his eyes narrow and glittering. "Where did you think we would stow him? In a water cask?"

One of Sigurd's eyebrows went up slightly. I looked at Skarp-Hedin, and his lips had tightened into bloodless lines. Why was Helgi betraying Thrain now? Then I realized that perhaps he thought if they found Thrain, they would spare him and his brothers. But what of the oath? Maybe Helgi believed that if the Jarl figured out Thrain's whereabouts from a mere hint, their oath would still be unbroken.

The Jarl returned Helgi's gaze steadily. "Perhaps. And perhaps we should search the ship again, with those words in mind." Jarl Sigurd turned, called his commanders to follow, and strode off toward the harbor. He left the three brothers pinioned hand and foot in the middle of the Assembly Field, with two men to guard them.

I watched and waited for them to return, expecting to see them leading Thrain Sigfússon, but they returned in less than an hour with no prisoner. The Jarl's face was burning with wrath, and without saying a word he stalked off toward his house.

I caught up with one of the men who had accompanied him and asked him what had happened. He told me the Jarl and his men had boarded the ship and opened every cask, but Thrain was not there. I had to struggle to contain my astonishment. I did not want to say anything that would indicate that I myself knew where Thrain was. But perhaps that was no longer true. Maybe he really wasn't there anymore. But if not, then where was he?

All through that day, I watched and waited, unable to keep my mind off the Njálssons, still tied up in the Assembly Field, and the fugitive Thrain Sigfússon. My duties that day—helping with loading barrels of salted dried meat and fish into a storehouse for the winter—seemed to pass at a snail's pace. My eyes kept straying, first out toward the Njálssons' ship, at anchor in the harbor, and then up toward the Assembly Field. I wondered if tomorrow, there would be only three blood-soaked patches where my friends were now sitting.

The night fell, and I returned to my sleeping quarters, but I could not sleep. I tossed this way and that, and finally rose and dressed. A quiet, amused voice—my comrade Kol—said, "Enjoy her well, Kári, and then maybe when you return you won't keep me awake with your rolling about." I managed a forced laugh, and left, hoping that Kol would not find it strange that I was going to meet a woman while wearing my sword.

All was dark, and the settlement was quiet. I knew few guards were posted unless there was reason, but I did not wish to be marked by even those few. I walked up past the main cluster of buildings. No sound issued from Jarl Sigurd's house, for which I was very glad. From there, I walked out onto the Assembly Field.

In the light of the sliver moon, all that was visible were vague shapes. I could see the huddled form of the Njálssons, where they sat waiting for execution, and a guard standing near them, leaning on a spear.

The guard heard my footsteps. Even in the dark, I saw him move, catching up his spear and pointing it toward me. "Who is it?" he said, his voice challenging.

"Kári Solmundarson," I said, trying to make my voice sound authoritative. "The Jarl himself told me to relieve you, as you will be wanted first thing in the morning. You may return to your sleeping quarters for the night." It did not sound very plausible, but I was not practiced in deceit and could think of nothing better.

The guard sounded wary. "For what purpose does the Jarl want me?"

"I do not know. Ask the Jarl that tomorrow."

There was a pause. "The Jarl told me I was to guard the prisoners through the whole night," he persisted.

I shrugged, although I doubt he saw that in the dark. "Very well. Shall I go now and tell the Jarl you are refusing to follow his orders?"

There was another pause, during which the man shifted uneasily from one foot to another. "I will go." He still did not sound certain, but he walked past me, down the hill toward the settlement.

"Sleep well," I said to his retreating form. "I envy you your night's sleep, as I will get none."

As soon as his footsteps had retreated back toward the settlement, I heard Helgi's voice saying, "Kári? Is that you?"

"Yes," I said, and went over to them and cut their bonds with my sword. They stood, rubbing their numb hands and stretching their eased limbs.

"Have they captured Thrain?" whispered Skarp-Hedin.

"Not that I've heard," I answered.

"No thanks to you, Helgi," Skarp-Hedin said irritably. "With that remark of yours about the water casks, I'm surprised that Thrain isn't tied up here next to us right now."

We left the field quietly, skirting the edge of the settlement, and made our way down to the harbor. It was a peaceful night, and the waves lapped the shore sleepily. I saw with relief that the skiff was still there, pulled up onto the gravel. We dragged it into the water and cast off toward the waiting ship.

The slap of the oars sounded rhythmically in my ears as we approached the ship. I found myself wondering what I should do. By identifying myself to the guard, I had made myself complicit in the Njálssons' escape. Surely the Jarl would kill me when my part in the deceit was discovered. I had no real desire to go with the brothers to Iceland, but the thought crossed my mind that I did not have many other options.

Helgi and Grím pulled in their oars, and there was a harsh scraping sound as the edge of the skiff rubbed against the side of the ship. Skarp-Hedin reached out and grabbed the gunwale, and we prepared to board.

There was a voice from the ship. "Who is it?"

Without thinking, Helgi looked up and said, "Thrain?" Instantly Skarp-Hedin tackled Helgi and pulled him down into the skiff. It was fortunate that he did so. At the same moment, a dark figure leapt down from the ship into the skiff, and I heard the whistle of a sword pass where Helgi's head had been only seconds before. I pulled out my own sword as a second man jumped into the skiff.

Brief though it was, that was the most terrifying battle of my life—in a rocking, unsteady boat, in nearly total darkness, and with three of my closest friends beside me. When I struck out I could not be sure of who I was striking at. In the end, we killed both of them, but I am not completely certain of who killed them or how. Within minutes, however, both of our attackers had been slain and tossed overboard.

I faulted myself for not realizing that the Jarl would post guards on the Njálssons' ship, to prevent just such an escape. There was no time for blame, however, and the four of us climbed aboard the ship, pulling the skiff up behind us. Skarp-Hedin had been grazed on the leg by a sword thrust, but it was shallow, and he took no notice of it. The rest of us were all unharmed.

"You know, Kári, that you can't stay here in Orkney now," said Skarp-Hedin.

"I suppose not."

"You will be welcome at our father's house," Helgi added. "Come to Iceland with us. Or if not, we will bring you wherever you wish. We owe you our lives."

"You haven't gotten away with them yet," I said wryly.

"Where is Thrain?" Skarp-Hedin asked.

"We stowed him in a cask in the hold." Helgi pulled up the wooden cover over the ship's hold. He reached down and rolled one of the casks back and forth. "This is the one, but it's empty."

"One of Jarl Sigurd's men told me they'd opened every cask on the ship, and found nothing," I said.

Suddenly, there was a rustling sound from underneath the floor planks. I drew my sword again, wondering if there was a third guard in hiding. But in a moment, there was a bump, and Thrain Sigfússon's head popped out through the trapdoor. We all gaped for a moment, speechless.

"How did you escape the Jarl's men?" demanded Helgi. "They were right on top of you."

"I think we should discuss that once we are at sea," said Grím, and that seemed good sense. We drew up the anchor and set to the oars with a will.

Even Thrain did his part. Within less than an hour, we were around the headland and out of sight from the settlement.

"Now, Thrain Sigfússon," said Skarp-Hedin, pulling on the oars with an easy motion of his thickly muscled arms, "How did you escape from the Jarl's men?"

"I stayed in the cask until I heard the Jarl's men leave the first time," said Thrain. "After they left, I assumed they would not be returning, and I was cramped in the small space. So I got out, and climbed into the end of the hold in the bow. It was narrow, but you had a bundle of wool blankets down there, and there was a piece of loose wood on the floor, so I pulled the blankets around me, and propped up the wood on the other side so it looked as if the hold ended there. When they came back the second time, I was tucked away safe and snug, and they didn't have any idea where I was. But then they left two men behind. Until I heard your voices, I didn't know what I was going to do. I was wondering if I might starve down there in the hold."

"Starvation might have been preferable to what the Jarl would have done to you," said Helgi. "I would prefer starvation to having my balls cut off and shoved down my throat."

Thrain ignored that, but he couldn't hide a tremor in his voice when he spoke. "Do you think the Jarl will pursue us?"

"We will have to wait and see," I said. "It wouldn't surprise me. Jarl Sigurd is not a man to trifle with."

We pulled in the oars and brought up the sail. The wind caught it, and it billowed out before us. Off to Iceland, with all of us. Who could have predicted it? I had once more had a sudden change of fortune, from one day to the next. But yet again, the gods had held their hands over me and I had come through without a drop of blood lost.

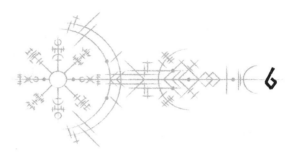

IT TOOK US TWO MONTHS TO reach Iceland. The journey was one of the most unpleasant I have ever taken, and all that remains in my memory of it is hard work, tedium, and the endless, aching cold.

Winter came early that year. We left at summer's end, thinking we had time to reach Iceland before the cold weather began in earnest, but by the time we reached the Shetland Islands, and our last chance to restock with water and food before the long final leg of the voyage, the last traces of summer's warmth were already gone. We had brought warm clothes, but the bitter wind and the constant, drenching waves made them hardly better than nothing at all.

At first, we were concerned that Jarl Sigurd would try to follow us, for surely he must have known we would head for Iceland. I had no doubt that if we were overtaken, he would not be content until all of us were slain—Thrain for his liberties with the Jarl's daughter, and the rest of us for conspiring in Thrain's escape, not to mention the deception of one of his guards and the deaths of two others. But days passed, and no sign of a pursuit came.

It was shortly after our hasty departure from Orkney that Skarp-Hedin, surely the strongest one among us, took ill from the wound that he had received in fighting the Jarl's guards. It was a shallow cut, beginning on the inside of his upper left leg and going down at an angle nearly to his knee, but it had been a clean cut, and not deep enough to cause any serious loss of blood. Many men have taken far more serious injury and ended with nothing worse than a scar to show for it. Skarp-Hedin himself had seemed hardly to notice it at first, but on our third day out, he winced when he stood, and we saw that his upper pant leg was stained red with blood. He still made light of it, and said it was a trifle. Nevertheless, we made him remove his pants to examine the injury, and saw that it was inflamed and oozing, and red streaks radiated from it both up and down his leg. Grím, the gentlest of us, cleaned it with fresh seawater. Skarp-Hedin cried out and writhed when Grím touched it, and this more than anything made me realize that the injury was more serious than we had thought.

The next day, Skarp-Hedin was feverish and delirious, and too weak to stand. Grím cared for him, as all day a knife-edged wind whistled over us, making the sail snap, and jarring the ship with its gusts. When we once again stripped him to check his wound, his upper leg was swollen and tight, and the wound itself was a bright, angry red. At every pitch of the ship Skarp-Hedin groaned, and he responded to us only when we shook him and spoke loudly. I felt certain that the next day he would be dead.

"Do you know nothing that could save him?" I asked Grím, who seemed to understand something of healing.

Grím shook his head. "I have no healing herbs here, and little enough skill with them if we did. My grandmother used to say that wounds should be kept clean and open. This one has closed up, and I fear that some foul matter is trapped in there. Perhaps if we could let it out, he would get better."

"Wound him again, you mean?" said Helgi.

"That would kill him," said Thrain, with finality.

"You know nothing about it, Thrain Sigfússon," snapped Helgi.

"As little as you yourself," Thrain responded coolly.

But I was still thinking about what Grím had said. "Do you think it's the only chance?"

"I fear that it might kill him," said Grím, "but my fear is outweighed by my certainty that he will be dead by this time tomorrow otherwise."

"If we must do it, we should do it now," I said.

"Only if all agree," said Grím. "I would not have it said that I killed my brother by acting against the wishes of all of the rest of my companions."

"I see no other way," I said. "I love Skarp-Hedin like a brother. But if this kills him, he would soon have been dead of the wound regardless."

"Kári speaks for me," said Helgi.

Although none looked to Thrain for his opinion, he said, "It is all one to me what you do, but for that matter I think that Grím is right."

We cleaned Grím's knife with seawater. Helgi held Skarp-Hedin's arms and head, and I held his legs, so that he would not thrash about and injure himself further. Grím looked at Helgi, and then at me, uncertain, but then Skarp-Hedin opened his eyes, and looked up at us with an agonized expression. He said weakly, "Do what you must do. Just be quick about it, I beg of you."

Grím breathed in deeply, and then placed the point of the knife against the place where the wound began, on the inside of Skarp-Hedin's leg. With a single, quick motion, he slit open the skin.

Skarp-Hedin shrieked, and his back arched so that only his head and heels were touching the floor of the boat. His body strained against us so that the cords stood out on his neck and limbs. With all of my strength, I could barely hold down his feet. His eyes rolled about, staring unseeingly at the gray sky. Blood flowed from the cut, along with streaks of whitish fluid, and spattered the floor of the ship. Grím pressed against the muscle of his thigh, to force more of the matter to escape, and Skarp-Hedin thrashed his head back and forth, his curling chestnut-brown hair drenched with sweat. Then he gave a great cry and went limp. I thought at first that he had died, but his massive chest continued to rise and fall slowly. With a rush of relief, I realized that he had simply passed out.

Within a few minutes, the wound had finally cleansed itself, and only gave forth pure, clean blood when pressed. Grím looked up at me, and I saw that his face was also beaded with sweat, despite the icy gale sweeping across us. Wordlessly, we washed Skarp-Hedin's leg and then bound it with clean strips of cloth, covering him with the warmest skins we had. I felt that we had done the best we could do, but even so, I doubted my friend would reach Iceland alive.

At sea, when night comes, it is with a terrible totality. When it is cloudy and there is no starlight or moonlight to see by, you are cut off from everyone in a way that never happens on land. Before night fell, the wind was blowing so hard that we reefed the sail to keep it from tearing out, and all that night we worked blindly in the black wind, baling out the water that came curling over the gunwale, trying desperately to keep the ship afloat and all of its men from being washed overboard. We tied Skarp-Hedin down—whether it was Skarp-Hedin or only his dead body I did not know. I could not see to tell if he was breathing, and the wind took away any breath for me to feel. The rest of us kept going by some kind of instinct that would not allow us to quit. Our bodies continued moving long after our minds and hearts, numbed by the cold and blasted through by the ceaseless wind, had shut down completely.

I remember noticing at some point that I could see again, that the gray sky had opened up above me, and that on the horizon there were streaks of blue and gold. Thrain Sigfússon was slumped near me, his long hair snarled and knotted and dripping, and his skin chafed and red from the salt water. I wondered what the Jarl's daughter would think of him now, and then realized with a wry smile that my chances with her would be no better—I must have looked as bad or worse than he did.

The wind had dropped, and we untied the reef and let the sail billow out. I stood and looked around me. Grím was kneeling next to where Skarp-Hedin lay, still tied down under his skin covers. I moved over towards them.

"Is he dead?" I asked.

At this, Skarp-Hedin half opened his eyes, and said in a faint voice, "Not yet. I take a lot of killing." Then he grimaced. "What a thirst I have."

My heart gave a bound. I had truly not expected this. I hastened to get him water. "How is the wound?" I asked Grím, as I returned with a cup.

Grím pulled back the coverlet, uncovering Skarp-Hedin's leg. The cut still looked ugly, and had bled more, but the horrid redness and swelling from yesterday had gone down. We held the cup of water to his lips, and he sipped it and seemed eased.

Helgi was standing behind me. "I think any of the rest of us would be dead by now." His voice was uncharacteristically solemn.

"You speak truly," I answered.

Skarp-Hedin lived, but was afterwards slightly halt on his left leg, especially when he was tired. He had an ugly, knotted scar that ran the length of his upper leg.

"Now my leg matches my face," he said some days later, grinning his crooked grin and touching the scar on his cheek.

It was more than a week before he could do even light work on the ship, and that made the duties for the rest of us heavier. For myself, I did not mind. I was so glad to see him alive and healing. I know that Helgi and Grím felt the same.

As for Thrain, I cannot say.

I have little to record about the remainder of the voyage. It was, as I have said, cold and unpleasant, but I have no desire to dwell upon that. It suffices to say that we sighted Iceland two months after we had sailed, and two days later anchored near the mouth of the river that passes Bergthorshváll, the home of the Njálssons.

We rowed the skiff onto the beach southeast of Bergthorshváll, and there I first stood upon the soil of Iceland. It is a strange, barren place. Not the same as the barrenness of Scotland, craggy and weathered like an old man's face, nor yet like the grassy, treeless Orkneys and Hebrides. It is a wilderness of black rock, and ragged, broken mountains, higher than any I had yet seen, with rivers of ice pouring down from them. In places were lush meadows, and sheep and goats especially seemed to flourish there, but overall hung the dark, threatening mountains, like thunderclouds in the distance. On occasion, steam rose from their summits, and Helgi told me that there were times when there was smoke like that of a great burning, and fire and ash poured in glowing rivers down from the mountain heights. I never saw it happen, and I do not know if anyone would believe it was true, but that is what Helgi said.

Thrain Sigfússon had chosen to leave us when we reached land, saying that he wished to rejoin his family as soon as he could. As unpleasant as he had made himself during his stay on Orkney, none of us could find fault in him for that.

"We will come to speak with you soon regarding your price for passage to Iceland," said Skarp-Hedin as Thrain was gathering his belongings and preparing to leave.

"We will discuss it when you do," said Thrain.

The rest of us walked along the west bank of the Hvit River, which is the river at whose mouth we had anchored, and then turned to the west and crossed the broad plain. We were in places wading through calf-high grass. It was dry and rustling because of early frost, but still I felt cheered. The meadows we walked through reminded me of my home island, as long as I did not raise my eyes to the brooding mountains in the distance.

Suddenly Skarp-Hedin gave a shout and pointed. Off in the distance, we could see Bergthorshváll, standing dark against the pale blue sky.

"Does it please you to return home?" I smiled at his excitement.

"Yes," said Skarp-Hedin. "Although I would be happier at our homecoming had we not had to betray the Jarl of Orkney in order to do so."

"And had we not had to help Thrain Sigfússon in the bargain," said Helgi.

"Do you wish that you were home yourself?" Skarp-Hedin asked, unexpectedly. On most occasions, he was not a man to speak of feelings.

My smile vanished, and I responded simply, "Sometimes."

Bergthorshváll was a large, sturdy house built on a little dome-shaped hill in the midst of a meadow stretching away on all sides. I could see immediately why the site was chosen. It offered a good view of the broad, grassy plain which surrounded it. Anyone approaching could be seen at a great distance. Besides, the plain around it was wet, so the forage for animals was excellent, but it would not have supported a house.

Distances are deceiving in that strange land, and it took us nearly an hour to reach the house on the hill. That was partly due to Skarp-Hedin's leg, which tired easily, though he did not like to admit it. We had to walk slowly, especially on slopes and where the terrain was uneven. Finally, we came to the hill, and climbed up its side to a broad yard at the top. The brothers strode up to the door, but I hung back a bit, out of courtesy. There, two people stood waiting for us.

Njál Thorgeirsson was a tall, slender man, with the same gentle features as his middle son Grím. His hair, once dark, was now streaked with silver, and unlike most older men, he had no beard. His wife, Bergthóra Grímsdóttir, stood beside him, her hair tied back and covered with a linen cloth. She was a big woman, with a square, determined face, and clear gray eyes that looked as if they would brook no nonsense. I did not find it hard to believe that she had driven one side of a blood-feud.

"I send away three sons, and four come back," she said, the corners of her mouth quirking upwards.

Njál came up and embraced his three sons, and then, gesturing at me, inquired of Skarp-Hedin, "And who is this young man who accompanies you? Some wanderer you have acquired? He hasn't the look of a slave about him."

Skarp-Hedin grinned, and motioned me to come forward. "Not a slave indeed, Father. His name is Kári Solmundarson, and he is a great friend of ours. He has saved the three of us from certain death, and at no small risk to himself. I ask that you welcome him here."

Njál smiled at me. "Welcome, indeed, Kári. Even did my sons not owe you their lives, that they count you as a friend would be enough. I must have all the story later, after we have eaten. Kári, you are welcome to stay in our house as long as it serves you to do so. But I must know, Skarp-Hedin my son, why you now go lamely when I sent you out two years ago on two sound legs."

"It is only a trifle, Father," said Skarp-Hedin.

"A trifle that nearly killed him," interjected Helgi, "and a trifle whose account you may lay at Thrain Sigfússon's feet."

Njál looked mildly surprised, but Bergthóra's expression grew pinched and peevish. "He dealt you this blow, then?" she said, her voice harsh.

"No, Mother." Skarp-Hedin flashed an irritated glance at Helgi. "But I received it during a fight while rescuing Thrain from the Jarl of Orkney's wrath."

"Why did you not leave him to the Jarl's wrath, as he deserves?" demanded Bergthóra.

Njál interrupted, placing his hand on his wife's arm. "Because I asked them to help Thrain if he needed it, as you well know. There is no need to keep this feud in motion, and perhaps their rescue of Thrain Sigfússon will stop it."

Bergthóra did not seem impressed. A difficult woman to impress, I thought. "It was over a woman, was it not?" She gave her wry, little half-smile again.

"What was, Mother?" asked Helgi.

"Thrain's dispute with the Jarl. It was over a woman."

"Yes, it was," said Skarp-Hedin.

"I *knew* it," she proclaimed. "I have no great love for Thrain's wife, because of her mother if for no other reason. But here she stayed, raising their son all alone, while Thrain sailed off where he would, to warm the beds of as many women as he could manage." She spat on the ground. "You should have left him for the Jarl to deal with, promise or no." She gave a haughty look at her husband, who either did not see it or ignored it, I do not know which.

Njál reproved her gently. "We do our sons and their friend ill, to keep them standing after their long voyage, while we rehash old quarrels. Come inside and we will give you refreshment. Bergthóra, find Ingrid, and set out meat and drink for all of us."

WE WENT INSIDE AND WERE SEATED around the great table in the house, which was almost as big as the one in Jarl Sigurd's hall. I realized then what a wealthy man Njál must be. Soon Bergthóra entered the room with a platter of food of various kinds—roast mutton, fish, goat cheese, and oat cakes. We all began eating and talking merrily about our adventures. Njál listened and asked many questions, a broad smile on his face, obviously proud of our exploits. Then another woman followed Bergthóra in, carrying an earthenware pitcher of mead. I glanced up to see who she might be.

And I was struck silent.

I knew immediately that this was no servant but must be my friends' sister. Her resemblance to the three brothers, especially Helgi, was striking. Even now, thirty years later, I can unhesitatingly say that she was the most beautiful woman I have ever seen. She had long, shining hair of reddish gold, and high, finely-cut cheekbones. Her crystalline blue eyes were like the sea on a cloudless day. She saw me watching her and, setting the pitcher on the table, she cocked an eyebrow at me, though she did not blush. I, however, blushed deeply enough for the both of us, to be caught staring thus.

All three brothers jumped up from their seats and embraced their sister, and Helgi gestured at me and said in a jubilant voice, "Ingrid, this is our friend, Kári Solmundarson. We've brought him back from Orkney especially for you."

Ingrid slapped at Helgi playfully, and said to me, in a clear, musical voice, "Welcome, Kári. I had hoped that they would learn more of manners while they were away, but it was a forlorn hope, I guess."

I could think of nothing to say in response, but simply smiled at her. A foolish smile, I thought, chiding myself for having so little presence of mind. She seemed amused by my muteness and gave me a smile of such sweetness that if it had been possible for me to become more dumbstruck than I already was, I would have no doubt have done so. I could not help glancing up at her every so often for the remainder of the meal, as furtively as I could manage, but each time it seemed that she was aware, and one corner of her mouth would turn upward in an amused fashion.

Afterwards, Skarp-Hedin and Grím stayed behind to talk with their father, while Helgi and I went outside to look out over this strange land that my friends called home. We talked of our adventures together during the two years I had served the Jarl of Orkney, and of our narrow escape. Helgi spoke of the adventures we would have in Iceland now that they were back home.

Then, he looked over at me, grinning broadly. "You like Ingrid, don't you?"

I looked away. "I hardly know her."

"Well, you like what you see of her, in any case."

"What man would not?"

Helgi gave one of his ringing laughs. "True enough. Be warned, though. She has our mother's temper. I will say that she seemed pleased enough that we had brought a handsome fellow back with us, however."

I scowled. "Handsome, after being at sea for two months? I'm chafed red by the salt, my clothes stained and dirty, my hair tangled like a drift of seaweed. She surely did not look at me twice."

"Well, that's true," Helgi said.

I looked up at him, the disappointment clear in my face, and he laughed again, and clapped me on the back. "Don't worry. She looked at you far more than twice."

7

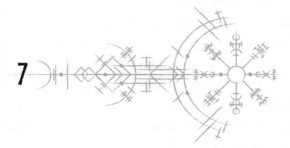

WE HAD BEEN IN ICELAND FOR about two weeks when one frosty afternoon, a man I had not yet met came riding up on a sleek brown stallion. Helgi and I were in the yard of Njál's house, splitting wood, and we had seen him approaching from some distance away.

Helgi shaded his eyes against the sun, which was low in the sky with the approach of winter. "It is Mord Valgardsson."

The name meant nothing to me. I had never heard the brothers speak of him. I watched him canter easily into the yard, and then dismount with a quick, practiced motion. Mord was a lean, wiry man with black hair and very fair, almost white, skin. His eyes were restless, always darting here and there, giving him an appearance of being constantly ill at ease. His voice, however, was warm and friendly, and he strode to Helgi and clasped his forearm.

"Welcome back, my friend. I am well pleased to see you back from Orkney."

"We are pleased to be here ourselves."

Mord regarded him with one eyebrow raised. "I hear that the Jarl did not make it easy for you to leave."

Helgi grinned. "He'd have been happier had we stayed, although it wasn't our company he wanted, but our heads."

"So I am told." Mord turned his dark eyes on me. "And this must be your friend Kári, who helped you escape."

"It is indeed. News travels fast. What brings you here, Mord? My father tells me that your father is unwell."

"It is true, although no worse than other times I can recall. I can surely spare a day to ride up to welcome you home. Where are your brothers?"

"They are helping my father bring in hay for the winter. But they will no doubt wish to greet you now that you are here."

The three of us went around to the back of the house and looked out over the fields. Njál and his two older sons were bundling and stacking the hay that had been lain out to dry. Helgi called out to them, and seeing who was with him, all three of them stopped their work and came up toward the house.

"Greetings," said Mord as they came nearer, and Skarp-Hedin and Grím both greeted him warmly.

Njál inclined his head to Mord. "We see you little enough these days, Mord Valgardsson."

"Less than I wish myself. My father is ill, and I must look after him and keep the household in order. I am glad to see all are well here, and your sons safely returned home."

Njál nodded. "We are glad of it as well."

"But not all of you have returned unscathed, I think." Mord turned and gave a frown to Skarp-Hedin. "I saw as you approached, my friend, that you seem to have gone lame."

Skarp-Hedin scowled, and seemed reluctant to speak.

"My brother doesn't like to be reminded of it," interjected Helgi. "It was a little gift given to him by one of the Jarl's guards, who didn't like it that we were helping Thrain Sigfússon to escape."

Mord shook his head. "That is the most amazing thing to me of all. I will say truthfully that I have heard of it before now, but it still strikes me strangely to hear it from you. That you were wounded in helping Thrain, does it not sound odd to hear it?"

"It does," said Helgi.

"We were doing simply what our father asked of us." Skarp-Hedin sounded as if he were tired of the subject.

"Thrain should have rather expected the point of your own sword, than you take the point of someone else's for his sake."

"That's true enough," said Helgi.

"At least he surely paid you well for your trouble." From Mord's voice, it was apparent that he already knew the opposite was true.

"He has paid us not at all," said Helgi, warming to the topic. "And after lavish promises of a rich reward should we get him safely home."

Njál made a small gesture with his hand, as if to cool the flames he saw rising in his son's eyes. "You have not gone to speak to him about it yet, Helgi, my son. I am certain that he has had his own affairs to get in order upon his return, just as you did."

"And no doubt wanted to spend as much time as possible in bed with his wife, since he was so sorely deprived while he was away," said Helgi, and all of us laughed except for Njál, who looked at us in a disapproving fashion.

"If you wish payment for what you have done, and since Thrain has promised such to you," said Njál, "then you should go to him and discuss it. But it should be enough that you were fulfilling your promise to me."

"It would be enough," said Helgi, "were it anyone but Thrain."

"It is not my place to say," said Mord, "but were I you, I would go as soon as possible. People like Thrain have a tendency toward short memories."

"You speak truly," said Helgi, and I must say that I agreed with him.

In the end, the three brothers agreed they would go to speak with Thrain the next day, and asked if I would accompany them, as I had played a major role in their escape from Orkney.

The following morning, we set out on horseback for Grjót, where Thrain Sigfússon lived with his wife, son, and mother-in-law. It was only about an hour's easy ride north, upriver from Bergthorshváll, and we chatted amiably on the way, as we had done so often before. The path wound away before us, up and over rocky hills, and always with the river rattling over its stony bed beside us, the mountains like shadows in the distance. Before long, the house came into view, not so large as Njál's home, but a respectable and well-kept farm house.

There was a little blond boy of about ten years tending a goat in the field near the house when we rode up. At first, I thought he must be a servant, but as he looked up at us, I saw in him his father's features, and realized that here must be the son whom Thrain's wife had been raising alone, while her faithless husband was abroad dallying with noblemen's daughters.

Skarp-Hedin called to him. "Hoskuld, we wish to speak to your father."

"I'll tell him," said the little boy in a high, clear voice, and ran off behind the house.

We dismounted and tied our horses' reins to a rail along the side of the house. I felt strangely ill at ease, and so must the Njálssons have felt as well. Our cheerful conversation of the ride up had fallen into an uneasy silence. For a time, there was only the sound of the horses shifting restlessly, and the goat munching dry grass in the yard.

Then came a voice from the house, one filled with a bitter contempt verging on hatred. "Well, what brings the three sons of Old Beardless, and their hanger-on from Orkney?" We looked up and, standing in the open doorway, was one of the tallest women I have ever seen. She was dressed in an embroidered linen dress fine enough for a feast day, although she had evidently been doing household work before she came outside. I could see a butter-churn standing in the room behind her, with milk pitchers beside it. She had a finely sculpted face, and clear blue eyes from which pride flashed brightly. She must once have been strikingly beautiful, but a habitual expression of scorn had drawn lines down from her mouth, so that she looked as if she were scowling.

Helgi regarded her with an evil expression, but Skarp-Hedin was unflustered by her discourteous remarks. "Our visit here is not to you, Hallgerd," he said in an even voice. "However, if we ever have need of trading ill-mannered taunts, your presence will be most welcome. For now, we are looking for your son-in-law."

"You have found him." Thrain came around from the back of the house, drying his hands on an old rag. I looked at his face, and was immediately struck by the fact that he, too, seemed hostile and prideful, far more so than I had ever seen him. Then I realized that before, when he had been on the Njálssons' ship, he was one man against four, in the middle of the ocean. Here he was on his own ground. I recalled the blood-feud between his family and the Njálssons' and wondered if Skarp-Hedin was right about it not being over.

Thrain regarded the four of us unsmilingly and tossed the rag he was holding onto the ground. "What is your business here, coming in force against me?"

"Force?" Skarp-Hedin laughed. "Which of us is armed? You would not anticipate men coming in force against you if your heart were not full of misdeeds, Thrain Sigfússon."

Thrain stiffened and gave us one of his scornful looks. At that moment, the resemblance between his expression and his mother-in-law's was astonishing. "Then why are you here?"

"There is the little matter of payment for your transportation here from Orkney," said Skarp-Hedin.

"Not to mention the recompense for the injury my brother suffered because of you," said Helgi, but Skarp-Hedin held up his hand and Helgi fell silent.

"I do not hold you accountable for that," said Skarp-Hedin, "because at that time I was as much under the executioner's blade as you were, and I count it as an injury I received in freeing myself. Nevertheless, you were taken here on our ship, and used our food and supplies, and in fairness it must be said that you nearly cost us our lives in doing so. You yourself said that if we reached Iceland safely, you would reward us richly. We do not expect any riches, but simply a repayment for what we have done for you."

Thrain and Hallgerd exchanged glances, and I realized immediately that they had already discussed this at length. It was obvious that this was no unexpected visit.

"You have arrived back here safely against all odds, with honor and more from your expeditions at the side of Jarl Sigurd Hlodvisson. I can recall your saying many times that honor was more important to you than any wealth, and if that is true, you surely have come back richer than you went out." He gave Hallgerd a furtive smile, and I felt, rather than saw, Helgi bristling with fury beside me.

"It is true that we won great honor accompanying Jarl Sigurd," replied Skarp-Hedin, keeping his voice even with an effort, "but in my mind we left the largest share of it behind us in Orkney, repaying his kindness by assisting you in escaping from him. We gave our aid to the Jarl for two years and ended it not with feasts and gratitude and farewells, but by killing two of his men and fleeing in the dead of night like common thieves."

"A fitting escape for such as you," spat Hallgerd.

"Again, let me say, this is no concern of yours, Hallgerd, though you wish to make it so." Skarp-Hedin still struggled to keep his voice calm, but I saw his face color and knew that he was becoming angry himself. "Thrain, I am speaking to you once more, as someone who shared a long and arduous voyage with you and reached a successful end none of us could have rightly expected. We only come to ask for what you promised, and when we have agreed that it will be given us, we will depart as we have come."

Thrain laughed derisively. "And if I say that you have come like a pack of thieves, to demand what is not yours, who will gainsay me? Who has witnessed any agreement between us? We all escaped Orkney, to avoid execution. All of us equally under the sentence, with the exception of this hired sword you have taken up with, and I would advise you to watch him closely lest he turn his own blade against you as quickly as he did against the Jarl whom he had sworn allegiance to."

This needled me beyond endurance. "You speak of allegiance because you have none to any man but yourself," I shouted. "You speak scornfully to men who risked their blood to save your worthless life, while you hid among the dried fish in a cargo hold."

Helgi snickered, and even Grím's mouth turned up at the corners a bit. Thrain turned pale, and Hallgerd cast her proud gaze on me.

"You have no part in this discussion, whoever you are," she said contemptuously. "Keep silent before your betters."

"When he finds them, he will," cried Helgi. "Without Kári, your son-in-law would now be a crow-picked corpse riding a gibbet in Orkney."

Thrain gazed upon the four of us, one by one, and finally looked back at Skarp-Hedin. "I owe you nothing, for at your hands I have received nothing but disdainful treatment. I have already said that we all escaped from Orkney together, none of us above the other, and I will not give you one stone from my field in recompense." Suddenly he began to laugh. "And what will you do about it, I ask you that? Will you tie me up and bring me back to the Jarl in Orkney, where your lives are as forfeit as mine? Come back when you have more to do than to waste my time with idle words."

With that, he strode into the house. Hallgerd, giving us all one last, scornful smile, followed him in and closed the door behind her.

My heart was pounding with anger to hear my friends treated so, but I knew that it was not my place to speak or act if they did not. Helgi was clearly furious beyond words, and he leapt upon his horse and spurred it, and galloped off alone down the path toward Bergthorshváll. The other two brothers mounted their horses as well, and I followed suit, watching them as I did so. Grím as usual was impassive, and it was hard to read what he thought. Skarp-Hedin had gone white, but two spots of hot color glowed in his cheeks. Thrain had interpreted his courteous speech as weakness, but had made a grievous mistake in so doing. Skarp-Hedin was not as quick to anger as his volatile youngest brother, but as he turned his horse's head back toward his home, and his crooked grin slowly grew upon his face, he looked as fierce as any warrior I have ever seen. In that moment, I realized that while Helgi might have the hottest temper of the three, it was Skarp-Hedin who was by far the most dangerous enemy.

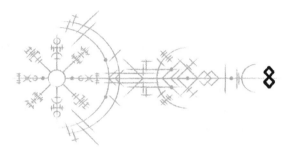

BY THE TIME WE RETURNED TO Bergthorshváll, Helgi was already in heated conversation with his father. We could hear their voices some way off. Grím, Skarp-Hedin, and I cantered up the hill, into the farmyard, and dismounted.

"I will not rest until Thrain has paid for his insults," Helgi said.

"My son, you must realize that this is not a simple situation." Njál's voice was patient, and at that moment, his patience angered me almost as much as Thrain's haughty words had, I was so eager to take action. "You must remember what has happened before this, how many have already died in this feud. Since you and your brothers left for Orkney, we have managed to maintain some sort of peace here. If you were to go now and slay him, it would be looked upon as unprovoked. And you will also recall that I have myself asked you not to harm Thrain, for the good of all of us."

"I think that it is time that you release us from this promise," said Helgi. "If you hold us to it, our only option is to swallow his insults, and be thought cowards."

"I do not ask that you ignore the insults. But instead of taking up a sword against him, let others make the judgment upon him. I recommend that you speak to as many as you can about what happened, so everyone knows what abuse they have heaped upon you." Njál looked at me, as I walked up to them.

"Perhaps Kári could go to Thrain alone and warn him about where his words are taking things. Kári speaks well and can hold his temper, I think."

I myself was not so sure of this, but I was heartened to hear Njál's high opinion of me.

"Now, you may hear people say you are afraid to act," Njál continued, "and you must simply bear that for the time being. Let people see that you must be sorely provoked before you will take action." His face became melancholy. "My advice from the outset was to leave this matter behind, and not ask for compensation from the likes of Thrain Sigfússon. Now that you have done so, you have committed yourself to this course of action, and cannot easily turn back. Either you will let Thrain Sigfússon alone, as I am asking, and be humiliated by your own inaction, or you will be forced to cut through your humiliation with your swords, and with terrible results, I think. We must cast our net wide and hope to capture as many hearts as we can. I fear if you act rashly, it may lead to all of our deaths."

This seemed good advice, and even Helgi was cooled by his father's words. We agreed to let the matter stand for a while and see what fell out from it. Soon we began hearing that people all over the area were discussing it, and most seemed to feel that the situation was now sure to end in violence, despite Njál's attempt to hold onto peaceful solutions for as long as possible. For myself, I agreed with them.

———————

THERE WAS A STRANGE OLD WOMAN who lived with Njál and his family. Her name was Sæunn, and she was the daughter of thralls who had worked for Bergthóra's parents. She had been given her freedom but had chosen to remain as a servant to the family, as she was unmarried and had nowhere else to go. Some said she had the second sight, and none could have begrudged her the gift, as she had little else. She was a hunchback and had one eye that always pointed inward so that one could never be certain of where she was looking. She was given to bursting forth with strange pronouncements, some of which seemed as perceptive as a seer's words, and others which were simply incomprehensible. Given her advanced age, she did little work, except for sometimes milking the goats or feeding them. But she was dear to the family, especially Bergthóra, and her oddities were overlooked.

I was bringing split wood into the house one day in the middle of that winter. Lost in my thoughts, I did not see that Sæunn stood just inside the door. She reached out with one claw as I came laden through the door and clutched at my sleeve with the wiry strength that old people sometimes have. I lost my grip and spilled much of the wood onto the floor, stifling the imprecations which came to my mind. As for Sæunn, she seemed not to notice.

"Get your axe and your luck ready, young man," she said.

"For what, Sæunn?" I began to pick up the fallen wood. "As you see, I have already chopped plenty of wood, and it takes little enough luck to accomplish that."

She did not respond, but simply continued with her own strange train of thought. "Sharpen it well, for soon the wolf will skate across the ice, and blood will be sprayed across his muzzle. And you will need to be behind him, with your axe at the ready."

I was by this time used to her crazy pronouncements and smiled a little. "What wolf, Sæunn? There are no wolves here."

"The wolf with the lame leg." She turned and hobbled away.

I frowned, and suddenly wondered if this would be one of the times that her words would prove prophetic. The wolf with the lame leg? "Do you mean Skarp-Hedin?" I called after her, but she either did not hear me or else ignored me. I soon forgot her words, for other events took them from my mind.

Later that day, three beggar women arrived at Bergthorshváll, while we were eating our midday meal, and they were greeted hospitably and given food. Bergthóra asked them about their travels.

"We have come from Grjót, where we were given food but little hospitality," said one of them.

"That does not surprise me," said Bergthóra.

"We asked where a night's lodging might be found," said a second, "and they told us to seek it at Bergthorshváll. 'For there, you will be among your own kind,' the elder woman at Grjót told us."

"The elder woman?" Bergthóra asked.

The beggar woman nodded. "A very tall woman, with an evil, scowling countenance, and thief's eyes."

Bergthóra's lips tightened. "Not many people are spoken of in the way they would best like. Least of all by the people at Grjót. But you came here directly afterwards, then?"

"Oh, no," answered the first woman. "Before coming here, we went to Hof, and spoke with Mord Valgardsson, who sends his greetings. We told him that we were on our way to Bergthorshváll, and he said that we should tell you what the people of Grjót were saying, and to send the following message—'Is it not time to stop these foul insults upon your honor? It is now time for you to act, this very day.'"

Helgi and I exchanged glances. I could see the anger building in him once again.

"What did the people at Grjót say of us?" asked Bergthóra.

"They seemed to have very high opinions of themselves," continued the first woman. "But they spoke ill of the people of your household. We have heard far and wide that here at Bergthorshváll you were hospitable and kind, and we thought it strange to hear your husband and sons insulted so."

Bergthóra had evidently had enough of the beggar women's rambling discourse. "What insults did they make?" she demanded.

The beggar women looked uncomfortable. "We do not wish you to think by repeating what they said, that we agree with them," said the second woman.

"Do not fear that, but tell us straight out what was said," said Bergthóra.

"They were saying that your sons had the hearts of rabbits and had been turned away by the taunts of women," said the third woman, who had not yet spoken. "They called your husband 'Old Beardless' and said that he was not the true father of your children, but that they had been fathered by a thrall."

I saw Njál look down at his food, his face stricken, as if he did not want to meet the eyes of his wife and sons.

Bergthóra looked around her with flashing eyes. "Do you hear this? You will sit still for these insults? Everyone in Iceland is thinking that you are all too afraid to lift your weapons and avenge your honor!"

All three brothers rose as one.

"I think you need say no more," I said quietly. "Your sons have been goaded well enough already."

"Where are you going?" Njál looked up at us. His face seemed despairing.

"To hunt for lost sheep in the countryside," said Skarp-Hedin.

"You have told me that once before," said Njál. "And that time the only sheep you found was Sigmund Lambason, and you killed him."

Skarp-Hedin gave his father a grim smile. "I think you understand me well. You are less innocent than you play at, father."

"What incident is he speaking of?" I asked Skarp-Hedin. "Who is this Sigmund Lambason?"

"He was one of the men who killed Thórd, my foster-father," said Skarp-Hedin, "as was Thrain Sigfússon. Two months before we left for Orkney, I came upon him in the hills, and he drew sword on me. We fought, and he was killed, and afterwards I told my father I had been hunting for sheep." Skarp-Hedin grinned. "It is time to catch the leader of the sheep now." He strode toward the door, and the other two brothers followed him.

"My sons," said Njál, his voice strained.

All three turned, and looked at their father, who stood up slowly and painfully, as if he were an old man.

"I hereby release you from your oath to me. I know what you are going to do, and I would not have it said that my sons are oath breakers as well as killers."

Wordlessly, the three brothers turned away from him—in shame, I think. They left the house without even saying a farewell.

I stood up and made to follow them. Ingrid, who had been standing nearby, watching us all silently, moved toward me and caught my arm. I looked down into her deep blue eyes and paused for a moment.

"Kári," she said quietly, "defend my brothers well. And come back to me unscathed."

"I will if it is my fate," I responded, and turned away and followed the brothers outside, but my heart beat a little faster.

Come back to me, she had said.

It was a fine, cold winter's day, only an hour or two past noon and already the sun was falling fast toward the horizon. We armed ourselves well, with shields and axes and swords, and set off for Grjót on foot. It was icy, and in places, the path was too slick to ride a horse.

"Do you think that those beggar women were sent by Thrain to lead us into an ambush?" I asked, as we wound our way up into the hill country along the banks of the frozen Hvit River.

"No, I do not believe so," said Helgi. "They said that they had spoken with Mord Valgardsson, and what they reported of him had the ring of truth. He has always spurred us on to take action against Thrain and his slander."

"Nevertheless, we should be cautious. Thrain and Hallgerd sent those women to Bergthorshváll and must know that we will respond."

"Why should he expect it?" asked Skarp-Hedin. "We have taken his insults meekly until now."

By the time we reached Grjót, the sun was setting, and the remaining light cast a weird glow upon the ice and black rock around the farmhouse. Skarp-Hedin went and pounded on the door, but there was no answer. After a moment, he pushed open the door, and carefully peered inside, but the house was empty. Not even Hallgerd and her daughter were there.

"I think you may have been right, Kári." Skarp-Hedin's voice was puzzled. "It seems that we were expected. How did they know we were coming?"

At that moment, Grím pointed. Across the frozen river, a polished shield caught the last rays of the sun and flashed towards us. "It is Thrain Sigfússon. He has at least six or seven others with him."

We walked down to the river bank and saw that Thrain was standing at the head of a group of men, fully armed. He was watching our approach, and when we were within earshot, he called out derisively, "Since you could not get what you wished by proud words, you now bring your rag-tag band with weapons. What are you, four against eight? Get yourselves home like the whipped dogs you are. Or, if you like, cross the ice and we will call Old Beardless to come and collect your dead bodies." The other men laughed.

Without warning, Skarp-Hedin exploded into motion. He brought up his axe, and leaping over the edge of the rocky bank, landed on the smooth ice of the river. He steadied himself, and carried by the momentum of his leap, he skimmed across the ice faster than a man could run. Thrain had turned to his followers, to laugh with them over his taunt. But as he turned back to us, still wearing his insolent grin, Skarp-Hedin swept down upon him and struck him in the head with his axe. Blood flew up in a shower and spattered Skarp-Hedin's face. Then, using one foot, he thrust against a rock and slid off once more down the ice, toward landfall a little downstream of where Thrain had fallen.

One of Thrain's followers slung a shield at Skarp-Hedin to trip him, but he leapt clear of it, and amazingly still kept his balance, reaching the bank without falling. It would have been an astonishing feat for anyone, but for a man with a lame leg it was something that I could hardly have believed had I not seen it with my own eyes.

Having reached the opposite shore, he then turned toward me with a fierce smile, and called out to us, "Now, brothers, it is your turn!" I saw his scarred, blood-streaked face, and only then recalled Sæunn's words.

Soon the wolf will skate across the ice, and blood will be sprayed across his muzzle, and you will need to be behind him, with your axe at the ready.

Giving a great cry, I drew my sword and struck off across the ice as best I could, and the other two followed me, not so gracefully as Skarp-Hedin had done, but we reached the other shore, and drove into the men on the other side.

I myself killed the one who had thrown the shield at Skarp-Hedin. He slung a spear at me, which missed striking me by no more than a hand's breadth, and I drove my sword into his chest. Grím and Helgi each killed two of Thrain's followers, and the remaining two, both of whom were quite young, threw down their swords. I seized hold of one of them, and Skarp-Hedin held the other, crying, "Well, we have caught two puppies! What shall we do with them?"

Helgi, his eyes blazing, brought his sword point near to the throat of the one I was holding.

"Gunnar Lambason," Helgi said. "And Grani Gunnarsson. You had no part in this quarrel. Why are you here?"

Grani, whom Skarp-Hedin held, looked at Helgi, his eyes glittering with hatred. "Men of your family killed my father. You deserve to die."

"And you, Skarp-Hedin, killed my brother Sigmund," cried Gunnar Lambason, struggling in my grasp. "How many men have died unjustly for the sons of Old Beardless?"

Helgi's eyes narrowed, and he swung his sword around, until the point was just touching Gunnar's throat. Gunnar's eyes widened.

"It is unwise to taunt someone whose sword is at your throat, Gunnar," said Grím, who had stooped to wipe the blade of his own sword clean on Thrain Sigfússon's cloak.

There was a moment of silence, as the last of the sunlight was fading from the sky. Then Helgi lowered his sword. "What shall we do with them?" Helgi asked Skarp-Hedin. "I will defer to your wishes as you are the eldest of us. Though my heart says that one day we will have cause to regret it if we do not kill them now."

"Grím, take their swords," said Skarp-Hedin. Grím walked over and picked up the weapons, and then Skarp-Hedin pushed Grani Gunnarsson down onto his knees on the rocky ground. "Our quarrel is not with them. They do not frighten me. Kári, release him."

I let Gunnar Lambason go, and he rounded on me. "We will remember this," he said bitterly.

"So will we," said Helgi.

We crossed the ice to the opposite bank of the river once more, as the full moon rose to cast its orange light over the land. Without speaking, we returned to Bergthorshváll.

When we entered, Bergthóra leapt up, her mouth turning up in her grim little smile. "You return with tidings, my sons? And I include you, Kári, for if the tidings are as I think, you shall henceforth be counted among my sons."

"Thrain Sigfússon is dead," Skarp-Hedin said. "With five of his lackeys. I myself split his skull. We will have to endure his taunts no longer." He seated himself at the table.

Njál shook his head. "I fear that this will lead to your death, my son. Or maybe the deaths of us all."

"You would have them simply hear his insolence without acting?" said Bergthóra angrily.

"It is out of my hands now," said Njál. "You have restarted the feud once more, and I feel that the blood-price will ultimately be paid by all of us here today. I have tried to hold off this fate as long as possible, but I fear now it is too late."

"Were all of them killed, then?" asked Ingrid, who was seated next to her mother at the table.

"No," said Helgi. "We spared Gunnar Lambason and Grani Gunnarsson. They had little part in Thrain's slander, and Skarp-Hedin thought it best to release them, as they had cast down their weapons."

Njál nodded. "Perhaps that mercy will be enough to stop the feud here."

"You would not say this if you had heard their words," said Helgi. "Grani still blames you for his father's death, although you had no part in it, and Gunnar has not forgotten that Skarp-Hedin killed his brother. They will not forget what happened tonight, either. It will come back at us sooner or later, I think."

"I find it strange," said Grím suddenly, "that Thrain and his followers were waiting for us. We thought to take them unawares, but the house was empty. Thrain's wife and child, and also Hallgerd, were already gone. I wonder if one of them had the second sight."

"It could be," I said. "But they knew that the beggar women whom they sent here to Bergthorshváll would tell us of their slander. Perhaps they also knew that we would respond."

"They have been slandering us for two months," persisted Grím. "Surely they have not spent all that time waiting for us by the riverbank."

No one responded. We all were deep in our own thoughts, but unable to answer him. As usual, when Grím spoke his words carried weight. As I prepared to sleep that night, I found myself still wondering how Thrain Sigfússon had known we would come for them that very afternoon.

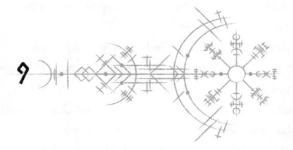

THE FOLLOWING DAY, SHORTLY AFTER THE midday meal, Grím came inside saying that he could see a group of men on horseback from a distance, riding across the plain toward Bergthorshváll. He seemed agitated—or as close to agitated as Grím ever got.

"I came in to get Kári, because he has the best eyesight of all of us."

I went outside, and the rest of Njál's family followed. Shading my eyes against the sun, I gazed out over the plain. There were four men, none of whom were familiar to me. All were armed, but something about the easy way they rode their horses gave me the impression that they were on their way to speak with us, not to attack. I said as much to Njál and his family.

"Nevertheless," said Skarp-Hedin, "we should have swords ready in case you read the signs wrongly."

This seemed good sense, and Grím and Helgi went inside to get our weapons. We did not strap them on, but simply lay them on the ground nearby.

As the horsemen neared, I heard Njál say quietly, "It is the Sigfússons."

"Thrain's brothers?" I asked, and he nodded.

"I enjoin you all to remain silent," said Njál, looking at all of us and speaking in a sterner tone of voice than I had ever heard him use. "I will speak for us all, unless a question is put directly to one of you. You must trust me to see that what is done is what must be done."

The four men rode into the yard but did not dismount. They simply reined in their horses, and remained there, looking down upon us with wary eyes.

"I can guess well enough why you are here," said Njál to the men. "I have been expecting you. I will speak for my sons, and you may hold my life to it, that if you do not draw sword against us, neither will we draw our weapons against you."

"Little enough good did that kind of promise do for our brother," said one of the brothers, a man of hawk-like features whose blond hair was his only similarity to Thrain.

"Nevertheless, Ketil, I can do no better than that," said Njál mildly. "I believe that you have come to speak with us, and not to fight. We are ready to speak with you and will only fight if pressed to it."

Ketil looked down at Njál for a moment more, and then dismounted. As he did so, he nodded to the others who did likewise. They tied their horses' reins to a rail in the yard and approached Njál.

"Your sons, and Kári Solmundarson who is living with you, are responsible for the death of our brother Thrain and four of his companions, as you know well," said Ketil. "We have come to ask if you intend to make compensation for it."

"You are also no doubt aware that my sons were sorely pressed, by the insolence and insults that your brother spread far and wide, and by the fact that Thrain refused to pay them compensation for his passage to Iceland."

"This is the only reason that we have not come against you in force," said another of the brothers. "Will you hear our demands?"

"I will. But let us discuss them civilly." Njál motioned for the four brothers, and also ourselves, to follow him into the house. "Helgi, tell Bergthóra to get us mead enough for all. Perhaps this may be settled peacefully yet."

We all went into the house and were seated around the large table. Bergthóra came in with two large pitchers of mead, and prudently chose to follow her husband's request that she remain silent. Nevertheless, she clearly did not care for these visitors, but regarded them with a pinched and peevish expression. For myself, I could not share her opinion. They seemed brave, honest, and straight-speaking, such men as might become friends and comrades if this matter should be settled peacefully. I was glad to see their manner had little in common with their swaggering brother's.

"We ask only for what is due us," said Ketil, who seemed to be the eldest and the spokesman for the rest. "And we have concern for the welfare of Thrain's son Hoskuld."

"It is well known to everyone present that I have no desire to see this feud progress further," said Njál. "I will happily pay your brother's blood price in full, and make arrangements for Hoskuld as well, to keep the peace between us all. We have seen what has happened because of your brother's refusal to compensate my sons. I do not wish such an outcome here."

"You slyly turn the guilt away from your sons' hands, and your words make our brother responsible for his own death," said another of the four brothers.

"Silence, Eirík," said Ketil, without anger, but nevertheless with authority.

I glanced over at Helgi, and his eyes momentarily met mine. I could see that he wished to speak, but was for now obeying his father's wishes, and remaining silent.

"He was, in a way, responsible," said Njál. "Such slander as he made against us is hardly to be tolerated, to say nothing of the payment owed my sons and agreed upon by Thrain before they left Orkney, which was paid only with contemptuous words."

"We have already told you that we are well aware of the reasons for which your sons killed Thrain," said Ketil, his voice patient. "That is not at issue here. We are here only to ask that you pay the customary blood-price for a man of Thrain's station, less a fair price for his passage to Iceland, to be split evenly between the four of us. If you wish for peace, that is its cost. We will leave it to his companions' families to come forward for compensation for their deaths, if they choose. That is up to them. We must also discuss Hoskuld's future. If you wish an arbitrator to determine the exact terms of compensation, that is acceptable, but let it be said outright that we are unwilling to agree to anything less than what I have stated."

"I am entirely agreeable to those terms, and will gladly pay Thrain's blood-price, as you have said. An arbitrator will be unnecessary, I think. As far as Hoskuld, what do you ask? Surely you have come here with some ideas in mind of how he should be dealt with."

"At present, he is staying with me," said Ketil. "His mother, Thorgerd, wishes him raised by men who can teach him well. At present, there is only herself and Hallgerd in their household..."

Here Bergthóra snorted loudly. One of the Sigfússon brothers laughed.

"…and it is not a place for a high-spirited boy," continued Ketil. "As for his remaining with me, he is a good child, but I have three of my own. Each of my brothers has children enough, and it would be a hardship on them to take one more."

"As I see it," said Njál wryly, "you are asking me to take the child myself."

Ketil shifted uneasily. "It would only be my wish if both you and Hoskuld are agreeable to it. For despite the feud which has torn our families and slain many of them, you are respected throughout this part of Iceland for your wisdom and gentleness. And perhaps, were you to take Hoskuld, it might prove to heal this rift which has done nothing but harm to both of our families."

Njál looked up at Ketil, and his face suddenly relaxed. It was as if a future that he had dreaded had suddenly been averted. He instantly looked ten years younger in my eyes. "Let me speak to the child. If he is willing, I am."

"One more thing remains to be said," said Ketil.

"What is that?"

Ketil again seemed reluctant, but nevertheless looked first into Njál's eyes, and then as he was speaking, his gaze passed around the table and he met one by one the eyes of each of Njál's sons, and finally myself. "It must be said that Thorgerd has requested, and we four brothers have sworn, that Hoskuld's life is ours, and ours alone, to avenge, should he be slain. We will accept no compensation for his death except the death of whoever kills him."

"That is reasonable," said Njál. "But even without this oath, you need have no fear for his safety."

The Sigfússons seemed satisfied, and arranged for Njál to meet with Hoskuld the following day. After Njál gave his word that the agreement they had made would be kept faithfully, and myself and each of Njál's sons had sworn to abide by the terms of the agreement, the four Sigfússon brothers left.

Afterwards, Njál was more cheerful than I had seen him since we first arrived in Iceland. Bergthóra, on the other hand, seemed ill-pleased by taking in Hallgerd's grandson into her household, but was prudent enough for once to remain silent on the matter. Although she was too proud to admit it, perhaps she too was relieved that an afternoon which might well have ended with her sons slain before their own front door had instead ended peacefully.

Njál set out the next day alone for Mork, where Ketil Sigfússon lived, and in only a few hours came back riding slowly, followed by a gray pony on which rode the same little boy we had seen tending the goat in front of Thrain's house.

Njál dismounted first and led Hoskuld's pony into the yard. Hoskuld then dismounted himself, and after carefully tying the pony's reins to the rail, Njál led him toward the house. The little boy looked about the yard, curious to see what his new home was like.

As luck would have it, Skarp-Hedin was the first one he met. I was feeding the goats when they arrived but stopped when I saw them meet. I could not help simply standing and watching them, curious at how such an awkward situation would proceed.

Hoskuld looked up at Skarp-Hedin towering over him, and said, in his high, clear voice, "You are the one who killed my father."

I winced at hearing the statement put so directly, and even Skarp-Hedin gaped at the boy for a moment. Then, he seemed to realize that honesty could only be met with honesty, and he knelt in front of him and said, "Yes, I am."

"I have heard that you are the best swordsman in Iceland."

Skarp-Hedin showed his crooked teeth in a wide smile. "No, I'm afraid that isn't true. My brother Grím is far better than I am, and my friend Kári is as well."

"That must be so. If you were the best swordsman, you wouldn't have that scar on your face."

Skarp-Hedin threw back his head and laughed uproariously.

"I would like you to teach me how to use a sword."

"You're a bit young," said Skarp-Hedin.

Hoskuld shrugged. "I could learn."

Skarp-Hedin grew serious. "Perhaps you could. But there are other important things to learn." Skarp-Hedin put his hand on Hoskuld's shoulder and looked the boy squarely in the eye. "I wish for your sake that your father had not died at my hands."

"So do I," said Hoskuld.

And thus was Hoskuld Thrainsson brought into Njál's home, and adopted as a foster-son.

Hoskuld was a slender boy with Thrain Sigfússon's startling handsomeness, but without his father's oppressive conceit. Everything about Thrain had been calculated and self-serving, while everything about Hoskuld seemed candid and straightforward. The little boy soon won everyone over, even Bergthóra, although I doubt she would have admitted it. He was honest and kind, and did not shirk from work, and strangely enough seemed attached to Skarp-Hedin most of all.

"How do you interpret it," I asked Helgi one day, as spring was approaching the following year, "that Hoskuld has come to look upon Skarp-Hedin as a brother, despite the fact that Skarp-Hedin killed his father? It seems odd."

Helgi shrugged. "Hoskuld probably knew Thrain little enough. Thrain was off chasing women most of the time and had no real interest in the boy. Hoskuld spent all his time living with his mother and grandmother. Hallgerd you've met, so you can imagine what life with her must have been like. As for Hoskuld's mother, Thorgerd, she's a pitiful meek little thing, caught between her rogue of a husband and her bitch of a mother."

"I do pity the child. But still, to befriend your father's killer? I have never heard of such a thing."

"I expect that Ketil Sigfússon is behind it," said Helgi. "Ketil is a good man, an excellent judge of others. I am sure that he has spoken with Hoskuld about what has happened. The Sigfússon brothers did not let on when they came to speak with my father about Thrain's blood price, but they all knew Thrain for what he was—a braggart and a woman-chaser, more often led by his balls than by his brain. They would have avenged him had we not agreed to pay them, but nevertheless they wish for peace between our families as much as we do. I am certain that in some fashion, Hoskuld too knows that his father's death was deserved."

"I wonder if he'd put it that way," I said.

"Probably not," admitted Helgi.

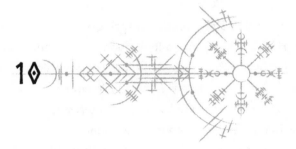

SEVERAL MONTHS PASSED IN PEACE, AND day by day I found myself more content to share the work of the farm with the Njálssons, throughout the short, cold days and long frosty nights of an Icelandic winter. I came to know them all so well that it seemed that I had always known them. Gentle Njál and dour, sardonic Bergthóra. Skarp-Hedin, honest and straightforward, and boundless in courage. Quiet, intense Grím, and volatile, funny Helgi. And, last in my words but first in my thoughts, Ingrid, whose presence was like spring after winter. I now looked upon them as much family as my own, and when I remembered my mother, and my brothers Oláf and Ljót, they seemed further removed from me than these people did.

Finally, spring did follow winter, and the meadows exploded into a riot of yellow, white, and emerald green. The air carried with it the freshness of growing things, and we opened up the house, still stuffy and dark, letting the wind blow the winter air away.

One bright spring afternoon I came into the area where the goats were milked, and found Ingrid sitting on a three-legged stool, speaking soothingly to an ill-tempered goat whose hooves had met my shins many a time. To my amazement, the animal stood quietly while Ingrid milked her, never stirring. I leaned against the doorway for a moment, content to watch Ingrid in silence. Even dressed in her simple working clothes, her red-gold hair plaited into a long braid, she was more lovely than any woman I had ever seen.

She must have seen me from the edge of her eye, and she spun around, nearly upsetting the milk pail in the process.

"Kári, you startled me! How long have you been standing there? You must walk as silently as a cat."

"Only a short time. I found it enjoyable enough simply to watch you. I have no need to say anything."

She cocked an eyebrow at me. "Strange words to hear from you. You've never been a flatterer."

"It wasn't flattery. Flattery is pretty-sounding falsehood. What I said was true."

For a moment we simply looked at each other, and an unaccountable discomfort came over me. My cheeks warmed with embarrassment.

She smiled at me and stood. "Did you come upon me by accident? Or find me in order to beguile me with your compliments? Is there something else you wish to say? You look like a little boy caught filching sweet cakes."

I shifted back and forth from one foot to the other, like the guilty child she saw in me, working up my courage to speak. "Ingrid, I have wished to talk with you for some time. But somehow the winter seemed the wrong time to mention it, and words have never been my strength...." I stumbled over my own voice, paused for a moment, then took a deep breath and went on. "It is in my heart to ask your father for your hand in marriage. But I would not... wish to do so, if you would not have me. I feel that your father will give his consent, should I ask him, but I do not wish to put you in the position of marrying someone who... what I mean to say is, I must know first if it would please you, to... to..."

Ingrid laughed, a sweet, bell-like sound. "Poor Kári. You always have been more comfortable fighting than speaking. I wondered how long it would take you to ask, and how you would go about it."

I goggled at her. "You knew?"

"From the first time you saw me, when you nearly choked on your food. I knew it was only a matter of time."

Somehow, I had not expected it to go like this. But directness is best met with directness, so I asked her, "And what answer do you give me, Ingrid?"

She smiled again, taking both of my hands. "Yes. Of course, yes. What did you expect?"

I leaned forward and kissed her on the mouth, ending it far quicker than I desired. Then, my face burning hotter than ever, I turned away to go find Njál and ask for his blessing.

Njál was checking on the health of some new lambs that had just been born the previous week, running his hand gently along the foreleg of one that had seemed to be slightly lame. When he saw me approaching, he let the lamb go and it capered off nimbly enough, bleating, to join its mother.

Njál straightened up and gave me a pleasant smile. "Kári, my friend."

I greeted him in response, and then, not knowing how to approach a topic other than straight ahead, I told him that I wished to ask for Ingrid's hand.

His expression grew serious. "Now, then, have you spoken to Ingrid about this?"

Mistaking him, I said, "I did, but I had no intent to discourtesy toward what is rightly your decision. I merely wished to ask if Ingrid were willing...."

Njál held up his hand, and I fell silent. "No need to defend yourself, Kári. I am not trying to trap you in any discourtesy. In fact, I had the same question in my mind. I would only wish for my daughter a marriage that is pleasing to her, and I take it as no discourtesy that you spoke with her first. She is agreeable, I would guess?"

"Yes, she is."

Njál broke into a wide smile. "Then, let us take it as done. I am pleased to welcome such a son-in-law into my family. I feel that Ingrid could have done no better had she searched for a mate for many years. It only remains to plan the wedding feast, which we will do as quickly as may be."

The wedding was set for a month following. There was to be no real ceremony, such as are practiced by men of the new faith now, thirty years later—simply a feast, at which we would be presented to kin, friends, and neighbors as married with her father's blessing. That month, between our betrothal and our marriage, seemed to me one of the slowest I have ever experienced, although it was filled with all manner of good things. There were good wishes and claps on the back from Skarp-Hedin, Grím, and Helgi. Helgi, for his part, claimed that he had known from the first that this would be the outcome. Even Bergthóra blessed me with a wry little smile. There were gifts and well-wishes from people roundabout, many of whom I barely knew. Best of all, there were many hours spent with Ingrid. Now that we were betrothed, I took advantage of my position to spend as much time as possible by her side, even when we were working. I came to know her better than ever, and more than ever, I loved her.

As the day of the wedding feast approached, the household began preparations. Bergthóra and Ingrid spent many hours baking, and the finest table settings were taken out and cleaned. Two days before the wedding, several sheep were killed and prepared for roasting. The storehouse was virtually emptied of mead and beer, such that I wondered if there would be anything to drink but river water in the weeks afterwards.

It will no doubt seem foolish, but it was only the day before I was to be married that the thought crossed my mind that I had no clothes of any quality to wear for the wedding feast. I had brought little but what I wore on my back from Orkney, and while Njál and Bergthóra had provided me well with serviceable clothing during my stay in their home, there was nothing that seemed to me fine enough for my own wedding. However, I did not relish bringing the problem to Bergthóra's notice.

I should not have worried. When I mentioned to her my concern that I had only my work clothes to wear, she laughed—she actually laughed!—the first time I had ever heard her do so. And she said, "Did you think I would let you go in rags to your own wedding? I have been at work, and Ingrid too, to make a fine linen shirt and pants for you. It is nearly finished, and fortunate that it is, for tomorrow you shall wear it." She went to a chest that stood in the corner of the room and opened it. Reaching inside, she drew out a snow-white linen shirt, intricately embroidered, finer than any I had ever seen. I was instantly reminded of my father's shirt, which my brothers and I had found in a similar wooden chest, in a little house in the Hebrides, many hundreds of miles distant. It seemed an age ago, another lifetime ago, that the three of us had sat around the chest in the dark house, wondering that my father owned a shirt so ornate. I suddenly realized it must have been his own wedding shirt, saved carefully all of those years.

I was speechless for a moment, and then reached my hand out to touch the complex stitchery around the collar. "It is beautiful. It was not necessary to go to such trouble...."

Bergthóra cut me off with a snort, and her face resumed a sardonic expression much more typical of her. "It is not only for your sake. I would not have Hallgerd say I dress my son-in-law in dirty gray rags."

"Hallgerd will be there?"

Bergthóra must have sensed the dismay in my voice. "I like it as little as you, but how should she not? Her grandson is a member of this household. The last feud began over an argument about who should have the higher seat at a feast. If she were simply not invited, I cannot imagine what she would do. Call down the gods to smite us all, I should imagine."

"If anyone could successfully do so, Hallgerd could."

Bergthóra signaled her agreement with that statement by patting me on the shoulder, none too gently, and replaced the shirt in the chest.

The next morning, I arose early, and dressed first in my work clothes to go out and do my daily work of chopping firewood and letting the sheep out into the fields. The sun was just rising over the slopes of Eyjafell, the mountain east of Bergthorshváll. The red-gold light spilled down the side of the mountain like a flood of fire. I sensed someone standing behind me, turned, and Ingrid was there, barefoot, wearing a light linen dress.

She looked out over the glowing mountain. "It is beautiful, is it not?"

"Only because it reminds me of you. The light is exactly the color of your hair."

She laughed. "You say you are clumsy of speech, but it does not seem so to me. Your words are as graceful as those of any poet."

I took her in my arms and kissed her, long and deeply, but was interrupted by a wry laugh from the direction of the house. I pulled reluctantly away from her, and found Helgi leaning against the door post, grinning.

"The wedding hasn't happened yet, future brother-in-law. Cool your fires for another few hours, and then let them burn as they will."

Ingrid looked at Helgi, her eyes sparkling. "Don't listen, Kári. He is only jealous because he can't find a woman himself." Then she turned on her heel and walked toward the house, slapping her brother on the chest as she swept past him.

Helgi then walked out toward me, still laughing. "She has a temper, Kári. I warned you the first day you met her."

Shortly before the time for the midday meal, the guests began to arrive, and I went inside to change into the new clothes Bergthóra had made for me. My delight in them when I had first seen them had evaporated a little—I now felt somewhat ill at ease in clothes so ornate. Then I saw that all three of Ingrid's brothers were dressed in equally fine clothes and felt less conspicuous.

Guest after guest arrived. Many I knew—Mord Valgardsson, then the four Sigfússon brothers, Ketil, Thorkel, Eirík, and Lambi. Shortly afterward Hallgerd swept in as if she were the queen of Norway, bringing in tow a frightened mouse of a girl whom I correctly guessed was her daughter Thorgerd, Thrain Sigfússon's widow. A dark-haired, broad-shouldered man came in after that, and was identified as Flosi Thórdarson, a kinsman of Hallgerd's dead husband, Gunnar of Hlidarend. Others came, filling the house to bursting, and names were called out which meant little or nothing to me—friends, neighbors, and distant relations from all over that part of Iceland. Then the feasting began.

I have never seen so much consumed so quickly. It snowed food and rained drink, as the saying goes, and there was much laughing and talking, and the afternoon wore on. I saw little of Ingrid, who had been swept away early on by the female guests, for what purpose I could not guess. I was pleased at the cordiality between all of these people, many of whom had been only recently facing each other across sword edges.

Only Hallgerd struck a slightly sour note, not that it was unexpected. She pointed out in a bitter voice to Bergthóra that she was deliberately selecting the lower seat, so as not to give offense to people who counted such things as important. Bergthóra gave her an outraged stare and was about to respond when her husband caught her arm and asked her to refill the pitchers of mead. Bergthóra had to content herself with a deadly glare and a contemptuous snort. I do not know if Njál intervened deliberately, but it was certainly fortuitous that it happened when it did.

The feasting went on until nightfall, and gradually the revelers dispersed, returning to their various homes. I was wondering how long it would take before all of them left when Njál came to me with a knowing smile and patted my back. "We will arrange for saying farewells to the rest and cleaning up. You may go to her, and my blessings with you. All has been prepared for you." He gestured toward a small side room that opened off the main sleeping area. I smiled at him, blushing a little, and he reached out and clasped my forearm.

"Welcome, my son-in-law," he said, and then gently pushed me off toward the little room.

I walked slowly toward the doorway, my heart pounding, and entered the room. Ingrid was there, as I knew she would be, still dressed in her wedding dress, her burnished hair flowing loose and shimmering by the light of an oil lamp. She had been seated on the bed but stood when I entered.

I quietly closed the door, and then went to her and took her in my arms. "Helgi is not here to stop us now." I kissed her again, this time letting it last as long as we wished it to.

Afterwards, she glanced up at me for a moment, and then looked away. "Kári..." she began and faltered. I saw that she was frightened.

I spoke soothingly. "There is nothing to fear. As long as you are with me, there is no reason to fear."

Her gaze met mine again, and in the dim light, her sea-blue eyes seemed endlessly deep. "I know that. I ache with desire for you. I fear only that I shall not be able to please you as you deserve."

I touched her cheek. "You are all I need or shall ever need. We shall please each other."

I reached out and undid the fastenings down the front of her dress, one at a time. My hands were trembling. The dress slipped easily over her shoulders and crumpled at her feet. I gently lifted her thin linen shift over her head, and she stood naked before me, her skin glowing fair in the flickering flame.

I have never seen a woman so beautiful. She was like a vision of an elf-maiden—alluring, completely unashamed of her own lovely nakedness, drawing me to her like a magnet to steel.

I ran my hands down her sides, amazed at her softness under my work-hardened fingers. I traced the curve of her breast with one fingertip, and she gave a little shiver of pleasure and smiled.

I picked her up. She seemed to weigh no more than a child in my arms. I lay her gently down on the skins that covered the bed, and her russet hair cascaded across the soft fur beneath her. I pulled my own shirt off, then the fine linen pants. Before I went to her, I stood for a moment, letting her eyes move over my naked body and the obvious sign of my desperate need for her. Then she reached out for me.

Even though I was shaken with a desire greater than I have ever known,

I went slowly with her, wishing to be as gentle as she needed for her first time with a man. My hands caressed every inch of her skin, and I followed it with slow kisses. I felt her passion rise, any apprehension she had felt disappearing in a flood of raw desire.

Finally, we lay belly to belly, bare skin against bare skin, and I was poised, ready to enter her warm depths. My lips brushed hers, feather-light. She responded with a deeper kiss, and our tongues danced against each other as our bodies merged.

I have never experienced such pleasure in my life as that first time. Her arms encircled me, pulling me deep into her. She moved her lips next to my ear, and said in a breathless voice, "Kári. My one, my only love. Take me, take me now, make me yours…"

No longer could I contain my need. She clung to me as we coupled, and we rode the waves of pleasure to their crest—pleasure so great that we both cried out at the end of it, not caring if the people in the next room could hear us. Afterwards, we lay there for some minutes, breathing in the cool night air in great gasps, my hair brushing the milk-white skin of her cheeks.

She ran her hands along the naked skin of my back, and I shuddered and held her close. She whispered into my ear, "I think I have been waiting for this moment since I first saw you."

I buried my face into her neck and nearly wept with joy.

That whole night long, we reveled in each other's bodies. In the depths of the night she woke me, her hand stroking me, reawakening the fire that had only an hour before been quenched. Afterwards we slept once more, but then I was roused, this time by my own need, and moved one hand to slip between her legs, where she was still wet from the last time we made love.

She gave a little laugh, and said in a sleepy voice, "So soon, my love? How long has your lust been dammed up, that it all needs to be released in a single night?" But she turned toward me and slipped into my embrace with a moan of pleasure.

Dawn came far too soon.

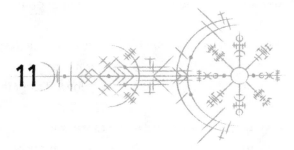

11

AFTER OUR MARRIAGE, INGRID AND I continued to live at Bergthorshváll, and for some years there was peace between the families in our area of Iceland. The Sigfússons continued to pay respectful visits to Njál and his family, in order to see that all was well with Hoskuld in his new home. The boy was prospering, and they saw that. The visits gradually decreased in frequency as the years passed. Ketil Sigfússon and his brothers were always cordial, but never stayed long, and there was an odd tension that hung in the air as long as they were there. Although peace had been established between the families, they would never love each other. No wonder, considering the strife that had torn them for so many years prior to my arrival.

The only frequent visitor to Bergthorshváll was Mord Valgardsson, whose father had died that spring. Once that duty was gone from his life and his time was freer, he came often to visit with Njál and his family and was always welcomed warmly. Compared with his manner at our first meeting, he seemed a little distant and preoccupied on these visits, which I attributed to grief over the loss of his father. Also, I thought he treated young Hoskuld with unnecessary sternness, hardly ever speaking to him in a friendly tone. The only time I questioned him about that, he responded that he had no personal dislike for the boy, he simply had little love for the Sigfússons and did not like the way in which they had foisted their kin off upon Njál's good nature.

"My father thought it was the best way to seal peace between our families," Skarp-Hedin had replied on that occasion.

"Perhaps," said Mord. "I wonder if it will work, in the end. Foster children do not always grow up to love their foster-parents' blood sons."

"Hoskuld has never shown us anything but devotion."

Mord regarded him with a raised eyebrow. "Thus far."

Spring turned to summer, then summer to an early autumn. Cold weather came earlier here than in the Hebrides and Orkneys. My love for Ingrid grew daily, and the life of toil on the farm seemed not so bad when I was able to lie in her arms each night. There was only one thing that was unfortunate—for some years we were not blessed with a child, for which we both wished heartily. That, however, was a small thing, and I recall those years fondly, a memory of joy long since departed.

It is strange in the telling, that peaceful and happy years have the appearance in a story of consisting of nothing at all. "I was happy." "Ingrid and I loved each other well." How inadequate those words seem, to convey a depth of sweetness that I would give anything to recapture. The years of strife, that make the far more interesting story—would anyone choose to live through those, however thrilling they are to hear of? I would be happy now if I could stop here and leave anyone who will read this in years hence with a story that ended when its characters had everything their hearts desired. Should I fall silent here, and leave them to think that we kept it all, and lived in peace and joy until old age quietly closed our eyes? Are sweet-sounding falsehoods sometimes a kindness?

I am no deep thinker, and I have no answers to these questions. I have always been a man who acts first and thinks second, sometimes to my grief. Perhaps my life would now have a different end had I not been born that way. Perhaps, I say—perhaps, perhaps, perhaps. It is all a pointless game to question one's fate.

However, I must now take a step aside from my story to speak of an amazing thing that happened during these years of peace. We had heard through traders and merchants that there was a new king in Norway, named Oláf Tryggvason, and he had espoused a new religion called Christianity that came up from the lands to the south. Word came that he had sent missionaries to many of the western lands which held allegiance to Norway, and many men of the Orkneys and Hebrides had pledged their lives to a new God, abandoning the old ones. Hearing this, I found myself wondering about my mother and my brothers, and whether they had accepted this new religion, and ceased their devotions to Odin and Thor and the gods we had all worshipped before.

That spring King Oláf Trygvasson sent missionaries to Iceland, including one named Thangbrand who was reputed to speak with great power about the new God. Njál, for his part, seemed eager to hear about the new faith. "If it seems better than the old one, as it surely is, from what I have heard, then I shall accept it willingly."

"Many people round about are still devoted to the old ways," I said.

"That is true. But if the new faith is true, which I believe it is, then it will win over the people even if some choose to fight against it."

Shortly after that, Thangbrand and his followers came to Bergthorshváll, and I was able to see them for the first time. Thangbrand was a quiet spoken man, clean shaven, with very light-colored hair that he kept cropped short. He had pale blue eyes that seemed to pierce through to your heart when he looked at you. His companion Gudleif was the opposite—a bear of a man, with immense hairy arms he usually kept folded across his massive chest, so that he looked like a great, forbidding statue. Unlike Thangbrand, he had long hair and a beard that identified him as the Icelander he was. Njál had been waiting for them to come and had heard much about their travels. He welcomed them warmly and said that he had already decided that he would accept the new faith willingly.

"I will accept baptism today, if it is possible. I wish the rest of my family to do the same, but I will not force them. This seems a decision a person can only make for himself."

Thangbrand wondered greatly at Njál's gentle disposition. I was also much moved by his fervor and felt in my heart that I should follow his lead. "I, too, will take baptism under this new God, for, as I hear, he gives great protection to those who pledge to follow him."

"That is true," said Thangbrand.

In the end, everyone in the household was baptized that day. We knelt before Thangbrand as he told us the words to recite—that we would follow God the Father, the Son Christ Jesus, and the Holy Spirit until the day we died. We promised to keep certain fast days and feast days, and he taught us which those were. The two most important were Christmas in the dead of winter, and Easter in the beginning of Spring. He poured water over our heads and made a gesture with his hand over our heads in the shape of a cross.

"Why do you make the shape of a cross above us?" Helgi asked him, after all of us were baptized.

"Because the cross is the instrument by which Christ Jesus shed his blood and died, and afterwards he came to life again. Since that time, the cross has been the symbol of all that is holy among Christians."

"He came to life again?" asked Skarp-Hedin, a little incredulous. "How can any man live again who has once died?"

"Christ Jesus did so." Thangbrand fixed each of us in turn with those curious pale eyes. "The old gods were subject to death, and all the legends say that they too will one day die. Death has no power over the new God. He offers this unending life to all who follow him truly."

We were all quite impressed by this.

Many families in our area of Iceland willingly embraced the new religion. The Sigfússons were baptized, I heard, and so was Flosi Thórdarson, the dark-haired man to whom I had been introduced at my wedding feast.

Only one family nearby resisted strongly. Mord Valgardsson refused to speak with Thangbrand and his followers, saying that he and his household would not accept the new God.

"Let the new God show his face to me," Mord told us one day while he was visiting Bergthorshváll, "and I will accept him."

"Have the old gods shown their faces to you?" Njál asked mildly.

"They have been worshipped for centuries," Mord snapped, his voice uncharacteristically sharp. "I will not change what I do because of an upstart king in Norway, nor because my neighbor has been taken in by his lackeys."

I looked at Mord with a frown. I had never heard him speak to Njál like this before. But immediately afterwards, he apologized for his harsh words, and his voice regained its customary warmth. Although, as always, his eyes darted around the room as he spoke, as if he were a caged animal looking for a means of escape.

Thangbrand passed on about the land. His following increased, and so did the tales of astonishing events which were accomplished in the name of the new God. The following spring, Thangbrand's ship, the Bison, was wrecked off Bulandsness in the east part of Iceland, and many of the adherents of the old religion rejoiced, saying that Thangbrand's disrespect for the old gods had finally caught up with him. However, Thangbrand and the others on the ship were rescued without the loss of a single life, and Thangbrand and the Christian converts interpreted it differently—that although the ship had been destroyed, the new God had held his hand over his faithful followers.

Despite miracles worked in the name of the new God, there was still great opposition to Thangbrand and his men on the part of many, and it looked likely to break out into violence. Both sides made plans to present their cases at the Great Assembly that summer. It was decided that to maintain peace it was essential that Iceland have only one religion, and the Law Speaker at the Great Assembly would decide which it would be. However, it was not known how he would decide what to do, since there were many powerful men among both the Christians and the adherents of the old religion.

Njál and his whole family decided to attend the Great Assembly, as all were devoted to the new faith and had great interest in the decision which would be made. Njál especially seemed eager to see what the outcome would be.

"I am certain that the events of this summer will be long remembered by the people of Iceland, whichever way the decision goes," he said, as we prepared our horses and gear for the journey.

"And which way do you think it will go, Father?" asked Helgi.

"I believe that the new faith will triumph, although it may not be without a fight."

We left Bergthorshváll on a warm summer morning, and rode fairly slowly. That evening, we made camp by the Thjorsa River, which lay about halfway between Bergthorshváll and our destination. We were met there by a number of other people from our area, all alike in our intent to attend the Great Assembly and see what the outcome would be for the adherents of the two faiths.

We arrived two days after our departure at the Thingvellir, the great plain of the Assembly, which is a sprawling, flat valley between rocky cliffs. Already there were great numbers of people who had erected their booths and tents on the plain, and we joined them.

The first task of the Assembly was to choose one man to be the Law

Speaker, the person whose job it would be to make the final decision regarding any matters at issue. It was a source of great argument as to who should be the Law Speaker at that Great Assembly, for obvious reasons—every man there wished the Law Speaker to be chosen from men of his own party.

In the end, the man chosen was Hall of Sida, who had been the first Christian baptized in Iceland. The men who still accepted the old religion were angry at this choice and felt that it made the Christians certain to win dominance over the Assembly. The first day of the Great Assembly was taken up mostly in shouting. There was such an uproar that none could be heard. For myself, I went to listen and not to speak, but from the angry words I heard I felt sure that soon there would be bloodshed.

Hall of Sida listened to what the people were saying, both the Christians of his own beliefs and the men of the old ways. And then, Hall did an amazing thing. He said that despite the fact that he had been chosen as Law Speaker, he would not be the one to proclaim what the law was on the subject of the new religion. "I have selected another who shall speak the law for us," he told us, and he designated Thorgeir Tjorvason, a chieftain respected for his wisdom, to rule on this issue.

Now there was an uproar among the Christians, for Thorgeir was a believer in the old gods, and the Christians shouted out that Hall of Sida had betrayed them. Still, the Law Speaker's words are unassailable, and none could gainsay his choice. Hall of Sida demanded that everyone there take oaths to abide by whatever Thorgeir spoke. Everyone did so, but there was much consternation among the Christians who were there.

After this matter had been settled, Thorgeir went off and sat apart from the people, with a hood drawn over his head, for an entire day. Then he rose, and went and stood upon the Law Rock, from which all such decisions are made, and gave his answer.

"This shall be our law," he said in a great voice, and all were silent, so that nothing could be heard but his words and the wind whistling among the rocks on the Thingvellir. "All men in Iceland shall take the new faith and take oaths that they will believe in the Christian God—the Father, the Son Christ Jesus, and the Holy Spirit. All worship of the old gods shall henceforth be abandoned, and the penalty for continuing them will be outlawry."

The adherents of the old religion were aghast, but all had taken oaths to abide by the new law, and in one stroke, without a drop of blood shed, the whole land became Christian.

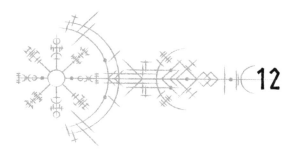

12

IT IS SAID THAT IF A man has children, then his blood will outlive him—that a man's children will carry part of him, and their children as well, so that as long as he has descendants, he will never truly die. Watching Hoskuld Thrainsson as he grew, I sometimes wondered if the blood of his dead father would eventually show itself. I certainly did not hope for this, as in my mind Thrain was not a man whose character deserved immortality. But thinking about the old belief that a son would follow his father, willing or no, made me perhaps more aware of Hoskuld's temperament as the years passed. For the first few years, it appeared that Hoskuld was an entirely different person than his father had been. He was kind and gentle, yet straightforward with an open heart. All of us, and Skarp-Hedin the most, had great hopes for him as he grew toward manhood. But as this event approached—during his fifteenth or sixteenth year, just as a boy is beginning to feel himself as a man—a change began to take place.

It was subtle at first and directed for some reason primarily at Njál and Grím, the one of the three brothers who was most like Njál in personality. Perhaps he interpreted their quiet dispositions as weakness, or perhaps even at that young age, he had begun to harbor some secret grudge against them, the two calmest members of the family. He began to speak haughtily to them, taking advantage of their reserve to speak his mind when it was not his place to do so.

One day, Njál asked him to go fill the water jugs at the river, and Hoskuld regarded him with one raised eyebrow. The expression immediately reminded me of his grandmother Hallgerd. The similarity was like a chill in my heart.

"Send one of your own sons. I am no servant to labor so, and your own sons do little enough real work about this place."

Njál was taken aback but said nothing in reproach. He had to be pushed far before he would scold. In the end, I went down to fetch the water myself.

As I was bringing the jugs into the house some time later, I saw Hoskuld idling about the yard. "Hoskuld, my lad," I said to him, trying to keep my voice friendly so as not to seem a threat, "it sounded ill that you refused your foster father so. You should think of the debt of gratitude you owe him."

"A debt I would as soon pay off and not have to my account," he said in a gruff voice.

"That was unkindly said."

He turned to me, and his expression seemed to lack some of its customary warmth. "You should understand how I feel, being yourself a guest in this man's house. We are little better than servants, you and I, workers paid only with food and a bed, to do the chores his own sons disdain."

This surprised me greatly, both because it was discourteous toward the man who had taken him in, and also because it was completely unjust. The Njálssons always shared in the daily work gladly, usually with their father working beside them as well.

"I do not see it that way," I said. "I feel as if we are both treated as if we were blood kin, and that there is hardly any difference between our treatment and the treatment of Njál's own sons."

Then his expression changed and became a little wary. "I should not have spoken this way to you. I am sorry."

I wondered at the time whether there had been some conflict between Hoskuld and Njál that I was unaware of. I thought back over the previous days, but try as I might, I could not recall any reprimand that Hoskuld had received, that he might have taken ill.

I soon forgot about it, and seemingly, so did he. That afternoon, I saw Hoskuld and Skarp-Hedin play-fighting using two long sticks as swords, much the way my brother and I had when we were children. Both laughed as they lunged and parried and turned, and Skarp-Hedin acted like the biggest child of the two of them. I smiled and decided that whatever had been the cause of the strife, it was over.

One night in autumn, Ingrid and I lay next to each other, skin against skin. We had just made love, and I felt her warmth and sweetness still surrounding me as I lay, sated and half asleep, with my arm resting upon her flat belly.

"Your strong arm encircles me," she whispered in the darkness, "to keep your son safe."

I did not hear her clearly, and said, my voice still drowsy, "What do you mean, my love?"

"Your arm," she said. "It rests against your son."

Suddenly, I was wide awake. My heart pounding, I sat up in bed, the soft skin coverlet slipping from my bare shoulders. "My son?"

I looked down at her, barely visible in the darkness. Her voice came quietly, like a breath of wind. "You are to be a father, Kári Solmundarson of the Hebrides."

I sat there for some time, trying to think of something to say, and failed completely. Ingrid laughed softly at my confusion.

"A son?" I asked again, when I had recovered sufficiently to find my tongue. "How do you know it is to be a son?"

Ingrid reached up and pulled me back down to her, and curled into my body, sighing deeply. "I simply know. A little boy, fair-haired like his father."

Drowsiness is a strange thing. After her mysterious pronouncement that we were to have a boy, Ingrid took my hand in hers and pressed it against her belly and was asleep within minutes. As for me, although I had been nearly asleep when Ingrid spoke, it was deep in the night before sleep found me again.

———————

THE NEXT MORNING, I WOKE AND wondered if it had been a dream, but Ingrid assured me that she was quite certain, in that strange way that women sometimes have, that we were indeed to have a son some time the next spring.

Dazed, I got up and dressed, with hardly a word. In truth, I did not know whether I was elated, confused, or terrified. Perhaps some of all three. It is an amazing thing, I reflected, as I ate and prepared for my day's work. All humans begin in this fashion, but does it not seem strange to consider it? Some night, not too long before, we had clasped and twined naked together in the dark, interlocking. Then our breath quickened, there was a moment's shuddering against each other, and a rush of the sweetest pleasure. From this, a child will come. It is hardly to be believed.

It was Helgi, of course, who brought me out of my reverie. That morning I was feeding the goats, hardly aware of what I was doing, my eyes vague and distant, when his voice cut through my dreaming.

"What's the matter with you today? You look like a seer in a trance. Or perhaps you are just sick to your stomach. Which is it?"

I looked up at him and grinned sheepishly. "Helgi, Ingrid is to bear a child."

He stared at me openmouthed for a moment. I felt good to have caught him unawares for once. Then he gave a great whoop and clouted me on the back so hard it nearly took my breath away, and called out for his brothers.

Soon all three were standing in the yard, giving me their congratulations. "It's high time." Helgi grinned broadly.

"What do you mean by that?"

"I mean, it's been six years since you married. You've taken long enough to father a child."

"It's not been from lack of trying," I said, giving him a broad grin in response. Skarp-Hedin laughed loud and long, and even Grím chuckled a little.

All of the household soon knew about the baby, and all were pleased for Ingrid and I. Sæunn, now well past her eightieth year and toothless as a baby herself, patted Ingrid's flat belly with her wizened hand and gave her own version of a blessing: "Good seed in there—good father, good mother. Good parents bring forth good sons."

At hearing this, I glanced surreptitiously at Hoskuld, who was standing nearby, a distant and unreadable expression on his striking, handsome face.

And arrogant, dishonorable fathers, what do they bring forth?

Hoskuld caught my eye, and I looked away, but not before seeing a new expression grow in his face as he saw that I had been watching him, one that I had not seen before. It bordered on open hostility. It was an expression that said, Look at Kári, standing there, playing the dutiful son-in-law, crowing about fathering a child on the old man's daughter. He's one of them now.

Once again, I wondered at the change, and could not imagine what might be the cause of it.

It seemed others had noticed how Hoskuld's formerly warm and open personality had altered. Shortly thereafter, Mord Valgardsson was at Bergthorshváll, on one of his frequent visits. It so happened that at that time Hoskuld was away for several days, visiting his uncle Ketil Sigfússon at his home at Mork, and Mord mentioned that even he had seen a change, despite the fact that his contact with Hoskuld was intermittent.

"The last time I saw him, he came up to me and complained bitterly about being sent to live with you and spoke the name of Njál in a tone that made it sound like a curse," said Mord, wonderingly. "I had heard traces of contempt in his voice before that time, but I was astounded to hear him speak so openly about a man who has never shown him anything but kindness—especially to me, as I am your friend, Njál, but neither kin nor a close friend of his. I hardly knew how to respond."

"Do not wonder at it too greatly," said Grím. "He has been nearly that open with us."

"He is as haughty as his father and his grandmother," said Helgi. "None would have expected him to turn out so, seeing what he was like as a child six years ago."

"Six years can be a long time," said Njál. "Much can happen in that span."

"That is true, but I wonder what it is that has happened," replied Mord. "As I see it, there is no cause for his attitude towards you."

"He minds his tongue around me," said Helgi, "only because he knows that I would clout the little pup if he gave me insult—as I have once or twice before, I might add. Mother tolerates it as little as I, using her words as I do my fists. But Father and Grím are slow to anger, and it is toward them that he directs the greatest share of his contempt, especially when Mother and I are not there."

"I do not understand it at all." Skarp-Hedin sounded greatly distressed. "I am sure that none of us have given him reason to treat us so."

"Have any of you spoken to him about it?" asked Mord.

"I have," I responded. "He said, not in so many words, that he resented his position here and felt himself to be a servant. He seemed surprised I did not feel so myself, as I am not a blood relative. When I said I felt great kinship with the family, I thought he became warier, as if he thought I might not be safe to confide in anymore."

Njál shook his head. "I have never treated him as less than any of you. In fact, because of the circumstances by which he came to us, I have perhaps laid work more lightly upon his shoulders than upon any of us."

"I wonder," said Mord, "if his uncle has been poisoning his mind with these falsehoods and scornful words."

"Ketil, you mean?" asked Helgi.

"He, or one of the others."

"It seems hard to believe," said Njál doubtfully. "There has been peace between our families for six years now, and although I do not think we will ever love each other, the feud is long over and buried. I see no reason for them to poison the boy's thoughts against us, after so much time has passed."

"People here have long memories. I would watch how Hoskuld's manner appears when he returns from his visit with Ketil. Perhaps he is the source of the disdain."

"I cannot believe it," said Njál. "Ketil has always been straightforward and spoken his mind openly."

"How do you know that? You are open-hearted yourself, so you assume all others are the same. Trust me. Hoskuld did not learn these disdainful words all on his own. Perhaps it was not Ketil, but someone taught them to him."

No one responded. I thought that Njál and his three sons all looked deeply concerned, and Skarp-Hedin seemed almost stricken, as if he were unable to comprehend how this boy whom he had loved had grown scornful and cold.

"I would advise you of one thing further." Mord's voice sounded almost reluctant. "Hoskuld has not forgotten that Skarp-Hedin killed his father, and that Grím, Helgi, and Kári were there and fought by his side. He will never forget it. He has told me as much. That he has forgiven it, I seriously doubt. These old wounds have a way of becoming infected again, and when they do, there is usually blood spilled."

"Surely you cannot believe Hoskuld would take up arms against one of us," said Njál incredulously.

"Skarp-Hedin has taught him how to handle a sword," said Mord. "I hope that he will not regret it one day. I am no seer. I do not foretell, I merely warn. Nevertheless, I think that all of you should be cautious around him, especially you, Skarp-Hedin. The likelihood is that his words are only words, but I do not wish for you to discover they were more than that as you lay dying."

THE SENSE OF CHILLY TENSION CONTINUED to grow, but slowly. Upon returning from his uncle's house, he seemed no worse, but certainly no better. Over time, however, Hoskuld's bitter contempt became more marked, and more than once I saw him wearing a bruise on his cheek, placed there by one of Helgi's fists. Then the winter came and gripped all of the northern part of the world in its claws, as my son grew within Ingrid's belly. Ingrid herself seemed to either be unaware of the increasingly open war of words between Hoskuld and his foster father and brothers, or to be simply ignoring them. Since she had conceived, her mercurial temperament had become more placid, and she wanted to concern herself only with our child, and not with petty conflicts between her brothers.

When spring came, the discord seemed to abate a little, thawing with the snow that lay on the fields about. As the weather warmed, all of us—Hoskuld as well—seemed to feel the pleasant, sweet air flowing around us, and to forget for a time any grudges as we ventured once more into the greening meadows around Bergthorshváll. Ingrid, by this time, had grown so large that she was uncomfortable walking far, but sometimes came to sit on a grassy hillock while Njál and I sheared the wool from the sheep. I watched her as I worked, marveling at how graceful she still looked—at a stage when many women seem ungainly—in her long, loose dress, her russet hair tied back under a white linen scarf, smiling at me as she noticed me looking her way.

A few days later, I was working in the field with Skarp-Hedin and Helgi when I looked up, and much to my astonishment I saw Sæunn tottering out toward us.

She came directly up to me, but when she reached me she was so winded that she could not speak for a time, but simply gripped my upper arm with one claw and breathed wheezily. "Master Kári, your wife's time is here."

I needed no further urging, but sprinted off toward the house, leaving the poor old woman by herself, swaying on her unsteady legs.

I had almost reached the house when I heard a voice call from behind me.

I stopped, my hand on the door handle, and turned. Skarp-Hedin had run after me, and stood in the yard, smiling a little.

"Perhaps you should not go in. My mother is with her and will help her through the birth of your child. Women do not wish their husbands present at this time."

I looked at him narrowly. "And how would you know?" I went inside.

The house, as always, seemed dark after the bright sunshine. After my eyes had adjusted, I went quietly into the little room where Ingrid and I slept. Bergthóra glared at me as I entered, an incredulous look on her face. Clearly, she had not expected me to barge in this way. As I looked warily at her narrowed eyes and tightened lips, the thought occurred to me that perhaps Skarp-Hedin had been right, and I prepared to retreat. But then Ingrid looked up at me from the bed, her face beaded with sweat, and she gave me a sweet, but weak, smile. "Kári, I want you with me."

I stayed with her through that afternoon, as she went through what seemed to me terrible, wracking pains, worse than any I have ever received in battle. I would gladly have taken them upon myself had it been possible and spared her the suffering. Bergthóra would not let me assist her, so I simply sat near Ingrid's head, wiping her face and speaking softly to her as she groaned in anguish. Toward sunset, the pains seemed to grow suddenly stronger, and she writhed and cried out. It wrenched my heart to hear it. Bergthóra placed her large, strong hands between Ingrid's legs, and there were a few moments when Ingrid gasped as if she could not catch her breath. Then she cried out again, and Bergthóra lifted up a baby, wet and pink and crying, and placed the little boy on Ingrid's chest. To my astonishment, Ingrid looked down at our son, and then up into my eyes, and smiled, as if the pain had never been.

A little son, with fine hair as white as flax, just as Ingrid had said.

I kissed my wife, and laid my hand on my son's head, then went to find Njál and my brothers-in-law.

We named our son Thórd, after Ingrid's foster father who had been slain. It seemed a fitting tribute to a man whom Ingrid and her brothers had loved dearly. Within a few days, Ingrid and Thórd were able to come outside into the sunshine, and it cheered me to know that my work was done under the watchful eyes of my wife and my new son.

Two more years passed. The winter following our son's birth, old Hallgerd died, defiant and bitter to the end. Her last words before her eyes closed were, I am told, "I am ready. Has this life been so kind to me that I should wish to have more of it?" Bergthóra seemed almost saddened by the death of her old rival, I thought. She was silent and withdrawn for some days after Hallgerd's funeral feast, but I never spoke to her of her feelings, and to my knowledge neither did any other. Sometimes, losing a bitterly hated enemy can be as disconcerting as losing a friend.

Over those two years, Hoskuld continued to grow colder towards us all. He was distraught at his grandmother's death. During his childhood, she had been the strongest person in his life, and I know he admired her courage and intelligence greatly. Perhaps, now that she was gone, he felt even more cut off from his blood kin, and this fanned the flames of his resentment against us—his foster family. I also think that my son's birth triggered him to become less cordial toward me. Before, he had directed his cutting words primarily toward Njál and his sons, but now he included me in his scorn. Perhaps he felt that now that I had provided Njál with a grandson, I was as bad as the rest. I do not know for certain. But Thórd grew strong and healthy, as bright and handsome a little son as any man could wish for.

When Hoskuld was eighteen years of age, he came to Njál and said that he wished to marry. I heard from Skarp-Hedin—I was not there when Hoskuld broached the topic—that he spoke his request quickly and stiffly, as if ashamed to have to ask such a thing from Njál, whom he disdained. He was in a peculiar position, to be sure—fatherless, and therefore dependent upon a foster father to arrange for his marriage. Interestingly, he asked specifically that his wife be chosen from landholding families. It was a strange request, because there were no families of our rank in the area who did not own at least some land, and therefore any wife chosen for him would have come from such a family anyway. I think he felt that by marrying, he would achieve status as a man and thus be justified in leaving Njál's household. He wanted to ally himself to a landholding family because he wished to assure himself of having a place to go to when he left.

Njál seemed to be not averse to his marrying, although Hoskuld was still quite young. I think that he was relieved that Hoskuld might soon be gone and felt that this would be an easy way for everyone out of what had become a very unpleasant situation.

Njál was well-liked and respected, and it was not long before he was able to arrange a marriage for Hoskuld which seemed to be pleasing to all concerned. The young woman's name was Hildigunn, and she was the daughter of Flosi Thórdarson, the dark-haired man who had come to my wedding. Flosi was a shrewd and intelligent man, although not particularly wealthy. He knew that her dowry would have to be somewhat small, and therefore recognized a good opportunity for his daughter when he saw one. Still, Flosi was a well-respected farmer, and his daughter—and only child—was certainly considered to be worthy of a husband who came from a family of equal status. Hoskuld was a good choice from either standpoint. The marriage feast was set for a month later, a date that fell near midsummer's day.

Njál, his sons, and I all felt greatly relieved that Hoskuld would be leaving soon. Hoskuld, however, suddenly began behaving even worse toward us all, as if the fact of his wedding being arranged and the date set meant that he was already no longer part of our household, nor even bound by the laws of courtesy. Helgi spent the majority of the month in a state of high fury, and it was only his father's request for peace within the household that kept him from pummeling Hoskuld until he was bloody.

The day of the wedding feast arrived, and we all rode to Flosi's house at Svinafell, where the feast was to be held. Thórd we left at Bergthorshváll with old Sæunn, who was delighted to care for him for the day. They loved each other dearly, perhaps because her babblings were quite as incomprehensible as his were.

On the way there, and still more after we arrived, Hoskuld strutted in his finery, resembling his father more than ever. His disdain of all of us was all the more cutting because it was displayed before guests.

Hildigunn, for her part, seemed a quiet, unsmiling girl. I watched her as she sat in her place at the feast, unable to tell if Hoskuld's arrogance attracted or repelled her. Ingrid and Bergthóra spent a great deal of time speaking with her, as did Flosi's wife Steinvor Hallsdóttir. I was not near enough to overhear what they might be saying, and it was not my place to join in conversation with women at such a feast, but I must admit curiosity was burning inside me.

Once during the feast, I found Ingrid apart from them, replenishing the platters of food, and I caught her arm.

"Is Hildigunn pleased with the petty nobleman she has been given?" I asked in a whisper.

Ingrid gave me a little smile. "She is more than his equal. It is Hoskuld who may soon have cause to wonder who has the loftier self-opinion, him or his wife. She may be just what the scornful young fool deserves."

There was a note of glee in her voice that I found quite encouraging.

I caught Mord Valgardsson's eye several times during the feast, once after Hoskuld had made a backhanded reference to his position in Njál's household, saying that he would be "glad to bend his back under his own loads for once." A few men laughed, but Njál looked embarrassed, and Mord looked at me with silent wonder in his eyes at Hoskuld's cheekiness, shaking his head.

The remainder of the feast passed off without event until Flosi announced that Hoskuld and Hildigunn would stay with him at Svinafell. This was already known to most of the guests, but I still felt a measure of relief at hearing it spoken aloud.

"For which I am very grateful." Hoskuld gave the assembled guests a glittering smile. "For my father-in-law's generosity and fairness is well known throughout the area, and I am fortunate indeed to finally find myself in such a household."

This statement was greeted by silence, and even Hoskuld's uncles, the Sigfússons, were shocked at the extreme discourtesy of his words. Hoskuld seemed to realize that he had overstepped the boundaries, and stammered a bit, adding—reluctantly, it seemed to me— "And my thanks to my foster father, Njál, to whom I owe much as well."

Njál stared at his plate, unwilling to raise his eyes to meet Hoskuld's. His three sons were in varying stages of anger, with Helgi of course near white-hot fury. Of the other guests, Mord especially looked aghast, and leaned over from where he was sitting and whispered something into Skarp-Hedin's ear. Skarp-Hedin nodded, his lips tightening into a bloodless line. For a long while, there was no word from any guest. No one wished to be the first to speak.

"I meant no discourtesy." Hoskuld's voice sounded strained, but if he had intended to say more he was interrupted by Helgi, who stood up suddenly, overturning his seat with a crash. I did not know what his intentions were, and perhaps he did not, either. In the end, he simply gave Hoskuld a withering glare, and strode from the hall, swinging the door shut with a resounding bang as he left.

I released my held breath as the room erupted in talking. I was relieved that Helgi had not fought with Hoskuld. Besides the impropriety of such an action at a wedding feast, there is no telling where it might have led. Still, it was clearly time to leave. I motioned for Ingrid to follow me. She nodded and bent her head to say her farewells to Hildigunn and Steinvor. Njál, Skarp-Hedin, and Grím also prepared to leave, and I saw Njál approach Hoskuld, to say farewell.

The room quieted. Everyone wished to hear what would be said. Ingrid paused, her face still close to Hildigunn's, and both women turned their eyes up toward the two men who had met in the center of the room—one young and defiant, and one older and clearly grieving.

"Hoskuld, my foster-son," Njál said, and I thought that he was near weeping. "I wish you everything good. That has always been my wish, and I hope that one day you will see that it is so."

Then, without waiting for a response, he turned and walked from the room. I thought that he looked older in my eyes than he had ever seemed before. Bergthóra followed, her face taut and proud, trying to retain whatever dignity remained to her after the ill-treatment of her husband at the feast. It seemed a mercy that Hallgerd had died, as she would certainly have been there. To have been so humiliated before her old rival would have been more than Bergthóra could have borne.

The ride home was silent. As at the feast, no one wanted to be the first to speak. Helgi had ridden off for home alone, and the other two brothers, cantering slowly along the path in front of me, were lost in their own thoughts. Njál and Bergthóra had fallen a little behind, but I heard no sound of a voice from them either. Ingrid rode pillion behind me, her arm slipped around my waist. It wasn't until we were almost home that she said in a whisper, "I wonder who has been feeding Hoskuld the poison he spat upon my father tonight."

"I have wondered the same thing myself."

"And why?" Her voice trembled near tears. "Does someone hate him so much?"

"I do not know."

There was a long pause. "Is it possible that Hoskuld still hates him because of Thrain's death?"

"It is possible, I suppose."

Her arm tightened about my waist. "I am afraid. I am afraid that this feud will never end."

"Perhaps now that Hoskuld is married and living with his in-laws, his scorn will be tempered by time."

"I hope you are right."

So do I, my love, I thought, as Bergthorshváll became visible in the distance, lit by the eerie half-light of an Icelandic summer night. *So do I.*

13

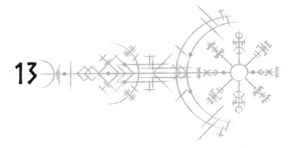

THE WORD BEGAN TO SPREAD ALL around our area of Iceland that there was bad blood between Njál's family and Hoskuld Thrainsson. Some people sided one way, some the other, but most recalled the old feud, and spoke in fearful words about its being resurrected, and wondered how many more lives it would cost.

Njál, for his part, seemed withdrawn and in despair, and would not speak to anyone about Hoskuld and how he had been treated at the wedding feast. I am not sure if it was shame or grief—or perhaps both—which so silenced him.

Only once did I hear him refer to it, and not directly. It was in the middle of the following winter, as Njál and his sons and I were finishing our evening meal.

"I feel in my heart," he said, as the wind of a winter storm whistled around the house, searching with its thin fingers for cracks through which to enter, "that this will be the last winter I will have to endure."

Skarp-Hedin looked up, alarmed. "What do you mean, Father? You are as healthy as ever."

Njál looked at his eldest son, his eyes curiously devoid of emotion. "I have survived these many years, healthy and hale for the most part, but it is my fate to be destroyed instead by discord, and sooner rather than later."

Skarp-Hedin did not respond, and neither did anyone else. We all knew exactly what he was referring to, and none of us wished to ask him to speak further about a topic that so obviously caused him pain.

It was the following spring that the Njálssons and I were riding to the spring District Assembly, as there had been a dispute over the ownership of some unmarked sheep between the Njálssons and Asgrím Ellida-Gríms-son, a neighbor to the north. It was not a great affair, and none of those involved was particularly concerned about the outcome. We rode easily toward the Rang River Plain, where the District Assemblies were held. We reached the ford of the Grjót River by midday of the first day out, and stopped there for a while, to rest and have some food. It was a cool day, with a south wind promising rain to come, but so far it was dry and pleasant enough. We stretched out on the grass, looking up at the ragged clouds scudding across the sky, content just to be motionless for a while.

We rested for a short time, and then forced ourselves to get up from the soft grass with some reluctant groans. Helgi was standing close by me, adjusting the girth-straps on his horse, when we heard the sound of horses. Both of us turned simultaneously to see who might be approaching.

Two men were riding down the near bank of the river, one on a lean gray mare and the other on a handsome chestnut stallion. They were still some distance away when I recognized them as Grani Gunnarson and Gunnar Lambason, the two men we had spared the day we killed Thrain Sigfússon.

I told the Njálssons who they were.

"They are riding as if they knew we were here," said Skarp-Hedin. "Very well. We will wait and see what they want."

Soon the two men came up to us and sat looking down on us from their mounts. Their horses stepped restlessly on the soft turf, and one whinnied softly, as their riders remained silent.

"Well, you have seen us all before now," said Skarp-Hedin finally, with some impatience. "You cannot have ridden all this way just to sit upon your steeds and gaze at us."

Grani and Gunnar exchanged glances. "Indeed, that is not our intent," said Grani, with a trace of a sneer. "We have little enough desire to see you even when it is unavoidable. We do not seek you out. We are on our way to see our cousin Hoskuld Thrainsson at Svinafell."

"Then we will not detain you," said Helgi. "Be off to Hoskuld, who is the only person I can think of whose discourtesy exceeds your own."

Skarp-Hedin frowned briefly at his brother but remained silent.

The two young men looked at each other once more. They seemed to me to be unsure of what to do. Then, without speaking, Gunnar Lambason turned his horse's head northward, and they both rode off upriver toward Svinafell.

"We should have slain them when we had the chance," said Helgi as he remounted his horse, and we continued our journey toward Rang River.

The decision at the Assembly came down without incident, and we were back at Bergthorshváll the following week. The meeting between ourselves and the two horsemen seemed to weigh on Skarp-Hedin, and he spoke to us about it some days later.

"It strikes me as strange to meet them so. Unless I misjudge it, they knew we were there."

"Many men knew that we would be going to the Assembly, and when we were to leave," I responded. "We made no secret about it. It needs no ill purpose to explain that they knew where to find us."

"And yet, what did they want? They simply looked at us and went away."

"It was a chance meeting," said Grím, with some finality.

"It did not seem that to me," said Skarp-Hedin. "It smelled of an ambush."

"An ambush in an open place, and of two untried twenty-year-old's against four seasoned fighters?" I smiled a little.

"All I say is, that is what it seemed." Skarp-Hedin's voice was still completely serious. "And let us remember whom they said they were off to visit."

"Let us ask Mord Valgardsson what he thinks," said Helgi suddenly. "He will be coming to visit here soon. Mord is intelligent and keeps his ear to the wind. If Grani and Gunnar are hatching treacherous plans with Hoskuld, then he will no doubt know of it. Even if he doesn't, he can at least tell us if he thinks you're reading the reasons behind our little encounter correctly."

This seemed good counsel. Mord came for a visit to Bergthorshváll late the following week and stayed for two days. In the second evening, after Njál, Bergthóra, Ingrid, and Thórd had all gone to bed, the Njálssons and I lingered late into the night over cups of mead. We told Mord about our odd meeting with Grani and Gunnar.

Mord raised both eyebrows and looked much taken aback. He did not respond for a moment and seemed to be trying to think of how to frame his thoughts. "Indeed," he said finally, speaking slowly and gravely, "this is the very reason I have come here today."

"What do you mean?" asked Skarp-Hedin. "Are you saying that you knew that we had met them before now?"

"I did not know that you had met. But that you were certain to meet Grani and Gunnar soon, I was sure. I am glad indeed that no worse came of it than some scornful words."

"How can you have known this?"

Again, Mord considered his words carefully. "I was speaking with Snorri Thorgrimsson of Helgafell two days ago, regarding this strange feud between yourselves and Hoskuld Thrainsson. He told me that Hoskuld had boasted at a feast that he had asked his kinsmen, Grani Gunnarson and Gunnar Lambason to find and slay the four of you."

"They did not draw sword on us," said Skarp-Hedin.

"They have rabbit's hearts." There was a trace of contempt in Mord's voice. "They came upon you and saw the four of you there, armed. They realized that they might wound or slay one of you, but if so they would never escape being killed by the other three."

Skarp-Hedin considered for a moment. "There is much that is strange about this. I cannot understand why Hoskuld would do such a thing."

"Have any of Hoskuld's actions made sense, since he began to turn cold toward us four years ago?" asked Helgi suddenly. "He began with scornful words. His father's son, the blood running true at last. Now he has turned to plotting ambush and murder. Is it not time for us to put a stop to this?"

"Kill him ourselves, you mean?" asked Skarp-Hedin.

Helgi was silent for a moment. "I do not wish it. I would not go with that intent. But if it comes to that, then yes."

Mord turned his dark, restless eyes on Helgi. "Consider carefully what that would mean. You would instantly have four mortal enemies, Hoskuld's uncles. Would it not be better to let the matter be...?"

"And be killed ourselves?" asked Helgi, his voice rising. "I do not mean to go after him as we did Thrain, intent to kill. But perhaps to go to speak with him first, to see if words might prevail upon him."

"I think that might be best," said Mord. "Still, do not go unarmed."

Helgi seemed suddenly to realize the impropriety of his planning such an action, without his elder brothers' approval. "What do you think, Skarp-Hedin, Grím? And you also, Kári, whom I count as a brother?"

Grím looked from one of us to the other. "My heart misgives me. There is more to this than meets the eye, and I fear to misstep. However, I see no other way, now that ambush and murder have been planned. If we are not to suspect every rock and hollow of hiding an enemy, we should have this out with Hoskuld soon. Perhaps he would be willing to place it before the Great Assembly this summer."

Skarp-Hedin nodded. "Grím speaks for me. However, I think what Mord says, not to go unarmed, is reasonable. Hoskuld's hatred of us must run deep for him to plan murder, and I would not wish to face ten of his friends without my sword by my side."

All of them looked at me, and I only said, "What you have said seems good sense."

At that moment, there was a ragged intake of breath from the direction of the doorway that led into one of the side rooms. All of us turned. It was Sæunn, standing there, near the little room where she slept. How long she had been there I do not know, nor how much she had overheard. But she spoke, her voice a hoarse whisper, and a shudder ran down my backbone as I heard her words, although I did not understand what they meant.

"Good sense, you say? A thing can make sense and still be folly. Desperate folly! I, too, see no other way, and will not gainsay any of you. Yet you rush forward to meet your fate like blind sheep led by a blind shepherd, and we are all dragged along with you. Every word you say hastens us on to the knife. When all paths lead to bloodshed, how shall a man choose?"

We all stared at her, where she stood panting a little with the exertion of speaking so many words, one wrinkled hand clutching the door. Mord's eyes flitted about the room, and he gave me a fearful glance, as if he were before a seer who could know others' thoughts. Then the moment passed. Sæunn retreated into her room, muttering.

"Is she a seer or is she simply crazy?" asked Mord after a moment's uneasy silence, keeping his voice light with an effort.

"It is hard to say," said Helgi. "I am not sure how to tell the difference."

There were a few chuckles, and the mood lightened a little.

"If we are going to speak with Hoskuld, let it be soon," I said. "There is no reason to wait, particularly if Hoskuld has an ambush in mind for us."

"When, then?" Skarp-Hedin asked.

"Perhaps the day after tomorrow," said Helgi.

"If I may make a suggestion," said Mord, "do not tell your father of your intention. He has been deeply grieved by this affair, and your going to Hoskuld would only upset him further."

"That seems like a deception," said Skarp-Hedin tentatively.

Mord shrugged. "As you wish. I simply want to spare Njál more anguish. If you tell him where you are going, you will have to tell him about the attempted ambush by Grani and Gunnar, and it will burden him further. But you know your father, and the decision whether to tell him or not is certainly yours."

Skarp-Hedin considered for a few moments. "We will go to speak with Hoskuld the day after tomorrow. It remains only to decide whether or not Father should be told."

"I say no," said Helgi. "Mord is right. If we are successful, then we can tell him that we have spoken with Hoskuld and agreed to settle."

"And if not?" asked Skarp-Hedin.

"If not," said Helgi, "he will find out soon enough."

And so, we all agreed that in two days we would ride out to Svinafell to confront Hoskuld Thrainsson.

———————

THE MORNING OF OUR DEPARTURE, I was readying my horse in the yard. It was still very early—just past sunrise—and I thought none but the four of us had yet risen. I heard a noise from the direction of the house, and turning, I saw Sæunn standing by the front door of Bergthorshváll, behaving very strangely. She was using a long stick to beat at some weeds that were growing near the door. She was doing so with great vigor, pausing every so often to catch her breath. I went to her, trying not to smile.

"Sæunn, what are you doing?"

She looked up at me, and to my surprise her eyes were wide with fear. "This plant," she said, still panting, "has threatened to kill me. To kill all of us."

"How could a plant do such a thing?"

She brushed my hand away with surprising strength. "This plant will be the death of the whole family." She glared at me. "I cannot uproot it, I lack the strength. You must help me."

I tried not to laugh, but the amusement must have shown well enough in my face. "Well, Sæunn, there is no need to uproot it. You are doing well enough in flogging it to death," I replied, looking at the shredded weed lying bent and twisted against the wall. "It is in no condition to threaten you any longer."

She simply looked at me in frustration, as if I were a very small child. "I do not need your reassurances, young Kári. I know what I know."

"Well, I will leave it to you, then. You seem to be making a good job of it."

At that, she threw down her stick in exasperation, and walked away.

Soon after, the three brothers joined me in the yard, leading their horses.

"Sæunn is beating the weeds with a flail," I said, chuckling and pointing to the bedraggled clump. "I think she has finally lost whatever reason she had."

"I hope she did not wake Father," said Helgi. "He and Mother were both asleep when I left the house."

No one else came outside, however, as we prepared to leave. I had left Ingrid sleeping peacefully with little Thórd beside her. She had hardly stirred when I kissed her forehead before I left the room. Njál and Bergthóra were normally early to rise, but we saw no sign of them as we cantered off downhill toward the plain.

We reached Svinafell shortly before noon. It was located on a high hill, within sight of the sea. A lonely place, far from other dwellings, with the high mountains on one side and pounding surf on the other. The horizon looked ten thousand miles away, and the ocean was dark and forbidding. Above it, the wild birds cried forlornly as they dipped and soared in the constant wind.

As luck would have it, we saw Hoskuld while we were still some distance from Svinafell. He was alone in the fields, between us and the house. He was standing at ease, tending some of his father-in-law's sheep, which were grazing in the rich pastureland. I knew the moment when he saw us coming, as his body suddenly stiffened. I could not see his face distinctly, but I could tell from his movements that he was frightened. He turned to look back at Svinafell. I thought at first that he was going to run, but he evidently realized that he could not outrun four men on horseback and turned back to us. By this time, we had come close enough that I could see his face. He looked afraid, but defiant and angry as well. He was wearing a sword.

We rode up to him and reined in our horses. As we sat there on our mounts, he looked up at us, his mouth tight with a mixture of apprehension and distrust. "Such dishonorable men you are, that you come, four against one." He kept his voice from shaking, it seemed, only with an effort.

"That is hardly a courteous greeting, Hoskuld Thrainsson," said Skarp-Hedin.

"As courteous as men such as you deserve," Hoskuld shot back.

"You sound more like your father every time we meet," said Helgi angrily.

"And why should I not?" Hoskuld cried.

"Silence, both of you," said Skarp-Hedin. "This is not why we came here. Hoskuld, we have come to speak to you about the words and rumors which have passed between us for the past few years. They have come to the point of threatening bloodshed, and we ask you to answer to them."

"You come to me to discuss them, wearing your swords? Your discussions have always been carried out with the edge of a blade, as my father found out."

"Your father had ample chance to settle with us," said Skarp-Hedin, and his voice sounded weary. "He left us no choice."

"And you are doing little better, it seems," added Helgi. "What have we done to deserve ambush?"

Hoskuld laughed, a high, ringing laugh, filled with contempt. It brought hot blood to my cheeks just to hear it. Then he said, smiling fiercely, "And what is this, if not an ambush? I have never gone out without wearing my sword in the last year, and I have usually tried to make sure that I was accompanied. I thought that tending my father-in-law's sheep would be a safe enough occupation. I never thought you would be bold enough to come to slay me on Flosi Thórdarson's own land. I did not think I would need my friends beside me here."

"Yes, where are your comrades, Grani and Gunnar?" asked Helgi. "They fell back soon enough last week, when they saw us by the Grjót River. Did you really think it was wise to send two against four?"

Hoskuld gave Helgi a withering glance. "I don't know what you're talking about."

"This accomplishes nothing," said Skarp-Hedin, and began to dismount.

I believe that he simply intended to propose that we sit down and have a more reasonable discussion—afterwards he would never say what had been in his mind to do. However, Hoskuld thought that he was being attacked. There was the ring of a sword being unsheathed, and Skarp-Hedin turned and found himself facing the edge of a blade.

Helgi gave a great cry, and jumped from his horse, drawing his sword as well to defend his brother. Within a moment, he was upon Hoskuld, and the two were fighting furiously. I shouted out for them to stop, but no one heard me. I was not sure of what I should do, but then Grím dismounted, and I followed.

Helgi stumbled, and Hoskuld aimed a savage stroke at his sword-arm. In a motion almost too quick to follow, Skarp-Hedin pulled out his own sword, and brought it up to meet Hoskuld's blade with a great clang. Instead of striking Helgi's arm, the point cut upwards and slashed a great rent in Helgi's cloak.

Hoskuld rounded on Skarp-Hedin, his face twisted with anger, and started to raise his sword. Before he could do so, Skarp-Hedin drove the point of his blade into Hoskuld's chest.

Immediately, everything stopped. Hoskuld fell to his knees, and the sword point wrenched free, the bright metal covered with crimson blood. Hoskuld looked up at Skarp-Hedin standing over him. Suddenly his face changed. He looked like a frightened child, and in that moment we all saw in him the innocent little boy who had spoken so frankly to Skarp-Hedin the day he arrived at Bergthorshváll. Skarp-Hedin himself looked stricken, as if he could not believe what he had done.

A trickle of blood was running from the corner of Hoskuld's mouth, and spattered onto his shirt front, to join the widening scarlet stain that was there. His wide blue eyes looked from one to the other, and then, softly but very clearly, he said, "God help me, and God forgive you."

And then he collapsed forward onto the ground and died.

We all stood staring at his crumpled body, and there seemed no words to say. The wind tugged at our clothing, and the birds keened overhead, but none of us moved. After some time, Skarp-Hedin finally stooped to wipe the blood from his sword onto the grass and re-sheathed it. Then, without saying anything, he remounted his horse and turned its head back toward Bergthorshváll.

It was a grim ride home. Usually, when the four of us rode together, we were full of cheerful talk. This time, we were all silent, and there were no sounds but the horses' hooves and the constant, searching wind.

We arrived back at Bergthorshváll in the late afternoon. Njál was in the yard when we arrived. He had evidently seen us coming from far off.

"Where have you been this day?" I could see the apprehension in his eyes.

Skarp-Hedin dismounted, and tied his horse to the rail. "Father, Hoskuld Thrainsson is dead by my sword."

I do not think I have ever seen any man look so stricken as Njál did now. His face seemed to crumble as I watched him, and he put a hand on Skarp-Hedin's arm.

"I tell you truthfully," he said, his voice trembling, "I would rather have lost two of my own sons and had Hoskuld still alive."

By this time, we had all dismounted, and Helgi walked up to his father. "Father," he said, and the dismay showed clearly in his eyes, "how can you say that?"

"I say that because I see far more clearly than you do where this action will lead."

"Where, Father?" asked Skarp-Hedin gently.

"It will lead to my death, and your mother's death, and the death of all of my sons," he said.

There was a moment of silence. In a quiet voice, I asked, "And do you foretell the same fate for me?"

Njál looked up at me, his deep eyes filled with grief. "Perhaps not. When they come for us, they will not find it easy to cope with your luck. I think it may yet carry you through. But for the rest of us, I think it is the end of all things."

14

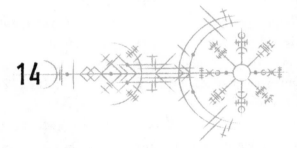

THE DAY AFTER THE KILLING OF Hoskuld Thrainsson, Njál sent
a servant man to Ketil Sigfússon at Mork, to inform him of what had happened. Njál also instructed the servant to tell Ketil that he proposed to put
the issue of compensation before arbitrators at the next Great Assembly,
which was scheduled for three weeks afterward, and urged him to let the
matter rest until that time.

"We will see what he says," said Njál. "I do not hold out much hope, as
the Sigfússons have all sworn an oath to accept only blood vengeance for
Hoskuld's death, but it is the only chance we have of reaching a settlement."

"I am not afraid to die, Father," said Skarp-Hedin. "If that is the price of
my actions, then let it be so."

Njál rounded on his son, his eyes flashing. It was the only time I ever saw
him speak in anger. "Yet you are willing enough to take us all with you. Your
action has doomed not only yourself. Trust me, when the Sigfússons and
Flosi Thórdarson come for your blood, they will not spare your brothers',
nor Kári's, nor mine."

I retired into my sleeping chamber, where I found Ingrid seated on the
bed, weeping bitterly. Thórd, who was then four years old, was sitting on the
floor in the corner, playing with a polished wooden ball that Helgi had given
him, but he kept his eyes on his mother, concern furrowing his small forehead.

"You have heard what has happened?" I placed my hand on Ingrid's shoulder. She nodded.

"Do you weep for your brothers and I, or for Hoskuld's death?" I asked, as gently as I could.

She looked up at me, and I saw a glimmer of the same anger that her father had shown. "There is no difference. When Hoskuld came to us, you all swore to treat him as a brother. Why did Skarp-Hedin slay him? Why, can you answer me that?" She shook her head in exasperation. "What foolishness!"

I was stung by her anger but kept my voice calm. I knew that she spoke the truth, and that hurt me worse yet. "Hoskuld drew sword upon us first, and attacked Helgi," I said, and knew that it sounded a pitiful defense of our actions.

"And the four of you, strong men that you are, could not disarm one boy? I do not understand it."

I bowed my head, the grief and shame overwhelming me. "It was over before we knew what was happening. I do not think that Skarp-Hedin had time to consider the consequences. Hoskuld brought his sword up, and Skarp-Hedin reacted. That is all."

Ingrid shook her head and raised her tear-stained face to me. "I dreamed that we would have a long lifetime together, Kári Solmundarson. It is not to be, I think. Our years so far together—they are like a reflection in a still lake, a lovely picture that breaks up and vanishes if you drop a stone into the water."

"Do not give up," I said, desperately trying to find some words of hope. "Your father has sent a message to Ketil...."

"Ketil and his brothers swore blood vengeance against whoever kills Hoskuld," she cried. "I heard them as well as you. My father knows that. He is simply buying time, time to put his affairs in order before it all ends." She began to weep again. "What shall I do when they come for you, Kári, my love, my only love? I would gladly throw myself upon their swords if they would spare you, but it would do no good. They would only kill you as well. God alone knows what I shall do when you are gone...." She dissolved into tears, helpless, despairing tears that I could do nothing to stem. I simply held her and felt her racking sobs shaking against my body.

Thórd came up to her, placing his little hand on her arm and asked her why she wept.

She forced her weeping to quiet, and after a moment was able to meet our son's eyes. "Your foster uncle has died, Thórd," she said gently, "a grievous blow, and one that we shall all regret bitterly soon enough, I think."

"Father, can't you help Mother to feel happy again?" he asked.

"I cannot, Thórd," I responded, my voice heavy with sorrow, "as I am partly responsible for her grief."

———————————

THE SERVANT DID NOT COME BACK until the next day, but the news that he brought was somewhat encouraging. He reported that Ketil had said that he would speak for his brothers, and that they would be willing to bring the case before the Great Assembly but could not promise anything further regarding acceptance of compensation, nor speak to what action might be taken after the case was heard. Njál sent the servant back to deliver his agreement to those terms and seemed satisfied that he had done all that was possible.

That evening, as I tried vainly to sleep, I became aware that Ingrid was awake beside me, and I felt her hands moving lightly over my body. She whispered into my ear, "Make love to me, Kári," and for a time we clung desperately to each other, like people from a wrecked ship cling to the broken pieces of floating wood that are the only things between themselves and drowning.*

Although it seemed strange, through the next three weeks, the work of tending animals and the performing of farm chores at Bergthorshváll continued the same as before. To an outsider, it would have seemed that nothing was different, that the men and women of the household were acting like any ordinary family. After the servant had been sent back to Ketil with Njál's agreement, nothing more was said by any of us about the death of Hoskuld and what might happen after the case was heard at the Great Assembly. It was as if there had been a silent agreement by us all not to speak of it.

I suspect that much, however, was being pondered by everyone at Bergthorshváll. What the others were thinking, I cannot say. I spent my time thinking about one thing only. Of emotions, I felt many—anger at my brothers-in-law, anger at myself, shame at being part of Hoskuld's killing, fury at

the scornful words he had used against us. Recriminations and self-recrimi-
nations came unbidden to my mind, however much I tried to keep my mind
on another subject. Many emotions, but all circling around one focus, like
eagles circling the dead men on a battlefield—dead men whom, when I saw
them in my mind's eye, all wore the face of Hoskuld Thrainsson. Late into
the night I would lie in bed, searching for sleep that would not come, as my
mind returned again and again to one unanswerable question.

Who was truly to blame for this? At whose feet should this matter be
lain? Skarp-Hedin had held the sword that slew Hoskuld Thrainsson, but
many others had done their part in driving it into his heart. What part of the
guilt belonged to Helgi, the first of the Njálssons to draw sword against Hoskuld? What part was mine and Grím's, simply for being there? And strange
it may seem to ask, what part belonged to Hoskuld himself, who had for
years acted towards us all with such bitter contempt, wholly undeserved?

The guilt did not end with the people who had been there at Hoskuld's
death. No, it spread like the roots of some evil tree, far across the plains and
mountains of Iceland. What part of that guilt should be held to the accounts
of those already long slain in the many fights which had gone before, back
and forth—men who had refused to give over their claim to vengeance? Even
old Bergthóra's hands were not clean of Hoskuld's blood. She had heard of
his death with a bowed head and closed eyes and was silent and downcast
ever afterwards. I believe that finally, after all the long years since the feud
had begun, she was gripped by remorse for the part she had played. It had
started over a petty squabble with Hallgerd over a matter of honor. Now
that her antagonist lay sleeping beneath her burial mound, did she question
whether all the bloodshed had been worth it? I do not know. But I think that
Bergthóra at least realized that Hoskuld's death was the last and most grievous stroke of a chain of revenge that she and Hallgerd had begun.

THREE WEEKS PASSED, AND THE TIME came to go to Thingvellir Plain for the Great Assembly. We prepared for the journey with no joy.
Even Helgi's usually buoyant personality was quelled. Everyone seemed certain that vengeance against us all would not be long in coming, despite any talk

of arbitration. Njál alone seemed to draw strength from our sense of hopeless-ness, and I found myself admiring his courage. There was a toughness in his quiet disposition that did not show itself except in extreme adversity.

We left for Thingvellir on the first day of summer, arriving there three days later. Bergthóra and Ingrid remained behind with Thórd. The parting from my wife was grievous, and there were bitter tears from both of us, which I have no real desire to recount. Our journey began on a dark day that reflected my mood, and we rode in silence for the most part. The contrast from the cheerful, easy conversation of most of our travels together was apparent and disheartened me further. I had little hope that life would ever be the same again.

And what life we all had left was likely to be short enough.

We set up our booth upon the Thingvellir when we arrived, as was the custom for all who were bringing petitions or cases to be heard. Njál seemed calm, almost detached, but his sons—especially Skarp-Hedin and Helgi—paced the ground like caged foxes looking for a way to escape.

"Content yourselves to wait until our case is heard," Njál finally said. "You cannot hasten it by indulging in your impatience."

Skarp-Hedin stopped, and looked at his father in silence for a moment. "Nevertheless, perhaps there is something that can be done before our case is put before the court. Could we not try to garner support from the other men at the Assembly?"

"I do not see what that would accomplish," said Njál.

"If it is seen that we have many powerful men behind us, perhaps the Sigfússons and Flosi Thórdarson will be less likely to attempt any sort of blood vengeance."

"I think what you plan to do is useless, yet I will not stop you from doing it," replied Njál with a sigh. "The fates set this in motion years ago, and it was a foolish notion that any of us could deflect its course."

Skarp-Hedin scowled. "If it is my fate to be gripped by death, then it too will have to fight me, as I will not give up so easily as you have, Father."

We left the booth and went to booths of a number of men nearby, who were known to the Njálssons. I closely watched Skarp-Hedin, whose face was grim and set. He and his brothers spoke to the men earnestly, reminding them of past loyalties, and times the Njálssons had supported each of them. We went from one to the next, every time getting the same answer—that we had exhausted the good will and tolerance of our friends by our willingness to continue this bloody feud, and now we could only count on each other for support.

One of them was Snorri Thorgrimsson of Helgafell, the man whom Mord Valgardsson had spoken of in regard to the ambush that Hoskuld Thrainsson was planning. Skarp-Hedin reminded Snorri of this and asked him to support our case by bringing this to light.

Snorri gave us each an appraising look, one after the other. "Words, words," he finally said, waving his hand in a dismissive fashion. "One man says one thing, and another says another. Mord and I did speak about Hoskuld and his alleged plans for ambush, but I do not recall exactly what Mord said on that occasion. As for what plans Hoskuld actually had, we will never know now, because you have silenced his tongue with your sword. I think that Mord knows more about Hoskuld's plans than I, but he is not here, is he?"

"He is here at the Great Assembly," replied Helgi, "but we have not seen him since we first arrived."

Snorri shrugged. "Your friends seem to be fewer and fewer, as the years pass. Were I to judge your case, I would say you have little evidence to support a judgment in your favor."

"Nevertheless, will you not speak in our support?" Skarp-Hedin persisted.

"You are a ruthless and formidable man, Skarp-Hedin, but I think that you have used up whatever supply of luck you were born with, and I suspect you haven't long to live. I have little wish to ally myself with your cause."

"That may be true," said Skarp-Hedin, his cheeks coloring, "and death is a debt you shall pay as well as I, Snorri. I need your support more than your prophecies. But I am surprised to find your concern for your own welfare exceeds your loyalty."

Snorri seemed unperturbed. "You are not the first man to say that," he responded with a bland smile. "It does not anger me, for it is the truth. If we were at sea, and you chained yourself to the anchor and leapt overboard, no man would feel I was obliged by my friendship to cling to you and drown as well. This is no different."

Skarp-Hedin did not reply but turned and left without a word.

It was like that in every booth we went to that day. None would support us, and some even refused to hear us out. Skarp-Hedin's face became sterner and more despairing after each conversation, and as we passed a group of men, strangers from another part of Iceland, I heard one of them say, "Who is that tall man, with the fierce, set face, and the crooked mouth? He is not one I would wish to face in battle."

"I do not know," said one of his companions. "But I doubt he has many battles left. In his face are the signs of one who is already marked for death."

We returned to Njál in the evening. He did not seem surprised by the outcome of our day's work.

"As I have said, the fates have already decided what will happen," he said. "We have only to wait."

The following morning, we went before the Law Speaker, who that year was again Hall of Sida, as he had been in the year that Christianity was declared the faith of all Iceland. He directed Njál to name the arbitrators whom he had chosen to plead his case. Njál named six men, and I was dismayed, although not surprised, to find he named several of the men who had refused to support us the previous day. I wondered how arbitration would proceed, when our own representatives were unwilling to give us their show of support.

Then Flosi Thórdarson, Ketil Sigfússon, and the other three Sigfússon brothers also chose six men as their arbitrators.

Hall of Sida then turned to the twelve chosen arbitrators to give them their instructions, but before he could do so, Njál stood and asked for permission to speak in his own behalf. Hall seemed surprised at this request, but nevertheless granted it.

Njál drew himself up proudly and gave a sweeping glance at the men before him—some faces hostile, others friendly, many neutral. He spoke eloquently, far more so than my faltering memory records here, but still it seemed to me as the last speech of a man before his execution.

"I appeal to you, all who will arbitrate this case, and also those of you who have come to hear the outcome of the arbitration. Listen to me now, and do not turn your ears away because you see me as arguing for my own side. I am not surprised that I am standing here. It was fated that the deadly seed planted many years ago would finally come to fruit, and I only regret that I am still alive to witness it. I want you all to know that I loved Hoskuld as I did my own sons, and when I learned he had been slain, and by my own son's hand, it was as if the light before my eyes was snuffed out. I tell you truth-fully, I would rather have seen one of my own sons lost, than to see Hoskuld so slain, by the hand of one who was his own foster-brother. I beg all of you who will be arbitrating, both on my behalf and on the behalf of Hoskuld's family, to give me a chance to make a settlement over this killing. I ask you to consider the decision well, and to weigh not only the immediate conse-quences to myself and my sons, but to consider what the ultimate outcome will be for all the families involved."

Hall seemed impressed by Njál's speech, and said, "Flosi Thórdarson, as spokesman for Hoskuld's family, do you agree to consider carefully the ac-ceptance of any settlement which the arbitrators determine is appropriate?"

Flosi looked at Njál, his eyes registering no emotion, but he did not so much as glance at Skarp-Hedin and the rest of us, who were standing right behind Njál. "I will consider it. As far as accepting it, I make no promises."

The twelve men selected as arbitrators retired into the area designated as the Court of Legislature, and everyone else was directed to leave. We re-turned to our booth, and awaited judgment.

The arbitration went on all that day, and into the evening, and no de-cision was reached. I have never been a patient man, and I do not think the Njálssons were either. I have always been better suited to action than to idleness. But here there was no action to perform, nothing we could do to hasten the process, nothing to do but wait. The night dragged on and I only slept restlessly, my dreams filled with words, words, endless arguments over guilt and fate and retribution.

It was not until the middle of the next morning that Hall of Sida sent for us, and we went to the Law Rock to hear the decision. My heart was pound-ing. In such cases, anything from death to outlawry to a simple fine could be imposed, and I had no idea which it might be. Might we die here, myself and these men who had become my family and my friends? I had faced death in battle many times, while working for the Jarl of Orkney, and had never felt fear of death. But somehow, having my head struck from my shoulders by an executioner's sword was a different matter.

Then Hall stood, and his voice rang out above the hushed crowd on the plain.

"It is the decision of the arbitrators that a compensation of six hundred ounces of silver should be paid by Njál and his family, to be split between Flosi Thórdarson and the four Sigfússon brothers, in payment of the blood price for the death of Hoskuld Thrainsson. It is furthermore decided that this amount must be paid here at the Great Assembly, and the debt not carried back with you to your homes, where it will sow further dissent. Because it is unlikely that such an amount of silver was brought here by Njál, his sons, and Kári Solmundarson, it was agreed that to keep the peace, the arbitrators would share the debt, and add to the amount which Njál and family have, to make up the entire six hundred ounces."

The crowd erupted in excited whispers. Whether of approval or disapproval, I could not tell. I let go of a great breath that I had not been aware I was holding. Then Njál and his sons and I took out all of the silver we had with us. It totaled a little under two hundred ounces. Hall brought forth enough silver, contributed by the arbitrators, to make up the rest.

I gave Helgi a sidewise smile of relief. He grinned back. All three brothers were smiling, even Grím. Then I looked at Njál. His face was still tight. His eyes registered surprise at the decision, but I saw no relief there. I did not understand why.

While we were counting out the fine, Flosi had been speaking with Ketil in an agitated fashion, gesturing with his hands in quick, sharp motions. Finally, he finished what he was saying, and Ketil nodded, a grim expression on his fierce, hawk-like face, and both men turned to face the Law Speaker. After all the coins were arranged in a pile on a bench, Hall motioned Flosi forward, as the eldest of the complainants. For a moment, he did not move, and I wondered what he was thinking. Then finally he went up to the bench, and his face was blank and unreadable. The crowd fell completely silent, waiting to hear his words.

He stood before the bench, and looked up into Hall's grave, gray-bearded face for a moment. Then, without warning, he reached forward, and with one angry motion swept the pile of coins onto the ground, where they fell clinking and rolling in all directions. His eyes suddenly flashed with fury, and he glared at Hall and the twelve arbitrators.

"You were selected to arbitrate for us, not to buy peace from this man and his sons, that they may do anything they please and be given no more than a penance to perform," he shouted. "Two hundred ounces of silver have

Njál and his sons paid? Five of them there are. That is only forty ounces each, a fit compensation for a slave's death, not for the death of a man of high standing such as Hoskuld Thrainsson. Our arbitrators are willing to fund Njál and pay the rest. Is that what your purpose was? Njál speaks a few fine-sounding words before the deliberations and pleads for peace. What good will those words do for Hoskuld, struck down for no reason, four men against one? What good will they do Thrain Sigfússon, killed for no better reason than some ill-mannered taunts? How long will we allow this family to escape justice?"

He turned and met Ketil's eyes, and then looked at the other three Sigfússon brothers, who were all standing nearby. "I speak for myself. I do not wish to speak for any other. But not one ounce of silver will I accept for Hoskuld's death. I will accept nothing but blood vengeance."

Hall looked down toward the Sigfússons. "And since he does not speak for you, what do you say?"

"We have sworn no less than blood for blood," said Ketil fiercely, and his brothers all added their assent.

Hall stood silent for some moments, looking gravely at each of us in turn. "I have nothing more to say to you," he said finally, and he seemed grieved by the turn things had taken. "I had hoped that this case would turn out differently. All has been done according to the law, and compensation offered and refused. I can do no more."

Njál turned to his sons and I, and I understood now why he had not seemed relieved after hearing the judgment. Somehow, he had known it would not be accepted. "Let us return to our booth," he said, his voice heavy with resignation. "There is nothing more to be done here. That it would end in disaster, I knew already."

We turned and followed him.

The five of us went back to our booth, where we collected our belongings together and made ready to leave the Assembly.

15

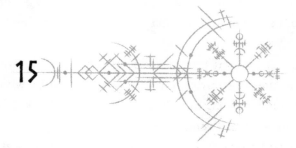

WHEN WE RETURNED HOME, BERGTHÓRA and Ingrid were waiting for us. They were downcast and silent, even before we told them what had taken place at the Great Assembly. Both of them seemed to know without being told what the outcome had been.

"I do not know when or how the axe shall fall," said Njál, "but fall it certainly shall. I will now commit myself to my duties and my prayers, as long as I have life. You should do the same, my sons, and you also, Kári. There is little else to be done."

Bergthóra met this pronouncement with stony-faced silence and would not meet anyone's eyes. Ingrid bowed her head with grief.

The work of the farm proceeded. Njál would allow nothing less. I found myself often scanning the horizon for horsemen and starting at shadows. My cheeks burn with shame to admit it. I have many faults, but I have always thought myself courageous. Now I saw that there was one thing at least that I feared—being taken unawares, by ambush. A fair fight in the open, or even an unfair, unwinnable fight, alone against ten men, I would have preferred. But once again, we were forced into inaction, waiting for the next move by Flosi, Ketil, and the rest. It was nothing short of maddening, and it took its toll.

Then, one night, about two weeks after we returned from the Assembly,

Bergthóra spoke to us all as she served our evening meal. We all looked up at her in surprise, as she had hardly said a word since Hoskuld's death.

"All of you should eat your favorite food at tonight's meal. I am certain that after this evening, I will never again serve food for my household."

"Mother," said Helgi in a hushed voice, "you cannot mean that."

"It is so, nonetheless." She would say no more. But I saw Sæunn, the old servant woman, standing in the shadows nearby, nodding and muttering to herself, and I remembered her strange seer's gift, and wondered if Sæunn had made this prophecy to Bergthóra.

We ate in silence for a time. I could think of nothing to say. The air felt heavy with apprehension, stifling all conversation. I looked about me at my wife, her head bowed, and my little son, who sat on the bench swinging his legs and staring at his plate, his forehead creased in a frown. Then over at the Njálssons, all lost in their own thoughts. Grím looked up suddenly and glanced around him.

"They are here." He got up, went to the door and out into the yard.

We all were frozen to the spot for a moment, and simply sat there, looking at one another. Ingrid paled, but I thought that Skarp-Hedin seemed almost relieved that the time was here at last. After a moment, we all got up and followed Grím, and peered out through the growing gloom.

In the hollow below the hill, men were gathering. I could see about twelve men and as many horses, but it was hard to be certain in the failing light.

"Can you see who is there?" asked Skarp-Hedin.

"I see Flosi Thórdarson," I replied, "and Ketil and Eirík Sigfússon. The other two Sigfússon brothers are certainly there, as well, although I cannot see clearly. I also see Grani Gunnarsson. Other than that, I am not certain."

"If Grani is there, then Gunnar Lambason is sure to be," said Skarp-Hedin. "They are seldom apart for long, and both of them feel they have accounts against us to settle."

"We should all go inside," said Njál. "We must barricade the door. When Gunnar of Hlidarend was killed, he remained within his house, and held them off for long, although he was one man against many. This house is as strong as Hlidarend, and we are many. Once we are within it, they will not be able to overcome us."

Skarp-Hedin looked at his father with a curious mix of admiration and impatience. "I mean you no disrespect, Father, but you are wrong. Remember who the men were that killed Gunnar. Our foster-father, Thórd Freedmansson, was among them. Men of high character and pride. I do not defend their actions, and I feel that Gunnar should not have been killed, but nevertheless, they fought him fairly and openly, as befit men of their rank. I do not have the same opinion of the men before us tonight. If we go inside, we will never leave again. They will use any means to destroy us, even burning down the house. I, for one, do not wish to be suffocated like a fox in its den."

Njál looked at Skarp-Hedin and the rest of us, tight-lipped with displeasure. "I have never been able to stop you and your brothers from doing what you would, and that is clearly what you intend to do tonight. It is not the first time you have disregarded my advice. Perhaps if you had listened to me long ago, we would not be here tonight, facing death at the hands of these men."

Skarp-Hedin bowed his head and did not reply.

"Let us do what Father says," said Helgi. "It would be best."

We all turned back toward the house.

As we were passing through the door, Skarp-Hedin leaned over, and said softly into my ear, "Now it is hopeless. But my father is right. We have disregarded him often enough, and the penalty will be that we will die together tonight." I looked up at him, and he gave me his crooked grin. "Nevertheless, if you survive, Kári, then avenge our deaths. We will do the same for you, if we survive."

I briefly clasped his forearm and nodded to him. We shut the door behind us.

Shortly afterward, there was a noise, and we looked out of the small windows, and saw that Bergthorshváll was surrounded. Flosi Thórdarson was there and was clearly the leader. He stood in front of the front door, an axe in his hand. All four of the Sigfússons were there, as were Grani Gunnarsson and Gunnar Lambason, and Gunnar's brother Sigurd. Ketil Sigfússon's son Modolf, who was only seventeen, was there as well, holding a spear and trying not to look scared. Three cousins of the Sigfússon brothers, Glum Hildisson, Arni Kolsson, and Kol Thorsteinsson, also guarded the house, armed with spears and swords. I had seen them only a handful of times during my years in Iceland, and I wondered if it would be my fate to be killed by men whom I barely knew.

There was a pounding on the door, and a voice—Flosi Thórdarson's—rang out in the stillness that followed.

"We have come for Njál Thorgeirsson, Skarp-Hedin Njálsson, Grím Njálsson, Helgi Njálsson, and Kári Solmundarson," he said, and he sounded as if he were reading out a pronouncement of law. "There has been bloodshed enough at the hands of these men, and we mean to end it this very night. We ask you to give yourselves over, and our claim against this family will be ended."

Skarp-Hedin roared with laughter. "You will end your claim against our family when you have destroyed it, you mean? A fine offer, I am sure. You may speak your words as prettily as the Law Giver, Flosi Thórdarson, but I will never willingly bow my head for you to strike it off with your axe."

"Then you are all doomed," said Flosi.

"We were already," replied Skarp-Hedin. "But if I can, I will not sink down into death before I have caught up a few of you to sink along with me." And, snatching up his axe, he burst through the door, and threw himself against Flosi, who fell back, amazed at the onslaught. Four other men came up immediately and drove him back inside, but not before he had succeeded in shattering Thorkel Sigfússon's shield and giving him a deep cut on the upper arm.

We slammed the door shut as Skarp-Hedin came back inside, breathing hard, grinning his crooked grin and shouldering his axe, the edge of which was stained scarlet.

"You have the most courage of all of us," I said. "You may yet escape death."

"I do not believe it," he said, but he did not seem frightened in the least at the prospect.

For a time, there was no sound from outside but an uncertain muttering, and we all wondered what they were plotting. By now it had gotten quite dark, although there was a three-quarters moon and it was completely clear. Then I heard scratching sounds near the front door, and went closer, kneeling by the door to listen. I could hear a soft tearing noise, and rustling, but could not think what they were doing.

Sæunn came forward then, and put her wizened hand on my shoulder, pressing down with a weight I did not think her frail body could manage. Her face glowed like a sepulcher in the flicker of the oil lamps, and she was breathing hard, either with excitement or with fear. "The plant," she said, her voice hoarse. "They are tearing up the plant. It will be the death of us all."

I looked up at her, uncomprehending. "What could they do with a plant, Sæunn?" I asked. Then I heard the noise of feet on the roof of the house, and I understood.

One broad, single wooden beam ran the entire length of Bergthorshváll, and the roof was shingled with wood. Skarp-Hedin's grin flashed out again. "They intend to burn us."

As if in answer, there was a crackle of flame as the dry weed caught fire on the roof, and we looked from one to the other, not knowing what to do, not knowing if there was anything we could do. Bergthóra dropped to her knees and crossed herself, then buried her face in her hands. Ingrid came to me, very close, holding Thórd, her eyes wide with fear.

Njál looked at his wife, as motionless as a stone statue, and at his daughter and grandson. Then he strode to the door, and pounded on it, and shouted, in a voice louder than I had ever heard him use, "Flosi Thórdarson!"

There was a pause, and Flosi's voice said, "What is it?"

"Will you not allow the women and children to leave? Your quarrel is not with them."

Flosi's voice came back quickly, "We will allow them to leave."

I thought his voice sounded shamed, that he had to be asked.

Bergthóra's head snapped up. "I have no wish to leave."

Njál went to her, and knelt on the floor in front of her, gently taking her hands. "There is no need for you to die with me."

She looked up at him, and her face softened. For one brief moment, I saw what she might have looked like as a young woman, and a quick smile graced her lips, then vanished forever. "I was given to you in marriage when I was young, and I promised you that I would share your life, share your bed, share your fate. Do not ask me to leave now."

Njál looked into her eyes for a moment, and then kissed her forehead. Then he stood, and Bergthóra resumed her stance, face in her hands.

By now, we could see flames dancing across the inside of the roof. A fine mist of smoke was swirling down, stinging our eyes. Njál looked at Ingrid, his face torn with pity. "My daughter...."

My wife did not let him finish. "Father, ask me to do no less than my mother has," she said, near tears but holding her head up proudly. "I too have no desire to live if the only man I have ever loved is to die here."

Njál sighed deeply, and said, "Then this is farewell." Now the entire roof was in flames, and smoke was filling the house. Coughing shook Njál's slender frame, but he stood and took Bergthóra's hands, helping her to rise. They.went into their sleeping chamber. We followed them into the chamber, to see what he was going to do.

Without another word, they lay down upon their bed, and pulled an oxhide cover over them, and crossed themselves.

"I commend our souls to God," said Njál, his voice steady, and closed his eyes.

We watched them for a moment in silence. It seemed to me that the roof above the sleeping chamber was burning the most strongly, and so I drew my wife and child away. There was nothing more to be done. Helgi and Skarp-Hedin came with us, but Grím, who of the three brothers most resembled his father, stayed behind, unwilling to leave Njál's side.

When we returned to the central hall, embers were falling from the roof, and catching the wooden benches and table alight. The heat was excruciating, the air acrid and searing, and Thórd was crying with every breath. I looked at Ingrid and Thórd, and suddenly I felt as if my heart was being wrenched in my chest. I drew them into my arms, and pulled my cloak about them, as if to shield them from the smoke and flames which were flickering nearer with every moment.

"I love you." I choked. I felt suddenly desperate to say, in the few minutes we had left, all that was in my heart. "I love you both..." But at that moment, there came a great cry from the sleeping chamber—I think that it was Bergthóra, but I am not certain. Thórd wrenched himself free of our grip, and crying, "Grandmother!" he ran toward the chamber. Ingrid twisted in my grasp, turning away from me, her eyes wild and panicked. "Thórd, come back to me!" she cried, and dashed off after him. For a moment—a moment I shall regret so long as I am allowed to live—I stood frozen to the spot, not knowing what to do. Then I started forward.

And, at that moment, half of the roof collapsed, including the part that lay over the sleeping chamber.

A great shower of sparks, smoke, and cinders flew up, blinding me. I reeled backwards, coughing and blinded. When my eyes had cleared sufficiently, I saw that the great beam of the house had split in two, and lay fallen, tilted upward from the ruins of what had once been the great table in the main hall. At that moment, I knew that my wife and child lay dead underneath it.

I shrieked, "No!" but the word strangled in my throat, turning into a cry of inarticulate grief. I would have wept, but the smoke turned my sobs into coughing. I heard a sound I have never forgotten and shall never forget—the sound of the men outside, laughing, laughing at my outcry. Every part of my grief turned to blind rage in that moment.

I turned around to look at the house. The fall of the roof beam had torn a great rent in the roof, letting in a little fresher air. It was suddenly easier to breathe, but the flames were roaring now as they consumed the roof and licked the walls. Grím must have been killed in the fall of the roof beam as well. He had been with his father and mother when it fell. I never saw him alive again. Helgi and Skarp-Hedin were both still alive, however, and we exchanged glances.

"There is no chance of escape," said Helgi. His voice was wild. His eyes glittered unnaturally in the billowing smoke, and his cloak was blackened and smoldering. He held his sword in his hand. Behind us, the door was still accessible, and Helgi gave a great cry, threw it open, and flung himself upon the first person he came to.

We watched through the open door as Helgi used his last strength to cross swords with one, then two, then four men—and then Flosi Thórdarson strode forward, and without so much as a word, drew up his axe and struck off Helgi's head.

Skarp-Hedin showed his teeth in a grin that was more like a snarl. "Now it is just you and I, brother. There is only one way out. Up the roof beam."

"It is aflame," I said. "And I doubt it will support us."

The grin widened. "Would you rather stay in here?"

There was no answer to that.

"You go first, and I will follow," Skarp-Hedin said. "Take a flaming brand and throw it at them when you reach the top, and do not hesitate, but jump. I will be right behind you."

I had no expectation of surviving, but I caught up two blazing pieces of wood, and walked to where the beam had struck the floor. I ran up it. The heat of it burned my feet, and the flames singed my clothes. I reached the top within seconds, and the cool, clean night air blew in my face. I slung the flaming wood at the men below, and they ducked. Then, as luck would have it, one of the walls caved in to one side of me, and there was a great rush of smoke and cinders and sparks. The men jumped back from it, and hidden by the cloud of smoke, I leapt from the roof.

I hit the ground running, downhill and away from Bergthorshváll, expecting at every second to feel a spear or an axe strike me and end my life. None came. I had only gotten a little way away when my curiosity could not be denied, and I turned and looked. Silhouetted against the night sky I saw Skarp-Hedin, standing on the end of the beam, holding aloft a torch like one of the elder gods in a battle rage. He lifted it to throw, but at that moment the beam split asunder, and he fell downward, back into the crumbling house, and the torch he had held was tossed straight up into the night air. It spun flickering against the black sky, flipping end over end, and as it fell back down toward the ruined house, it went out.

I turned and ran. Only then did I realize how badly burned I was, especially my feet and lower legs. I did not stop until I reached the Hvít River, downstream of Bergthorshváll. I plunged my legs into the icy water, and the shock of it took my breath away. I quickly pulled my legs out, and then crawled a little way into some sheltering bushes where I would be hidden until morning.

I lay there all night, sleepless. The pain in my legs was excruciating, but I could have borne it had it not been for the pain in my heart.

The burns on my legs have long healed, but that other pain has been there ever since that night and has never lessened or grown dim with time. I have known the pain of battle wounds, but this was far worse. It is like an invisible knife, making a wound that does not heal, but is torn open and left raw again and again.

This knife that so wounds me, and that will wound me forever, is fashioned from the vision of my son and my wife, dashing back into the sleeping chamber, and the vision of the great roof beam breaking in two above them. It is kept sharp by the knowledge that I should have died by their side and would have had I only acted more quickly. It is honed to a fine edge by the regret that I never was able to give Ingrid a last kiss, and never saw Thórd grow to manhood.

Such regrets are all I have. So, should people still call me 'Kári the Lucky'? Should I still bless the luck that has carried me here through fire and sword, against all odds?

That night, I did not. I curled up underneath the bushes, and put my hands over my face, and wept like an orphaned child.

II

THE OATH

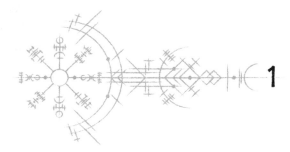

1

I AWOKE WITH THE SUNRISE THE next morning—an Iceland summer morning, of the kind that seems to come when night has only just fallen. My legs and feet ached. When I looked down at them in the reddish half-light, they seemed to be on fire again, seared and blistered so that I could scarcely walk on them. I pulled at my shoes and found that the leather was burned almost all the way through, and it fell apart in my hands. The soles of my feet were covered with raw blisters. How I had been able to run so far on them I could not imagine. My clothes were scorched, and my hair was singed and brittle. I looked like a man who had journeyed from the edge of hell.

Perhaps I had.

I washed my face in the icy river, and then plunged my feet into it. It stung and numbed them at the same time, and afterwards the pain lessened for a while. I stood and looked about me. There was no one to be seen, and I surmised that Flosi and the others did not realize that I had escaped. To the northwest, tendrils of smoke still curled into the clear air, and I knew that embers still smoldered at what had once been Bergthorshváll. The tears came anew, but I forced them back.

Where could I turn, now that my family was dead, and the only home I had ever had in Iceland destroyed? I had no doubt that if the men who had burned the house found me where I was, they would kill me without hesitation. But even if I were to find a haven somewhere, when they found out that I was still alive, what would they do?

I pondered this question long, as I sat by the river, every so often plunging my feet into it to dull the pain. I was sorely grieved and sorely wounded, but alive. Now that I had escaped, there was a part of me that fervently desired to stay that way. I reasoned that if I could find a place to be, where there was someone whom I could count on as a friend, perhaps Flosi and Ketil and the rest would not dare a further act of violence. Since they had succeeded in destroying Njál and his sons, they might let me be, alone and friendless as I seemed. That would leave me free to plan my vengeance, the seeds of which were already forming in my mind.

All at once, I realized to whom I should turn. There was one person who had always supported the Njálssons in their troubles, and whose advice, it seemed to me, had always been good. If anyone could assist me now and lend me aid to deal with the men who had burned Bergthorshváll, it was he.

I turned and began to walk, as quickly as my scorched feet would carry me, toward Hof, the home of Mord Valgardsson.

It took me the better part of a day to walk there, the most difficult ten miles I had ever walked—barefoot, stumbling, with searing aches flickering along my legs like a second fire. Yet although none was there to hear me, I was determined not to cry out. I walked along the river and then up into the hills, the harsh rocks tearing at my wounded feet. Once, I looked back, seeing my footprints, wet and scarlet on the black rock, but I did not stop. Much of the journey I do not even recall, or remember only as one thinks of a dream, which upon waking fragments into nothing but ashes and dust and a memory of unspeakable agony.

Mord was tending his sheep and saw me coming from far off. He knew by my limping stride and the fact that I was alone that something was amiss. He leapt upon his horse and rode out to me.

"Kári, my friend, what has happened to you?" he cried, when he saw my state. "Has there been a fire at Bergthorshváll?"

"You may well ask it, Mord." Suddenly I felt that my legs could no longer carry me, and I collapsed. I felt the weak tears rising in my eyes, and with an effort forced them back. Mord swung his leg over his horse's side, and jumped easily to the ground, then knelt beside me.

He looked with pity at my bleeding feet and scorched legs. "You are in terrible pain, I am certain, but even so, I fear the others have not been so lucky as you." His face was grave as he spoke, but still his dark eyes never rested upon mine for long.

"Indeed, none other has survived. All are dead under the burned timbers of Bergthorshváll. All dead."

"How has this come to be? That none survived except you?"

I met his eyes, but they again flitted away from mine. "The doors of escape were blocked by the swords and axes of Flosi Thórdarson, Ketil Sigfússon and his brothers, and their kin. It was their fire which consumed Njál and his family."

Mord's voice dropped to a horrified whisper. "They burned the house? How could they dare?"

"I do not know, yet they did."

"And they burned the women and children along with the men of the household?"

"Yes. Bergthóra, Ingrid, and Thórd were offered the opportunity to leave, but the women refused it, and my son died with his mother."

Mord shook his head in astonishment. "Do Flosi, Ketil, and the rest know that you escaped?"

"I do not think so."

He considered for a moment. "I will bring you to Hof, and my wife will tend your wounds. When you are better, you will tell me the whole story. After I have taken you to my house, I will ride abroad and discover where these men have gone. They must be brought to justice."

I had no further words within me and let Mord help me onto his horse. He then led the horse back across the field to the little house. I climbed down, wincing in pain as my feet touched the ground, and hobbled through the dark doorway. Mord's wife, Thorkatla, met us at the door. If she was surprised to see me standing there in such a state, she did not show it. She took me to a soft bed, and I felt her dressing the burns on my legs, but I had hardly lain down when I fell into a restless sleep.

It was then that I had a strange dream. At the time, I thought that it was a creation of fever and pain, and perhaps it was. But I have since then had the same dream or one much like it at other times, when no wounds troubled me. Some men have dreams that foretell, I am told. I am no seer, and have never had one that did, except perhaps for this one. If it prophesied in truth, I cannot say, but I will tell the dream in its entirety, and others may judge.

I was standing on the seashore. The cold salt wind of the sea struck my face and blew my hair out behind me, and my cloak billowed from my shoulders and snapped in the wind. Behind me was a great cliffside of solid rock, and above me the seabirds dipped and soared and cried. Suddenly, there was a noise as of a clap of thunder, and the cliffs opened up, and out of the rent in the rocks there came a huge man. He wore only a goat skin about his loins, and in his hand, he carried a great iron club. He stood on the shore, looking out across the sea toward the gray horizon.

"Who are you?" I asked him, wondering that I had the courage to speak to such an uncouth creature.

"I am called Iron-Grím, and I am here to call out the chosen warriors to follow me."

"Sigurd Lambason," he called, in a deep voice. I turned, and saw Sigurd, Ketil's nephew, walking toward us. His stride was jerky, as a man who does not wish to go to where his body is taking him. He was a young man, barely seventeen, and he looked as if he were being pulled by a rope invisible to my eyes. As I watched, he passed me, and gave me a wide-eyed look of unabashed terror, and vanished into the great opening in the cliff.

"Thorkel Sigfússon, Eirík Sigfússon, Lambi Sigfússon, I call you," said Iron-Grím, and Ketil's three brothers came in the same fashion, although they looked more angry than afraid, and they followed Sigurd into the opening.

"Modolf Ketilsson," he called, and the young son of Ketil Sigfússon came as well, crying out and twisting as if to escape, and he too was pulled in and disappeared.

Next came Ketil Sigfússon himself, then Glum Hildisson and Arni Kolsson, two of his cousins. Then Grani Gunnarsson and Gunnar Lambason, the two young men we had spared when Thrain Sigfússon was killed, and who had met us on the way to the District Assembly. Gunnar spat at me as he passed, and his face was twisted with hate. He put his arm around Grani's shoulders, and they followed the others into the cliffside. Finally, the name of Kol Thorsteinsson was called, and I heard his voice cry out with anguish, as if he had thought that he would escape—and Kol, who was one of Ketil's kin, was likewise dragged past me and into the opening.

I looked at Iron-Grím, and waited for other names to be called, but he turned away and made as if to go.

"Are there no others?" I asked. "These are the men who burned my home and killed my family, but there is one missing. Where is Flosi Thórdarson?"

"I do not know him. I only know those men who are mine."

Iron-Grím then came closer and looked at me, his eyes pitiless. I sensed then that there was no warm blood coursing beneath his skin, and he was a man in the shape of his body only. In his expression, there was nothing even remotely human. I wondered if he was like the frost-giants of the old stories, who have icy ocean water in their veins instead of blood.

He studied my face carefully. "You have the appearance of one who has cheated me. What is your name?"

My grandmother had told me stories of men and women who had been tricked into giving their real names to trolls or witches, and they all seemed to come to bad ends. "I am called The Luck-Bearer."

His expression did not change, but he seemed displeased. "Perhaps I will break your luck one day."

There was a question I wished to ask, and my curiosity was great, despite my fear. "What will you do with the ones whom you have called?"

"There is no need for you to know that."

"If you are like the old Valkyries, taking men to die glorious deaths in battle, then take me also. For I am weary and grieved and bereft of my wife, whom I loved more than any other, whom I loved more than my own life's blood. And my only son is taken as well, leaving me nothing. I long for death."

"Perhaps that is so, but I am not the one to give it to you. Nor am I a Valkyrie, judging men's worthiness. I simply call whom it is appointed for me to call. But shall I show you your fate, Luck-Bearer?"

I did not reply, but in the dream, I was afraid. To my surprise, he called out Flosi's name. I turned to look, and Flosi Thórdarson walked out toward me, willingly and not dragged like the others. He was looking at me with his typical stern, steady expression. Then, Iron-Grím picked us both up, one in each huge hand, and bound us together in fetters of bronze. Then with one swift motion, he threw us up into the air, out toward the sea. I saw it below

me as we fell together, green and deep blue, gray streaked with white, eter-
nally moving like enchanted, liquid glass. I recall thinking the sea seemed
as pitiless as did Iron-Grím. Little did either one of them care for the lives
of men. Flosi did not utter a sound as we plummeted downward and struck
the sea with a tremendous splash. The cold salt water surged over my head,
roaring in my ears like thunder. At that point, I woke.

THE NEXT DAY, MORD CAME BACK in the mid-afternoon. He
came in to see me. My feet had swollen so that I could barely walk. He sat down
to speak with me, as I could not easily rise. He seemed thoughtful.

"I found Thorkel Sigfússon," he said, "and asked him about the burning
of Bergthorshváll. Thorkel did not seem proud of the deed but admitted that
he had helped in it, and it was clear that he believed that all had perished."

"Did you tell him that I had survived?"

"I did. At first, he did not believe me. He said, 'How can that be, since no
one left through door or window after the fire was kindled, except Helgi Njálsson, and he was slain?' I myself did not know how you escaped, so I could
not answer that. But I said that you had escaped somehow, that you lived and
breathed and that I had spoken to you myself. He was quite shaken."

"Not as shaken as he will be. I will visit vengeance upon his head, and
upon the heads of all of them."

"Easy, my friend. One man against twelve? And that one man, grievously
injured? You would be throwing away your life. Listen—there is a better
way. Now that they know you are alive, they will fear for themselves. Not
for your sword, but for your words. If all had perished, as they intended, who
would bring an action against them? But you survived, and my advice is to
wait. Let them worry and wonder what you will do. You may stay the winter
with us, and you will be welcome. I know these men well, and they will not
dare another killing. They have already done a thing so horrible that it will
still be spoken of a thousand years from now. They will leave you alone, as
long as you do not provoke them. And then, next summer, you should bring
an action against them at the Great Assembly, and you will be certain to win.
They will be lucky if they are only outlawed for what they have done. If you

ride against them now, or even next spring, you will simply be killed and that will be the end of it."

"Who will support me? We could get little enough support at the Great Assembly this summer. Everyone we spoke with seemed to side with Flosi and Ketil and their men."

"That was before they burned your family in their house. You can be sure that they have lost any support they ever had by this action. I have already spoken to Hjalti Skeggjason and Asgrím Ellida-Grímsson, and they have agreed to help you. They are powerful chieftains. You must be careful not to act rashly, and to maintain the support you have."

"It galls me to spend the winter in idleness, while my beloved and my little son lie dead in the ashes of Bergthorshváll, and my father-in-law and brothers-in-law also, who were as much my family as my own blood relatives were."

"We will go to Bergthorshváll when you can walk easily again," Mord said, his voice soothing. "We will find the bodies of the dead and arrange for proper burial. Then spend the winter planning your case. Asgrím and Hjalti are brilliant men, Asgrím especially. He will see to it that justice is done. I know you well, Kári. You are a man of action, and you dislike waiting. But now you must wait with patience. Nothing will be accomplished by your going off in a rage, but the loss of your own life and of any hope for bringing Flosi and Ketil and the rest to justice."

Mord spoke persuasively, and I could see nothing in what he said that was arguable. In the end, I agreed to do what he advised.

A week later, my feet and legs were sufficiently healed that I could ride a horse, and Mord and I went to Bergthorshváll.

As we rode up the little hill on which the house had sat, my breath caught in my throat. The house, once one of the most beautiful and strong in the district, was nothing but a pile of broken and charred timbers. Fine white ash had blown from the burnt wood out into the yard. The grass has been blackened by the heat in a great circle around the base of the house. I sat looking at the ruins for a moment, and then wordlessly dismounted. Mord followed, watching me closely.

Helgi's headless body lay crumpled in front of the door, where the burn-ers had left it. I looked down on him, and pity welled up in my heart. I recalled the many adventures we had seen together. Of the three brothers, I had always felt the closest to Helgi. He was open, straightforward, quick to laugh and quick to anger, easy to like. Seeing him like this brought anger to me, which rose up and smothered the pity, but I remembered Mord's words about biding my time. I pulled Helgi's body away, and arranged it on the grass, gently placing his poor severed head with it. Then we went forward into the house.

Our feet crunched on the burnt wall timbers as we made our way over the wreckage. I began to pull the beams up, tossing them aside, and in this way made my way to what had once been the side wall.

"I climbed up the beam," I told Mord. "This is where I leapt down, when a cloud of smoke hid their eyes, and thus escaped."

Together we lifted a piece of the wall, and underneath was the body of Skarp-Hedin.

His legs were nearly burnt off at the knees, but his upper body was merely scorched. His face especially was almost untouched, and in death looked peaceful. All of the terrible tension of the last weeks of his life were erased, and his scarred features seemed almost pitiable. Beside him lay his sword, its blade softened and turned a dull blue-black by the heat. Together, we carried the body clear of the house and laid it on the grass next to his brother, folding his arms across his chest. We lay his sword next to him.

Afterwards, we pulled apart more of the wreckage, and for a time found nothing more than charred wood and ruins. Then, under a piece of the big central beam, we found Grím's body, where he had fallen. His skull was crushed, and he must have been killed instantly when the beam collapsed. Sæunn was near him, and both of their bodies were badly burned. We placed both of them out on the grass. Mord seemed sickened, but all I felt was the weakness of pity and the strength of anger, fighting for control in my heart.

Sæunn had fallen near the door to Njál's sleeping chamber. The wall that contained the door had split in two when the central beam had fallen. Mord and I had a difficult time pulling the beam aside to gain access to what was left of the chamber. It took both of us, straining and heaving, to lift the beam and toss it aside.

Mord then lifted up a piece of the wall, and it flipped over with a great crash. Then he stood, looking downward, and I saw a look of great horror come into his eyes. It was quickly swallowed in his normal restless, flickering gaze, but for a moment he looked thunderstruck. I stepped over to where he was.

There, lying on the floor among the ashes, was Ingrid. Her back was burned where the wall had lain across it, and on her fair skin was a great, cross-shaped welt. Wordlessly I knelt next to her, and smoothed her hair, scorched and made brittle by the heat. Then I turned her over.

Thórd lay beneath her, as if she had tried to shield him with her own body. His little body was quite untouched by the fire, and his face seemed as if he was sleeping, and would wake with a smile if I shook him.

I could not stop myself. Great, helpless sobs tore through my chest, shaking me like a fox shakes a rabbit. I could not move, could do nothing but stare at them and weep. My tears rained upon them, as if water could heal them and bring them back into life. Finally, my grief was poured out, and rage rose up to replace it. My fists clenched, and I screamed, roaring out my anger to echo from the sky, like the striking of a great bell echoing from the pitiless stone face of a cliff. Then I sunk down onto my heels and buried my face in my hands. I remained there for some minutes, then I felt Mord's hand on my shoulder.

"Come, my friend. Let us move them."

Mord and I carried Ingrid and Thórd out to join the others.

We cast about further into the wreckage. Finally, we found a place where two walls had fallen in and lay against each other like a tent. Beneath this lay Njál's bed, surprisingly unscathed. Mord and I pushed the walls over, and then we looked down upon where Njál and Bergthóra lay.

They had drawn the oxhide cover up over their heads. When we pulled it back, I saw their faces were untouched by the flames. They, too, looked asleep, and on Njál's face was a look of such gentleness and nobility that the fury in me died. I still desired justice, and to see vengeance meted out upon the men who had done this, but I suddenly felt in my heart that Mord had been right to argue that we should do it through the law. Njál had been, above all, a man of the law, and his honor demanded nothing less. I decided at that moment if we could bring Flosi, Ketil, and the rest to justice at the next Great Assembly, that I would let any further claims to their blood drop.

The two of us unaided could not hope to bring so many bodies to the church at Ossaby, which was the nearest to Bergthorshváll, about ten miles east. So, Mord and I rode there and told the priest to send men of his household with a wagon to bring them back, and to tell us when the burial might take place.

"We will bury them in the churchyard after the matins on Monday next," said the priest, and then he looked at me with a frown that held as much curiosity as puzzlement. "You look solid for a ghost, Kári Solmundarson. There are men about who say you are dead, along with Njál and his family."

"They are wrong," I said simply. I know he wanted to hear more, but I did not feel like explaining.

"Everyone always said that you bear more than your fair share of luck. But how you came to escape when all the others perished must be a story worth hearing."

I did not respond.

"A story worth hearing it surely is," interjected Mord, "but another time, my good priest. Kári is weary with our day's work, and grieved by it as well, as he has had to see the bodies of his wife and child, not to mention those of his wife's family, removed from the ashes of the house where they were unjustly slain. How many men have had to live through such a sorrow? I ask your forbearance, that you ask us no further questions, but simply aid us in seeing that these good people have fitting Christian burials."

The priest seemed ashamed of his prying and acquiesced quickly to Mord's requests.

"We will return for the burials," said Mord, and without any further talk, we mounted our horses, and turned their heads back towards Mord's home at Hof.

As we left the church land, I turned to Mord. "I recall when you alone in the district would not accept Christianity, even though it had been demanded by decree, but now you are friendly with the priest of Ossaby and talk eloquently about the need for Christian burial as if you had been a believer since birth."

Mord shrugged. "Does it matter what one believes?"

"I think it does," I responded.

Mord gave me a curious glance. "I only agreed to become a Christian when it became obvious that Christianity was here to stay. Even after the decree at Thingvellir, I thought in a short time, the followers of the old religion might once more gain the upper hand. It was not so, and I consented to be baptized."

"Are you not concerned with what is the truth, then? All that matters is what is in your best interest?"

Mord shrugged again. "Is there a difference between the two?"

I did not respond. Indeed, there seemed to be little I could say to that. But I pondered it much on the way back to Mord's house.

THREE DAYS LATER, MORD, THORKATLA, AND I left at sunrise for Ossaby, to attend the burial service for those who had died in the burning of Bergthorshváll.

I have no wish to recount the day of their burial—the day when I felt that my entire life passed into the cold, dark ground of a churchyard in Iceland. Should I be ashamed of having stood there, weeping helplessly as they covered over Ingrid and Thórd with black earth? I do not know. All I know is that now, as I dictate this thirty years later, the tears still rise up to take me, as hot and fresh as ever, a supply as inexhaustible as the ocean.

THE WINTER I SPENT WITH MORD Valgardsson at Hof was unremarkable. Mord was a gracious enough host, and I was as undemanding and as helpful as I could make myself. Still, it was a strange household. They had no children. Thorkatla, Mord's wife, was an odd, silent woman, quite unlike her earnest, talkative husband. She struck me as a deep thinker, but one who kept her own counsel. I recall watching her closely once, after the evening meal, as she cleaned the table. Her lips were tightly shut, and her eyes distant and vague, as if her mind were many miles away from the task at hand. I remember thinking at first that perhaps she was a little like Grím Njálsson, but then the comparison seemed strangely inapt. Grím had been silent because that was his nature. Thorkatla seemed to be silent for some other reason, and her face was always tense and guarded. I think there was much she would have said, had she decided to speak. I had no reason to dislike her, but still she always made me feel uncomfortable.

My body quickly recovered from the injuries I had received, as I was young and strong and healed easily, but my spirit did not prove so resilient. During the first few weeks the pain, and then the itching as my burned legs healed, reminded me constantly of what had happened. Memories rose up to take possession of me without warning, and my sorrow was a spring that never ran dry. With great effort, I busied myself with work on Mord's farm, and managed to distract myself for the most part.

Only once did Mord catch me staring blankly into nowhere as I was supposed to be forking up hay for the goats. Suddenly, without my willing it, before my mind's eye was the smiling face of my wife, as I had seen her the day I asked for her hand in marriage. My eyes flooded over with tears before I could stop them, and in some embarrassment, I looked over at Mord, who was watching me without seeming to watch, the way people do when they are curious but do not wish to be thought prying. I heard him whisper something to the servant man who helped him and heard the name of Ingrid mentioned. I knew he could read my thoughts and pitied me. His pity felt like a gift I did not wish to receive. I took care never to be caught grieving again.

The nights, however, were the worst. After we retired, Mord and Thorkatla to the alcove where they slept and I to my simple mat on the floor, I found myself longing for the joy in which I had dwelt when Ingrid was alive, and the longing was more painful than any injury I had received. It was not only for that pleasure in women which all men crave, for that is quick to come and quick to pass, and by itself gives little comfort. It was simply a need for the presence of a warm, loving body close by, with the knowledge that at any time I could press up against her, skin on skin, and breathe in that joy until it filled me. I craved her utterly and desperately, and in my terrible loneliness I pitied myself beyond enduring. It was the only time in my life I have indulged in that weakness. My empty mat each night was a reminder that I was alone in the world, crawling on the face of the earth like a solitary ant on a mountain, with no connection to any other. Some men relish being disconnected and call it freedom. I do not. I would trade all of my freedom of the past years if I could spend this night in Ingrid's arms.

Only once during that winter did I see any of the men who had burned

Bergthorshváll. I was accompanying Mord to visit Asgrím Ellida-Grímsson, one of the chieftains who had promised to help us, and we came upon Lambi Sigfússon, Ketil's youngest brother, out riding on some errand. When he saw us, he reined up his horse immediately, and stared at me as if he wished to look away but could not.

Mord and I continued to ride on, and I met Lambi's eyes steadily but without letting my anger show. As we passed, Mord said, "Good morning to you, Lambi Sigfússon," in a pleasant tone, and then looked at me and gave me a wry little smile, hardly more than a twitch of his lips. Lambi turned and looked at Mord, as if seeing him for the first time. His expression changed from discomfort to puzzlement, and back again. Then he seemed to become completely unnerved, and rode away without responding, a little faster than necessary, I thought.

"You can be sure that this meeting will be discussed thoroughly among the Sigfússons and their comrades." Mord reined in his horse and turned it to watch Lambi disappear into the distance. "Many things will they wonder at. What did it mean that I greeted him? That you said nothing, neither in anger nor in forgiveness? Where were we going this winter's morning? There will be much speculation about your plans, Kári. And how I am involved. They knew already that you were living with me, I would guess."

"That does not mean that you would be involved in any action I will take."

"That is true. I have always remained on friendly enough terms with them. I have never given them cause to think I had any reason for vengeance. Now, they see us riding together, and it will remind them that I took you in after the burning, and they will worry at it, like a dog worries a bone. What are we planning? This is what they will want to know."

Mord seemed to relish this, but I found myself feeling uncomfortable about it. I had nothing against taking revenge on them, but I was not then, and still am not, a weaver of intricate plots. Direct action has always been my natural tendency. "Should we make our intentions public now, rather than waiting until the summer? I dislike all this secrecy and scheming."

Mord seemed surprised at the question. "Certainly not. We will give them as little time as may be to plan their defense. No, Kári. Let them worry. Let their sleep be haunted by it. They deserve that, and far worse. With luck, far worse will be their fate when they are judged at the Great Assembly this summer."

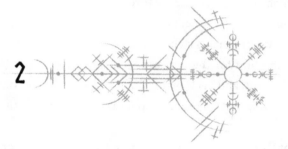

2

LATE THE FOLLOWING SPRING, AS THE time of the Great Assembly approached, Mord and I went once more to the home of Asgrím Ellida-Grímsson, to discuss what action was to be taken.

Asgrím was a tall, stocky man, with long brown hair shot through with gray. He was considered to be one of the best lawyers in all of Iceland. His blue eyes flickered with a keen intelligence, shrewd and far-reaching. I was pleased to have him on my side.

"I believe that you know," I told him, as we sat before the great fire in his house after a fine evening meal, "that it is my desire that you represent me at the next Great Assembly."

"It was not unexpected," said Asgrím with a faint smile.

"My skill lies not in words. I wish to have my case presented by someone whose voice carries weight. I would like to bring an action against all of them, but I do not know my rights in the matter."

"It is your right to bring an action against the men who burned Bergthorshváll for the deaths of your wife and son, but you cannot bring an action against them on the behalf of Njál or the rest of his family, as you are not a blood relative. That is the right of the nearest blood relative."

"I suppose," said Mord, "that the nearest relatives now are Njál's nephews."

Asgrím nodded. "There are three, are there not?"

I nodded. "Njál had a younger brother, called Thórir the Lame, who was weak, and died shortly after I arrived in Iceland, but he had fathered three sons before his death, who would support us now, I think."

"A pity they did not support you earlier," said Mord wryly.

"None of them lives nearby, as they were fostered by their mother's family, which comes from the southeast of Iceland. It is likely they did not know of their uncle's troubles until it was too late."

"Are they already planning an action of their own?" asked Asgrím.

"Not that I am aware of, but there is no reason why they would tell me if they are."

"What do you know of these men? If we involve them in this, will they stand firm, do you think?"

"I have met them once or twice. They seemed stout enough, and certainly fond of their uncle. The eldest is a little younger than I am, and the youngest would be just turned twenty, I believe."

"What are their names?"

"The eldest is named Thorleif, called the Crow because of his black hair. The middle son is Thorgrim, and the youngest is Thorgeir Skorar-Geir."

"I will have messages sent to them," said Asgrím. "We should meet again, soon, with the three brothers. It would be well if we could plan our arguments carefully before we present them at the Great Assembly. I know your opponents well, and they are no fools, especially Ketil Sigfússon and Flosi Thórdarson. Even if we give them little time to plan their defense, they will still do so skillfully. Do not underestimate them. I do not."

The following day, Asgrím sent word to the three brothers, asking if they would be willing to meet with us and discuss an action against Flosi, Ketil, and the rest. Only a week later, he received an answer. Thorleif Crow, speaking for the three, said that they would be agreeable to participating in an action against the men who had burned Bergthorshváll, and that we should combine our efforts rather than pursuing our separate courses. Scarcely ten days after our first meeting, I was once again sitting in Asgrím's hall as I surveyed the men before me.

Thorleif Crow was very tall, and his hair was a shiny blue-black, unusual in Iceland. He had a relaxed, easy manner, and was soft of speech and quick to smile. From the way he sat with his long legs stretched out before him, he looked like a simple working man enjoying a cup of mead at the end of a hard day. Only his eyes betrayed a steely glint, the sign of a quick mind and a fierce sense of justice.

The middle brother, Thorgrim, was called Hammerfist, and it did not surprise me. He lacked something of Thorleif's height and easy grace, but he was powerfully built and was every inch a warrior, although still courteous and friendly. He seemed ill at ease sitting in discussion at a table, and I understood his discomfort immediately. Here was a man who, like myself, was happier in action than in endless speech. I liked him immediately.

The youngest brother, Thorgeir Skorar-Geir, had neither the height of his oldest brother nor the girth of his middle brother, but he was subtle and quick-witted. I had once heard Njál say that his youngest nephew could see into men's hearts and read what was written there. Njál seemed to value this gift as highly as his own sons' skill in sword fighting. Thorgeir's pale blue eyes, set in a face made all of angles and sharp edges, certainly gave the impression of far sight. If his eldest brother was a crow, then Thorgeir was an eagle, a bird of prey whose vision stretched to the horizon. I cannot say I liked him, but I was nevertheless glad his restless, piercing intelligence was on my side.

"Well, Kári," Thorgeir said, after we had finished our meal together. "Your luck has carried you through once again. Against all odds you sit here, to bring an action against the men who burned Bergthorshváll."

"I wonder if it is luck," I said. "Some days I wish that I was now at peace in the churchyard beside Ingrid and Thórd."

Thorleif Crow looked at me with sympathy in his eyes. "Let us not dwell upon that. What has happened, has happened, and it is up to us who are left behind to deal with it and see justice done. What exactly is to be done, Asgrím, my friend? I am unschooled in the law and will need much in the way of guidance from you, as will my brothers—and Kári also, I suspect, although I do not wish to speak for him."

"You speak well enough, Thorleif," I said.

Asgrím placed his index fingers together, and studied them as if they held some great secret. I noticed that he wore an ornate ring on the right one, and I realized then he must be a very rich man. He did not speak for a moment.

"It is only necessary to show that Ketil, Flosi, and the rest inflicted a mortal injury on Njál and the members of his household, in order to claim compensation or retribution from them."

"That should be obvious, and hardly worth arguing," I said. "Even Flosi would not argue that he was responsible for their deaths."

"True," replied Asgrím. "They will not argue that point. They are guilty, and everyone knows it."

"Then what argument will they have?"

"The judgment," said Asgrím. "For such killing, what should it be?"

"Is not the penalty for such an action outlawry or death?" asked Thorleif.

"Surely it is," said Asgrím. "But should such a judgment be passed, you realize what their response will be."

"I don't know about the others," I said, "but I don't."

"It will be a quick response, and a hard one to counter. They will claim that the deaths of Njál and the rest should be weighed against the deaths which have gone before."

"Have not those already been fully compensated for?" asked Thorgeir Skorar-Geir.

"They have," said Asgrím, "all but the death of Hoskuld Thrainsson. This killing is viewed by almost everyone in the district as unjustified, and therefore will be weighed against everything else that has happened. I believe I can predict how the argument will go."

"You must tell us." Thorgeir leaned forward and fixed his intense blue eyes on Asgrím.

"I will present the burning of Bergthorshváll as a heinous crime which took many innocent lives, and as a barter of eight deaths in exchange for one—for on their side, only Hoskuld was killed, while in one stroke they killed Njál and his wife, their three sons, their daughter and grandson, and their old servant-woman. They will then counter that the figuring is wrong—that it is only one death in exchange for one."

Thorgrim picked up a cup of mead in his huge hand and drained it. "How do you see that?" he asked, his voice a deep growl.

"Njál is the only one whom they will want counted against them."

I stared at him for a moment, an uncomprehending frown on my face. "I don't understand."

"It's quite simple, really. Skarp-Hedin, Grím, and Helgi will be looked upon as an exchange for Hoskuld's death. Yes, it is three to one, but given the bad name the three Njálsson brothers had made for themselves, it is likely that the judges will let any imbalance there be set right with a small fine, to be divided up between the twelve men who were at the burning. Now, Kári, am I correct that Flosi Thórdarson asked for all of the women and children to leave the house?"

I began to see where he was going with his thoughts. So, rather reluctantly, I answered, "Yes."

"But the women all chose to stay, and your child, Kári, stayed with his mother, am I correct?"

"Yes," I said again.

Thorleif's eyes narrowed. "Therefore, they will say that they cannot be held accountable for their deaths, because Bergthóra, Ingrid, Thórd, and Sæunn chose to stay."

"Precisely. Njál is the only one who was neither guilty of Hoskuld Thrainsson's death, nor given the opportunity to leave. It is one undeserved death against one. Unless they are far less clever than I think they are, that is what they will argue. I do not see an easy way to argue against it. Unless an opportunity opens up to win the judges' favor, I am afraid that the best you can hope for is the payment of a fine in compensation, and probably not a large one."

"That seems to me entirely unjust," said Thorleif.

"And to me as well." I felt angry, and my anger was first toward Asgrím. He seemed so impassive about it, reducing the deaths of Njál's family to a matter of exchange, like coins passed back and forth between a merchant and a customer. But I quickly realized that he was merely doing what any man should in his place—attempting to predict what his opponent's argument would be. My anger then turned outward, toward Flosi and his band, and the thought of their being let off with a mere fine enraged me. I could barely sit there any longer. All I could think of was my sword, striking down Flosi Thórdarson and the rest, and the image filled my mind with a hot glee.

Mord broke into my scarlet reverie by patting my shoulder. "I know that look, my friend. Don't worry. They will be brought to justice somehow. The Sigfússons and their band will be broken."

Asgrím turned toward Mord, his blue eyes glittering. "And who will break them, Mord Valgardsson? You? It is precisely this kind of talk that has created this situation. I will give you some advice now. The first and last time I will do so. If a fine is offered in compensation, take it and make an end of this. Even if it is four copper pennies, one for each of you. Take them, and go your way, and leave this behind. How long does this cycle of bloodshed go back? Twenty years? More? I remember when Gunnar of Hlidarend was killed, and a better man has never walked the ground of Iceland. Just remember that Flosi, the Sigfússons, and the rest of them are not bad men. They are decent men who have done an evil action. There is a difference, although hot blood tends to obscure it. These men were not strong enough to forebear from this evil action when their anger and passion for revenge said, 'Go on! Go on!' And now that the sword has switched hands, will you be strong enough to forebear? If not, I fear for another twenty years of blood, and more good men like Gunnar, sent untimely to the grave because no one was willing to cry out, 'Stop!' I have spoken. Will any of you listen?"

No one spoke. A strange thought floated through my mind, seeming to come from outside of me, that if none of us heeded him, we would all regret it bitterly. A picture formed in my mind of the judge at the Great Assembly handing me a single copper penny in compensation for the deaths of Ingrid and Thórd, and Flosi Thórdarson standing nearby, smirking with satisfaction.

But which of us would forebear in such a circumstance? Not I, certainly.

After speaking with such passion, Asgrím sat with his eyes closed for some moments, and then, quite suddenly, opened them, and looked around at all of us.

"I have said all that needs to be said. You are all welcome to pass the night in my house, and we will meet again at the Great Assembly, in two weeks' time."

MORD AND I RETURNED TO HOF. My heart was restless inside me, and I longed for action. The two weeks' wait stretching before me seemed endless. Despite Asgrím's words, I was anxious for the Great Assembly to take place.

Mord only remained at home for a day after our return from Asgrím's house. That evening, he told me that he would be setting out again the following morning.

"For what purpose?" I asked.

"I am going out to ask for support among the local men who will be attending the Assembly."

"I wonder if that is necessary. Surely we have enough support already."

"One can never have enough support, especially among these folk, with whom allegiances change daily," said Mord with a touch of acid in his voice.

I looked at him curiously. What "folk" was he referring to, that he himself did not belong to? His restless eyes crossed mine briefly, and he seemed to recognize my perplexity, and smiled.

"If it is seen that you have powerful allies, then the judgment will be more likely to go your way. You know how these things go. Sometimes, it matters less who is in the right than who owns the most land. In any case, I can do more good there than I can here."

I glanced at Thorkatla, who was serving the evening meal. I wondered if that comment had been aimed at her, but there was no response on her impassive face, and I dropped the subject.

Mord departed at sunrise the next morning and left me behind to begin the preparations for our journey to Thingvellir for the Great Assembly. There seemed little enough to do, actually. It was an easy three days' ride, and the food, extra clothing, and such which we would need were quickly assembled. Early that afternoon, I was standing in the little yard in front of their house, finishing the packing of one of the saddlebags, when I became aware that Thorkatla was watching me from the house, her face expressionless as always.

"Do not fear, Thorkatla," I said, feeling myself in unaccustomed good spirits. "You shall have your husband back in good time. Even after we go to the Assembly, you shall not be left alone for long."

"I hope you are right, and I am trusting you to keep him out of any wickedness while he is gone."

I looked at her with a frowning half-smile, not knowing whether she jested. It did not seem in her character. "I will do what I can, but more likely he will have to manage me than the other way around. I have a hot temper, while he always seems to have the rule of his."

She simply regarded me for a moment with her somber eyes, and then turned and went back into the house.

Three days after his departure, Mord returned. He seemed elated and said that a number of wealthy and powerful men, led by Hjalti Skeggjason, had committed to voicing their support for our action.

"I think that your action, and that of Njál's nephews, is assured of success. Let the Sigfússons tremble."

I recalled how alone I had felt the morning after the burning of Bergthorshváll, and I was glad that Mord was such a staunch ally, but I gave him a shrug and a smile.

"I do not know what our chances are," I said truthfully, "for I know little of law. It is far too subtle for me."

He waved his hand in a dismissive fashion. "It isn't necessary to understand law. It is plain to see what the outcome will be."

"Asgrím didn't think so."

"Asgrím is a stodgy, careful old man. When he walks, he checks the ground twice at each stride, to make sure that there are no hidden pitfalls. It is a good trait in a lawyer and a chieftain, but you need have no fear. It is a thing accomplished. Two weeks from now, the Sigfússons will be destroyed, just as they destroyed Njál and his family."

"I am glad you are so confident. I feel confident as well, but hearing your optimism makes me doubly so."

Mord flashed a quick smile at me. "Just let Asgrím handle things, and you watch if it doesn't all fall out in your favor."

A week later, we left Hof early on a bright, sunlit morning. The weather seemed to me to be a good omen, as much of the previous week it had rained. The journey was unremarkable, and after an easy three days' ride, we arrived at Thingvellir. We found Thorleif Crow and his two brothers, and together we set up our booth upon the plain.

"Asgrím Ellida-Grímsson is already here," Thorleif said, "planning his battle strategy. He is a crafty old fox. I do not see what could go wrong. I believe he has the entire argument assembled in his mind already." Thorleif gave me his open, warm smile. "Better him than me, Kári, my friend. I don't have a subtle enough mind to make a lawyer."

"Nor I," I said, returning his smile.

"Thorgeir might have, had he turned his interest that way. But not I. And Thorgrim only argues with his fists. It's good that we have Asgrím to speak for us."

"Do you know where Asgrím's booth is? I should speak with him, if for no other reason than to let him know we have arrived."

"Let us all go," said Thorleif. "We should all be present when he describes what course he is to take."

Thorleif called to his brothers, and we all walked over to a richly decorated booth nearby.

"He certainly knows how to announce his presence," said Thorgrim, looking at the fine hangings with an appreciative smile. "I wonder if it is to intimidate his opponents."

"Asgrím Ellida-Grímsson has no need to intimidate," said the youngest brother, Thorgeir Skorar-Geir. "I have heard him speak before. His words carry weight enough of their own. This is simply his way. He likes fine things, and wishes to be surrounded by them, even here."

Asgrím was inside, and welcomed us all warmly.

"I will present your action to Hall of Sida tomorrow morning. Hall will no doubt call for arbitration between yourselves and the Sigfússons. I am told that Eyjolf Bolverksson is acting as their representative. You will want to give thought to which six men you wish to arbitrate for you. I would expect that I will be one, and I suggest Hjalti Skeggjason as another, but the remaining four are up to you."

Thorleif Crow began discussing with Asgrím who the arbitrators should be. As an elder member of the group, I should have participated in the discussion, but I could not keep myself focused on what was being discussed. I kept looking about me at the many booths clustering the broad plain, and the hundreds of men milling about on their own business. It seemed that I had traveled back in time to the previous summer, when I and the Njálssons had come here to be judged for our lives over the killing of Hoskuld Thrainsson. It seemed a lifetime ago.

With some effort, I forced my attention back to the present. Now I was once again here with three brothers, but a different three, and I was on the opposite side of the executioner's sword. It was a strange, disorienting feeling.

The selection of arbitrators was completed—I did not contribute a single name, bemused as I was by my memories, but I do not know if anyone noticed. The four of us then returned to our booth, bidding Asgrím good night with hopeful hearts.

I saw Flosi Thórdarson once that evening. We passed each other wordlessly, and Flosi gave me a stern glance that communicated nothing. Lambi Sigfússon was trailing along behind him, and I heard him snarl at me, "You should have died with the rest of them."

I kept my temper with an effort. "Whether or not I should have, you see that I did not. And now I am here to see that you and the rest of your family are dealt justice."

Lambi spat on the ground at my feet and then turned and strode away. I clenched my fist, and my heart leaped within me to strike him, but for once my mind took control.

It was not time yet. Let the law deal with them, as I promised to Njál's dead body.

The next morning, I awoke early. Thorgrim and Thorgeir were both awake already, and Mord Valgardsson was gone. Thorleif, the eldest of the three brothers, still slept, his long legs stretched out in an attitude of complete relaxation. One would never guess that he was here on a matter of such gravity.

I nudged him with my foot. "Thorleif Crow. It is time to go to the Assembly."

He stretched luxuriously, like a cat, and yawned, and then sat up. "Is it already?" He gave me a little smile. "Let us go, then."

We dressed in our finest clothes, and the four of us left our booth a scarce quarter-hour later. Together we walked to the Law Speaker's Rock and found Asgrím already there, standing in the front of the crowd that was beginning to form. He seemed to notice us from the corner of his eye and turned, nodding to us as we arrived.

"Let us hear what petitions we have before us today," Hall of Sida said, in his clear, deep voice. Hall was now quite an old man, with silver hair falling to his shoulders. From his position, high up above our heads, his voice carried a long way.

Asgrím was the first to speak. "Law Speaker," he said, and his own voice swelled to a deep roar, silencing the murmuring crowd, "I bring forward an action on the part of Kári Solmundarson, and another on the part of Thorleif, Thorgrim, and Thorgeir Holta-Thórirsson, that last summer a band of men led by Flosi Thórdarson and Ketil Sigfússon deliberately killed Njál Thorgeirsson, his wife Bergthóra, his three sons, Skarp-Hedin, Grím, and Helgi Njálsson, his daughter Ingrid Njálsdóttir, Ingrid's child Thórd Kárason, and the family servant, Sæunn, by burning them inside their house. On their behalf, I ask for arbitration to be conducted to determine an appropriate judgment against these twelve men, whose crime is terrible and cries out for retribution."

I do not believe that this was unexpected, for Hall did not so much as raise an eyebrow. "Very well. I presume that arbitrators have been designated by Kári and the others?"

"They have," Asgrím said, "subject to your approval and the acceptance by the arbitrators representing Flosi and the Sigfússons."

Hall nodded gravely. "Are Flosi Thórdarson and the four Sigfússon brothers here?"

There was a stirring of the crowd, and the five men summoned stepped forward. I looked at their faces. Flosi showed no apprehension at all, nor did Ketil, but I thought I read tension on the faces of one or two of Ketil's younger brothers. None, however, looked afraid.

"You have heard the accusation levied against you, and against others of your family," Hall said, looking down upon them.

"We have," said Ketil. "And we were aware before now that it would be made. We have asked Eyjolf Bolverksson to represent us, and he has been given the names of the five other arbitrators whom we appoint to decide the outcome of these actions." Ketil exchanged glances with Flosi and smiled a little. I wondered at that.

"Eyjolf Bolverksson," said Hall, "please come forward."

A tall, lean man, perhaps fifty years of age, with very light-colored hair and a ruddy complexion, stepped forward out of the crowd. He strode up to Hall, and then his eyes swept over the people standing around the Law Rock. He, too, wore a small, superior smile.

"Do you accept this position of representative for the men charged in this action?" Hall asked.

"I do," said Eyjolf. "And," he added in a loud voice, "I do not wish to waste the time of the Law Speaker nor of the good men called upon to arbitrate this case, so I will speak out now. There is good reason to throw out both of these actions without arbitration. Indeed, I think that there is no other course."

There was a sudden rush of murmurs from the crowd. Thorgrim Hammerfist, who was standing to the right of me, exchanged glances with me. He seemed as mystified as I was. I looked at Thorgeir Skorar-Geir, who was standing to my left, but his cool blue eyes were staring straight ahead, and his face wore no expression at all. For myself, I felt the beginnings of dismay in the pit of my stomach, but I did not know why.

Hall, too, seemed caught off guard. "Indeed?" he said, and now an eyebrow went up. "Please tell us what that reason might be."

"I submit to you, Law Speaker and men assembled here," said Eyjolf in a loud voice, "that the twelve men who have been accused have come here to the Great Assembly, knowing full well that they might be judged against harshly. Nevertheless, they came in good faith because that is the law. However, their accusers have not been satisfied with the due course of judgment here, and thought to take matters into their own hands, in the most dishonest possible fashion. I know not which of the four accusers it was. Perhaps more than one in conspiracy, or perhaps all. But whoever it was has sent a henchman to me with a bribe, asking me in return to make certain that the case be judged against the men I represent, and to see to it that they were one and all sent to their deaths at the hands of the executioner, or at the very least outlawed for life."

Now, the crowd erupted into such a fury of shouts that Hall's call for silence could not be heard. It was several minutes before order was restored, and Hall stood, gazing out over the crowd with flashing eyes. He looked at Eyjolf. "And who is this henchman, sent to do this? His name at least we will have."

Eyjolf paused for a moment, savoring the tension in the air. Then, he swung his arm up and pointed out over the crowd with one long finger at a figure standing on the edge of the milling group of men.

"It is he," Eyjolf said. "Mord Valgardsson."

We all turned. I saw Mord only for a moment, his eyes wide in his pale face. I have never seen anyone look so surprised and dismayed.

For myself, I was struck dumb with astonishment.

Mord gaped only for seconds, and then he turned and fled. No one pursued him for a moment. The crowd was thick, and those nearest to him were not certain what to do until Flosi's deep, stern voice rang out, "After him, you fools!"

The men fanned out after him, but I was not watching anymore. I was watching Hall of Sida, who was standing on the Law Rock, his eyes wide in disbelief at what had happened. Eyjolf Bolverksson, still smiling at the way in which he had destroyed all our efforts at one stroke, turned, and said, "By the law, if such a bribe is made, any action connected to it is considered void..."

If he spoke further, I did not hear him, for at that moment my heart exploded within me. I saw Eyjolf's smirking face superimposed upon the cross burned into my Ingrid's back by the fallen timbers of Bergthorshváll. I saw Thórd's innocent little face twisted and altered by some strange magic into the face of Ketil Sigfússon, smiling his secret smile in anticipation of our destruction. I gave a great, snarling cry of rage, and drew my sword ringing from its sheath. Then I leapt up onto the Law Rock, and before anyone could hinder me, I had cut down Eyjolf Bolverksson and thrown his body down to the ground below. I then flung myself into the crowd, growling like a wolf, or like a man gone mad. Other men tried to stop me, with words or with blades. Some fell back, but others I slew, not knowing if they were friend or foe, acquaintance or total stranger.

All the time, one name rang inside my skull. Mord. Mord Valgardsson. No wonder he had been so sure of success. He had undone all that we were trying to do, in attempting to make a likely victory into a certain one. Had he been standing before me then, I would have struck him down as well, but he was gone, and probably well away by now. He was slippery and would have no difficulty evading the men who had run in pursuit of him, many of whom probably had little enough idea of whom they were after. Failing him, whom could I slay? That was all that was in my heart. A red fog clouded my wits. I knew whom I wanted to kill, but I could not find them. I searched in vain for Ketil, Flosi, and the rest. I ran among the crowd seeking them, the blood running from my sword, but everywhere I turned it seemed that I saw only terrified, unfamiliar faces drawing back from me in horror.

Finally, I was grabbed from behind and disarmed by strong hands. I struggled like a wild beast, but there were too many, clutching at me from all sides. I cried out in impotent rage as I was dragged to the Law Rock. I saw

Asgrím Ellida-Grímsson there, looking at me sternly, and the three brothers, Njál's nephews, were there as well. Thorleif Crow's eyes met mine for a moment, and then he turned away from me in sorrow.

Hall of Sida was still there upon the Rock, his face a shifting mask of incredulity, anger, and despair. When he saw that I had been subdued, he called out, "Are the accused men still here?"

There was some stirring among the crowd, and Flosi, Ketil, and the rest came out, a little hesitantly, from where they had been hiding. I roared and thrashed about when I saw them. I must have been a fearsome sight, my long hair hanging before my eyes, and the blood of others spattering my clothes. My struggles ceased, and Hall spoke again.

"There is no arbitration to be had here," Hall said, his voice stern. "Since one of the representatives is now dead, and several other men wounded or slain, including men having nothing to do with these actions at all. I need hear no further discussion of this. I will pass judgment on all of you myself."

He straightened, and his voice rang out over our heads, echoing from the blue sky like a great bell. "Iceland has seen violence enough from these two factions over the past thirty years. Too many good men have died, and good women too. It is time to end it and end it I shall. I hereby outlaw the twelve men who were at the burning of Bergthorshváll—Ketil, Thorkel, Eirík, Lambi Sigfússon, Flosi Thórdarson, Sigurd and Gunnar Lambason, Grani Gunnarson, Modolf Ketilsson, Glum Hildisson, Kol Thorsteinsson, and Arni Kolsson. You are to leave Iceland for a period of ten years, upon pain of death should you return before that time. You have two weeks in which to make your preparations to go."

"And what of Kári Solmundarson?" I heard someone call. I do not think it was one of the outlawed men, but it may have been. Soon, others took up the shout. "Yes, what of Kári?" "He killed my brother." "Kill him!" "He should die."

I looked around at the men near me through my tangled hair fallen in front of my eyes, and I felt from them a solid wall of hot hostility. Never before had I felt anything like it.

Hall looked down upon me, and in his eyes, I think I saw sympathy, but there was a fierce sternness there as well. He said, "Kári Solmundarson, you are to leave Iceland and never return, upon pain of death. I hereby command all men here neither to help, harbor, nor injure you. You are likewise given two weeks to go. If you are in Iceland one hour past that time, any man may strike you down without fear of penalty or retribution."

I looked at him for a moment, and his eyes met mine. Then I turned my gaze out to the twelve men who had just been judged, the men who had destroyed my life. Most of them showed no emotion at the judgment of outlawry, but several of them, especially the younger ones, were pale and distraught. I looked at them, standing there in a dense little knot only a few feet away, and the hatred, wild and uncontrollable, flared up in my heart. It was not hot. It was cold, bitter cold like iron in midwinter when the cold can burn what it touches. I bared my teeth at them, and the nearest ones backed away in fear.

"I swear," I said, and my voice started out as a husky whisper but rose as I spoke until it became a cry so loud I could scarcely believe it was my own voice, "I swear that I shall see every single one of you dead, and dead by my sword. I shall not rest until I have struck every one of you down, and you lie in a pool of your own life's blood. I swear this by the old gods and the new, and if I do not follow through upon it, let me be struck down by the vengeance I now call upon your heads!"

Men drew back from me as I spoke. Even Hall of Sida paled as he heard these words, but he regarded me with an unflinching gaze, and said, "Kári Solmundarson, I charge you not to further defile this hallowed place with bloodshed. If you bare your sword here again, I shall not lift a finger to judge against the man who cuts you down."

I met his eyes and looked steadily at them. "I understand, and I will obey you," I said. "Give me back my sword."

Hall motioned for someone to retrieve it. Then he said to the men who held me, "Release him."

I took the sword, and wiped it clean on the grass, and returned it to its sheath. Then I turned, and without a glance behind me, returned to the booth. Thorleif and his brothers were not there. Neither was Mord Valgardsson, not that I expected him to be. I went to my horse, untied it, mounted it, and rode away.

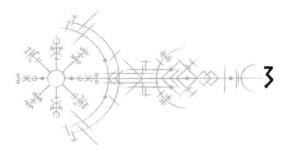

I RODE FROM THINGVELLIR IN WORSE despair than I had ever known. I had thought that my sorrow at the death of my wife and child had been the very trough of despondency, that there could be none deeper, but that day I felt the loss of Ingrid and Thórd return a hundredfold, compounded by a terrible sense of helplessness. I felt like a man might feel who has fallen into a swift-moving river. I was being swept along, and my own feeble efforts to ward off disaster were unavailing. In fact, it simply drove me faster toward the plunge over the waterfall which awaited, and the sharp and deadly rocks below.

What saved me then was my anger, a bitter well that seemed to have no bottom. Had I not been propelled by my hatred for the men who had destroyed my family, I would probably have let my horse run free, and fallen onto my own sword, as I have heard that men did of old when there were no choices left to them. Perhaps it would have been better had I done so. Who can say?

The first night, I camped in a shallow valley south of Thingvellir. I lay on my back, staring up at the long, slow fade of the sunset, and then at the white stars wheeling silently over my head. Sleep eluded me. All that filled my mind were fears and questions. I had been declared an outlaw. I no longer had a family in Iceland, and after Mord Valgardsson's foolish scheme, I had no desire to go to him for help.

Where, then, could I go? I felt that now I truly had nowhere to call home. I had abandoned my own home in the Hebrides over fifteen years before. It seemed like an eternity ago. Going back to the Orkneys seemed suicidal. If Jarl Sigurd was still alive, he would certainly remember the part I had played in the escape of Thrain Sigfússon and the Njálssons. He did not seem to me to be a forgiving man, nor one who would easily forget a wrong done to him.

Where else was there to go? The men I had served with under Jarl Sigurd had traveled widely—some as far as Norway and Denmark, and settlements still further east, and others had traveled far to the south. But I had no knowledge of those places, nor how to get there, nor did I know what I would do if once I arrived. To set off there alone was impossible. What ship could I find to bring me there, or anywhere? At that moment, it seemed to me preferable simply to wait until the two weeks had passed and let the first man who saw me strike off my head. To rest in death, to sleep in peace in the churchyard beside Ingrid and Thórd, seemed like a sweet dream.

But what of the oath I had sworn? Just thinking of it made my fists clench and my heart pound. I could not rest yet. I had sworn to hound them to their graves or die in the attempt. But the impossibility of carrying out what I had promised weighed upon me like stone. How could I, alone, kill twelve men?

I lay on my back, the white stars glittering coldly above me, and I remembered then a story that my grandmother had told me, when I was a small child. It was about a man whose life had been saved by a troll. The man had then sworn to repay the troll by giving him enough gold to fill whatever container that the troll chose. The troll brought to the man a narrow drinking horn, and the man thought, "Excellent! Look at this horn and see how little it can contain. This foolish troll will get hardly anything from me." But the man found that however much gold he put into the drinking horn, it never filled up. It was a bottomless horn whose end went down to the depths of the sea and could never be filled. My grandmother said that the man poured every bit of his own wealth into the horn, and finally grew old and died, bound always to his impossible promise. Even now, his spirit was still there, stealing people's gold—he had long since run out of his own—and tossing it into the drinking horn. For once sworn, my grandmother said, an oath will hold you, and even in death you will find neither release nor solace unless it is completed.

At that moment, I did not fear dying, but the thought that my words had bound me to an endless and impossible quest terrified me beyond imagining. Death I could accept, but not ceaseless, fruitless wandering without end.

It was the most despairing moment of my life. I brought my arm up over my eyes to block out the sight of the stars, and locked myself into the dark, hopeless world within me. It was thus that sleep finally found me.

———————

THE FIRST LIGHT OF DAWN WOKE me. I stretched and drank a little from a small stream nearby. Feeling somewhat ashamed of my nightmarish despondency the previous night, I prepared to journey on toward Hof. I had no wish to see Mord Valgardsson, but I had a few small belongings at his house that I thought to take along with me, wherever it was I was going. I was just preparing to mount when I heard the sound of hooves and looked up to see who it might be. My hand dropped automatically to my sword hilt.

It proved to be a young man of about twenty whom I had never seen before. He was riding a young chestnut stallion and was coming from the direction of Thingvellir. He slowed when he saw me and reined in beside me. His horse continued to move restlessly on the short turf, a nervous, spirited young animal. I thought the horse seemed well suited to his rider, who was fine-featured and bright-eyed, with a sparkle of adventure and intelligence in his clear gray eyes.

"I am Thorfinn Karlsefni," he said. "I am a friend of Thorleif Crow. I was sent with a message for Kári Solmundarson."

"I am Kári Solmundarson. What is your message?"

"Thorleif and his brothers send you greetings and say that despite the ruling by Hall of Sida, they will give you what help they can. They have sworn to Hall they would take no revenge upon the twelve men who burned Bergthorshváll, and they said that they will not break their word in this matter. Nevertheless, they said that they still count you as a friend and will not forsake you. They sent me because my father owns a ship, and it will be leaving from the harbor at Holt for the Hebrides in eight or nine days' time. Thorleif tells me to say to you that they will pay your passage there, if you are willing."

I stared at him for a moment, struck dumb with amazement.

The Hebrides!

Suddenly it seemed to beckon to me, like a dream of all that is desired. Was it possible to return there, after all this time? Would anyone there remember me? I pictured myself landing at the beach from which I had set out so many years ago and being greeted by my brothers. Perhaps I could stay with my brother Oláf for a time and renew old friendships to which I had never expected to return.

My luck, once again, had opened a door where none had seemed to be.

Thorfinn seemed distressed at my silence, and his clear young eyes showed concern. "Is that unacceptable to you?"

I straightened up. "No. It is far more than I had hoped for. I will gladly accept their help. Please tell them they have proven to be far better friends to me than I have to them, and I regret bitterly my actions yesterday, and hope that no ill will befall them because of it."

"Do not worry. They are not being held responsible."

"Have they caught Mord Valgardsson?"

"Not that I am aware."

I nodded. "I thank you for delivering this message, Thorfinn Karlsefni. I will remember your friendship to a man who thought himself friendless."

He smiled, an open, warm smile which lit up his handsome, even-featured face. "You are not friendless. Even after yesterday, there are still many who are in sympathy with you. But Thorleif Crow has asked me to give you one further message."

"What is that?"

"He says that the Sigfússons, Flosi Thórdarson, and the rest have split up, going to their respective homes, to gather what they will of their belongings and make arrangements to leave Iceland. He said that Sigurd Lambason and Thorkel Sigfússon left this morning for Kerlingardale and will be there within two days. You might intercept them there, if you wish. Eirík, Lambi, and Ketil Sigfússon, and Ketil's son Modolf, left yesterday afternoon for Ketil's home at Mork, and are probably already there. He said he was told that they would only stay a day or two at Mork, and then were going on to Hornafjord, where Ketil has a ship that they will take when they leave Iceland. But Thorleif said that between Mork and Hornafjord is the river crossing at Skapt, and that it is a narrow place, where one man alone might well be at an advantage over several adversaries."

A slow smile spread across my face. "Tell Thorleif that I understand him well."

"Of the others, Flosi Thórdarson left midday yesterday for Svinafell, and has such a long start that you would be hard pressed to catch him up. Where he intends to go afterwards, Thorleif did not know. Arni Kolsson, Kol Thorsteinsson, and Glum Hildisson went the other way, toward the ports on the bay of Faxaflói, where I have heard they plan on finding ships to take them from Iceland. Grani Gunnarson and Gunnar Lambason were still at the Great Assembly when I left. I do not know where they will be going."

I nodded. "I thank him for the news, and also for his help. You may tell Thorleif that if it is in my power, I will be at Holt in eight days' time, to take your father's ship to the Hebrides. I thank you as well for faithfully bearing his message to me."

Thorfinn Karlsefni's quick smile flashed out again. "I am pleased to help you. I have been told that you are a fierce warrior of great renown, and have been to many places, far away from Iceland."

I returned his smile, and in doing so, I felt some of the tension relax out of my body. "Whether I am a fierce and renowned warrior I cannot say, but it is true that I have traveled. There are, however, many places which I have heard of and never seen, and countless more, I do not doubt, that I have never heard of."

His eyes shone with a childlike curiosity that I found completely disarming. "What places have you visited?"

"I was born in the Hebrides, and I have been in the Orkneys, and also in Scotland and England."

"What is it like in the wide world?"

I thought for a moment, trying to find words to sum up the places I had been. Finally, I just said, "It is large. Larger than you can possibly imagine. And the sea fills the greater part of it."

This description, simple and inadequate as it was, seemed to fill him with awe. "I am going to see the world when I am older."

I looked at him, into his honest, guileless eyes, and said only, "I hope that you may find it a kinder place than I have."

We bid each other farewell, and he rode back toward Thingvellir. I watched as he and his horse disappeared over the crest of a hill, and then I mounted my own horse, but sat for a moment in indecision.

Eight days. I had eight days to accomplish whatever I had left to accomplish in Iceland, before Thorfinn's father's ship left. If I failed to take that journey, less than a week afterwards my time ran out and I became a hunted man. Thorleif Crow had made it plain that he supported me in my oath against the men who had burned Bergthorshváll, but Hall of Sida had made him and his brothers swear that they would take no action against them. In the little time I had known Thorleif, Thorgrim, and Thorgeir, I had found them to be unswerving in their honesty, and I could not imagine them breaking such an oath.

And so, the revenge was mine to take. That had clearly been the message—by telling me where each of the burners had gone, Thorleif had as much as said, "Now, Kári, go and kill them."

In that moment, I felt my oath sink its claws deep into my soul. It was as if I no longer had any power in the matter. Before I knew what I was doing, I had turned my horse's head toward Kerlingardale, which lay a day and a half's ride east of where I was. Sigurd Lambason and Thorkel Sigfússon were heading there, Thorfinn Karlsefni had said. Sigurd lived there, and Thorkel and he were good friends. They no doubt wished to return there to make preparations for leaving Iceland. Karlsefni had said that they would be there in two days' time. I knew the lay of the land well, and already had a day's lead. I reckoned that if I did not delay I could arrive there before they did.

I rode my horse hard all day long and camped that night along a rocky stream which chuckled and laughed along the stones throughout the short night. It was a soothing sound, and I slept well. More than anything, however, the fact that I had decided to take action kept me from despair and gave me the will to keep going.

I passed north of Bergthorshváll early the next day. From a distance, I could see the rounded hill which had once been crowned by Njál's house, the house in which I had lived in happiness before it had been destroyed. I did not pause in my journey, but kept on, hardening my heart and forcing myself not to stop and gaze at it in sorrow. I felt that if once I stopped and looked upon it, I would never move again. Soon I crested a hill, and it disappeared from view.

Kerlingardale lies east of Bergthorshváll, and I reached it by mid-afternoon. The river there was running high, rushing white and foaming between its rocky banks, but there was a shallow place which was much used
as a ford, and I crossed it without difficulty. I then rode a bit further, until I
was in sight of Sigurd Lambason's house, to see if perhaps the two men had
arrived before me. But, other than an old servant man who was in the yard
tending some goats, the house seemed empty.

I then returned to the place where I had forded the stream and dismounted. I tied my horse's reins to a bush and sat down to wait.

It was a clear, cool day, of the kind so common during the short Icelandic
summer. I could hear the distant calling of gulls and terns, and high in the
pale blue sky above my head, an eagle soared. It was a peaceful place. I leaned
back against a cool-sided boulder and fixed my gaze upon the ford.

I have said that I am an impatient man. But no predator has sat in wait for
his prey more patiently than I did that day. I did not move from that place for
five hours, as the slow summer sun banked and began its long, tilted swoop
toward the horizon. I knew that they must come that way sooner or later.
Only two hours before sunset, I heard the sound of approaching hooves.

Thorkel Sigfússon came into sight first, riding his horse around a hump
of dark rock which lay on the other side of the river. He seemed tired and
was riding slowly. Sigurd Lambason, his nephew, came next. When I first
saw him, Sigurd was speaking earnestly to his uncle about something, but
he noticed me at once and fell silent, pointing. Thorkel reined in, and sat
motionless on his horse, staring at me in silent amazement.

I stood up, unsheathing my sword, and faced them across the water. "You
have heard me swear to kill each one of the men who burned Bergthorshváll
and killed my family," I said in a voice loud enough to be heard above the
roar of the river. "You two will be the first. Unless you turn and flee like
cowards, you will not leave this place alive."

Sigurd glanced at his uncle. I saw fear in his eyes, and my heart rejoiced
in it. Thorkel did not seem impressed, however. He was a big, heavy man,
with massive arms and legs. I had never seen him fight. I knew from experience that such men are often slow, but that if a blow he struck landed, it
would be with killing force.

"Kári, you may be a warrior, but you are no prophet," he said, his voice disdainful. "I have killed men before, just as you have. There are two of us, and you are alone. Hall of Sida enjoined us all not to injure you, and I would not break my promise to him. But if you do not get out of our way, I will slay you as you stand there."

"Your word means nothing to me, killer of women and children that you are," I sneered at him. "As for your threats, I do not fear them. Fight me if you are as unafraid as you seem."

Thorkel half-turned to Sigurd, all the time keeping an eye on me. "Let us rid the world of this lout. It will not change our outlawry, but at least my brothers will praise us for it."

At that, he dismounted, and drew his sword, and strode toward the river. Sigurd, a little less certainly, did the same.

The icy river water curled around his thighs as he crossed. It was running so high that it was hard for him to keep his balance. I did not want it to be said later that I struck him while he was at a disadvantage, so I waited until he had stepped upon dry land. Then I launched my attack upon him.

I do not think that Thorkel expected me to fight with such fury, but my heart was aflame. His eyes gradually became wider and wider as I beat against him like the waves beat upon the shore, relentless, battering him with sword blows. Sigurd Lambason stood nearby, with sword drawn, but I kept Thorkel between myself and him. Sigurd, obviously inexperienced, did not know what to do.

Thorkel's extra weight proved a hindrance to him. He was slower than me, and tired faster. I have always been quick, and my white-hot hatred gave me endurance. It was over in minutes. He parried one of my blows too slowly and brought his elbow up too far. I slashed upward savagely and cleaved off his sword arm at the shoulder.

Thorkel gave a terrible shriek, and his sword clattered away onto the rocks. Then he stepped backwards, and pitched over into the river, and struck his head on a stone. His cry was stopped instantly, and his life quickly bled itself out and was carried away downstream, staining the churning water scarlet. I looked up at Sigurd Lambason, who stood watching me, his sword hanging from nerveless hands, his face white. He could not tear his eyes from mine and seemed to be in the far reaches of terror.

"How old are you?" I walked towards him until I stood only a few feet away.

"Twenty-two," he answered, his voice trembling.

My gaze was cold and pitiless. "You could have lived another forty years."

At that, his nerves failed him, and he dropped his sword onto the ground, and fell to his knees. "I beg of you, have mercy on me!" he cried, and almost choked upon his words.

"I will show you mercy, Sigurd Lambason. As much as you showed to Ingrid and Thórd." I raised my sword and struck off his head.

It may be that this brands me as an evil man, to have struck a young man down so, and one who had not even drawn his blade. But I can say that I felt no remorse in my heart, but only a kind of savage glee when I looked at their bodies lying there, and the ground splattered with crimson, glowing in the failing light. At that moment, there redoubled in my heart the desire to do it again and again, to strike them all down thus.

What do I feel now? Am I a different man, so many years later, have I grown and changed and become wiser? Perhaps, perhaps not. I have lost the ability to discern. I will say only that as I sit here now, in the night of another Icelandic summer, having the priest's boy of Hvitaness record these events, I still do not feel any real remorse. I feel only a sadness at the circumstances that would drive a man to such actions.

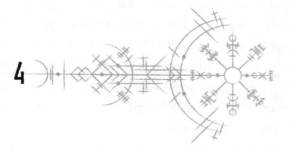

4

IT MAY SEEM STRANGE, BUT IMMEDIATELY after I killed Thorkel and Sigurd, I found myself suddenly swaying with weariness. Exhaustion seemed to seep into me from the very air I breathed, and it overcame the vengeful joy I had felt. Suddenly, all I wanted to do was sleep. I wiped my sword clean, and then found a small patch of dry turf which looked more comfortable than the stones all about and threw myself down and fell immediately into a deep, dreamless sleep.

I have heard that men have been at times haunted by the specters of the men they have slain, and that these apparitions are especially likely if a man spends the night in a place where he has killed someone. I do not know if that is true, but that night I lay not ten paces away from the blood-drenched bodies of Sigurd Lambason and Thorkel Sigfússon, and I slept like an innocent child, waking refreshed with the first rays of the sun.

When I awoke, my mind was gripped even more strongly by the talons of the oath I had sworn. It is a terrible thing to admit, but I gave no thought to the men I had killed, nor to the grief of their families, but only to whom I would kill next. More than any of the others, I desired to find Flosi Thórdar-son, but Thorfinn Karlsefni had said that Flosi had left the Great Assembly early and had too great a lead on me, and that I would not be able to catch up with him before he was safe at his home in Svinafell. There, surrounded by the men of his household, I would not stand a chance against him, alone as I was. Reluctantly, I put aside my desire to find Flosi.

Later, I thought. I would not forget him, not in a hundred years' time. I would kill him as well. But others would have to come first.

Who, then? The Sigfússons' cousins, Kol Thorsteinsson, Arni Kolsson, and Glum Hildisson had gone the opposite direction, west to the bay at Faxa-flói, and might well already have taken ship. There was no point in pursuing them now.

Later, my mind said again.

I wished greatly to fight the sneering and hateful Grani Gunnarson and Gunnar Lambason, whom we had spared when Thrain Sigfússon was killed, so many years ago, but Thorfinn had said that they had remained behind at the Great Assembly and had not known where they would go.

Then I thought of Ketil Sigfússon, with his haughty expression and fierce, hawklike face. He had been the other leader the night they burned Bergthor-shváll. I saw him in my mind, exchanging a smirk with Flosi Thórdarson as they awaited our defeat at the Great Assembly. Ketil, I thought, was certainly as guilty as Flosi was. If I could not fight Flosi, then Ketil was the next most worthy of my revenge.

Two days' ride east of Kerlingardale is the little, tumbling Skapt River, which comes down from the huge ice walls in the high mountains and final-ly plunges into the sea at Skaptafjord. It is, as Thorfinn had said, a narrow place, and there is only one easy ford. Too far north, and one would find steep rocks and hard going on foot, impossible on a horse. Too far south, and there are the treacherous sandy marshes of Kringlumire and Skeidar. Ketil, along with his son and two of his brothers, had returned to Mork, but Thorfinn had said they would soon set out again for Hornafjord, which was still further east. To get there, they would have to cross the Skapt River, and there was only one place to do it easily. I knew what path they would take.

It was only a matter of waiting.

So I turned my horse's head east and rode toward the Skapt River.

I had only gone a half-hour's ride when I once again came upon Sigurd Lambason's house, which I had seen from a distance the day before. The same old man was out in the yard, and I did not see any other people about, so I rode up to him. He squinted up at me from under bushy brows.

"You have the look of one with ill news," he said in a creaky voice.

"Indeed. I am both the cause and the bearer. Is your mistress within?"

"She is."

"Get her."

The old man tottered inside, and shortly afterward came outside with a young woman of about twenty, fair in a simple sort of way, drying her hands on a coarse, linen apron.

"Who are you?" she asked, and I heard a note of fear in her voice.

"I am called Kári Solmundarson," I said, looking down upon her from my high seat, and she blanched. She evidently knew the name.

"You are the one they thought dead," she said, in a weak voice.

"Indeed. I fear that I have ill news, and I regret it, for you seem a good woman. But your husband is dead, and his uncle Thorkel Sigfússon as well. By my sword it was done."

Her blue eyes grew wide, and she said only, "Why have you done this?"

"I have sworn an oath that all of those men who were there when my wife and son were killed would die by my own blade. I have begun with these two. Let it be known that Kári Solmundarson has done this and send someone to fetch their bodies and give them a decent Christian burial."

But the woman said nothing, and in a moment had fainted dead away on her doorstep.

The old servant man knelt beside her to help her, and then looked up at me, a mixture of fear and reproach on his weathered face. I returned his gaze silently, challenging him to speak. He looked away from me, down toward his mistress. I left them there and rode toward the sun still lying low in the morning sky.

The land between Kerlingardale and Skapt is rough and rocky, even for Iceland. I was impatient with my progress, for I did not know if Ketil and his band were before me or behind me. I did not want them to cross the ford at Skapt before me. Once past that, the way to Hornafjord was largely open and flat, and four men could easily hold their own against one. But the ford was reached through a narrow cutting in the black mountain rock, and Thorleif had shown his characteristic shrewdness in pointing out the one place where a single attacker might have an advantage.

I camped the first night deep in a cleft of the high mountains. It was as sheltered a place as I could find, but even so the wind whistled disconsolately past me the whole night, and I pulled my cloak about me for warmth. My horse, too, seemed ill at ease and tugged unhappily on his tether in the darkness. It is strange to think of how soundly I had slept the previous night, with two of my foes fallen close by. Here, alone in the mountains, I felt uneasy, as if there was some dark magic near. I tossed about restlessly, and finally fell into a disturbed sleep, filled with strange and forbidding dreams.

I dreamed that I was in a room with Ingrid, and she was lying on a bed, dressed in her light linen shift, her lovely red-gold hair arrayed about her. I smiled at her, and touched her face, saying to myself, "She is asleep." I caressed her smooth cheek, and felt my blood grow hot with desire in my veins. I called her name, and greatly wondered why she did not wake. Then, like an ice-cold claw clutching my heart, I knew that she was not asleep, but dead, and my passion turned to ashes within me. I stood in horror and saw that there were tallow candles surrounding the bed, lit and burning steadily with a shimmering golden light. I wept for her, crying out her name, as if my pain and grief could undo her death, as if my voice could call her back and wake her, and she would lift her arms to encircle me once more.

As I stood weeping, a chill wind came and blew out the candles, and I smelled bitter smoke. The darkness became complete, and rain began to fall. Thunder snarled in the distance like some huge beast of prey. I stumbled about, the rain pouring off my drenched body and running in my eyes. I called for Ingrid, and reached out to find her, but her body was gone, or else I had lost my sense of direction and did not know where it was.

Then, in the distance, I heard Lambi Sigfússon's voice sneering the words he had spoken to me at the Great Assembly. "You should have died with the rest of them." I knew suddenly that all of them were out there, all of my enemies, and that they knew where I was, but I could not see them. Panicked, sensing that I would be attacked at any moment, I reached down for my sword, and felt my knuckles scrape against something rough and grating. The pain woke me up, and I found myself groping blindly for my sword in the hours before dawn, lying on my back in the little mountain cleft in which I had camped. I had rubbed my knuckles raw against the rock beside which I was lying. The rain was pouring down in sheets from a sky the color of cinders, and I was soaked and chilled to the bone.

I ate a few morsels of food and prepared myself for another day of journeying. It rained all morning. I could see out over the western end of the flat,
treacherous Skeidar marshes, and a gray veil of rain hung over it as far as I
could see, seemingly motionless. Rivulets of water leapt across my path, and
everywhere there was the hiss of droplets falling on stone.

It was not until the early afternoon that a wind came up in the west, and
the rain stopped. Then the clouds were torn to shreds, and the sun came
out. Despite my haste, I reined in my horse, and dismounted. I stripped off
all my sodden clothes and spread them out on a rock to dry. I lay for a while
in the sunshine, simply glad for being dry myself, for feeling the warmth
seeping back into me, for the play of the sunlight on my bare skin. It is
strange how even in the throes of sorrow, dire oath, and desperate haste,
a simple pleasure like this could enter my darkened mind and cheer me, if
only for a little while.

I allowed myself only an hour's rest before I rose and dressed again. My
clothes were still damp but at least were no longer soaked and dripping. I
remounted my horse and continued my journey toward Skapt.

It was about mid-afternoon that I saw a farmhouse in the distance and
realized that I had veered somewhat to the south, but was making better
time than I had expected. It was the house of Hjalti Skeggjason, a staunch
friend of Asgrím Ellida-Grímsson, and one of the men who had promised
to help me in my action against Flosi and Ketil and the rest. The path I was
taking would lead me right past the farmhouse. I knew that Hjalti would
undoubtedly still be at the Great Assembly. The fight and my banishment
would probably have disappointed him, but he surely had other business to
conduct there and would not have left early because of it. However, I still
decided to stop for a little while there, to leave a message with his wife and
to find out any information I could about where my foes had gone.

When I rode into the yard, I was greeted by a cheerful shout of, "Kári!
Greetings to you!" from old Askel, their servant, who was in his eightieth
year but still hale and fit and never without a smile on his face.

"My greetings to you, as well, Askel." I swung my leg over and jumped to
the ground. "Your master is still away, I guess?"

"He is, but I am always glad to see you. Your business at the Assembly
must have gone well, for you to be away so soon."

"You know of it?"

He laughed heartily. "My master has such a loud voice, what he says carries all the way down to the sea and the gulls there repeat it. I know something of your troubles, and that you hoped to have them recompensed at the Assembly."

"Well, Askel, old friend, I fear that I have ill news. My action was destroyed by the foolish attempt by a friend to make our victory a certain thing, and I am now outlawed and in ten days will be a hunted man. One reason I come here is to say farewell."

Poor Askel's face fell. He truly was a kind-hearted old man. "Now, Kári, it is unbecoming of a man like you to jest with me."

"I do not jest. If I am in Iceland a day longer than ten days hence, you may well have to see to it that I am given a Christian burial, and no man may seek my blood price in compensation. My life is forfeit, old friend. I would speak to your mistress before I go."

He went into the house, looking dejected, but shortly afterward came out again, and Hjalti's wife Gunnhild came out behind him.

Hjalti was, as Askel had said, a big man with a loud voice, but his wife Gunnhild was a match for him and more. She was not much to look at, all curves and roundness beneath clothes that never seemed to fit properly, with dust-brown hair and muddy green eyes—but she had the quickest wit of any woman I have ever known, and a voice loud enough to shout down even her husband. Nevertheless, she was a good-hearted person, open-handed and generous. The smile that lit up her plain face when she saw me cheered my heart greatly. "Kári!" she cried out, much as Askel had, "what brings you here, with such goings-on at the Assembly, and all concerning you and what happened at Bergthorshváll last year?"

I told her what had happened at the Assembly.

She shook her head. "I told Hjalti that it would not be so simple as he thought. That Ketil Sigfússon, he is a crafty one, and Flosi is no fool either, although I think that he is a good enough man and am still surprised that he allowed himself to get caught up in this evil. And now you are outlawed. What a terrible thing."

"That is not the whole story, Gunnhild. In the heat of my anger, after the destruction of our action at the Assembly, I swore an oath to kill all of the men who were at the burning of Bergthorshváll. I have already killed two of them and am pursuing four others."

Gunnhild raised an eyebrow. "Which men have you killed?"

"Thorkel Sigfússon and Sigurd Lambason."

She nodded. "It is no great loss, those two. Thorkel was a lout and Sigurd a coward. Who are you after now?"

"I have been told that Ketil, Lambi, and Eirík Sigfússon, and Modolf Ketilsson, are journeying to Hornafjord, and I wish to stop them at Skapt."

Gunnhild grinned but gave me an appraising eye. "You take them on four to one? I know that you are not lacking in courage, but I have sometimes had reason to wonder where courage ends, and foolhardiness begins."

I returned Gunnhild's smile. Her frankness was refreshing, after the life of tangled plots and schemes and duplicity in which I had lived for the past year. "I do not know, myself. All I know is that I have sworn to fight them, and if I die, I will die in trying to find justice for Ingrid and Thórd, since no justice could be found for them at the Assembly."

"Is it not enough that the men who killed them were banished for ten years?"

My smile faded. "No, it is not."

"I understand you, Kári. You have always had hot blood, but do not forget the warm heart that drives it. You have never been a man of evil. You should stop now before you become more snarled in this web. If you kill them all, what then? Will it bring back your wife and your little boy?"

I did not know how to respond to that. In the end, I just said, "No."

"I am sure that my husband would counsel you the same way as I do. Leave Iceland, since it has been decreed so. You have said that Thorleif Crow and his brothers will pay your way to the Hebrides. Stay for a few years, then return and petition the Assembly to overturn your outlawry. There are many who support you, and I do not doubt that it will be an easy thing for you to return in a few years if you go away peacefully now. If you are responsible for more violence.... I do not know."

"You mistake me, Gunnhild. I do not wish to return. I have no life left here in Iceland. The oath is all I have left."

The old servant, Askel, who was still standing by, murmured something under his breath, and turned his face away. Gunnhild herself seemed filled with sorrow at the despair in my voice. "In that case, my friend, I pity you."

"I thank you for your kindness, Gunnhild. Kindness is all I have ever been shown here, and I value it greatly. I regret I cannot take your counsel. Maybe it was fated thus years ago, and I am only acting out a part laid out for me since the day of my birth."

To my surprise, her eyes flashed, and she gave me a wry smile. "That is an excuse, Kári Solmundarson. You have chosen your own course, none other. One day you will look back on all of this and realize that I am right. Every day we do what we do, and then something results, for good or bad, and we say, 'Look what has happened, it was the fates at work.' What foolishness! Anyone who says we could not have chosen differently, and the fates rule our lives, is simply looking for a convenient place to lay the blame."

"I did not ask for the sorrow I have had to bear," I said, feeling curiously like a small child being lectured by his mother.

"No, no, you misunderstand me. No one chooses sorrow. But sorrow is part of life. I have lost two children as babies. Do you think I wished it? My father was killed at sea by Vikings who took everything on his ship but the bodies of him and his crew. Do you think I wished that?"

"Of course not. But did you not want to see the Vikings who murdered your father brought to justice?"

She shrugged. "I did once. But I soon realized that it would not have brought my father back from the dead. It would not have dried a single one of my mother's tears. I grieve like any human, but I do not need to place blame. My father died because of a chain of events so complicated that no man alive could say where the blame lay. If he had delayed his voyage, if his crew had been better armed, if the Vikings who killed him had been raised to abide by the law. *If, if, if.* When evil happens, it is everyone's fault, and no one's fault."

Listening to her words, I once again pictured Flosi and Ketil smirking at one another, and remembered my dream of Ingrid, and I rejected her argument. Surely, they were to blame!

"I am sorry, Gunnhild, but I do not believe it."

Once again, she shrugged. "I did not think you would. Hjalti does not either. Perhaps it is the sort of thing women understand and men do not."

Despite my dark mood, I burst out laughing at her audacity. "Gunnhild, truly Hjalti is a lucky man to have a wife like you. He will never want for wit and intelligence when you are around."

She gave me a wry smile. "You flatter me, Kári, and here in front of Askel. Now he will tell Hjalti, and Hjalti will be mad with jealousy, and then the two of you will fight over me, and I will be grieved whichever of you wins."

Askel blushed all over his lined face, and I laughed again. "Hjalti would have to give me chase, and he'd never catch up with me. I must continue on to Skapt River. Have any of my enemies passed this way in the last day or two?"

She nodded. "Kolskegg, who tends our sheep, said that Flosi Thórdarson came riding by here yesterday morning at a great pace, making for his home, I would guess. He was alone. None other has passed, at least that we have been aware."

I thanked her for her help.

"Help? All I have done is loaded you with a woman's worries. I wish you good fortune in your journeying." There was a twinkle in her muddy green eyes. "And I hope that you have the courage to face whatever those fates of yours have in store for you."

I bid Gunnhild farewell, and Askel as well, and left a message of farewell for Hjalti Skeggjason. Then I mounted my horse and resumed my journey toward Skapt.

I reached the river valley late in the evening. The mountains there draw very close to the sea, and the ground is rough and black rocks stick through the patches of grass. The sun was just skimming below the horizon for its short night's journey when I came to the Skapt River ford, and as before, I sat down to wait.

The darkness swept over me, and I must have slept. The next thing I remember is the gray light of dawn and hearing the soft neigh of a horse close by. I thought it was my own, but even half asleep as I was, I recalled that I had tied my horse to a low, gnarled tree to the left, and the sound was coming from my right. I opened my eyes and sat up.

Standing around me, with grim expressions, were the men whom I had planned to stop at the ford—Ketil, Eirík, and Lambi Sigfússon, and Ketil's son Modolf. All had swords drawn.

"Get up, Kári Solmundarson," said Ketil in a harsh voice, "and draw your sword like a man, so we may kill you and be done with it."

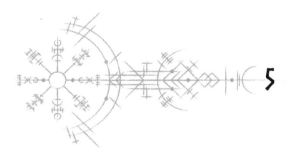

I LEAPT UP AND FOUND ALL four sword points turned toward me. I was certain that I would be cut down within moments. I threw a defiant taunt at them, thinking it would be my last words.

"Such honorable men you are," I snarled, looking upon each in turn, "to ambush a man, four against one. I should have expected no less from men who would slay an entire household, women and children included."

Modolf Ketilsson's sword dropped a little, and I caught a look of guilt flash across his young face. But his uncle, Lambi Sigfússon, continued to stare at me coldly. Lambi was the father of Sigurd and Gunnar Lambason.

"You would talk about honor, after slaying my brother and my son," he said, between clenched teeth.

"There is no stain on my honor from it, for the innocent blood of my wife and my son calls out for retribution. The deaths of Thorkel and Sigurd were but the beginning."

Eirík Sigfússon grinned at me, his pale blue eyes glittering harshly. "It is looking like being the end of it, as well, Kári Solmundarson. You will not leave this place alive."

I had no doubt that he spoke the truth, but I was not willing to show them any fear. I backed away a little. The narrow cut in the rock that led down to Skapt River ford I kept at my back, as that way they could not get behind me. I faced them defiantly. "I have had a dream," I said, and my voice rose to a shout. "I have dreamed of the twelve men who burned Bergthorsh-váll, and I saw eleven of them gathered up by the hand of Death." I pulled my sword from its sheath and held it before me. "Two have already gone into death's grip. Which ones of you will follow?"

Again, I saw Modolf Ketilsson's expression change a little. "Which of the twelve escaped, in your dream?"

His father scowled. "Quiet. Pay him no heed."

I met Modolf's eyes, and held them. "I will say the one who escaped death was not you," and without warning I launched myself at him. He seemed the weakest, and was certainly the least experienced of the four, and I thought that his dismay would further distract him from defending himself. Even so, I knew that the three older men, especially Ketil and Eirík, were experienced fighters, and that I would be hard pressed to remain on my feet for five minutes. I threw myself into fighting with a desperation that was almost a kind of freedom. I had no fears, no thought of anything but the world of the senses. All that I recall was the ringing of metal on metal and the harsh cries of enraged men fighting for their lives.

I did not want to move away from the rock walls that protected my back, but I was slowly being drawn away. Seeing that, I was sure I was lost. Eirík Sigfússon came up from one side, attempting to sweep my legs from beneath me with a great swing of his sword. But I saw him and leapt over the blade as nimbly as I had over that of the first man I had ever fought, so many years ago in the Hebrides. His eyes widened, whether with surprise or apprecia-tion, I do not know. I drove once more against Modolf, moving quickly to avoid the furious blows of his father and uncles.

Suddenly, Modolf seemed to lose control. I do not know if it was the extremity of his fear, or wild rage that did it. Whichever it was, it proved his undoing. He came at me, his young and handsome face twisted out of all recognition and aimed a heavy blow at my head. I dodged it easily and drove the point of my sword into his chest. He pitched forward without making a noise and was dead before he struck the ground.

His father, Ketil, gave a great cry of grief and fury, and fell upon me. Here, once again, luck took my hand. I raised my sword to parry a deadly blow from above, and when our swords met, there was a grinding clang, and Ketil's sword blade shattered in his hand. With a furious snarl, he threw away the useless hilt, and stepped back, knowing he could do nothing further.

Eirík then made the mistake of looking over at his brother to see what had happened. He had his face turned away from Ketil when the sword broke. I seized the moment of his distraction to strike at him, and the edge of my blade sliced across his throat. He shrieked and dropped his sword, clapping his hand to stem the rush of blood. He collapsed to his knees, looking at me with astonishment as the life drained away from him. Then the chilly blue eyes rolled upwards, and he slumped to the ground.

Ketil still stood there to one side, making wordless noises of impotent rage, but did not dare to attack me weaponless. Encouraged by my unexpected success, I threw myself upon Lambi. Lambi was the worst sword fighter of the Sigfússons and knew it. He soon realized that what had seemed a certain victory was now looking like a certainty of defeat and death. We had hardly crossed swords when I heard Ketil behind him shouting, "To the horses! You cannot win!" All of a sudden, my sword was cleaving the empty air. Lambi had turned and fled, and he and his brother had leapt astride their horses and were galloping away as fast as they could.

I raised my bloodied sword into the air and gave a great shout. "And such payment will I give you, as well. You shall not escape!" I laughed then, at the turn of fate that had given me the victory over four men, and I began to think that I was unable to be defeatede.

Ketil and Lambi fled south, rather than returning the way they had come. I sat down on a stone to clean my sword and watched them until their retreating horses could no longer be seen, disappearing over a rocky hill some distance away. The path they were following lead to the marsh of Kringlumire, formed where the Skapt River fans out into a broad flat land of reeds and grass before it finds the sea at Skaptafjord. It is a treacherous country, but with luck and surefootedness it can be crossed. No doubt they intended to ford the river there and continue on their way to Hornafjord.

I looked up at the blue sky and savored the silence after the battle. What should I do? I had been given eight days to reach the harbor at Holt, before the ship belonging to Thorfinn Karlsefni's father would leave with me on it or not. I had taken two days to reach Kerlingardale, and two more from there to the Skapt River. I could easily spend another two days searching for

Ketil and Lambi in the marshes, and that would leave me only two more to get from there to Holt.

I considered my options, and held a heated argument with myself, there on the hill above Skapt River ford. Should I let them go? Ketil was weaponless, and Lambi a poor swordsman. An unfair fight at best. But a fierce voice within me responded that Ingrid had been weaponless as well, and my heart pounded at the memory of her death beneath the burning timbers. What fairness had there been about the death of my wife and son?

I should pursue them, then. But could I safely cross the marshes on horseback, without getting mired in some muddy bog? I did not know this part of Iceland well, but I reasoned that I had only to follow their trail. If the ground could support their horses, it could support mine as well. I reminded myself that I had two days only. I could give myself no more than that. After two days, I would have to turn back west toward Holt, whether I had found them or not.

With that, I untied my horse, mounted, and rode off southward along the path that they had taken.

At first, the path was hard to follow, being through a rocky country whose bare bones break through the shallow soil, black and stark and rough. Southward, the hills quickly descend toward the plain, ever lower as they sink toward the sea. When I crested the top of a low rise about mid-morning, I was greeted by the sight of a vast expanse of green, with streaks of brown, blue, and black wandering across it. The marsh of Kringlumire. Very far in the distance was an indistinct gray line that I knew to be the ocean. There was the continual calling of birds of many kinds, and the wind made a constant sighing in the grass, like the breathing of some great beast sound asleep. From my high vantage point, I could see the swath that my foes' horses had made in the fresh greenness, and I rejoiced at having such a clear path to follow. My heart pounded within my chest, and I gave a great cry, and urged my horse on down the hill and into the plain.

I rode on all that afternoon and into the evening, as the sky turned purple, gold and blood-crimson. The horizon was awash with colors more brilliant than any jewels. When it became too dark to follow the trail, I dismounted and prepared to sleep for a while. I rested uncomfortably that night, on damp ground. The moisture seeped into my clothing and my skin felt clammy. Insects whined around my ears and stung my face and hands until I was nearly mad. I was desperate for the day to come, but not primarily because of my discomfort, more because only then could I continue the chase. Despite my state—muddy and tired and journey-weary—I truly felt invincible.

However, when I rose early the next morning, I found that fog had rolled in, borne on a southerly wind. My heart sank as I realized that the path of bent grass before me only went on for ten yards or less before it vanished into a heavy white cloud that obscured everything. The wind rolled it about, and ghostly curtains parted and then shut again, making my search that morning slow and painstaking. I went most of the way on foot, leading my horse, for fear of losing the trail. I knew that if once I lost it in the fog, I would waste valuable time trying to find it again, and in fact might not find it at all. The ground grew wetter and squelched unpleasantly under my feet.

I will admit that I have never liked fog. It is common both in the Hebrides and in Iceland, but I am always uneasy until it lifts. When I am outside in the fog I feel isolated, and at the same time strangely exposed, as if I am naked to my enemies but hidden from my friends. I journeyed that day in increasing anxiety, wondering whether at any moment Lambi Sigfússon might leap out at me, sword drawn, and catch me unawares. And still the path led on, further south toward the sea.

I crossed a small, muddy-bottomed stream at about midday. The thick mud clung to my feet and fouled my clothing. I found myself wishing heartily for the harsh, inhospitable mountains I had traveled in only the day before. My nerves continued to fray as the afternoon wore on and the fog remained thick, and when my presence startled some small brown bird into a flurry of wings past my face, I drew my sword before I knew what I was doing and gave a great cry of alarm. Then I stood for a moment, drawing great breaths of air, half laughing in relief at my own foolishness.

Another night approached, and the path veered toward the east and crossed a second small stream. I followed it until it was too dark to see, and then lay down for another sodden night among the reeds.

Lying there, while wisps of fog slid silently past me like the shades of men long-dead, I began to wonder if I had not been foolhardy to chase Lambi and Ketil into Kringlumire. I was ill-at-ease and could not get comfortable. I felt I was being watched by many pairs of unseen eyes, just out of my vision's reach. I have heard since that there are parts of Kringlumire that are said to be haunted. I do not know if that is true, for I saw nothing, and heard nothing, neither man nor ghost nor demon. Still, I felt it to be a hostile place at night and rejoiced to see the sun rise.

As soon as it was light I took up my pursuit once more and told myself I had only until midday before necessity would force me to turn back toward the west and my final journey in Iceland, to the harbor of Holt. The fog lifted a little by mid-morning, enough that I was able to remount and follow the trail on horseback. However, at the same time, the ground became still wetter and more treacherous, and my horse was hard-pressed to negotiate the mud flats and bogs, which looked grassy and solid but were nothing but quagmires. I soon stopped looking for the trail and concentrated on looking for ground solid enough to support me.

The sun, a mere white blotch in the grayness, reached its zenith. I had decided, with a mixture of disappointment and relief, to turn away from my search when I heard the whinny of a horse ahead of me. I reined up immediately and dismounted as silently as I could. Then, unmistakably, I heard men's voices ahead, murmurs whose identities I could not recognize with any certainty. Still, who else could be out here in this horrible marsh? I pulled my sword smoothly from my sheath and made my way stealthily toward the voices.

I came upon them with the suddenness that only happens in the fog. The white veil parted, and I was almost on top of them. Ketil Sigfússon was standing a little away, and Lambi was kneeling on the ground, peering into a saddlebag. Lambi's horse was beside him, holding up one foreleg. It had evidently gone lame in the clutching mud, and they had stopped to bind the animal's leg.

When he saw me Ketil froze, soundless. Lambi did not realize I was there at first, and continued what he was saying. "I believe that there is something in here I can use to bind the splint fast."

Then he looked up, and saw me standing there, and with a great cry leapt up and drew his sword.

As I have said, Lambi Sigfússon was no great sword fighter, and within minutes he was lying dead at my feet. Ketil had not moved all that time, and simply watched me mutely, his fierce, hawk-like face caught between anger, grief, and admiration of my skill. He gazed with stern pity upon his younger brother's body, and then up at me, and we looked at each other in silence for some moments.

"I will show you no mercy," I said finally, and found myself regretting the harshness of the words.

"I expect none," he said plainly. In that moment, I found myself saddened that he and I had ended on opposite sides of this feud. I felt here was a man I could have liked, whom I could have worked beside and fought beside. But I was caught in the web of my oath, and still held hostage by my grief and anger. I advanced toward him, until I stood in front of him.

"Why did you burn Bergthorshváll?" I asked suddenly. Looking into that proud face, I felt that I needed to know, that I could not simply cut him down as I had the cowardly Sigurd Lambason.

"Blood demands blood." His voice was steady and showed not the slightest trace of fear. "I regretted the death of your wife and child, and I regretted Bergthóra's death. I regret them still, and if there had been any other way, I would have taken it. You and the Njálssons had to be stopped. By all rights, you should have died with them, Kári. Your wife was innocent, but so then was Hoskuld Thrainsson."

I did not answer for a moment. Finally, I found the words to respond to him, but I still felt a strange reluctance, now that the final confrontation had come. "I regret the part I played in Hoskuld's death. But the blood price on your family's head goes further back, much further. And your regrets will not return my Ingrid and Thórd their lives, taken from them by men too cowardly to face me and the Njálssons sword to sword, like warriors should. Fire is the weapon of cowards, but you shall use a better one now. Take your brother's sword and fight me, or I will strike you down where you stand."

Ketil looked at me with, I think, a measure of respect, and he went over and picked up the sword still lying in the limp hand of his fallen brother. "I will fight you, but without any hope of living to boast of it. For I know of no better sword fighter in Iceland than you. I only wish our swords could have been drawn together instead of against each other."

"As do I," I said, and then I fell upon him.

It was not long before I landed a blow. My sword bit deeply into the muscle of his left leg and crippled him. He winced but did not cry out. His leg buckled and he almost fell. It would not bear his weight. At that moment, he looked up at me and knew that the fight was over. He threw down his sword.

I touched the point of my sword to his throat, and his clear blue eyes showed no fear. "Do not beg for mercy, Ketil Sigfússon," I said, still breathing hard. "For you shall find none."

"I know it. And in your place, I would do no less. Give me but a moment to prepare myself."

He knelt on one knee in the mud, favoring his injured leg, from which came a steady trickle of blood, and he closed his eyes. There in the dim, mist-shrouded marsh, that toughened warrior said a brief prayer for strength to face death. Then he stood and stripped off his shirt. "Do not strike off my head as if I were a common criminal," he said. "But strike me to the heart like a warrior. And, I pray you, be quick about it. I believe you to be a man of great spirit, Kári Solmundarson. Show it now. You may say to anyone who asks that I told you that my blood price, and that of Modolf my son, were forfeit to you, for my part in the death of your wife and child. You may say you took my life and my son's with justification. But I only ask that you do what you must do quickly."

He clasped his hands behind his back, and threw back his head, and closed his eyes. I stood there for a moment, not knowing what I should do. Then the oath's claws bit into me deeply, and I drove my sword into his naked chest.

Thus died Ketil Sigfússon, of all my enemies the bravest and best, and the only one whose death I truly regret. I have killed many men in the long tumult of my life, but when in my dreams I am faced with the horror of having taken another man's life, it is always the face of Ketil Sigfússon I see upon the bloodied corpse.

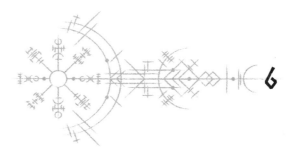

AFTER MY FIGHT WITH LAMBI AND Ketil Sigfússon, I stood there in the swirling mist for a time, contemplating what I had done. I still felt driven by my oath and by my desire to revenge my beloved wife and son, but I felt none of the wild glee that had swept me when I had killed Thorkel Sigfússon and Sigurd Lambason, the first two I had slain. Ketil, one of the ringleaders of the men responsible for the burning of Bergthorshváll, lay dead at my feet, and I felt no joy in it.

I wondered at this change.

I knelt by him and looked long at his body. His face had relaxed in death and looked far less proud and haughty than in life. Gone was the eagle-like fierceness that had lain beneath every gesture, and without it his features seemed more handsome, and he looked younger.

The thrust of my sword had plunged the point of the blade deep into his chest, but the wound looked astonishingly small—a narrow gash in the middle of his breastbone, between the nipples—but there had been a great flow of blood. I tried to stir my heart to the feelings of hot satisfaction I had felt before, but they were gone. I found that I could not even rouse myself to the anger at the deaths of my wife and child that I had felt only days before. All I felt was a deep, deep weariness, and the sight of Ketil's body, wounded to the death, brought only a sudden and unexpected upwelling of pity. At that moment, I realized that Ketil, as much as I, had been caught in an intricate web of death and revenge whose spinning had been no work of his, and had begun long ago.

It was a strange idea. Standing there, in the mist-shrouded marsh, I looked upon him with wonder dawning in my eyes. I had always held myself blameless for the acts I had committed, but in that moment, there awakened in me the thought that if I was to be held blameless despite the killings I had done, then should not my enemies' actions be looked upon in the same fashion? But this thought was too disturbing, so I forced it down. I once again embraced my oath and my desire for revenge, although with far less eagerness than before.

I remounted my horse and turned his head toward the west, beginning to thread my way back through the marsh.

I guessed that I had perhaps a little over two days to reach Holt, and no assurance at all that Thorfinn Karlsefni's father would wait for me even an hour past the time he wished to leave. I was still fog-bound and on wet land by nightfall, and I made a third uncomfortable camp in the midst of the mud and rustling grass.

The next day, the sun seemed to be making an attempt to show his face through the clinging mist. By noon, the land had begun to rise and I saw the familiar stones of Iceland poking through the grass. Before long I came to a little farm, standing alone in a broad field. A few sheep raised their long, silly faces to look at me as I passed, and the sun was finally coming out as I rode up to the house.

No one seemed nearby, but I could see several figures far distant in the field, and I dismounted and tied my horse's reins to a rail in the yard. Then I went up to the door and rapped it sharply with my knuckles.

Within a few moments, the door was opened by one of the oldest women I have ever seen. She was bent nearly double, and looked up at me through squinting, watery eyes. Still, her embroidered linen scarf told me she was no servant—more likely the mother or grandmother of the master or mistress.

"Yes?" Her voice creaked like branches rubbing each other in a windstorm.

"I am called Kári Solmundarson, and I wish to speak with the master of the house."

She nodded. "That is my grandson," she said, pointing with one gnarled finger out toward the distant figures in the field. "He is called Gudmund Thoroddson. He is working there with his two sons."

I thanked her for her help, untied and remounted my horse, and rode out toward the men.

Three curious faces turned to look at me as I approached—a man in his mid-forties, stocky and powerfully built, with sandy hair going to gray about the temples, and two young men, younger versions of their father, with the knotted and sinewy arms so common among farm folk. They had been cutting the long grass for hay, laying it on the ground to dry, and all three held long, curved sickles. One of the sons regarded me with an expression of amazement as I rode up, but I did not know why.

I rode into their midst, and said, "I am looking for Gudmund Thoroddson, and I was told that he is one of you here."

The older man squinted up at me. "I am Gudmund Thoroddson."

"I am called Kári Solmundarson. I am here to tell you, as our law demands, that I have killed four men and that two of them lie in the marsh there—" I pointed out east toward Kringlumire "—and the other two up north there, near Skapt River ford. I would not be thought a common murderer, and the law says that I must tell the first landholder I come to what has happened. Their names are Eirík, Lambi, and Ketil Sigfússon, and Modolf Ketilsson, and the four of them were responsible for the murder of my wife and child, and six others besides. I would not have them left unburied and ask you to send word to the nearest priest, that his men may retrieve their bodies for Christian burial."

"It sounds as if it was a great battle. You must have left companions of yours dead in the marshes as well," said Gudmund, in what sounded like a question.

"No. There was none there but me."

One of Gudmund's sons looked at me with awe. "You killed all four of them... by yourself?"

"Yes. I have some skill at sword fighting, but I must say that luck aided me in this endeavor."

"You must be lucky indeed to have killed four such men," said Gudmund. "But I do not doubt, young man, that your reckoning will be swift. I have heard of Ketil Sigfússon and his brothers. They were powerful chieftains and highly thought of."

"The reckoning has already been dealt out. I am outlawed and am now riding to the harbor at Holt to board a ship which will take me from Iceland, never to return. I did not wish to leave the Sigfússons' debt to me unpaid when I left, however, and I am content for the time being, although there are six others to whom I owe similar justice."

"I feel lucky not to be one of those men," said Gudmund's other son.

I gave him a smile. "As well you should. I do not wish to interrupt your work, good farmer, but only to perform my lawful duty on behalf of the men whom I have killed. Can I trust you to send word of what has happened to the nearest priest today, or tomorrow at the latest?"

Gudmund nodded. "I will send one of my sons today, and he shall do what you ask."

"I thank you," I replied, and prepared to resume my journey, but one of his sons, the one who had looked at me with such strange astonishment as I approached, called out to me.

"Kári!"

I turned and looked at him curiously. He came right up to my horse and looked up at me eagerly.

"When I looked at you as you came up, it seemed that the clouds parted, and a ray of sunlight shone down upon you and illuminated you and your horse alone, and a voice within me said, *'Here is a man who leads a charmed life.'* When you said you will never return to Iceland, the same voice said, *'He shall return one day, and only then will the accounts be balanced.'* I do not know what it means, but my mother was second-sighted, so they say, and I have some skill in that fashion as well, I am told." His cheeks reddened at the hint of boasting.

I smiled at him. "Perhaps you are right." I reached down and clasped his forearm in farewell. "What is your name?"

"Tjorvi Gudmundsson," he said.

"Well, then, Tjorvi Gudmundsson, I will say farewell. If your seeing proves right, perhaps we will meet again one day."

"Perhaps we will."

With that, I rode away.

There is little to say further of my journey to Holt. The sun came out in full that afternoon, and it turned to a fine day. I camped that night in sight of the sea and, following the shore, I reached the harbor of Holt by the middle of the following day.

From the hill above the east end of the harbor, I looked shoreward. Out at sea were several longships at anchor. There were a number of dwellings clustered about the shore, and little knots of men standing about talking, working, or both. I rode down the hill and onto the sand of the beach and dismounted. I walked up to the nearest group of men.

One of the men, who had his back to me, was very tall, with long black hair. I called out to them, wishing to ask of them which of the ships belonged to Thorfinn's father. The tall man turned around, and both he and I gazed at each other in surprise for a moment, and then he laughed and strode toward me. I was looking at Thorleif Crow.

"Well met, Kári Solmundarson," he said in a cheerful voice, and reached out and grasped my forearm. "I am glad to see you. Your ship awaits you." He raised his long arm and pointed out over the harbor. Then he grinned. "My young friend Thorfinn sent you out on the hunt. Were you able to overtake your quarry?"

My answering smile died upon my lips, and my gaze strayed back east, the direction from which I had come. "My quarry is overtaken. Six of them lie dead. Two of them at Kerlingardale, Thorkel Sigfússon and Sigurd Lambason. Two at the Skapt River ford, Eirík Sigfússon and Modolf Ketilsson. And two in the marshes of Kringlumire, Lambi and Ketil Sigfússon."

Thorleif's eyes grew wide. "Six of them! I did not know you were such a hunter. And one of the two king foxes you took, too? That Ketil Sigfússon was no fool, and an experienced fighter."

"I take no joy in it."

Thorleif's face became solemn. "Truly, I was wrong to jest. The taking of a man's life is a serious business. Still, I am glad things went in your favor. And what of Flosi Thórdarson?"

"Thorfinn gave me your message that Flosi was well ahead of me. That proved to be true. He is surely now safely in Svinafell. I wonder if he is waiting there to join the Sigfússons, and if they intended to sail together on Ketil's ship from Hornafjord. If so, he will wait long."

"Indeed," said Thorleif.

"Are your brothers here?"

"No. Both have returned home. Thorgrim has a beautiful wife, and he does not like to be long away, and Thorgeir also wished to be home, but he is a closed-mouthed one. He does not divulge his reasons, and I have learned better than to push him. But I wanted to be here to meet you, if you were able to come in time."

"When is the ship leaving?"

"Thorfinn's father is a prompt man. He wishes to leave as early as to-morrow. You should meet him—he is called Thórd Hesta. He bears the same given name as your son had. Thórd Hesta is a prickly individual, but you will not meet a better sailor nor a more honest man."

Thorleif led me down through the buildings near the shore. I led my horse along by the reins until I found a convenient railing to tie him to. I patted the horse's nose, and then turned to Thorleif. "Thorleif, my friend, I would be pleased if you would take my horse. I cannot take him with me, and I would sooner see you have him than to sell him to some stranger. He has borne me well and faithfully, and is a good-natured animal, no harm in him. It would repay some of the debt I owe you."

Thorleif gave me another of his infectious grins. "I will take him glad-ly, but I do not consider you to owe me anything. You have undertaken to achieve justice for both of our parts and have already dealt it out to six of the twelve men who escaped fair judgment at the Assembly."

He and I walked a bit further, and we came up to a man standing by a group of workers who were shaping a piece of wood, perhaps for a small repair to the gunwale of a ship. "Thórd," called Thorleif. "Here is the man I have told you about, whose way my brothers and I have paid."

Thórd Hesta turned around and looked at me appraisingly. He was about forty-five years old, with unruly chestnut-brown hair. He had a long, horsy face, much scarred and weather-beaten, and thickly muscled arms and legs.

I reached out my arm, and he briefly grasped it in a powerful grip. "What do you know of sailing?" he asked abruptly.

"I was one of Jarl Sigurd Hlodvisson's men for a time, and I sailed with him all over the east coast of Scotland and England."

"In other words, nothing," said Thórd.

Coming from another, I would have taken great offense at this state-ment, but somehow, I found myself disarmed by the man's frankness.

"You're probably right. But I will no doubt know more by the time I arrive in the Hebrides."

"Perhaps. We shall see. For now, simply stay out of the way, and be here on the shore at sunrise tomorrow. I'll have a skiff here to row you out to the ship. Be warned that I shall not wait for you."

"I will be there."

Thórd Hesta turned back to his business of overseeing the last-minute repairs, and Thorleif and I went back up to where the buildings were.

The two of us talked until the small hours before dawn, much as my brother Oláf and I had talked before I left the Hebrides, so many years earlier. Now, I was returning there, and I felt as much like I was leaving home as I had the first time. Thorleif and I spoke much of the past and little of the future. Indeed, what part of our future could with certainty be foreseen would diverge at sunrise the following day. He was staying in Iceland, while I was going back to the Hebrides and would not return. His future and mine would probably never be reunited, regardless of the predictions of some strange Icelandic farm lad.

I gave him my farewell the following morning, standing in the chilly predawn on the shore, and bid him give my greetings to his brothers and to everyone else I could think of whose lives had touched mine in Iceland— Asgrím Ellida-Grímsson, Hjalti Skeggjason and his wife, Thorfinn Karlsefni, even Mord Valgardsson, despite what he had done, and many others.

Then the skiff was ready, and I was rowed out to the waiting ship. Fifteen minutes later, the anchor was up, and the ship was putting out to sea. The last thing I saw of Iceland were the slopes of the high mountains, the black rock and white ice glowing like crimson in the light of the rising sun, so that the whole skyline looked as if it were drenched with blood. Soon even those were lost to view, and afterwards all that surrounded me was the immensity of the sea, and horizons as flat as the blade of a sword.

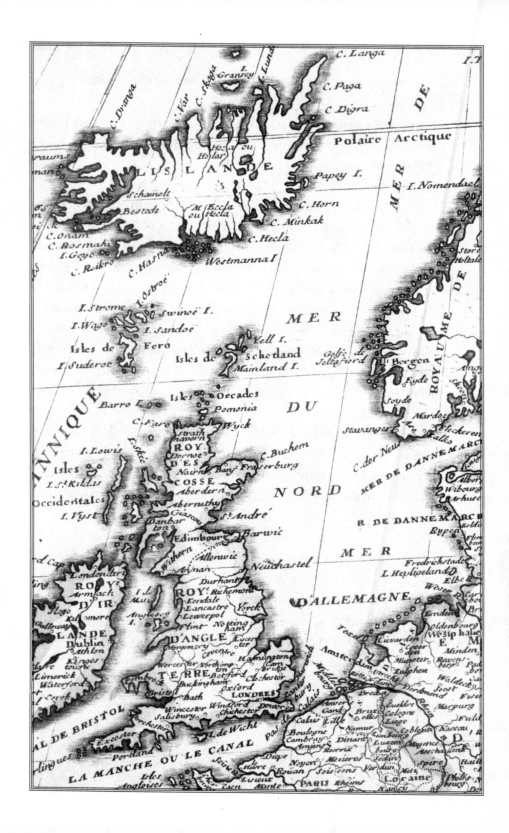

III

THE EXILE

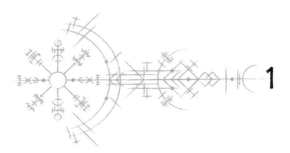

1

THE VOYAGE FROM ICELAND TO THE Hebrides took five weeks and was one of the least eventful sea journeys I have ever taken. Thórd Hesta's temper was far stormier than any weather we encountered. I had many occasions to wonder how such a man had ever fathered a lad like Thorfinn Karlsefni, who in my short time with him, had seemed as warm-hearted and good-natured as his father was sarcastic and given to snarling out commands. His crew respected his knowledge, however, and did what he asked without question.

This was the first time I had ever been aboard ship as a passenger rather than as crew, and I found it rather unsettling that Thórd not only did not expect me to work but did not want me to. I think he viewed me as an opportunity to make a profit from Thorleif Crow and his brothers, but otherwise as a nuisance who would probably do more harm than good if allowed to assist in the sailing of the ship. I would have preferred to work, but it was not an option. As a result, most of what I recall from this voyage is boredom. I spent countless hours sitting in the stern of the ship, watching the green ocean water slip away behind us, and contemplating my return to my childhood home.

Most of my thought was given to what I would do once I arrived. Would I give up my adventuring and settle down to the quiet life of a farmer? That

was the fate that Oláf had railed against so many years ago. I wondered greatly how he felt now, and how he would see things when he found out that my
own desire for adventure had ended tragically enough.

And what of my oath? I was already weary of revenge, but I had the sense
of having left a task incomplete. I had killed six men, including two—Sigurd
Lambason and Modolf Ketilsson—who were young and who surely had little
to do with leading the band which burned Bergthorshváll. They had simply
had the ill fortune to be sons of two of the leaders and had been there the
night of the burning. Others, far guiltier than they, were still alive—Flosi Thórdarson, of course, but also Gunnar Lambason and Grani Gunnarsson, whose fierce hatred of Njál's family had been evident since the death
of Thrain Sigfússon. How could I let them live? I felt I would be betraying
Ingrid's memory.

I looked about me at the endless expanse of green sea water, and the
hopelessness of ever finding my six remaining enemies weighed upon me
like a stone upon my shoulders. I had looked forward to reaching the Hebrides, but I realized then that it would not be the end of my journeying. I knew
at that moment that the words I had spoken at the Great Assembly were not
yet done with leading me on.

About three weeks out of Iceland, we were becalmed for almost three
days. The wind died to nothing, and the sails hung slack and useless. One of
the sailors, a seasoned veteran named Ozur, told me that this was extremely
unusual in these parts, and thought it might be an ill omen.

"How can it be ill," I asked him with a smile, "seeing the blue sky which
covers us? There is not a storm cloud to be seen."

Ozur was not amused by my lightness and looked at me with a scowl.
"There are other dangers at sea than storms. I feel that we are held in place
for some reason—a dark one, I do not doubt."

However, the only bad outcome was that within hours of the wind dropping, Thórd Hesta decided that there was nothing for it but to out oars and
row. He even allowed me to take part, but after a few hours of it I was regretting my eagerness to help. My hands were raw and my back aching, and
I was only too glad to allow another to take my place when my turn ended. I
had three more turns at pulling the oars before the wind picked up, the sail
billowed out, and we were underway once more.

I thought Ozur would be pleased. "Lucky for us that your dire prophecies did not come true," I said, once the ship was skimming forward on a stiff breeze. "We suffered no worse than sore muscles and blistered hands."

Still, I got no trace of a smile. "Don't mock the new God and the old," he said, in all seriousness. "If they have forgotten to smite us, well enough. Don't remind them of their oversight."

I thought he might be jesting, but when I looked at his scarred, stony face, I realized that he actually believed that we had escaped destruction simply because God had forgotten to strike us down.

"Do you believe that fate has such control over our lives?"

His eyes narrowed. I think he was trying to discern my motives in questioning him. Maybe he thought I was looking for a further occasion to poke fun at him. In any case, he finally answered, "I do."

"So, is it not possible to change one's destiny?"

He thought for a moment, and then shrugged. "I don't think so. My mother wept when I went to serve on Thórd Hesta's ship when I was sixteen. She said she was afraid I would die at sea. I told her that if I was fated to die at a given time, then I would die whether I was at sea or lying in my bed. She did not understand."

"Are some men born lucky, then, and others born unlucky?"

"It may be so. I have had my share of both." He regarded me appraisingly. "You have the look of a lucky one. I would guess that you have been through more than most men on this ship, however Thórd Hesta treats you like a child."

I smiled at him. "You may be right. From my childhood, folk have called me 'Kári the Lucky,' and that nickname has followed me wherever I have gone."

"You have no doubt seen your share of battles, then."

"No doubt."

"And unscathed, always?"

I looked out over the foam-flecked green expanse before us. "Unscathed in body, yes. I have hardly even received a scratch in compensation for all the battles I have seen. Yet my heart bears scars, so deep that I doubt they will ever heal." I felt the hot tears spring to my eyes, unbidden. Even after a year and more, how close they still were to the surface! I turned my face away, so that Ozur would not see.

But I heard his voice, gentler than before, saying, "So it always is. That pain is worse than any ever inflicted by sword, fist, or lash. Yet it can heal, given time."

"Fates willing?" I asked, still not looking at him.

"Yes. Fates willing. Do not forget that you have luck on your side."

I only said, "Perhaps."

There, the conversation ended. For the remainder of the journey, Ozur returned to his gruff demeanor. I looked upon him as a man who understood a little, at least, of what I felt, and I was grateful to him.

———————

IT WAS FIVE WEEKS TO THE day after our departure that we arrived in the Hebrides. Thórd Hesta had cargo to unload, merchandise for Jarl Gilli Klapa—who was still alive, and fatter and more dyspeptic than ever, I heard—and for other noblemen of the islands. I disembarked with his men and helped to unload it onto the shore. While I was working, he came up to me, and with no preamble at all, asked me which my home island was.

"It is called Kolnsey. It is south of here...."

"I know where Kolnsey is." He cut me off with an impatient gesture of his hand. "Do you wish to go there, or stay here?"

"I wish to go there, but you surely have business elsewhere. I can find transportation there, I am sure."

He raised an eyebrow. "Thorleif Crow paid for your transportation back to your home island, and to your home island you shall go," he said, in a tone of voice that sounded as if he expected me to argue with him. "It isn't on my way, but we will take you there."

Every word he said had a way of making me feel that I had been nothing but a nuisance to him. My pride was pricked by his contempt. "I do not need you to inconvenience yourself," I said, drawing myself up. "I am capable of finding my way home."

"You'd have done well enough without my help, I dare say," he said, his mouth wry.

"I didn't mean that—"

"Well, however it is, I am the commander of this ship, and we are taking you to Kolnsey. Re-board with my crew when you are done here. I must speak with Jarl Gilli about payment, but that won't take long. Be ready to leave within an hour's time."

I watched him walk away, feeling torn between anger and amusement. One of his crew, standing nearby, gave me a grin.

"If you travel much more with Thórd Hesta, you will learn. Don't ever argue with him. It isn't possible to win. He'll twist your words around to make it look as if you were arguing for the very thing you're arguing against."

"How can you stand it?"

He laughed. "The only way is to simply agree with him, and then do whatever it is that you know you should do."

Another man joined in. "It would be different if he was a fool, but he's not. He knows his business, none better. He thinks he's always right, which would be annoying in most people. But when it comes to sailing, he usually is right."

I shook my head. "I envy you both for your tolerance."

"Intolerant people on Thórd Hesta's ship," said the first man, "only last one voyage."

Not long afterwards Thórd Hesta reappeared, looking pleased with himself. I found out later that he had done quite well out of his ship's load of cargo and would be bringing home to Iceland a nice share of profit.

"He may have a sharp way with his crew," I said to one of his men as we were being rowed out to the waiting ship, "but he must be able to sweeten his tongue when needed. Gilli Klapa is as prickly as your commander is, and unless he has changed since I last knew him, is tightfisted besides. Yet Thórd seems to have persuaded Gilli to part with a sizable amount of money."

The crewman nodded. "You've said it, friend. He knows people as well as ships. He doesn't stand to make a profit from us, so to us he says what he pleases. He's a different man with a paying customer."

"It must be a subtle business, being a merchant."

"Far too subtle for me," the crewman said.

We were underway again by early evening and made use of the long hours of summer twilight to thread our way south through the islands of the Hebrides. When it finally fell completely dark and we were forced to anchor, I could feel that we were close to my home island. Something about the very air and the sound of the sea felt familiar.

The following morning, I saw it—Kolnsey, the island where I was born. It was still far away, just a line of distant cliffs, and yet I knew it for what it was. The memory of my departure from it, twenty years ago, was etched permanently upon my brain. Had it been fifty years, I would still have known it immediately.

I stood in the bow, my hand gripping the gunwale and the wind blowing my hair into tangles. I watched it gradually grow larger, until I could see the line of the shore and the gray of the cliffside. Finally, I heard the noise of activity behind me, and I turned to find that the crew had taken the sail in and were dropping the anchor.

Thórd Hesta came up to me. "Here you are. Come along, and we will row you out in the skiff. Unless you want to swim."

By this time, I knew better than to laugh at what would have been a joke coming from anyone else. "No, I prefer to take the skiff."

He grunted his assent, and I helped his men lower the boat into the water. Then I climbed aboard.

"Thank you!" I cried out to as many of them as were within earshot and was returned many smiles and shouts of farewell. Then the oarsman in the skiff began with long, practiced strokes to carry me to shore.

After a few minutes, the bottom of the skiff grated on gravel, and I gave the oarsman a brief word of thanks and leapt out into the water. It only came to my knees, and I ran splashing onto the shore, and turned to see the skiff already halfway back to the ship. As anxious as I was to go on, I watched as the oarsman pulled up alongside the ship and climbed back aboard. The skiff, looking tiny as a toy with the distance, was drawn up behind him.

Thórd Hesta wasted no time. Within minutes the anchor was being brought in by thickly muscled arms, and the sail was billowing out. I continued to watch until the ship disappeared around Kolness Head, and then I turned my back on the sea and began to walk inland.

It felt as if I were walking backward in time. The island seemed unchanged, as if every pebble were still in the same place it had been twenty years ago. With every step, the years fell away from me, and I felt once again like the callow nineteen-year-old I had been then. Everything that had happened since my departure—the slaying of Asbjorn and my joining Jarl Sigurd's men, the battle in Scotland, my rescue of the Njálssons and Thrain Sigfússon, all the feuding and death which had so entangled me in Iceland—it all seemed more and more like a waking dream. With some alarm, I felt Ingrid and my son slipping into that same realm of unreality. As I walked toward my brother's house, I could have easily convinced myself that Ingrid was a product of my imagination, a sweet and beautiful dream ended prematurely.

The gravel crunched beneath my feet as I crested the hill that overlooked the little valley where my brother's house lay. I saw it in the distance, and I began to run.

I was still some distance away when I knew that something was wrong. The house seemed lifeless. There were no sheep and goats, no servant boys doing chores. The fence that had surrounded the sheepfold had collapsed in several places and had not been repaired. The eagerness in my eyes died away, to be replaced by silent astonishment, and my run slowed to a walk.

The shingles of the roof were rotted, and there were gaping holes, showing nothing but darkness beyond. The door stood halfway open, sagging on rusted hinges. Everywhere there was a pervasive silence, broken by nothing but the calling of the gulls and the continual surging of the sea in the distance behind me.

I went forward, and pulled on the door to open it, and I stepped inside. The house was empty of furnishings, except for one or two broken pieces of old furniture, covered with dust and spotted with mildew. Sunlight streamed through the holes in the roof.

I stood in the middle of the house like one stricken dumb. Of all of the ends to my voyage, this was one I had never expected—to arrive home and find Oláf and his wife and son gone. Where could they be? And why would they have left this house, our father's house, to decay and ruin?

I turned, dazed and prepared to leave. There was no reason to stay here. Then I saw that someone was silhouetted in the doorway, and I froze. Whoever it was, was backlit by the sunshine, and I could not see who it might be.

Then a female voice spoke. It was a sweet voice, but sad, the voice of one who, like me, had lived through great sorrows.

"They are gone. All gone. But your brother told me that one day you would return, and he asked me to watch for you."

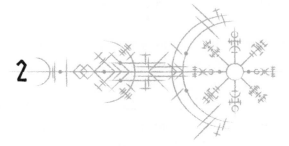

2

I STARED AT HER FOR SOME moments, as if what she had said made no sense. "Gone? How do you mean, gone? Where have they gone?"

She stepped forward into the desolate room. Now that she was no longer backlit by the glaring sunlight, I saw that she was about my age, perhaps a little younger. A fair woman, with clear gray eyes and long, straight, light brown hair. From the fact that she had her head covered with a scarf, I knew that she was married, and wondered greatly why she would have been set to watch for my arrival.

"I said 'gone' because it sounds less harsh than 'dead.'"

My eyes must have betrayed my dismay, although I think that I had half guessed the truth already. "Dead?" I said, in a strained voice. "All of them? My mother and grandmother, my brother and his wife and child? How?"

She smiled a little, a smile as sad as her voice had been. "You have been away a long while. You expect that everything will be the same after so long? Your grandmother died many years ago, of honorable old age. The rest were carried off by the plague that swept the island five years ago. Your mother, and your brother Oláf, and Ragnhild his wife, and their four children, Solmund, Thóra, Rannveig, and Bjorn."

I felt as if I had been struck in the stomach. The room seemed to spin. "Oláf had four children? And all of them dead?"

She nodded. "Solmund was a strapping lad of fifteen years when it struck, yet he was the first to die. The sweating sickness they called it. It came with fever, aching, and delirium, and copious sweats, and it killed in only a day. I remember when Thóra died..." Her vision turned inward, into her memory, and as she spoke she seemed not to see the world around her. "Only twelve years old she was. A sweeter child you have never seen. She was lovely and soft spoken, we all thought that in a few years she would capture the heart of every boy on the island. She came to get me when her mother took ill, and within an hour she was struck down herself. Both did not survive the night."

I had no words to speak. The news had knocked me sprawling, and I felt unable to answer her. She looked at me in pity.

"I am sorry to give you such tidings. But you had to be told. Your brother told me to watch for you, when he took sick and knew he was dying, the last one of his family. I cared for all of them, and before Oláf died, he asked me to keep watch for you. He knew you would one day return. So, every day I have gone out to the cliffs near my house, and I have looked down at the sea. And today, I saw the ship and the skiff. When it left one man behind, alone, I knew it must be you. So I came to meet you."

"But what of your own family, your husband and children? Why were you given such a task to do, when you had your own work to attend to?"

Again, the sweet, sad smile flickered across her face. "I cared for your brother's family because mine was struck down first. My husband and two children died of the sickness as well."

"And you never sickened?"

She shook her head. "By God's grace, I have survived. I do not know which is luckier, to have died and to be at peace, or to be left behind, alone and grieving."

"Nor do I," I said, with some vehemence, and she raised her eyebrows.

"I am sorry." Her voice was as gentle as the wind over the grass. "I spoke as if I am the only one who has ever grieved. I see that you have lived through sorrow as well. I recognize it in your face."

I looked at her in some perplexity and did not know how to respond to what she had said. "But I still do not understand. Why did you go to Oláf's house, where there was sickness, and more likelihood of your becoming ill with it yourself? It was selfless, but a little foolhardy, I think."

"I went," she said evenly, "as you would, I think, were it your sister's family who was dying."

Suddenly I understood. "Ragnhild... Oláf's wife..."

"Ragnhild was my older sister. I am Gudrun Thorvaldsdóttir. I remember you as a boy, but it is so many years ago, and appearances change.... You would remember me only as a girl of twelve or thirteen, when you were grown to manhood and had other concerns. Your nephews and nieces were mine as well, and I grieve their loss as you do. We have much in common, I think."

We went outside into the sunshine and sat down upon a rocky outcrop at the corner of what had once been the sheepfold. She asked me to tell her what I would of my life after I left the Hebrides, and I told her about my two years in the Orkneys, and then about meeting the Njálssons and going to Iceland, and the feud between the Njálssons and the Sigfússons, and finally of the burning of Bergthorshváll. I did not mention Ingrid and Thórd, however, for no very clear reason. I simply felt reluctant to discuss with a stranger what was for me the most tragic part of the whole story.

However, she looked up at me. "And you married as well, I suppose?"

I looked away, and said simply, "Yes."

Those clear eyes, gray as a cloudy day, caught my gaze and held it. "I would guess that your wife was taken from you, as my husband Geir was from me."

I nodded. "She and my only son died in the burning of the house, when my friends the Njálssons and their parents died."

She looked out over the brilliant green fields, toward the horizon. "There is much evil in the world."

I nodded again.

"What of the men who killed them all?"

"Six are dead. I killed them myself. I swore an oath to kill them all, but how I shall accomplish that I do not know."

I spoke this with some reluctance. I did not know how she would react to finding that I had killed so many men. However, all she said was, "There had been no judgment against them?"

"They were outlawed, but only after I spoke my oath."

"You would condemn yourself to a lifetime of wandering the world, looking for these last six?"

"I think I already have done so."

Gudrun looked at me curiously. "I wonder if your wife would have wanted you to do this."

"I do not know," I said truthfully. "Probably not. But justice must be done."

Again, she looked out toward the horizon. "I wonder if it ever really is."

Neither of us spoke for a time. Finally, I turned toward her. "What of my uncles? Did Gunnar and Magnus survive the plague?"

"Your uncle Gunnar is dead, but not of the plague. He was repairing the shingles on his roof after a storm damaged them and fell. It must be ten or eleven years ago. He lived for a few days, but finally died of the injuries. Magnus is still alive. Like me, he never sickened. His wife died, and so did their son and elder daughter. The younger daughter is alive still, one of the few who sickened and survived it. She is married to a man on the other side of the island, a kindly and handsome fellow, and they had five children. Four are still alive. One sickened and survived, like his mother, three never sickened at all, like their father, and one sickened and died. They are luckier than most families."

"You seem to have in your memory a record of each family's fate when the plague swept the island."

"I have had little else to do."

"I would like to speak with you further, but I would also like to speak with my uncle Magnus. Perhaps I could visit you..." I stopped, and my cheeks reddened. I did not know whether she would think it improper for me to be so forward. But she simply smiled, and said, "I would welcome you."

———

I TOOK MY LEAVE OF GUDRUN Thorvaldsdóttir and walked over the hills toward my uncle's house. I was struck then by how little the island itself had changed. It was only the creations of men which, left to themselves, crumbled away to nothing in only a few years. How proud we are of our puny little undertakings, while God's creations stand unchangeable.

I came up to Magnus's house, but saw no one about. He had never had but one or two servants, to help in the fields, but none was to be seen. I rapped on the door, and within a moment it was opened. The figure of a man stood in the shadowed doorway, silent for a moment. Then a voice said, "Kári Solmundarson. You have returned. I hoped you would, but I never knew if my hope was a foolish one…."

Then, Uncle Magnus stepped out into the sunlight, and it was still recognizably him—thinner, much grayer, but still with his characteristic quick, intelligent eyes and swift smile. He clasped me by both arms. "God's blessing that you left when you did. Such a horrible time we have had here, such a horrible time…. But before I say more, come in, Kári. Come in and rest yourself, and we will share a cup of mead."

Once we were seated at the table, in the dim coolness of Magnus's house, he resumed his story.

"The past few years have been horrible. Like we were cursed by God. A sickness came, and afterwards there was only one out of every five left alive on the island."

I nodded. "I saw Gudrun Thorvaldsdóttir. She told me of the plague, and about Oláf, and your wife and children."

He sighed. "My poor Gerd, my poor Auda and little Stein. Auda was married by then, you know. She and her husband and child all died. We thought the end of the world was come."

"I cannot imagine it," I said, and I meant it.

"It was horrible. Waiting to fall ill and watching everyone around you dying. Like hell come to earth. And then, every little twinge, every sneeze makes you think the sickness has taken you at last…. But some of us survived, and life goes on. We stopped all ships from sending men onto land and sent none of our own out. The plague did not spread farther, I think."

"Where did it come from?"

He shook his head. "Who can say? God alone knows."

There was a question I wished to ask, but after the terrible fate of my family on Kolnsey, I hesitated, wondering if there was more bad news to be told. It was with some reluctance that I asked, "And what of Ljót? Have you heard from him at all?"

The somberness passed from Magnus's face as if it had never been, and he smiled at me. "Oh, Ljót lives still. Still on Saudey."

"He stayed there? What of his woman, the one he wanted to marry? The chieftain's daughter?"

"Oh, he married her, all right. It was the year after you left Kolnsey. I always said that there was nothing about Ljót to dislike, and evidently the chieftain on Saudey eventually decided he could do far worse in a son-in-law, even if Ljót owned nothing but the clothes he wore. They were married with great ceremony, and even Oláf was convinced that he should attend, although he was still furious with Ljót for staying on Saudey. But they made it up, and it all ended happily enough. Ljót's father-in-law died about eight years ago, and Ljót is now chieftain of Saudey in his place, with his fine wife and a family of seven children."

"Seven?"

Magnus nodded. "He never was much for farm work, but there is at least one thing he seems to do well and often."

I burst out laughing, and Magnus joined me. I had forgotten how much I enjoyed his ribald sense of humor.

"Do you think we could go to see him?"

"Certainly. After the plague passed, we reestablished commerce between the islands. It should be easy enough to find a ship to carry us. I have been out to visit him several times, although only once since Gerd died. It would be fine to see him again, if you would like me to come along with you."

I smiled at him. "I was hoping that you would."

"What of you, Kári? What adventures have you found, what glory have you won for yourself?"

"Little enough glory, and my only adventures have led to not but tragedy and outlawry." I told him my tale, and how I had come finally to return to the Hebrides.

After I was done, he looked at me in silence for some moments, and then placed his hand on my shoulder. "I know it will not seem possible, but your heart will one day heal. It is good you have come back home."

I remained with Magnus for several weeks and helped him about his farm. He had only one old servant man left, and Magnus himself was growing old. The house and outbuildings had fallen into some disrepair from their inability to see to all the work that needed doing. He was delighted to have my help and said I could stay as long as I wished. Living with him was not the homecoming I had expected, but of all of my father's family, he was the kindest and the one I was closest to. It felt good simply to be in a place where there was honest work to be done, and no talk of feuds, plots, legalities, and revenge.

As I toiled, I gave much thought to the circumstances under which I had left, so many years ago. When I was young, Magnus had told me to fly as soon as I saw the cage door open, and I had done so. Now, the bird had returned to the cage, and found it greatly changed, but I began to wonder if the real change had not perhaps been in the bird himself.

———————

THREE WEEKS LATER, AS THE SEASON was turning toward the cool rains and cloudy weather of fall, Magnus and I boarded a ship belonging to Magnus's friend Ragnar Finnbogason, a fisherman who lived on the north side of Kolnsey. He had a hold full of salted fish to sell on Saudey and some of the other islands—probably the last he would be able to sell before the winter storms made fishing impossible. He was an old man, far older than Magnus, who nevertheless sailed his small ship with only three other men to assist him. He had thinning white hair, and a face weather-beaten and sunburned to the color of leather. His eyes, however, were an astonishingly bright blue, and his teeth showed white in his dark face when he smiled, which was often.

Ragnar clasped my forearm in a friendly fashion when we boarded and gave Magnus a hearty whack on the back that nearly knocked him into the sea. Magnus scowled at him.

"You see, Kári," he said to me in a loud voice obviously directed at Ragnar, "it is a strange thing that Ragnar's friends and enemies never know which is which, because he treats them all the same."

Ragnar grinned. "If I were not here to beat you every so often, old man, your life would be entirely too pleasant."

"I wouldn't complain of that," said Magnus, but he returned his friend's grin.

Saudey is only five or six hours' sailing north of Kolnsey, depending on the direction and speed of the wind. With the stiff autumn breeze filling our sails, we made the harbor on the east side of the island with plenty of daylight to spare. I offered to help Ragnar in unloading his cargo, but Magnus took my upper arm. "Smelly dried-out fish, and smelly dried-out old man. They belong together. You and I should go to see your brother."

Ragnar grinned and made an obscene gesture at Magnus.

"That's what he does whenever he can't think of a good response," Magnus said, and we walked up away from the shore.

"Be back in two hours," Ragnar shouted after us. "Unless you want to spend the winter on Saudey!"

We walked up toward a large, well-built house on a hill overlooking the harbor. There were a great many people about in the yard. Servants, mostly, but there were several children, better dressed than the servants in sturdy linen garments, who were doing various chores.

One fair-haired young man of about sixteen years had his back to us when we came into the yard but turned as we approached. When I saw him, my eyes widened. I could have been looking at myself at that age. Just coming to manhood, with blond hair to his shoulders, and sharp, probing gray eyes, he was so like me that I stopped, and said to him, "You must be the son of Ljót Solmundarson."

He nodded unsmilingly and came forward to us. He clasped Magnus's forearm, and greeted him as "Uncle Magnus." Then he looked at me appraisingly. "I am called Kári Ljótsson. And I was always told that I had an uncle who went away to sea before I was born, and whom I resembled closely. I was named for him..." He faltered, unsure of what more to say.

I smiled. "Your eyes do not deceive you. I am your father's brother, Kári Solmundarson." I reached forward, and we clasped arms.

At that moment, a man came around from behind the house. Before I knew what was happening, I was caught in an embrace of two strong arms, and when I was released, I saw my brother Ljót before me. He had grown stocky with good food and the rich life of a chieftain, but his eyes still had the same gentle, easy kindness as they always had.

"Kári, my brother, how little you have changed! I knew one day you would return."

"That is what everyone has said. You, and Uncle Magnus, and I am told that Oláf said it, too. It appears I am the only one who did not know it."

Ljót grinned at me and clapped me on the back. "It is fine to see you, and you as well, Uncle. Come inside and share some food and drink with us."

"We can stay a mere two hours," Magnus said, "for that is all that the miserly Ragnar Finnbogason will give us."

"A pity, but we will make of it what we can." Ljót turned to his son. "Kári, tell Helga and Thorgerd that your uncles Kári and Magnus are here. Send them to help your mother get food and drink for us, and then you may come in yourself and join us."

Young Kári nodded and went away silently.

"Serious lad," I said to Ljót.

"So were you, at that age. He is like you in more than appearance. I fear for him when he reaches manhood. I think we will lose him, as our mother lost you."

We went into the house, and there I met his wife, a smiling and lively woman named Thorhalla. I could well see why Ljót had been taken by her. She was still fair, and twenty years before must have been beautiful indeed.

"Magnus tells me that you have seven children," I said, as Thorhalla and their two eldest daughters served us with food and drink, the finest I had had since I ate at Njál Thorgeirsson's table. Soon afterward, young Kári came in and joined us silently. Throughout the meal, his restless eyes kept returning to me, filled with a strange mixture of longing and envy.

"Indeed," said Ljót. "I cannot keep up with them. Your namesake is the eldest, and the youngest is Leif, who is only four." He leaned toward me, his eyes bright with interest. "But tell me of yourself. You wished for adventure. Have you found it?"

"Found it?" I leaned back in my chair. "I did not so much seek it out as it found me, wherever I went." I told him, as briefly as I could, of my life since I left the Hebrides. All through my tale, I saw my young namesake watching me with a great eagerness.

Afterwards, Ljót looked at me with sadness in his eyes, and shook his head. "Strange how one can never tell which way a man's life will go. Who would have guessed it?" He paused for a moment. "Do you regret leaving the Hebrides? Do you wish now that you had stayed?"

I longed to answer him truthfully, that having once returned, I now felt myself a fool for having left in the first place. However, with my nephew's eyes upon me, I was not sure how I should respond. In the end, I answered him with a lightness I did not truly feel. "How can I say if I regret it, when I do not know what your own fate has been? How has it been these years? What stories do you have to tell of?"

Ljót shrugged. "There is little to tell. The years go by, all too quickly, each the same as before, except each year I am a little older."

"And each year you have fathered a few more children," added Magnus.

Ljót grinned. I guessed that this was a long-standing joke between them. "Well, when you do something well, keep doing it," said Ljót.

"Or, when you do something badly, you must keep practicing until you get it right," Magnus shot back, smiling wickedly.

"Which it is, you'll never find out, as I have sworn Thorhalla to secrecy. But Kári, how good it is to see you! Will you be staying on Kolnsey now? Are your years of adventuring over?"

"I do not know," I answered truthfully. "My hope of finding the remaining men who killed my son, my wife, and her family is slim. I have nowhere else to go, so I will stay here for a time, at least."

"I need his help," Magnus added. "A willing set of strong arms is hard to find on Kolnsey."

"It's not easy to find anywhere," added Ljót.

There was a sudden pounding on the door. It opened, and Ragnar Finnbogason thrust his head inside.

"Look at the two of you, feasting while I work. I will up anchor in fifteen minutes, and if you are not on the ship, you will swim home."

"You sound like Thórd Hesta. The captain of the last ship I was on. Except that I think that Thórd meant what he said, and I don't believe that you do."

"Find out for yourself." He withdrew his head and slammed the door.

We finished our meal quickly, and then Magnus and I stood, and Ljót did, as well.

I smiled at my brother and his wife and children. "I thank you, Ljót, and you as well, Thorhalla, for your hospitality. I am glad to see that you have been blessed with so many fine children. I am fortunate indeed to have been able to come to visit you."

Thorhalla returned my smile but said nothing, and Ljót said, "I only wish you could stay longer."

"It will not be our last visit," Magnus said. "And we would welcome you to Kolnsey."

"I will come. And perhaps on your next visit, Kári, you could stay behind for a time with us. We have so many here, one more will be no trouble."

"I will do that," I said.

Ljót beamed, and we went outside.

Ragnar met us on the shore, and he and Ljót spent some time dickering over payment for the shipment of fish. The sun had passed its zenith, and we stood looking out over the gray sea, churning endlessly under a sky filled with clouds. The sight saddened me, for some reason, and I turned toward Magnus to make some light conversation. I saw that young Kári had come up to us and stood waiting nearby. I could see in his expression that he was hoping to speak to me, and I smiled encouragingly at him. The corners of his mouth twitched upwards a little, in the first smile I had seen on his face. Again, I was struck by our uncanny resemblance.

"Uncle?" he said to me, and beneath his courteous voice I caught a hint of an undercurrent of restlessness, and I suddenly understood his father's fear of losing him.

"Yes, what is it?"

"I wish to ask you something." He seemed to search for the proper words. "My father told me long ago of what you did when you were a young man, and I have always remembered it. I have wanted for years to leave the islands and seek adventure as you did. If you go away again, someday, could you... would you be willing to take me with you?"

I looked down at his clean-cut face that was so like my own, and my heart nearly broke when I contemplated his question.

"Kári, you do not know what you are asking for."

His response came quickly, as if he had known what I would say. "I am not afraid of working hard. I am strong and brave and would be no hindrance to you. I know something of sailing and wish to learn the use of a sword. as well."

I shook my head. "I know all that. I am sure I could not wish for a finer companion, and if that were all there was to it, I would not hesitate to take you with me. But you do not truly understand what you are asking." I paused, considering my words carefully. "They call me 'Kári the Lucky', and yet were you not listening to my tale, earlier? What has my luck brought me but sorrow and loss, and what has it brought others but pain and death? I say to you truthfully, that were I to have the choice to make over again, I would be better off being an honest farmer than the warrior and outlaw I have become."

"An honest farmer?" I caught a hint of bitterness in his voice, and I was reminded then not of myself, but of Oláf, another eldest son whose fate to take his father's place was all but settled. "A caged animal, no more."

"Perhaps. But I tell you now, I would choose such a cage without hesitation, over all the adventures of fire and sword I have seen."

But still, I could see he did not believe me. At that moment, Ljót and Ragnar completed their dealings with a burst of laughter and claps on the back and came toward us. I was not able to speak further with him.

I took my farewell from Ljót and young Kári on the beach and embraced each of them. As I did so, I leaned over and said to Kári, in a voice low enough that only he could hear, "Do not disdain what you have. Each person is born to a certain fate, but that is not what makes him happy—it is whether he is willing to accept the lot he is given, or spend his entire life striving vainly against it. And in the end, what good does that serve?"

Then Magnus and I boarded the skiff with Ragnar and one of his men, and we rowed back out toward the waiting ship.

As the sails came up and we began to move away from the harbor of Saudey, I looked back. Ljót had gone, but my nephew was still standing there on the shore, still as a statue, looking out to sea.

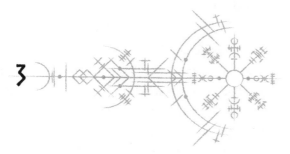

3

I SPENT THAT WINTER WITH MY uncle Magnus, assisting him in what needed to be done about his household, and relishing once again the feeling of leaving behind for a while the tangled intrigues of blood feuds. Magnus was delightful company, and rarely ever mentioned the tragedies in my past, my loss of family and friends, and for this I was grateful.

The one continual reminder of sorrow was Gudrun Thorvaldsdóttir. She had a way of showing up unexpectedly, coming silently up to me like a gray ghost as I was tending the sheep, or standing silhouetted in the door of an outbuilding, startling me when I thought I was alone. She hardly ever mentioned the loss of her own family, yet even five years afterwards, the grief she carried still surrounded her like a cloud. At first, I felt myself drawn to her through pity, and perhaps she felt the same way for me, but she reminded me too much of my own loss. After a time, although I remained friendly with her, I began to avoid her.

This, however, was not easy. Gudrun and Magnus were on friendly terms, and he frequently gave her the food and other necessities that she needed to survive. There was no way she could live off the few sheep and the small garden she tended, and the charity of her neighbors on the island was what kept her alive. She also was given to walking the hills and was a frequent sight in all sorts of weather, strolling about all dressed in gray and white.

As the weather warmed with spring's approach, it became even more difficult to avoid her, as she often came to eat her evening meal with Magnus and me. This had not been especially unusual even before my arrival, I was told—simply a case of two people, widowed and alone, looking to each other for company. However, her visits had become markedly more frequent since the previous summer, and this had not escaped Magnus's notice.

"Gudrun seems quite smitten with you," he said, with his typical lack of tact, one evening as we lingered over cups of mead.

I took a deep draught and looked into my cup. "She simply needs someone to assuage her loss."

"Who doesn't?" Magnus shot back. "Don't you? Or are you too much the stoic Viking to need a woman to warm your bed?"

I looked up and scowled at him. "I had one wife. It is all I have ever wanted, and there will never be one who can replace her."

"Replace her? Who said anything about replacing her? But everyone needs love and companionship and the pleasures of the bed."

"I don't see you pursuing the company of women," I responded acidly. "Gudrun was here long before I was, if you find her so attractive."

Magnus waved his hand dismissively. "I am far too old for her. If there were any older women about, however, they would have to beware the theft of their virtue, you can be sure of that."

I laughed heartily. "I don't doubt it. But I cannot see myself with Gudrun. She seems too sunk in her own sorrow, somehow."

He locked his sharp eyes upon mine. "And you are not?"

Again, I was nettled, because I knew that he spoke the truth. "I have grieved my loss and am done with grieving."

"That is nonsense." He smacked down his cup with a bang onto the table. "You and Gudrun both grieve still. You simply have different ways of showing it, that's all. She wears her grief like a cloak, you wear yours like armor. She floats about in a cloud of sadness, while you alternately rage and then act as if nothing has happened. Don't be derisive of Gudrun. At least she hasn't gone about killing everyone involved in her sorrow."

I bounced up out of my seat, furious, but Magnus just looked at me steadily. "Sit down, Kári. There's none here but you and me. There's no one to posture in front of, so stop indulging your anger and listen to me."

I slowly sat back down, but my heart was still beating hard in my chest.

"You have a choice, Kári. You always have. Life is a series of choices, and yours were not made for you by some fate beyond your control. You cannot go back and undo what is done, but you do have a choice here in the present."

"What is it?" I said, but there was a part of me that was already rejecting everything he was saying.

"You can put down your sword and your vengeance. You pretend to be happy here, to have given all that up, but I can see it in your eyes. Every time someone you don't know comes by here, your ears perk up to catch every word he says. Why? I know why, and so do you. You still hope to catch word of those six lost wolves you failed to slay. You seem happy enough, and no doubt it has been fine for you to have a time away from your feuding, but your heart still yearns to go out and begin it all again."

"That is not true," I said, then faltered and fell silent.

"It isn't? Then tell me, Kári. Tell me honestly, for I know you to be honest. In your heart, you have always been honest with yourself and with others. If that door opened right now, and standing outside was the leader of the six men who escaped you, what would you do? Would you say, 'Go in peace, for I have come home and have no more wish to fight?'"

I looked at him, and his words burned in my ears. I pictured Flosi Thórdarson standing there, smirking at me. I said, in a low, shamed voice, "I would pull out my sword, and slay him where he stood."

Magnus nodded. "I know it. But you need to know it is a choice you are making, to feel this way."

"I swore an oath!" I cried.

"Foolishness!" he shouted, louder than I have ever heard him shout. "An oath to whom? Words they are, mere words. If in a moment of grief and rage, a man swears an evil oath, but should he hold himself to it? Which is worse, to break the oath or to do evil?"

I could not answer that, and so I said, "I swore the oath to Ingrid and my son Thórd."

His eyes looked at mine with deep pity. He looked almost as grieved as I felt. He reached out and touched my hand gently. "Kári, Ingrid and Thórd are dead. They cannot hold you to this oath, and I do not believe they would want to. It is you, and you alone, who do it."

"I know that." My voice sounded hollow and empty in my ears. "But I cannot relinquish it."

Magnus leaned back in his chair, and he looked at me for a moment. Then he smiled a little, and said, "Then we will speak no more of it. But still, I think you should speak with Gudrun. There is more to her than you have yet seen."

MAGNUS'S WORDS HAUNTED ME OVER THE next weeks, as early spring with its fog and hints of warmth turned to full spring, and the pastures greened and the days lengthened. There were new lambs to tend and much work to be done, but always in the corners of my heart I could hear Magnus's voice, chiding me and calling me to consider what I had done. And always in the background, there was Gudrun—watching me, smiling at me, appearing at my side when my mind was occupied elsewhere.

One sunny afternoon in late spring, I was returning from five days spent on the north end of the island helping Magnus's friend Ragnar Finnbogason. His ship had been damaged in a winter storm and I had gone up to help him repair it. He was pleased enough for the help, although his way of showing it was to say that Magnus had only sent me because I was too inept to be of any real use. I responded that I had come, rather, because Magnus had said that I'd better watch over the repair and make sure that Ragnar didn't leave any gaping holes in the hull. Ragnar snorted when I told him this but accepted me immediately. Before a day had passed, we were fast friends.

After the ship was repaired and once again seaworthy, I said my farewells to Ragnar and his men, and headed back home to Magnus's house. It was a perfect spring day, cool and sunny—the kind of day not nearly common enough in the rainy Hebrides, but one to be savored when it happens. As I crested a hill and saw the low stone fence of my uncle's land in the valley before me, I also saw a lone figure, dressed in gray and white, sitting on a stone beside the road. Before I even saw her face, I knew it was Gudrun Thorvaldsdóttir.

I came up to her, and said, "It looks as if you are waiting for someone." She smiled. "I am."

I returned her smile. "Who?"

"You."

With an effort, I continued to smile at her. "Now, that cannot be true. You say it only to flatter me. How can you have known I would come this way today, when I have been gone for five days and did not myself know when I would return?"

She shrugged. "I didn't. It was a fine day, and I went walking, and thought, 'That looks a comfortable place to sit. Maybe Kári will come this way, and we can talk for a while.' That is all."

"Well, Kári is here." I sat down next to her, feeling that it would be discourteous simply to leave. "Now that I am here, what do you wish to talk to me about?"

She looked up at me, suddenly solemn. "It is difficult for you to talk, is it not?"

I frowned. "I do not know what you mean. Does my speech sound halting to your ears?"

She shook her head. "I do not mean it like that. Your voice is deep and rich and kind, and a pleasure to listen to. But you speak of things and events, always. 'I had this, and then I did that, then he did this.' It is not easy for you to speak what is in your heart."

I looked away, out over the hills. "That is true."

"Yet I think there is much that is there."

I did not answer for a moment, but finally said, "I do not know. My uncle says I deal with my grief by first raging and then acting as if all is well. My feelings change from one thing to another so quickly that I do not know which ones are real."

"Perhaps they all are."

My eyes turned toward her again, and she still sat with her hands folded in her lap, her gray eyes patient and kind. "Perhaps you are right."

"You could speak of your feelings to me, if you wished."

"What purpose would that serve?" My voice sounded harsh, and I regretted it.

She did not seem upset by my tone, and kept speaking in the same soft, kind voice as before. "I think I understand a little of what you are feeling, for I have felt many of the same things. Why did this happen to me? Could I have prevented it? And the sorrow, the endless sorrow. It is worst at night, is it not?"

"It is." My throat felt tight as I said it.

"The need to feel another person close by, it is a powerful need. And now there is no one, just emptiness...."

At that I sprang up, and cried, "Stop! My grief is great enough without your feeding on it. I just wish to forget."

She looked up at me, her eyes grown large in her slender face. "Why do you wish that? You will never forget, whether you wish it or not."

Without another word, I turned and walked away from her. I heard her voice behind me, still patient and sad. "Kári, come to me when you need me, when you need to talk about it, I will be waiting for you."

That evening, when I retired, I could not sleep. I tossed about on my mat of soft straw on the floor, thinking, thinking, as if my brain could never stop talking to itself.

Never forget. I would never forget. I would be haunted forever by the sight of Ingrid's naked back, with the mark the timbers of Bergthorshváll burned into it. By the sight of little Thórd, lying unmarked and beautiful, as if he were sleeping. By the sight of my friends—the best friends I have ever known—Helgi, beheaded before his own threshold, Skarp-Hedin, fallen into the burning like a stray thunderbolt, Grím, crushed by the fallen beam. By the anger, hot as the burning itself, toward the twelve men who did this thing.

Grief, sorrow, and bitter hatred coursed through my veins like a hot venom, and I jumped up from my bed, quickly pulled on some clothes and went out into the night.

It was still clear, and the stars burned down from the black sky. A quarter moon hung low in the sky, and by its light, I made my way over the hills toward the cliffs of Kolness, to a little house that stood there in a field by itself. I went up to the door and rapped on it with my knuckles.

In a moment, a voice said, "Who is it?"

"Kári Solmundarson."

The door swung quietly open, and Gudrun was there, in a thin linen night dress, and she smiled at me as sweetly as ever, as if the harsh words I had spoken to her that day had never been.

"Come inside," she said, and she lit an oil lamp.

We sat down at a little table at the back of the house, and she looked at me expectantly. I felt suddenly shy and tongue-tied.

"I wish to apologize for my words today," I said, fumblingly.

"There is no need."

"There is. I spoke to you in anger, and only because I knew you spoke the truth. I do need... I need..." And again I faltered, and fell silent.

"You need to talk to someone who will understand," she said quietly.

I nodded. "I couldn't sleep for thinking of it. There is so much anger and grief inside me, it burns my heart." The last words came out through clenched teeth, and my fists tightened with the terrible effort to contain myself.

Then she said, her voice nearly a whisper, "You must have loved her very much."

I looked at her in some surprise. She had a way of never saying what I expected her to say. There, in that dark little house, beside a woman I hardly knew, I began to weep. The tears flowed as if they would never stop, so that my entire body was wracked with it. The grief shook me, helpless as a rabbit in a wolf's jaws. I was so taken over that I was unable to even be ashamed. She sat next to me, and held me, and her slender arms encircled me, and she simply waited for the storm to pass.

When it finally did, she reached up, and stroked my face with her cool hands, to wipe the tears away. My eyes searched hers for a moment. Suddenly we were kissing, fiercely and passionately, and she took my hand and guided it along her bare leg and under her thin dress.

She broke our kiss long enough to say, "Kári... I need you, stay the night with me...." and I lifted her up and carried her to her bed, and lay her down gently upon it. Moments later, we were twined naked around each other, coupling so deeply that it seemed that we could not be close enough together, so that she cried out with the desperate pleasure of it. Then an explosive rush of pleasure shuddered through me and cried out as I clung to her warm body, and she to mine. And we held each other that way, without moving, until finally our awareness dissolved away into sleep.

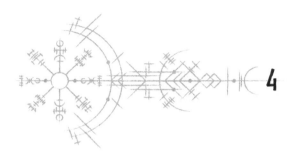

4

I WOKE THE FOLLOWING MORNING WITH the sun streaming in the small window above her bed, and Gudrun lying with her head upon my bare chest.

I stirred, and she opened her eyes, and smiled.

"I am sorry for showing you my grief last night," I said. "I should not have added to your burden."

"Is that what you believe you did?"

"You have your own sorrow," I began.

"Sharing it with another makes the burden less, not more. I need you as much as you need me."

"Yet you have not told me much about your own grief, Gudrun."

There was a pause, and the smile died from her lips. "Do you truly wish to hear of it?"

"I do."

She did not speak for a moment, and when she did, her voice was controlled. "I was married to a man named Eilif Asgrímsson, who raised a few sheep and goats. He was not a wealthy man, but he owned this house and a little land here on Kolness."

"You had children, you said."

"Two children. A daughter, Astrid, who was six, and a son, Eirík, who was four." I felt the warmth of tears running down my chest, but there was no sign of her grief from her voice, which continued quiet and steady.

"My little son Eirík woke in the middle of the night in summer. I will never forget it. He cried and thrashed about, and the cloth covering of his bed soaked with sweat. Eilif and I tried to quiet him, but he continued to cry in his delirium, until... it was the middle of the following day, he sank into a deep sleep and there he died."

Now, her entire body was trembling, and I held her closer, and she continued. "Eilif was next. He collapsed two days later while out tending our sheep, and I did not know it until Astrid came to get me. To think of him, lying there, alone, unable to rise...."

"No doubt he was beyond knowing what had happened."

"I hope that is so, but I cannot forgive myself for not being there to speak with him, to hold him. He died that night. For a time, I thought that Astrid would be spared, but she fell ill three days later, and was also dead within a day's time."

"It must have been horrible. I cannot imagine it."

"Even now, I dream at night of watching my children die." Her voice cracked slightly, the first I had heard. "It is the worst thing of all. I know that you understand, as it has happened to you as well."

I held her close to me for some time, and then she said, "I would like... I wish you to stay with me, Kári."

I did not respond for a moment. It was with some reluctance that I said, "I cannot do that."

She looked up at me, incomprehension in her eyes. "Why can you not?"

I pulled away from her, sat up, and I looked down upon her with pity. "I cannot commit to you or to any other, as much as I wish to. I have an oath I have sworn, and until it is fulfilled I cannot promise anything." I reached down and stroked her face. "But were I to promise to stay with anyone, it would be you."

"I cannot understand you. You would turn aside from peace and love for this?"

"Magnus doesn't understand it, either, yet I know it is what I must do. I cannot so lightly turn aside from my word, nor from seeing justice for the family I lost."

She was silent for a moment, and then said, "I find myself almost envying you. For you have the thoughts of revenge to bear you up in your loss. For me, there is no such comfort. How can one find revenge against a sickness?"

I kissed her lightly. "Yet you have survived these five years. There is a strength in you that you do not acknowledge. You have already given me a measure of healing. I only wish I could remain here, and perhaps I could find a full cure."

Later, I went back to Magnus's house, and when I came in he regarded me with one eyebrow raised.

"You went to speak with Gudrun, I take it."

I nodded, but the color rose in my cheeks, and he grinned at me.

"Oh, is that the way of it? I should have known. Well, good for you, Kári, good for you." He patted my shoulder. "Your heart will heal, if you let it."

"You mistake me, Uncle. I spent the night with her, yes. But I cannot do so again, and I told her that. My oath holds me, and I cannot leave it behind." I paused, and then said, "In any case, I do not know if I could truly love another, after Ingrid."

I expected him to give me argument, but though he looked saddened, he said nothing further.

After that day, I was not sure how Gudrun would act toward me—whether she would be angry that I had shared her bed and given nothing in return, or feel betrayed because I had left, or grieved because I could not stay with her. In fact, she seemed to feel none of these things. She was as courteous and friendly as ever, and I spent many hours helping her about her little farm, but I did not speak further of my past, and neither did she. I did not wish to mislead her further into thinking that I was trying to give her something that it was not in my power to give.

So as the spring matured into full summer, I spent my days helping both Magnus and Gudrun with the work that needed doing, and each night I returned to Magnus's house, to my empty bed. Still I dreamed of revenge, and I dreamed of Ingrid. Yet those dreams were more than ever tinged with questions.

Was I right to reject Gudrun? She was an offer of love and comfort and peace, such as I had never had since the burning of Bergthorshváll, and I knew that I had hurt her deeply. Yet my heart still yearned for Ingrid alone.

I have never truly wanted any other, and I have never warmed another woman's bed except for that single night with Gudrun. I felt some pangs of guilt about having done that, but I wondered if Ingrid herself would have so greatly minded—surely, she would not want the rest of my life spent in celibate solitude. Yet my heart was still filled with the thought of the men who had escaped me, and there was then no room for anything or anyone else.

Was I right to feel this way? I cannot say. It seems that the older I get, the less certain I am about everything I have done, and all I am left with are questions.

Ljót came to visit us that summer, with his oldest son, my namesake. Young Kári was growing quickly toward manhood, broad-shouldered and handsome, and still with the same serious demeanor I had noticed before. We spoke together much during that visit, about adventures and courage and gain and loss, and although he seemed to hear my words, I felt that he still sought escape from his home island.

"Are you really content here on Kolnsey, Uncle?" he asked me one evening, as we sat on the rocks on Kolness and looked out over the sea.

"For now, I am," I replied, choosing my words carefully. "I think I could be happy here."

"What of your oath?"

I broke off a grass stem and turned it between my fingers. After a moment, I smiled and said, "It still pulls at me. However, I do not know how I will fulfill it. I don't know where the six remaining men have gone."

"You sound as if you would be just as happy if you never heard anything more of them."

"No. I think of little else, but I have scant choice but to wait until I hear word of them. I cannot search the world over for them. It is a large place, Kári."

"The part I have seen of it is small enough." His voice held a trace of the same bitterness I had heard before.

"True. But if you went to another place, what would you find? Elsewhere there are people, just as there are on Saudey, some good and some bad. If you found some other place, you would find that the people there are just like the people everywhere."

"There must be more exciting places in the world than Saudey."

"Possibly. And perhaps you will see some of them one day. But always remember that your home is here in the Hebrides. It took me long enough to remember it."

Summer turned into autumn, and Ljót and Kári returned to Saudey, and the islands slipped into the dark sleep of winter. Thoughts of my escaped foes receded into the corners of my mind, and my determination to find them turned to a sense of hopelessness at completing my quest. Fighting and killing occupied fewer and fewer of my dreams. As the year turned once more toward warmth and light, I began to think that perhaps I would never be able to fulfill the oath I had sworn—that whether I wished it or not, I would not leave the Hebrides again.

———————

GUDRUN WAS VISITING MAGNUS ONE DAY the following spring to help him with the farm work that needed doing, as was becoming a custom with us. All three of us worked both farms, which made the tasks lighter and provided company and friendly conversation—a good arrangement for all involved. That day, all of us were indoors. Gudrun was churning milk, I was sharpening some knives used in butchering, and Magnus was rather halfheartedly grinding grain in a quern.

"Woman's work," he said, with some measure of scorn.

"Gudrun cannot be expected to do all of your work and all of hers as well," I responded with some heat. Magnus scowled at me, and Gudrun gave a little laugh.

Suddenly Ragnar Finnbogason, our fisherman friend from the north side of the island, pushed open the door and stuck his head inside.

"Greetings, and nice to see you all working so hard. Even Magnus is taking a hand in it for a change, I see."

Magnus regarded him sourly. "You're welcome to take a turn at it."

"I don't wish to interrupt, you're all doing so nicely. I just brought in a big haul of fish and thought I would share with my friends and neighbors." He nodded in my direction. "Perhaps this strapping young man would like to bring an empty creel up to the harbor, and I can fill it up for him."

I stood and stretched my stiff muscles. "I would welcome the chance to be outdoors. I have been inside most of the morning."

Ragnar and I went across the hills and around the base of Kolness, to the little harbor on the east side of the island.

"You have had good fortune in fishing so far this year, I guess?"

"Indeed. It is one of the best years I have seen. We cast out nets and can barely pull them aboard for the weight of the catch. Three weeks ago, we were up in the waters east of Skaraness off the island of Tyraey, and caught so many fish we came ashore and sold them to the chieftain on Myley rather than trying to bring them back here. Made a handsome profit, as well."

"Myley is north of here, is it not?"

"It is." Then he turned toward me suddenly, as if he had just recalled something. "Oh, I had nearly forgotten to mention something which may interest you. I met one of your adopted countrymen, a man who has made his way to Myley, and is in the employ of the chieftain there. It is seldom we get Icelanders this far south, although they visit the Orkneys at times, I hear."

My heart leapt suddenly, although for no very good reason. There were many Icelanders, after all. What chance was it that it was even a man I knew, far less one of my foes? "Who is he?"

"A tall man, very fair, with a loud voice and rough speech." He grinned. "Not so different than most Icelanders, I have heard."

"And his name, Ragnar?" I tried to keep the excitement from my voice.

"His name is Glum Hildisson."

At that moment, I knew that my time in the Hebrides had come to an end.

My agitation must have shown in my face, because Ragnar said, "You know him, then?"

"Oh, yes. I know him." But I did not say anything further to him about it, and he, seeming to sense that what he had said had affected me strangely, did not enquire further. We went onto the shore where he had beached his catch, and I filled the creel with fish. I thanked him, and then set off once more for Magnus's house.

So, completely by accident, Glum Hildisson was found. Not the greatest of my enemies, but even so, he had been there the night that Bergthorshváll was burned. He was one of them. Glum was a rogue and a lout and he had been loud in his abuse of the Njálssons as their house burned around them. A foolish, troll-like man. Was it worth leaving behind the fragile peace in my life to visit vengeance upon him?

I walked back over the hills, fresh and green in the spring sun, and all of the conflict came weighing back down upon me again. Once more, the internal argument began.

I swore an oath to kill him.

It was my choice. Magnus said that. If I threw away my chance to live in peace here to pursue Glum and the others, I would have chosen it. There would be no one else to blame. But what of Ingrid and Thórd, dead beneath the timbers of our ruined house?

They would want me to be happy more than they would want me to complete my vengeance. Leave it. Let God take care of revenge.

Could I let someone like Flosi Thórdarson live?

Foolishness. I didn't even know where Flosi is. This was Glum Hildisson, who was nothing more than a loudmouthed fool.

But he was there when Ingrid and Thórd perished in the flames! Surely, I must kill him as well.

If I lived so long.

But still, I must do what I must do.

And with that, the decision was made.

What made the decision? Was it the oath, come to life like some magical beast, driving me with claws and teeth that none other could see? Or was it me, and me alone, as Magnus had said, deciding at each step of the way, although I always felt as if I had no choice? I do not know. Whichever it was, when I arrived at Magnus's house that evening, my face was so changed that both Magnus and Gudrun looked at me in perplexity, as if I were a total stranger.

"Kári," Gudrun said, in a hushed voice, "what is it?"

Magnus regarded me in silence for a long moment. "I knew it would happen eventually. You have found a trace of one of your six lost wolves, is it not so?"

I nodded.

"Where is he?"

"Serving the chieftain on Myley."

"So, now, you are faced with a choice."

"It is no choice, Uncle!" My voice was filled with a fierce anger that was not directed toward him. "I swore an oath to kill him!"

I looked at Gudrun, who was sitting, stricken, her face pale. I realized then, with some measure of shock, that she loved me, even though I had told her I could not love her in return. My heart felt heavy with shame because of it.

"It is what I must do." My voice sounded dull and lifeless in my ears.

"Have you not listened to anything I have said to you?" Magnus shouted, and I saw Gudrun cringe. "Who is it saying that you have to do this? Who?"

"*I* am!" I cried. "Is that not enough?"

Magnus regarded me for a moment, no discernible emotion on his face. "It will have to be, it seems."

Gudrun stood, and ran from the house, weeping, into the twilit fields. I followed her, calling out her name, but she did not slow or stop.

I caught her up halfway to her little house. I stood before her and placed my hands on her slender shoulders. My heart ached to see her face wet with tears.

"Do not grieve. Perhaps one day I will come back here, and we will sit and talk as before."

Her eyes looked searchingly into mine. "After the night we spent together—and I do not regret it, I never will—I thought perhaps with time, you could come to love me, even though you told me you never could. I love you, Kári Solmundarson, and I thought we could together build a life here and leave our past sorrows behind. I was a fool."

"You are no fool, Gudrun." My words sounded empty and worthless in my own ears. How must they have sounded to her? "I wish my fate was otherwise. But I have a task I must see through to the end, bitter though that end may be."

"Do you wish then that you had never come back here?"

I shook my head. "It has been pleasant enough these two years, to be home on Kolnsey. I do not regret it. It is far more than I ever expected to have when I was outlawed."

"Will you not come back? When it is all over?" She sounded pleading.

"I cannot say."

She looked up at me, and I saw the grief, which had over the previous year gradually been fading from her, rush with aching suddenness back over her face. "It is over, then. You will go to Myley, and if you are not killed by this enemy of yours, will you not then continue to pursue your quest elsewhere? And on and on and on."

"Yes. If it is possible, that is what I will do."

"I thought I understood you, but I do not. I never shall."

With that, she turned and walked away in the gathering dusk, on toward her house. I watched her until I could no longer see her, and after a time I turned, and made my way back to Magnus's house. My heart was doubly heavy, at leaving my home again, and also at having hurt someone who had only wished me well.

Magnus was waiting for me. When I walked in and sat down dejectedly in a chair by the little table, he came over and sat down nearby. His face was kind, but I still expected him to chide me further about my decision. I sat like a cat about to spring, with my argument ready upon my lips should he try to dissuade me.

However, he merely said in a gentle voice, "Decisions are never easy. I hope you will not regret this one."

"I truly did not know she loved me."

"Odd how sometimes we are blind to things that all others can see clearly."

Even though he had uttered no criticism, I still felt stung. "I have no desire to hurt Gudrun."

"I know that. And so does she. It is simply that you each desire different things. You, justice against the men who wronged you, and Gudrun, love and peace and companionship with you. The two are incompatible. No man can tell you which to choose, and no man who has not been in a similar situation should criticize you. I am sorry if I have tried to lead you toward one choice. It was not my place. I have never walked the road you have walked, and in your place, I do not know what I would do."

"I myself do not know if I am doing rightly." My face sank into my hands.

"Most men do not," Magnus replied. "The difference is that few men seem to care."

"That is true. But I cannot understand why so often those men who care little for justice live long and prosperous lives, and those who care the most have nothing but sorrow and grief and tragedy. Why does God treat his people so?"

Magnus shrugged, and gave a little smile. "I don't know. I am not a learned man who has such answers. Truly, I have less often had cause to question how God treats men than how men treat other men."

I looked up at him. "If you are trying to persuade me not to kill Glum Hildisson, then come right out and say so."

He shook his head. "I am not trying to persuade you at all. I have always known you to be an honest and just man. I know you have done what you have done from a desire for justice, and because of this, I have hope God will shield you through your quest so that you may return unscathed."

"It does not always happen so."

"I know that," he responded.

Two weeks later, I prepared to leave Kolnsey. Ragnar Finnbogason had agreed to give me transportation to Myley, and I accepted with thanks. He did not inquire too deeply into why I was going there and seemingly not returning, for which I was even more thankful.

The evening before I left, I went to Gudrun's house. It was the first time I had gone there since I had told her I was leaving. I had wanted to see her, but each day I found myself delaying, believing I would not know what to say to her. The days slipped through my fingers, and it was only when my departure was imminent that I finally forced myself to go to her to say farewell.

She was on her knees in her little patch of garden, pulling weeds, when I came up. When she saw me, she looked up with the same patient, grieving expression that she had worn when I had first seen her, in the ruins of my brother's abandoned house.

"Kári," she said.

"I have come to say farewell, Gudrun."

"I know."

She stood and brushed the dirt from her hands. "I have no very great hope that I will ever see you again."

"Nor do I. Yet I want you to know that I have never wished you ill. My uncle said were I not blind, your love for me would have been obvious."

She smiled a little. "Perhaps. But even if I do not really understand you, I do not blame you for it. I do not believe it is in you to be unjust."

"I hope you are right."

She looked into my eyes. "Farewell, then. And may God protect you."

I kissed her once on the cheek, lightly. "And may he look after you as well." I turned from her, with some reluctance, and walked away.

When I crested the little hill above her house, I turned, and she was still standing there, watching me, like a white ghost glimmering in the half-light. I raised my hand in farewell, and she did the same. Then I turned and walked away, down the other side of the hill. As I did so, I felt as if I was severing the connection to my life on Kolnsey and had turned irreversibly toward whatever awaited me on Myley.

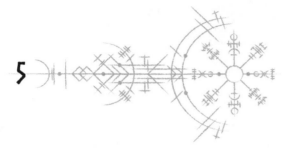

I AWOKE EARLY THE NEXT MORNING as the sun was just coming up over the hills to the east, staining all the sky scarlet. I dressed, went outside, and stood watching the colors gradually pale into clear blue. I turned to go back inside, to collect the few belongings I wished to bring with me—my sword, a small leather bag with food in it, and a leather flask filled with water—and found Magnus standing behind me, hands clasped behind his back.

"Do you wish some company walking down to the harbor?"

"I would welcome it."

After I had gathered my things together and bound my sword at my waist, we walked down toward the harbor below Kolness. Neither of us spoke except about light things, things of no consequence. The weather, plans for enlarging the sheepfold, what to do about the persistent leak in the roof at one end of the house. All unrelated to the business at hand, but all somehow more important, now that the time had come to part.

Ragnar's ship stood in the deeper water off shore, and one of his men had rowed a skiff in to pick me up. He and it were already waiting for me when we arrived, there on the shore where I had first trod upon my return to Kolnsey two years earlier.

When I turned to bid farewell to my uncle Magnus, much to my astonishment I found that he was silently weeping.

"Do not grieve, Uncle. Perhaps I shall return."

His voice was rough with his tears. "Perhaps you shall, but I have no hope that I shall see it. I am an old man, Kári, an old man, and to old men every day is precious. Your presence here has brought me back to life. When you arrived two years ago, I had reached the point where I no longer cared whether I lived or followed my Gerd to the grave. Now you are going again, and I stand here weeping like a foolish child because of it—and I shall miss you, Kári. I truly shall."

The tears started to my eyes, as well, but I fought them back, and embraced my uncle. "May God look after you."

"And you as well, Kári."

I turned and helped Ragnar's crewman to pull the skiff out into the waves, then together we rowed out toward the waiting ship. We drew up alongside, and climbed aboard, and pulled the skiff up after us. I turned and waved farewell to my uncle, who was still standing on the shore. He waved back, heartily, and I shouted, "Farewell!" at the top of my voice. Perhaps he shouted back, but I heard nothing but the echo of my voice bouncing off the cliff of Kolness, and the distant crashing of the surf. I thought that from a distance, Magnus looked like a little, wizened old man, and I feared that he might be right about my never seeing him again, even if I did return one day to Kolnsey.

Then at a shout from Ragnar, the anchor was raised, and the sails billowed, and we began to move out of the harbor. As we did, I had a strange feeling of the past and the present being superimposed. I felt that another Kári Solmundarson was there, only nineteen years old, standing in the prow of a ship sailing out from Kolnsey, with the salt wind in his face and excitement in his heart—and the other Kári, forty-one years old, standing in the prow of a different ship sailing the same waters, doggedly facing a grim job to be done. I wished for a moment, foolish that it might seem, that the two Káris could speak with one another. What might they say? And how would it have changed all that had happened?

Such was the absurd dream I was immersed in as the hills of Kolnsey dipped behind us into the surrounding sea and were lost to view.

———

MYLEY IS A LARGE ISLAND, FAR larger than Kolnsey is, and nearer to Scotland. The chieftain there pays tribute both to Jarl Gilli of the Hebrides and to the King of Scotland. As a result, he is, in a sense, subject to both and trusted by neither. Ragnar told me something of him as we sailed toward the island, a day's sailing northeast from Kolnsey.

"His name is Skapti Oláfsson, and he is a shrewd man. A clever bargainer, but fair enough. He recognizes his position for what it is. Caught between the King of Scotland and the Jarl of the Hebrides, he watches his step carefully and does little to attract attention. He does not wish any interference in island affairs by either side. Thus far, he has done well enough. But be honest with him, should the need arise. He will not tolerate liars."

"I do not lie in any case."

"No, I don't suppose you do. Nevertheless, you are being closed-mouthed enough with me about what exactly you plan to do there, and I thought it only fair to warn you."

I sighed. "Ragnar, my friend, I would not burden you with the whole tale. Suffice it to say that this Glum Hildisson, whom you found for me on Myley, is one of the twelve men who were responsible for killing my wife and child, and my wife's entire family, by burning them in their house."

Ragnar regarded me impassively for a moment. "You seek revenge."

"Yes."

"Good fortune to you. Such a man deserves whatever you plan to give him."

The night fell, and we anchored near the Scottish coast, but out of bowshot. There was peace with Scotland at this time, but it was never a relaxed one, and we did not wish to take chances. I slept fitfully onboard ship, and woke before dawn, as we once again moved northward toward the coast of Myley.

It was near noon of that day that we drew into the main harbor of the island. It was a sheltered place, and a number of low buildings clustered along the shore, reminding me of the main settlement on Orkney. However, there were many other ships at anchor in the harbor, and there seemed to be much more activity on the shore than I had seen in other harbor settlements. It had the look of a thriving market town. I gave my thanks and bid farewell to Ragnar Finnbogason and his crew, and once again was rowed to shore.

I looked around me. This was a new experience, to be deposited upon the shore of a strange place, to search among strangers for an enemy to kill. I was wary, as I did not know how I would be looked upon even before I made my attack upon Glum, much less what my fate would be if I killed him.

On the first count, it appeared that I had little to worry about. The people of Myley seemed to be used to comings and goings onboard ship, and none spared me a second glance. Merchants argued in loud voices over goods of various kinds, workers laughed and sang as they unloaded and loaded cargo, and crew from various ships saw to repairs and fittings for their vessels. I suppose that everyone assumed I was simply a sailor, merchant, or fisherman from another island, and paid me no heed at all. It was easy to wander about the island unmarked.

I asked a young boy of about twelve years where the chieftain's men lodged, and he pointed up to a group of long buildings on the south end of the harbor shore. I thanked him, and walked toward them, determination building at each step as I pictured Glum Hildisson's face, and his astonishment at seeing me approaching him when he probably expected never to see me again.

As luck would have it, the guards, workers, and other men in the employ of the chieftain were at their midday meal when I arrived. In a large, open hall, the central building of the men's lodgings, a hundred or so men were gathered around tables in a noisy throng, eating and drinking and laughing. There was much coming and going, and none marked my entrance into the hall. I walked up and down the aisles between the tables, scanning the people there for the face I wanted to find.

"Who are you looking for?" said a friendly voice at my elbow. Startled, I turned to find a young man of about twenty standing next to me, holding a cup of mead and smiling broadly. "You look like you are searching for someone."

"I am. I seek a man named Glum Hildisson. He is an Icelander, and is tall and fair-haired, with a ruddy complexion."

He nodded, and his smile broadened. "Oh, him. Yes, I know who you mean, although mostly folk seem to want to get away from him rather than find him." He laughed at his own joke, and then continued, pointing with his free hand across a sea of heads. "I saw him earlier at the far table. Perhaps he is still there."

I thanked him, and then threaded my way through the crowds toward the table he had pointed out.

I saw him before I had even gotten halfway there. He was telling some story, laughing loudly as he ate and drank. The people around him, it seemed to me, were laughing less than he was, but he continued undaunted. I approached slowly, never taking my eyes off him. I was only a few feet away when he caught sight of me, and the laughter died upon his lips. He grew ghastly pale, as if he had seen a specter of the dead rising from the floor.

"Glum Hildisson," I said grimly, and I drew my sword, "no doubt you did not expect me to find you."

There was a great commotion of sliding of chairs and benches, as men all around us saw me standing there with a naked blade, my expression fierce as I faced my enemy who had escaped justice for two long years. Many men nearby stood, and I heard the ringing of swords being drawn. Glum did not stir, no doubt fearing that I would kill him instantly if he moved.

"*Slay him!*" he shouted to his comrades, and I heard the edge of terror in his voice. "This man comes to kill me!"

In response, I shouted even more loudly, "Slay one of us, at least, men of Myley, and you choose which it should be! For before you, you see a man who has killed my wife and innocent child, and I come seeking him to bring him to justice at the edge of my blade. If you think it just to kill me so that you can protect such a man, then go ahead and do so." None moved. And Glum, I think, knew that he was lost.

"Stand up," I told him, motioning with the point of my sword, and he did. I moved the point until it was right before his throat. It was dead silent in the hall now, and all eyes were upon us.

"Tell them," I said. "Tell them what you have done, or I will slay you without hesitation."

Glum, who was a bully when he had the advantage and a coward when he did not, swallowed, and his windpipe moved convulsively in his throat. He then said, his voice unwarrantedly quiet, "I was there at the burning where Kári's wife and son died. But I did not set the fire, and I killed no one."

"Nevertheless, you heard me swear an oath, did you not? I swore to kill you all, all twelve of you who were there. Six I have slain already. You will be the seventh. Have you anything to say?"

His eyes grew wider until the whites showed all the way around, and he cried out, "Kári, spare me and I will tell you where the others have gone!"

I raised one eyebrow. "How would I know you spoke the truth? A man who would betray his comrades might also lie."

"No, I swear it! I know where they went, because we left together, and went to the Orkneys. We only split up the following spring, each going his separate way. Arni Kolsson went on to north Wales, and Kol Thorsteinsson to Jorvík, in England. Grani Gunnarsson and Gunnar Lambason went to a settlement called Dyrness on the north coast of Scotland."

"That is not all of them," I said, and I touched the point of my sword against the skin of his throat, so that a small bead of bright blood welled up around it. "What of Flosi Thórdarson?"

"I do not know, I swear it!" he cried, and he was trembling, but did not move at all. "Flosi did not leave from Faxaflói with the rest of us. I did not see him again after we left the Assembly!"

I regarded him for a moment through narrowed eyes. I had not agreed to his request to spare him if he told me where his comrades had gone. In any case, was it just to spare such a man, who in his cowardice had betrayed his friends, while I did not spare Ketil, who would have died a hundred times and never done so? Also, he had not drawn his sword. I did not wish to strike down an unarmed man. Everyone watched us in complete silence while I stood, unsure of what to do.

Then with a swift motion, almost too quick for the eye to follow, Glum picked up a metal drinking horn and slung it at my head. It grazed my scalp, and I cried out, more in surprise than in pain, and my cry was echoed by the shouts of the hundred men watching us, but still none came either to attack me or defend him. Glum reached to pull out his sword, but luck once more took me by the hand. The hilt of his sword tangled in his cloak as he grabbed for it. In the moment while he fought with his own sword, I brought up my own blade and struck off his head.

There was a great cry from the men assembled there, and as I knelt to wipe the blood off my sword on the hem of his cloak, I felt strong arms grab me and disarm me. I expected no less.

I was dragged, none too gently, from the hall, and, accompanied by four strong guards, was brought into another building, a smaller but better-built structure in the center of the settlement. The inside was dark, but as my eyes adjusted, I saw that it was an ornate lodging, obviously meant for the chieftain. Seated at a table, enjoying his own midday meal, was Skapti Oláfsson, the chieftain of Myley.

Skapti was neither fat and suspicious like Gilli Klapa, nor was he immensely tall and fiercely energetic like Sigurd Hlodvisson of the Orkneys. Skapti was a small, wiry man, with finely sculptured features and dark, intelligent eyes. He leaned back in his chair when he saw us enter, and folded his hands across his chest, quite unperturbed by the interruption.

"What is the matter?"

"This man, a stranger, has killed one of your workers. The Icelander, Glum Hildisson, who came here last fall."

"Oh?" He looked at me questioningly. "Who are you, and why have you done this? What have you to say for yourself?"

My eyes met his steadily. "My name is Kári Solmundarson. I am from Kolnsey, but I lived for a time in Iceland, and three years ago this Glum Hildisson was part of a band of men who burned down the house in which I lived, and I was the only one who escaped death. In this fire, died my wife and child, my wife's parents and her three brothers, and their servant woman. I swore to pursue and slay all of those who were there that night, as there was no justice to be found at the Assembly."

"At sword point, Glum admitted as much," said one of the men who held me.

Skapti continued to look at me without changing his expression. "Now that you have killed him, you are no doubt expecting me to clap you on the back and say, 'Well done,' and let you go."

I shrugged. "I have no expectations. I simply am doing what I swore to do, and I cannot dictate what you will do in response. That is for you to decide."

"It is well spoken," he admitted. "And should I say to my guards, 'Take this man away and strip him to the waist, tie him to yonder railing, and mark his back well with fifty lashes for disturbing the peace of my settlement, what would you say?"

"I would willingly bare my back to your whip and consider the exchange well worth the price."

"Perhaps. But if I said, 'Take him now and strike off his head, for he has killed one of my men,' what would you say then?"

Still, my gaze did not waver. "What could I say, Chieftain, when I am disarmed, and your men stand about me with swords? My head is yours to take, should you choose to do so. I came here knowing that I might die. Were I given the chance, I would kill Glum Hildisson again without hesitation. As I said, I did what I must do by the oath I swore. Now you must do what you must do, and I simply wait to hear what that might be."

There was a moment's silence, and despite my brave words my heart skipped a beat within my chest, as I wondered whether in moments I might be facing a flogging or even death by the edge of a sword. Then Skapti laughed, and said, "Release him, and return his sword. He is honest, I think, and has too noble a spirit to suffer a whipping and is too just and straight-forward to deserve death." The men let me go, and I found my sword back in my hands. I sheathed it and thanked the chieftain for my release.

"I spoke once with Glum Hildisson, and I find it all too easy to believe that he did what you said he did," Skapti said. "In any case, he admitted it, it seems."

"He did. He was not the greatest of my enemies, but I swore to kill them all. He was the seventh. Before he died, he told me where four of the remaining men had gone."

"A cowardly thing to do, to betray his friends in an attempt to buy his life. Truly, if any was worthy to be put to the sword, he was." He looked at me, and the intelligent dark eyes glittered. "Where did he say that his four comrades had gone?"

"One to north Wales, one to Jorvík in England, and two to northern Scotland."

He nodded. "You have no small amount of searching ahead."

"I know it."

"How do you expect to go to these distant lands? Do you have a ship which might bring you there?"

I shook my head. "A friend from Kolnsey brought me this far, but he would not have been willing to go further, and I would not have asked him such a favor in any case. Truthfully, I have given no thought to that. My only thought has been to get to Myley and kill Glum Hildisson. I did not even know where the others had gone until I got here and spoke with Glum myself."

"Ah, yes, I had forgotten," said Skapti. "But now, here you are on Myley. What will you do?"

I shrugged. "I would offer my services to you for a time, maybe in exchange not for payment but for transportation to Wales, for it is the nearest of the places I must go to. Perhaps when I have worked for you long enough to warrant such a payment, I might be given transportation there."

He considered my words. After a few moments, his smile flashed out at me. "You are an amusing fellow. Your ideas entertain me. We do have ships in from Wales from time to time, so what you ask is possible. My mother was Welsh, so I know the land well. And also, your revenge on Glum Hildisson has given me a man to replace, and it may as well be you to replace him as another. I will accept your offer and take you as a worker here for a period of nine months. After that time, if you have given me good service, I will see to it that you are given transportation to Wales."

And so, for the second time in my life, I killed a chieftain's man, and as a result was given not death but a post serving the chieftain himself.

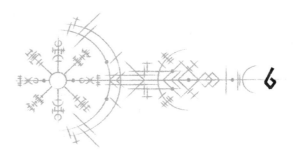

THE FOLLOWING NINE MONTHS WERE SOME of the slowest I have ever experienced. I am not a patient man, and the thought that four of my foes were found and I was left on Myley, loading and unloading endless amounts of cargo and doing minor repairs to ships and buildings, was difficult to endure. There was no help for it, however. Nine months of hard labor was my price for transportation.

Skapti Oláfsson was much as Ragnar had told me—wily, intelligent, and cautious. He was neither an inspiring war leader like Sigurd Hlodvisson, nor was he a suspicious grouch like Gilli Klapa who found it necessary to surround himself with flatterers and relatives from fear of betrayal. Skapti was secure in his knowledge that he was more intelligent than most of his men, and he made certain he used to the utmost the wits of any who showed special abilities. His second-in-command, a one-eyed veteran from Jutland named Asbrand, seemed with his single eye to see everything that went on in the settlement, and everyone knew it. Only a fool would have attempted thievery or plotted any sort of ill-doings with Asbrand about. I found out later that it was only the fact I acted so swiftly that allowed me to succeed in killing Glum Hildisson without being challenged. It turned out Asbrand had already gotten wind of my arrival and was in fact notifying Skapti of my presence as I was striking Glum's head from his shoulders. My odd mode of arrival was duly noted—that I had been rowed in and deposited alone on the beach from a strange ship that immediately turned and sailed from the harbor. Skapti had apparently just given word for me to be brought before him when I was dragged into his presence. Had I taken fifteen minutes more to find Glum, it is likely that I would have been captured first and my revenge would have miscarried.

Skapti did a thriving business with both the Scots and the Hebrideans. A phenomenal amount of cargo passed through his harbor, for such an out of the way place as Myley—ships from Wales and England, fishing boats from Scotland, longships from the Orkneys and many islands in the Hebrides. Merchants of many places knew Myley as a place to sell goods of all kinds. Trade was brisk, and each ship and every merchant paid a toll to Skapti. As a result, he was at least as wealthy as the far more powerful Jarl Sigurd. His personal fleet of ships was overseen by a shrewd and resourceful ex-merchant named Herugrím, who seemed to have the ability to mint gold coins with the tips of his fingers. Skapti, unlike many rich men, was open-handed with his wealth. Because of this, the people at the settlement on Myley, from the officers to the humblest workers, ate far better and lived more comfortably than many a wealthy man I have known.

Still, I am no merchant, and the work from day to day was sheer boredom. There was no danger to me except for sore muscles. I would be more likely to be killed in a single day working for Jarl Sigurd than in a whole year working for Skapti Oláfsson. It may seem a foolish thing to say, but I would have much preferred fighting beside Sigurd than being a warehouser for Skapti, safe though it was.

The autumn passed, and winter closed in, not with ice and snow as in Iceland, nor even with the storms we often had on Kolnsey, but with fog and mist and endless drizzle. My spirits grew as damp as the weather. I was surprised at how little my comrades seemed to be affected. Through the winter they passed the long evenings gaming and swapping stories and dallying with any available women, and for the most part seemed happy enough. For my part, I had no desire to take part in any of their sport.

Their games were mostly dicing and centered about winning and losing money. I had no money to win or lose, for I was working for a different sort of wage, which I could not add to nor lose from even had I wanted to. As for their stories, what story did I have to tell but the one story that was my life, and who would wish to listen to it? It was tragic and bloody, and not finished in any case. The women in the settlement were of two kinds—either honest and married, or the type who would willingly open her legs for any man who would drop a gold coin into her palm. I had no place befriending the first sort, and any man's interest in the second was over and done in minutes. I avoided both.

As a result, I have never been in a place where I was so surrounded by people, and yet felt so completely alone. My dreams were all of Magnus and Gudrun, whose company now seemed to me to be infinitely desirable, and of my Ingrid and little Thórd, and my dear lost friends the Njálssons. In the morning when I woke to another day of hauling cargo, my hope of completing my oath and finding rest seemed utterly beyond my reach.

Eventually spring did come. It remained wet and cool, but the fog lifted from both the land and from my brain. One day, as I unloaded yet another of the seemingly endless number of ships that came through Myley harbor, a man came to say that Skapti Oláfsson wished to speak with me.

I found him standing in front of his house, hands clasped behind his back, as he watched me approach with his characteristic keen expression. His one-eyed comrade, Asbrand, stood next to him, arms folded across his massive chest.

"So, Kári Solmundarson, you have served your nine months with me, and served it well," he said, as I came up to him. "Did you not realize that your time was at an end?"

"I knew that you would keep track, so there was no need for me to remind you."

Skapti laughed heartily. "You are a shrewd judge of character, Kári. You are right, I know where every copper penny of mine goes, and what every man here does to the last minute. But did you not consider that I might cheat you, and keep you here longer than we bargained?"

In my arrogance—how foolish it seems to me now!—I responded, "Sir, I know a cheat well enough when I see one. I have known many a man who was dishonest, and I can tell such a man for what he is. I know you are honest, and I knew I had no need for concern on that account."

He raised his eyebrows a little. "It is well for you that I am indeed honest. Would you care for a little advice on that account, however?"

"I would listen carefully to any advice you wished to give me."

"Do not be so trusting. You are clearly an intelligent man, and no doubt a fair judge of character. However, you will one day learn that there are men who, under a guise of friendship, will play you false so completely that you may not realize it is so until it is too late to mend the situation. A man like this is careful, careful enough that you, being a trusting man and an honest one yourself, may not recognize such a person for what he is. It is a lesson I have learned by harsh experience. The least trustworthy men may seem the most to be trusted, for it is in their interest to appear honest and true."

"How can one tell, then, who is to be trusted?"

Skapti's smile flashed out. "Trust no one completely, for there are few who deserve complete trust, and how is one to know who those are? Toward those whom you trust partially, keep your eyes open and your brain working."

"I thank you for your concern. As far as trusting others, I will have little enough chance to do so in the future, as I look forward only to further opportunities to complete my revenge upon the men whom I know to be scoundrels and murderers."

Skapti nodded, and his dark eyes searched mine. "I hope for your sake that your struggles are all of this kind. Out in the open, such as one may settle in a fair fight. In the nine months you have been here, you have shown yourself to be unafraid of hard work and able to work well with men of many dispositions and attitudes. If you wish to stay, I would welcome it. If you still desire to go, I will keep my end of the bargain, although I will add that you would be welcome back here should you desire to do so when your quest is over."

"I thank you for your kind words, and even more for your assistance in a matter that is truly no concern of yours. I must go now, and with luck will find this next of my foes, Arni Kolsson by name, who has fled to Wales."

Skapti nodded. "You are single-minded, and I thought it unlikely you would be turned from your path. There is a ship from Wales that put in yesterday. It will be leaving tomorrow morning, and I have arranged with its captain to pay a price of fifty silver pieces for your transportation to the Norse settlement of Asktún on the north coast. Unless he is hiding among the Welsh, which I think is unlikely, there are few other settlements there to which your man can have gone." He frowned thoughtfully. "There is a large island, however, on the northwest tip of Wales, called Öngullsey, which the

Welsh call the Isle of Mona, and there are scattered Norse settlements there. Should you not find him in Asktún, you might search about on Öngullsey. It is a big place, however. It will probably not be as easy to find him as it was to find the unfortunate Glum Hildisson."

"That may be, but my oath leaves me no choice. With your permission, I will go and collect my belongings together in preparation for my departure."

Skapti grinned, a little mischievously. "To be sure, and I wish good luck to you, Kári. I can give you little more in the way of advice, but I will give you the rest of your salary. You truly are either too trusting or have had few dealings with money." He dropped into my hand a little leather bag full of coins. "Fifty silver coins is little enough payment for nine months' hard work. With this, I have compensated you fairly and deducted the fifty coins I paid the Welsh ship captain. The rest is in that bag. It may be useful to you."

I blushed a little from having been caught out in my own foolishness and ignorance, but I thanked him profusely. "My only thought in working for you was that I was working for my transportation. Continuing my quest is important enough to me that nine months' work seemed a fair exchange. Still, I thank you for your fair dealing. I will not forget it."

I took my leave of Skapti Oláfsson and made my preparations for leaving Myley. The next morning, I found myself upon yet another ship, sailing away southward to the strange country of Wales.

The crew of the ship I sailed on were all Welsh themselves, but the first thing I learned was that they did not like to be called Welsh, nor to hear their country called Wales. Those names were, I was told, insults of long standing, names applied to their people and their homeland by the English and meant "foreigners" and "foreign land" in the English tongue. Strange, as the Welsh were themselves here long before the English set foot on the island of Britain. The Welsh call themselves Cymreig and their land Cymru, and so I learned to call it whenever I was in their company.

About half of the crew, including the captain, spoke little Norse, and it was possible to communicate with them only by means of gestures. One young man, who was called Owain, became my friend in our three-week voyage, despite the fact that he knew nothing of my language and I nothing of his. Still, we were able to communicate after a fashion. I learned from him that he had a wife named Angharad, and missed her very much, and after this voyage he planned to stay home for a time and seek his livelihood in another fashion than going to sea. I, in turn, told him some of my own story. I cannot say how much he understood, but his expressions told me he caught at least the gist, for facial expressions go beyond the bounds of language. Some of what we said was translated by a crewman named Huw, who spoke both languages well enough, but most was not. We really had no need. Despite the barrier of language, Owain was a lively and intelligent fellow and a good companion. Strange that I felt less alone here, among men of another land who never spoke my language except when speaking to me, than I did on Myley among Norse Hebrideans like myself.

There was a storm two weeks out that concerned me far more than it did my shipmates. They simply pulled in the sails, tied everything down, and waited it out. I was amazed at how well the flat-bottomed Welsh ship lay on the rushing waves, compared to our narrow, sleek longships, which pitch and roll in even light seas. Longships are faster, but I was more comfortable on this Welsh sailing vessel than I had ever been on a longship, and probably safer as well.

Three weeks after our departure, I was once again set ashore alone, with nothing but the clothes I wore, my sword, a little food and water, and one thing more—the little bag of silver coins that Skapti had given me. Asktún is a little cluster of houses huddled in a cove on the north Welsh coast. It seems far from everywhere, and there are no other Norse settlements within fifty or so miles. Southward, the mountains and forests of north Wales lie forbidding and dark on the horizon. The settlement was completely isolated. Fortunately, it was in no real danger from attack, as the relationship between our people and the Welsh had always been fairly good.

The nominal chieftain of the settlement, although he did not call himself that, was a scurrilous fellow named Thorodd, and he was surrounded by companions even more evil-looking than he himself. I had hardly arrived in his presence before he began to tell me his own tale. All the men there had already heard it many times, I suppose, and he looked upon a stranger as an opportunity to take advantage of a new hearer.

He had come to Asktún, I understood, after narrowly escaping execution for murder in Jorvík, in the northeast of England. It was an interesting story. He had killed a man because the fellow had not paid up after losing a bet, and it was unfortunate for him that the man he killed was the son of a powerful nobleman. Within an hour, he found himself stripped to the waist, with his hands tied above his head to a tree branch and was flogged to within an inch of his life. He was then left hanging there to be beheaded the next morning, with the local headsman guarding him. Somehow, Thorodd was able to free himself and slew the headsman with his own axe, escaping into the woods west of Jorvík. There was a manhunt for him, but they never found him. He holed up in a deep glen near a river, and the search passed him by. Still, he almost died of hunger and from the wounds the whip had left on his back. But he recovered and fell in with some other outlaws and made his way to the west coast of England, and then crossed into Wales. Upon arriving in Asktún, he killed the former chieftain and set himself in his place.

"And here I am still, twenty years later. Alive and no less wicked than before." He looked at me with a challenge in his eye, as if he were expecting me to fight him for the chieftaincy then and there. "What could bring a handsome and noble man such as yourself to such a place as Asktún?" Some of his companions snickered quietly to themselves.

"I am here for one reason only," I told him, attempting to appear reassuring and self-assured at the same time. "I seek a man who has done me great wrong, to bring him to justice as there was no other justice to be found. He is a murderer of women and children and deserves death. He is an Icelander whose name is Arni Kolsson."

Thorodd's eyebrows went up a little, but he shook his head. "Arni Kolsson? I have not heard of any man by that name."

My heart fell, but it was not unexpected. Skapti had warned me that Wales was a large country in which to search for a single man.

"Do I have your permission to enquire among your men, if any have heard word of the man I seek?"

Thorodd shrugged. "Do as you please."

I took my leave of him. But I noticed that as I left, he called two of his evil-looking companions near to him, and they began to speak to each other in whispers, looking at me all the time as they did so.

I went around the village, asking everyone I saw if they had heard of Arni Kolsson, but none had. I was given many sidewise and suspicious glances, as if the inhabitants could not imagine what I was doing in such a place.

One man, somewhat more honest-looking than the others, told me that there were more Norse settlements on the island of Öngullsey, which Skapti Oláfsson had mentioned, and that it was a mere forty miles west of Asktún.

"But as it is an island, how will I get there, having no ship?"

"It is separated from the mainland by a narrow strait, and the Welsh have ferries which cross it, for a price."

I thanked him and said that I would continue my search there. After buying some food from a man who had fish and meat drying on a rack, I set off eagerly enough for Öngullsey, glad to have reason to leave Asktún behind me.

The coastline of north Wales is alternatively rocky and sandy, but it was not difficult walking. I cheered up considerably after I had turned the corner around a headland and could no longer see Asktún, which was one of the more disreputable places to which my quest had taken me. By this time, the sun was setting and I found a sheltered place among the rocks. After eating a little, I prepared to sleep.

It was a clear night with a full moon, and the moonlight glinted on the waves and cast sharp shadows in black and white all about me. I was restless and uncomfortable. When I heard the noise of a stealthy footstep, I was alert and on my feet, sword drawn, in a moment's time.

Facing me were five men, armed with swords and spears. The leader was one of the men who had spoken to Thorodd in whispers as I left his presence. There was also the man who had sold me dried fish and meat, and the honest-looking man who had spoken to me about going to Öngullsey. The other two I did not recognize but were undoubtedly men I had spoken to earlier in the day.

"Steady, now," said the leader, with a faint smile. "You can just put away that nasty-looking sword. We want your little pouch of coins, and we can settle this in a friendly enough fashion if you'll just hand it over. We don't want to have to spill your handsome and noble guts all over this coastline."

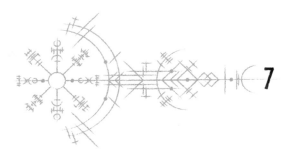

I LOOKED AT MY ASSAILANTS ONE after the other. "What guarantee do I have that you wouldn't kill me anyway, once I gave you my sack of coins?"

The leader put on an expression of mock hurt. "Oh, now, my handsome friend, you mistake us! We give you our word that we'll leave you be after you hand it over. Right, fellows?" His men, with many snickers and surreptitious smiles, all grunted their assent. I caught their unspoken thought toward me—*Here is a coward or a weakling. This should be easy.*

I drew myself up. "The word of a thief means nothing," I said in a fierce voice. "To take my coins, you will have to kill me first. But I warn you, I have killed many men myself, and a warrior of high standing accounted me the best sword fighter in Iceland, shortly before I slew him. So, get you gone before I stain the rocks with your worthless blood!"

The leader's mouth curled into a sneer. "A pity you aren't in Iceland any longer." He threw himself at me, and his fellows came at me from all sides.

I was at first certain that I was a doomed man. Five against one seemed impossible odds. However, I soon realized that the men I faced were inept fighters, and I found that I was able to hold them off. Their own numbers worked against them. The two men holding spears did not want to step back and throw them, for fear of pinioning one of their comrades, and a spear is not terribly effective if all one can do is to stand and strike out with it. Had I not had that advantage, I would undoubtedly have been struck through with a spear before a minute had passed.

I fought that night as hard as I have ever fought, and before long one of my foes had lost his sword hand, and his blade clattered to the ground as he howled and fell to his knees, shrieking with agony, clutching at his wounded arm. I did not want one of the spearmen to take up the fallen sword, so I grabbed it and flung it into the sea. One of the swordsmen, the man who had sold me fish and meat that day, was foolish enough to watch it as it flew out, glittering in the moonlight. His head struck the sand even before the sword disappeared beneath the surface of the pounding waves. At that, one of the spearmen, having no more stomach for fighting, turned and fled into the night. With the fury of battle on me, I gave a great cry and hacked the other's spear in half and struck him through the breastbone with the point of my sword.

That left the leader alone, who was standing, his face all pale skin and dark shadows in the light of the full moon, looking at his fallen comrades with a sick expression. The man whose hand I had struck off lay on his face on the ground nearby and had bled to death as I fought his friends.

The leader held his sword limply in his right hand, knowing full well that if he raised it he would die before it was waist high.

I brought the point of my sword to his throat, and I saw that great beads of sweat were standing out on the man's forehead.

"Did Thorodd order this ambush?" I asked through clenched teeth.

The miserable scoundrel's voice shook as he spoke. "He said that he would bless us if we succeeded but would claim to know nothing of the plan if it failed."

"Give me your sword," I ordered, "or I will gut you like a caught fish."

The man handed over his sword, and I flung it out to join his comrade's in the surf.

"Now, friend, give me a single reason why I should not end your worthless thieving life. In Iceland, your life would be fairly forfeit, and none would lift a finger to stop my striking you down."

"Please," the man gasped. "I beg you. Don't kill me." His eyes widened, and he nearly shrieked, "I can tell you where the man you search for went!"

I half expected something like this from such a man, but Skapti Oláfsson's words about trusting no one rang in my ears. I had already been far too trusting among these people. My blade point did not waver. "Where is he, then?"

"He came through here last year but did not linger long. Then he went on to the settlement at Presthólm, at the northeast tip of the island of Öngullsey."

"If you have seen him, as you claim, what did he look like?"

His eyes turned downward, as he frantically searched his memory. "He is a tall man, slender-built but lithe and strong, perhaps forty years of age. He had chestnut-brown hair which he wore very long, pulled to the back and tied. He was a quiet man, who spoke little, except when spoken to."

I nodded. "Fortunate that you speak the truth. It is indeed Arni Kolsson whom you describe. How did he come to visit your accursed settlement?"

"I can only say what he told us. He said that he had wandered among the Welsh for some time and had learned their language and taken a Welsh wife, but he came to Asktún, wanting to be among his own kind. He found it little to his liking…."

Here I interjected, "I cannot imagine why," but he did not seem to hear me.

"…and went on to Presthólm, where they have a priest and a real chieftain, not a villain like Thorodd."

I smiled grimly. "I wonder how Thorodd would like to hear himself spoken of this way."

His eyes widened with fear. "Don't tell him. He'd have me whipped to death or hanged. In fact," he added, a little desperately, "take me with you. I could be your servant…."

I threw back my head and laughed. Skapti's lesson in trust had been well enough learned. "Little chance of that. Take on as a servant the leader of a pack of thieves and murderers? I'd never sleep, for waiting to feel your knife at my throat over a matter of a few coins. No, get yourself back to your kind, before I change my mind and send you to hell to join your comrades." I waved my blade in front of his throat, and with a cry he turned and fled into the darkness.

I looked about me at the fallen men, and marveled that the weariness had fallen from me like a sodden cloak. I paused only to clean my sword, and, re-sheathing it, began walking again.

The men from Asktún had not yet finished with me, however. Before I had gone fifty paces, there was a rush of wind by my left ear, and a spear flew past, and struck the rocks a few feet ahead of me. The point snapped with a clang, and a shower of sparks flew from the rock. I turned to look behind me, and could not see anyone, but it was clear enough what had happened. Evidently the leader had met up with the spearman who had fled and wished to give one last attempt at stealing my coins. I picked up the spear, and flung it into the sea, and shouted the laughter of relief up at the stars at my narrow escape. Then I turned and once more made my way along the coast.

I walked most of the night, and only two or three hours before dawn did I stop to rest. I doubted that the two who remained of Thorodd's ambush party would have followed me this far, weaponless as they were. Still, I wished to take no chances, and went away from the shore a little, into a small wooded cove. When I was some way into the trees, I found a dry, warm place among last year's fallen leaves at the foot of a large tree and lay my weary body down. I was asleep within minutes.

———————

IT TOOK ME TWO DAYS' WALK to reach the sea crossing to Öngullsey. I saw the island itself before I realized what it was. It looked like a distant headland, on the other side of a wide inlet of the sea. As I followed the shoreline, however, I found that it curved further and further to the south, and I soon realized that what had seemed an inlet was actually a narrow strait. Skapti had told me that there were ferrymen who would take one across the strait. I had no idea where such a crossing could be made, so I kept walking. By the late afternoon of the second day out, I had reached a Welsh settlement along the strait.

As I approached, such a commotion began that I wondered if I could be the cause of it. After a moment, I realized with some astonishment that I was. Children ran away at the sight of me. Women bustled indoors with a great slamming of doors and clattering of shutters over windows. The men looked at me suspiciously, but neither ran away nor attacked. Many pairs of dark eyes flitted over me, and I was suddenly conscious of how different I looked from them. I must have seemed a pale, gawking giant, as they were mostly small and dark and stocky, and I tall, slender, and fair-haired.

I held up my hands, palms outward, in a token that I came in peace, and I pointed at them and said, "Cymreig," the word that my friend Owain had taught me, the word that the Welsh call themselves.

The men first frowned and then a few, at least, smiled, and nodded. I did not then know how to say "Hebridean," or "Norse," in their language. In the end I tapped my chest, and said, "Kári Solmundarson," but that seemed to be too much for them, so I just repeated the gesture and said, "Kári."

One man, older than the rest, came forward, and pointed to himself. "Griffith ap Rhodri."

I reached out to clasp his arm, but he took my hand instead. A strange gesture, but one which no doubt means the same thing. I then pointed off to the island across the strait. "Mona?" I asked, recalling the name that Skapti had told me that the Welsh call Öngullsey, and there was some raising of eyebrows. I had evidently impressed them with my knowledge of Welsh. I had no way to tell them, even had I wanted to, that having spoken those two words, I had exhausted my Welsh vocabulary.

I pointed to myself again, and pointed across toward the island, then I tapped my bag of coins. I knew that I was taking a chance that these men might be as villainous as had Thorodd and his men, but I wanted them to know that I could pay my way across.

Griffith nodded, and taking me by the arm, propelled me further down the shoreline. As we reached the south edge of the settlement, he pointed off further down the coast. There, perhaps a quarter-mile from where we stood, was a collection of little round black boats, drawn up on the shore. He said a few words to one of the men nearby in Welsh, and receiving a positive answer, clapped me on the back and pointed again toward the boats.

I walked off toward the boats. Only the man whom Griffith had spoken to followed me, although the others followed me with their eyes. Then the women and children, seeing that I apparently meant them no harm and was leaving in any case, came back outside, and by the time the Welshman and I had reached the boats, I was being followed by a procession of small children, all babbling and pointing and laughing. When I turned to look at them, however, the nearest scurried away, dark eyes grown large and frightened. But once I turned back they followed again, chattering and laughing.

We reached the place where the boats were beached, and the man who was accompanying me stopped suddenly, and then turned and faced me. I knew his look. It was the look of a merchant demanding pay. I took three silver coins from the pouch, and held them out to the man, not knowing whether they would be enough or were far too much. I reasoned that Skapti had paid fifty for my transportation to Wales, and three to cross a narrow strait seemed fair enough. But the man regarded me with a smile and narrowed eyes, and held up five fingers before my face. Instead I added a single coin to my hand, and looked at him with a smile and a flash of defiance in my eyes. The man thought for a moment, then shrugged, grinned, and took the money.

Together he and I pulled one of the little boats toward the surf, and I was surprised at how light it was. I looked at it more closely, and my surprise turned to astonishment when I found that it was made of animal hide stretched over a wooden frame, but the skin had been tanned by some process that I could not guess. Having grown up near the sea, I greatly wanted to ask how they were made and how seaworthy they were, but my inability to speak their language prevented me. The man recognized my interest as I ran my hand along the interior of the boat, and grinned broadly as we climbed in.

The little boat bobbed easily on the waves, and with a practiced hand the man rowed me across the strait. It took about a half-hour, and by the time I reached the opposite side, it was getting dark. Before getting out, I pointed up and down the coast and said, "Presthólm?"

The man nodded, and reached out and thumped me on the chest, grinning again. "Ah, Presthólm! Y Llychlynaidd." I later found out that this was what the Welsh called all Norsemen, regardless where they live. He pointed off to the right, northeastward, and I followed his finger with my eyes along the coast of the island, to where it was lost in the deepening dusk.

I thanked him in my language, and he responded in his own. We understood each other well enough, I suppose. Then he tossed his little boat back into the waves, and was gone back out into the strait, toward his home, without so much as a backward glance at me.

The evening had turned cloudy. The moon, just past full now, was simply a white spot behind a veil of gray, giving no light at all. I went far enough inland to be above the tide, and cast myself down to the ground to sleep the darkness away.

I woke the next morning long before the sun rose. The first signs of light in the eastern sky had just begun to show. After drinking and eating a little I went on in the direction that the boatman had pointed out. The day looked to be a dreary one, and summer though it was the wind was cold. Then it began to spit rain at me, and by noon it was as drizzly as a winter's day on Myley. My spirits fell with the turn of the weather, and once again the old voices started up, as so often happened when I felt cheerless and alone.

Why was I doing this? It was now four years since Ingrid died, and I was still pursuing this revenge. What good things had I given up to achieve this oath? And what would I truly have when it was done, if ever it was?

I growled aloud, "I will have the satisfaction of knowing that these men paid for the murder of my wife and child." But even that could not awake in my heart the fury that it once would have.

I felt weary of revenge, weary to the bone. As I walked, a strange and disquieting thought came to my mind. I pictured Arni Kolsson, living peacefully in Presthólm with his Welsh wife, and I saw myself coming up and killing him. That I might be killed myself did not even enter my mind, although I knew Arni to be a keen swordsman. I still felt invincible, as if success was inevitable if only I could bear the terrible weariness of carrying my revenge to the last. But then, I pictured Arni's dead body lying on the ground, and his wife weeping over it, and then in my mind she looked up at me, dark eyes cold and accusing.

At that point I realized that it was not twelve men I was destroying. I was destroying far more than that. What of the young wife of Sigurd Lambason, whom I had left fainted on her doorstep? She had probably counted on many more years with her man beside her, and now she was widowed before she had reached the age of twenty-five. What kind of life had I condemned her to, she who had never wronged me? What of the wives and children of the Sigfússons, now without husbands and fathers because of my hand and sword? My wife and child had been killed, yes. But was my revenge truly an even payback, or was I taking far more than had been taken from me, and exacting a terrible price upon women and children who had done nothing to deserve my hatred?

It was the second time that I had felt such misgivings. The first time had been when I looked down on the body of Ketil Sigfússon, noble still in death, and would have regretted what I had done had I allowed myself to do so. How many had tried to sway me from this course? Magnus had. He had called my pursuit of revenge foolishness, saying it was only an evil man who would follow an evil oath simply because he had sworn to do so. Gudrun had tried to heal me, but I would not let her. I recalled Gunnhild, Hjalti Skegg-jason's wife, speaking to me after I had killed Thorkel Sigfússon and Sigurd Lambason—it seemed decades ago—saying, "When evil happens, it is every-one's fault and no one's fault." She had urged me to forget my blaming and instead go live my life. Where would I be, I wondered, had I listened to her? Not walking down some rocky beach in Wales, toward yet another killing, toward yet another destruction of a family's happiness. Probably I would be on the island of Kolnsey, just waking up after a night's sleeping warm and secure in Gudrun Thorvaldsdóttir's arms. And Magnus, dearest Uncle, had you said I was the one who was choosing this? If so, only a fool would claim that I had chosen rightly.

Such were my thoughts as I walked into the settlement at Presthólm at sunrise, trying vainly to gather together what scraps of my anger and hatred were left so that I could justify what I was doing. And, God forgive me, I succeeded. I found Arni Kolsson mending a net on the seashore, and his eyes grew wild and wide when he saw me. The sight of his dismay made my heart leap within me. He snatched up an oar lying nearby, to defend himself with, and I hacked it in half, and slew him. At that moment I heard a great cry from nearby, and a little Welsh woman came running down the shore, and bent over Arni, sobbing bitterly. Then she looked up at me, as disbelief and fear and bitter anger chased one another across her face. Then I looked up toward the settlement, and I saw, framed in the doorway of the nearest house, a little boy of about three years, standing wide-eyed and gaping on the threshold, staring at me and at the two figures on the sand. He had his moth-er's dark eyes, but his hair was long and chestnut brown, just like his father's.

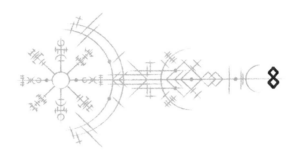

MY FACE BURNING WITH SHAME, AND my heart pounding in my chest as if it would burst asunder, I turned and fled from the accusation in the eyes of the wife and child of the man I had just slain. For some reason the woman had not given the alarm, and I was not pursued. Indeed, no one seemed to be about, to witness me flying back down the shore as if all the demons of hell were chasing me.

It was still early in the morning when I came back to the place where the boatman had left me. The mist was showing no sign of lifting, and I could not see the far shore, even though it was only a mile or two away. There was no way I could signal someone to come get me, and evidently the Welsh did not have a settlement nearby on the island side of the strait. I would have to wait until one of the ferrymen from the other side came across. This meant if there was a pursuit—which I was certain there would be—I would be easily found, waiting here for a boat to come and fetch me.

It is strange how little that thought affected me. The sight of Arni Kolsson's wife and little boy—a child only a little younger than Thórd had been—was like a hammer blow to my heart. I think if I had been approached by a band of men, and told I would be tortured and killed for what I had done, I would not have struggled against them. I now cared little for what happened to me. Rest, and freedom from the horrible oath I had sworn, seemed the only good. I sat down upon a stone and buried my face in my hands.

It was my fortune—I will no longer call it luck—that a ferryman came over from the opposite side only fifteen minutes after I sat down to await my fate. He was transporting three young Welshmen, who were all chatting cheerily among themselves and paid me little heed, but strode off down the shore line away from the settlement at Presthólm. I leapt up, and shouted at the boatman, who turned in some alarm. But I went through a series of gestures, similar to the ones I had gone through the day before, including tapping my bag of coins. The man looked at me curiously, but finally shrugged and allowed me to board his strange, round little boat.

As he rowed away, I looked back on shore, and saw first one, then another, then several more men arriving from the direction of Presthólm. All tall and fair, Norse like myself. They looked angry, and were shouting to one another. Finally one spotted the boat and cried out, "There he is!" and the others shouted, "Vile murderer!" "You shall pay with your life if we catch you!" But they had no boats, and no way to catch us. The Welsh boatman paid them little attention, but I could tell his thought—Crazy Norsemen, running around shouting and waving their fists. Best to ignore them. He looked back at me, a little suspiciously, but I showed no sign of imminent crazy behavior, and he soon turned his attention back to rowing.

As for me, I sat in the boat and bowed my head in shame at what I had done. Strange it is to say—I was one step closer to the completion of my quest, and yet sunk in worse despair than I had felt since the loss of my family.

Upon reaching the far shore, I considered for a moment, and then reached out and handed the entire bag of silver coins to the boatman. His eyes grew wide. It probably contained sixty coins, ten or more times as much as any fair price he could have charged. His suspicious expression altered to a narrow-eyed look of complete disbelief. He turned his palms upward, as if asking a question, and then held up five fingers. I shook my head, and dropped the little bag into his hand, and then left him standing in astonishment on the shore.

I began to walk, giving little thought to my destination. I knew I did not wish to return to Asktún. That would be to leap into the arms of death, after the fight I had with Thorodd's ambush party. On the other hand, walking southward down the coast of Wales would accomplish nothing more than taking me farther from my home. So I began to walk inland, away from the water, and almost immediately the land began to climb into rolling, rocky hills. Because of the fog I could see nothing further of my path, but I cared little, and only the restless energy in my body kept me putting one foot in front of the other. I had little food, and almost no water, but that as well struck no chord in my mind. Most of my brain had become numb, and there was only my body left, resolutely striding toward nowhere.

The only thing that remained in my thoughts was my oath. My wicked, evil, damnable oath, still dominating my mind. I considered what was left for me to do. My remaining enemies were far away. Flosi, the man I had most wished to slay, I had not been able to find the slightest trace of. Kol was in Jorvík in the northeast of England, Grani and Gunnar in Dyrness in the north of Scotland. I had little hope of reaching either of those places on foot, even if I wanted to.

Suddenly, with a measure of complete astonishment, I realized that I was no longer certain that I wanted to.

Every man I killed had brought me closer and closer to the truth—that I was accomplishing nothing by following this oath to the end. And if that was so, should I complete it at all? Kol Thorsteinsson was an arrogant braggart, true, but he was also a man of noble bearing whose participation in the burning of Bergthorshváll had come as a surprise to many people. Grani and Gunnar were petty men, vicious in a small way, whose exile to an out-of-the-way settlement in Scotland was certainly no loss to Iceland. But did they deserve death?

And lastly, Flosi Thórdarson. I suddenly recalled Gunnhild, Hjalti Skeggjason's wife, speaking to me after I had slain Sigurd Lambason and Thorkel Sigfússon, the first two men to die by my oath. She had spoken of Flosi, but at the time her words had passed me by, and had remained unremembered until now. I could hear her voice, as if she were standing before me: "Flosi is no fool either, although I think that he is a good enough man and am still surprised that he allowed himself to get caught up in this evil."

The idea that Flosi himself might not be evil came to me like a dash of icy water in the face. The leader of the men who burned my wife and child, not evil? If that was true, then it cast doubt on my own side of the conflict.

Once again, it was too great a thing to accept, and I forced my mind away from it.

Step after step, stride after stride, up into the trackless woods and rocky hillsides of north Wales. Occasionally I passed a cultivated field, and once or twice I saw a dark face with a pair of darker eyes peering at me curiously, but always with the characteristic suspicion that the Welsh seem to have for the Norse. Each time I did not slow and I was not, so far as I know, followed. I walked until it was so dark that I could not see my hand before my eyes, and then lay down where my last step had ended and fell asleep immediately.

The next morning I exhausted my supply of food. I would have also been without water had I not crossed several small streams which allowed me each time to replenish my little leather water-flask. Hunger sank its claws into me with vicious speed, as I had been on short rations for many days before, and now had nothing at all. But still I walked, and still the terrain rose before me. I left behind the trees and began to thread my way through a rocky land of dry grass and boulders. The rocks were gray and looked ancient in the misty half-light, not fresh and sharp and black as in Iceland, where they come new-forged from the fires of the earth. The air grew cold, although it was late spring. The mist soaked my clothes and they clung to me, dripping and sodden. My body trembled with chill and hunger, and still I went on.

A second day, stride after stride, foot before foot, and still the terrain rose. Another night, and yet another day, and little changed except that I grew hungrier and weaker and my mind became more numb, and still I kept on.

The next nightfall found me among the rocks of high peaks and moors, where the wind whistled disconsolately and unceasingly around me. I shivered painfully, hanging on the ragged ends of exhaustion and despair, as the night closed over me in that strange place, and I felt I was dying.

As I lay there, I thought I saw Ingrid coming to me. She was dressed all in her finery, as she had been the night of our wedding. She smiled, and the wind seemed not to touch the red-gold of her long hair, that fell loose upon her shoulders. She came to me, and uttered not a word, but I sprang up like a man newly awake and eager to meet the day. She placed her hands upon my arms, although I did not feel her touch upon me, and lifted her head to kiss me. I closed my eyes, waiting for the feel of her warm mouth pressed against mine, waiting to feel her soft embrace encircling me and to smell the sweet scent of her hair enveloping my face, but nothing came.

I opened my eyes, and I was alone in the dark. The vision was gone as if it had never been, and the wind was howling like a demon. I threw back my head and shrieked again and again in my torment, and the rocky sides of the sheer cliffs flung my cry back to me in mockery, so that it seemed that the air was full of despairing wails. Then I fell to the ground, senseless.

THE SUN WAS HIGH IN A cloudless blue sky when I awoke. How near to death I had come that night I do not know, but I believe that the warmth of the sunrise saved my life that day. Had another chill and misty day dawned, I would have died of cold up there in the mountains of Wales, with none to hear my last outcry or to witness my last breath. I was still very weak with hunger, and trembled uncontrollably, but after a time I was able to rise and stagger onward.

I cannot say how long I walked. It could not have been far, but it seemed to me to be longer than any trek I have ever taken. I became aware that I was going downhill, and that a green valley had opened up before me. I saw a little house by the side of a clearly marked path descending from the mountains. A man of about my age was standing before it, watching me with a mixture of disbelief and concern. I held up both my hands, palms outward, to indicate that I intended him no harm. Indeed, what harm could I have done him in that state?. But then I staggered, and collapsed to my knees, and just sat there staring stupidly about me.

The man shouted something in his deep, musical Welsh voice, and a woman came running out of the house, followed by a boy of about seventeen years. I half walked and was half carried into the dim interior of the little house, and found myself lying on a comfortable bed. Moments later I was helped to sit up. It was difficult enough even with help. They presented me with hot food. I was only able to eat a little before exhaustion overwhelmed me. I do not recall lying back down, but I must have slept, for the next thing I recall was my consciousness returning, by imperceptible degrees, like the way a distant speck of light, seen approaching from afar, becomes brighter and larger and finally becomes a flaming torch in the hand of a friend.

I opened my eyes to find the slanting rays of the late afternoon sun coming in through the little windows of the house. I do not know for sure, but I believe I had slept through a day and a night and another day. All I knew was that I was warm and alive, but so weak I could not sit up. I turned my head, and found the young man of the household sitting next to me, his eyes wide.

"I must eat." My voice was a hoarse whisper.

He shook his head, uncomprehending, but I heard a noise, and his mother was approaching, with a bowl of hot stew and a large hunk of coarse bread.

The boy helped me to sit up, and the woman placed a board across my lap and set the bowl on it, and I ate ravenously. All the time the boy watched me, his eyes filled with a combination of curiosity and mistrust.

When I had finished, and felt a little strength returning to me, I looked at the boy and smiled, and he ventured a small smile in return.

"Kári," I said to him, and lifting my hand—it felt as if it was fashioned of stone—I touched my chest.

"Dafydd," he said quietly, and touched his own chest.

The woman came up to me to take the bowl and the board, and I said to her, "Thank you."

The corners of her mouth turned upwards. She looked at me in a curious fashion. *"Diolch yn fawr."*

I stared back at her, and she repeated, *"Diolch yn fawr,"* and I suddenly understood that she wanted me to repeat her. So I did my best—the boy laughed at me, and I smiled a little myself—but it satisfied her, and she raised one eyebrow, and nodded to me, then turned and walked away.

I recovered my strength quickly, although my mind was still in darkness, and I dreamed much of my quest and of the killing of Arni Kolsson, and further back, that of Ketil Sigfússon. Nevertheless, I was soon fully myself again, within a week to the day that I had been found on the roadside by Hywel and Siân, which were the names of the man and his wife.

However, even when I was well, I found I did not wish to leave. It was pleasant to be in the presence of people who knew nothing and cared nothing about my past, and who could not have understood me even if I had wished to explain it to them. Dafydd, their son, followed me about and tried to teach me a bit of their language, but his efforts were, on the whole, a failure. Welsh is a subtle and musical language—far too subtle, I am afraid, for me. I did learn some names of things, and was able to put together a few simple phrases, after a few weeks had passed. I learned that the mountains I had crossed were called Eryri, and the part of Wales I was in was called Gwynedd. I learned the names of the various animals on the farm, and the plants they grew for food. I amazed, and no doubt amused, Siân one evening during the meal by asking for more beer in Welsh. Dafydd clapped his hands, and Hywel smiled at me broadly. Siân simply raised her eyebrows and refilled my cup, which was praise enough.

I found the Welsh to be a courteous and kind people, and I undoubtedly breached their laws of courtesy a hundred ways, not least by being unwilling to leave. I stayed with Hywel and his family for two months, until the high summer, and tried my best to pay for my food and bed by giving him help about his farm. It was a small farm, but produced enough grain and milk and meat to sustain their family. I reasoned, I hope rightly, that a farm can always use an extra set of strong arms and legs, and I did my best to serve them well.

Their land was also a place of breathtaking beauty, perched as it was on the shoulders of the tall gray mountains, and overlooking a brilliantly green valley. It stirred my heart every time I looked upon it. What I found there, for a little while, was peace, and escape from the burden of my oath. For now, I saw, I did wish to escape it, yet I felt I had no power to do so. As the summer turned the fields of grain to ripening gold, I knew that I had to leave once more, and despair came weighing back down upon me.

I tried to explain to Dafydd, who of the three seemed to understand the most from my halting, broken Welsh. I used copious gesturing, and failing that, supplemented my speech with Norse words that he certainly did not comprehend, but still I think he understood me well enough. I told him that I had to leave, that I needed to find a place called Jorvík—the name seemed to mean nothing to him—and that I did not want to be traveling here when winter struck. This he seemed to understand, and he made sounds like the wind and waved his fingers in the air. "Eira, llawer iawn." Then he wrapped his arms about his chest and mimicked a shiver.

I nodded. I wasn't sure what he had said, but cold, snow, ice, whatever it was he meant, would not bode well for traveling. I repeated his shiver, and pointed toward the east, and asked, "Is it cold in winter further east of here? Or only in the high mountains?"

He frowned, and pointed east himself, and said, *"Lloegr,"* evidently a name for a land that lay that way—far away or over the next rise, I did not know. I pointed down toward the valley, and said, questioningly, *"Lloegr?"* and he laughed a little and shook his head, then made a gesture with his hands— far away, far from here. I shrugged. What importance did the name have, I wondered? What he was telling me seemed unimportant, and I disregarded it.

I asked him if it was warmer there, further east. He evidently understood that, and tugged on his shirt front as if trying to cool himself, and laughed again. At this point, Hywel came up, and Dafydd began speaking with his father so quickly that I could not catch a single word, although I gathered that I and my questions were the topic of conversation.

I interrupted them, catching on Hywel's sleeve, and slowly began to say in Welsh, "I go, soon, tomorrow maybe. Must go before cold." I felt like I was a child again, forming my first sentences, but he understood, and his face became serious.

He went inside to get Siân, and she came outside, drying her hands on a cloth. There was a quick exchange, and then Hywel said something to Dafydd, who said to me, slowly in Welsh, "You may stay here if you wish."

I smiled at them. "I cannot."

Then, the question I had dreaded. Siân asked, with her typical bluntness, "Why?"

My smile faded. "I have work to do." I pointed off east. "There."

Hywel frowned, and I saw a hint of unease in his eyes. *"Yn Lloegr?"*

There was that name again. *In Lloegr,* he had said. I shrugged, and pointed east again.

Hywel made a motion toward me like someone striking with a spear. "They fight much there now," he said, speaking slowly and painstakingly. He looked at Dafydd for support, for more words to explain what he meant, but the boy simply looked back at him helplessly.

"How do you know?" I asked, but I evidently said it incorrectly. All that I got in response was silent bafflement. I could guess well enough where he had heard the news, however. His house was evidently a waystation for people traveling both out of and into the high mountains to the west, and he had

many visitors from both directions. Everyone who came through brought
him news. I had witnessed many such conversations, but the discourse was
always too rapid for me to follow.

He still seemed uneasy that I might be going that way, and so I smiled
reassuringly and patted the hilt of my sword. Hywel shook his head. "Many
men, much fighting. Not just one man for you to fight alone."

I did not know what to do. I was torn asunder, half of me wishing to
remain behind with these kind people who had saved my life, and the other
half pulled forward, for if I remained here my oath would never be completed. I shrugged again, and said, "I must go." He then shook his head, shrugged
as well, and gave up trying to dissuade me.

Thus it was that I found myself the following morning, taking my leave
of Hywel, Siân, and Dafydd, who stood before their doorstep solemn-eyed
and unsmiling. Siân had packed my food bag with as much as she could fit
into it, and my little water-flask was replaced with a larger one of theirs. I
had been embraced warmly and wished well, and I thanked them in their
own language and in my own. Then, under their dark, somber eyes, I turned
and went downhill toward the green valley and toward Lloegr—whatever
land that would prove to be.

I saw no sign that day of the fighting Hywel had warned me about, nor
for the next three days. I crossed the valley I had seen from their mountain-
side home, and kept on in the same direction as it swept upward into rolling,
tree-covered hills, dotted here and there with little farms. In the clearings
I saw sheep and cattle and goats. I was watched with amazement by many
pairs of eyes, and the amazement swelled to astonishment when I cried out,
"Bore da!" which is the greeting in their language. I helped an old man repair
a stone wall—an afternoon's work, and in payment he filled my bag with as
much dried meat, bread, and cheese as it could hold.

On the fourth day out, I left Wales.

The transition was a gradual one, yet I knew when it happened, when I
had left behind the land that its people call Cymru. I saw fewer small, dark-
haired and dark-eyed folk, and began to see faces that resembled my own,
light-eyed and blond. I saw many times from a distance clusters of buildings
that I knew to be towns, and I had seen nothing of the sort in Wales. There
people seem to live most often in separate farm houses, much as they do in

Iceland. I saw men on horseback, which I had also not seen since I left Iceland. Then I passed two men who were arguing heatedly while leading a cow away by a halter. They ignored me completely, but I listened to them closely until they passed out of earshot. The language was not Welsh. It sounded more like my own tongue, but I could not understand it.

So, this was presumably Lloegr, but what land, exactly, was Lloegr? There was none to ask the question to who could have understood me enough to answer it. Still I kept walking resolutely eastward, although I did not know where my path would end.

In the days that followed, I began to see signs of the fighting about which Hywel had warned me. I came across a burned village, filled with skeletons picked clean by crows. The branches of a spreading tree held odd fruit—three men in battle dress, hanged by their necks. Their hands were tied behind them, their heads pulled askew, and the wind made the ropes creak as they swayed and turned.

All through this land, there was enough food at hand that I never went hungry. The countryside seemed depopulated, and everywhere there was unharvested fruit on trees and berries on vines and bushes. At several burned-out houses I helped myself to what was left of the garden, and wondered what had become of the unfortunate owners.

One day I came across a great battlefield, where stray arrows and broken spears littered the ground like shingle tossed up onto the beach by a storm. Bodies lay everywhere, and in the armor and shields of some I saw designs like those I had seen in Iceland, and I wondered at the reason for the similarity. I picked up a bow and a few arrows as I crossed the battlefield, and for some days afterwards I ate well enough. I have little talent at archery, but still I was able to kill several rabbits and birds. The meat was savory and delicious, although I soon ran out of arrows.

About two weeks after I left Wales, I crossed paths with a young man whose long fair hair and ruddy complexion was so like to my own that I said, in my own language, "How did you find your way here, to this strange land?" before I could stop myself.

He looked at me, a little taken aback, and then smiled. "I live here."

His speech was a little different than mine, but perfectly understandable. I had not realized how much I had missed being with someone who could speak my language. It was infinitely comforting, and all I could think of was that I wished to speak with him for a long time, and sate myself with words. "What is this land called?"

He looked at me as if I were not in my right mind. "You walk in a land and don't know its name?"

"That is so, for I have come from Wales and do not know what this place is called."

"It is England. But where you stand now is the Danelaw, and is not under the rule of England's king but the king of Denmark, Sveyn Haraldsson, called Forkbeard, who has recently conquered all this land."

"You came with him, then, as a warrior?"

The man smiled. "No, I am no warrior, but a simple farmer's son. My family has lived here for four generations, and came to this land in the time of Eirík Bloodyaxe, a hundred years ago. Since then it has gone back and forth, back and forth, between England's rule and the rule of Norway, Denmark, Sweden... who can keep up with it? I don't much care who rules the land as long as they leave us alone, but at least King Sveyn speaks the same language as we do."

"Do you live near here?"

He nodded and pointed away north, the direction from which he had come. "I am going now to bring a message to my mother's father, who lives a mile south of here. My grandfather lives alone, and while the fighting was going on he thought himself safer, for some reason, in his cottage than with my father and mother, and he thought that if he left his little hut unoccupied, that the warriors might destroy it. I do not know what an old man such as he could have done to protect it, but old people can be stubborn and he refused to leave. But now that the battles are done, for the time at least, my father has sent me to ask him to come live with us on our farm near Jorvík."

"Jorvík?" I cried, and once again the young man seemed startled.

"Yes, that is what it is called. The city which lies in yonder valley," and here he pointed north, "about five miles up that way, along the banks of a great river. The English call it York, but Jorvík it has always been to me and my family." He frowned. "Do you know the place?"

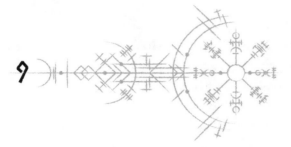

JORVÍK.

I stood there marveling at my fate after the young man had gone his way. I had ceased calling it luck, but it was nevertheless astonishing. It was as if there was a power that would not let my oath die. I had wandered the island of Britain, with no thought further than going eastward as far as I could, and had ended a mere five miles away from the place to which Kol Thorsteinsson had fled.

I turned and began to walk northward.

I had been to Jorvík once before, many years earlier, when I was in the employ of Jarl Sigurd of Orkney, but that time I had come from the other direction, from the sea. I had not recognized the place until I was told where I was.

Jorvík is a big city, one of the biggest I had yet seen, and as I approached it I began to see much activity. There were men on horseback, and others driving wagons, fields being worked by thralls, small houses near the road-side, some of which had been damaged in the recent war. I was not given a second glance.

I entered into the city of Jorvík not knowing where I would go, nor how I would find food. I had no money. There were no untenanted gardens to raid here. I walked through the muddy streets, hearing many voices—some speaking my language, some speaking what I presumed was English. And buildings, buildings, everywhere buildings! I remembered that from the first time I had come here, twenty years earlier. Everywhere I looked were houses, shops, taverns, smithies, and a good many buildings whose purpose I could not guess.

I thought to take care of my lack of food first, and found a merchant selling fruit and vegetables. I thought perhaps that I could pay for my food by working for him. But when I approached his roadside stand, he scowled and shouted something unintelligible at me, in apparent but inexplicable anger.

"He doesn't like our kind," said a friendly voice behind me, and I turned to see a tall, smiling youth with hair so light that it was nearly white, and crystalline blue eyes.

"How do you mean?"

"Eadric doesn't serve Danes, nor Norse either, and one of the two you clearly are."

"True enough. How can he tell? I have seen Englishmen fair enough, although none as fair-haired as you are."

He grinned. "I can't say, but Eadric can tell every time, before a man even opens his mouth."

"How can a stranger get food here? I am without money, and know no one here in Jorvík save one man, and he would be unlikely to give me anything but the sharp edge of a sword." I paused, wondering if I had said too much.

But the boy just grinned wider. "Well, you'll get nothing but harsh words and no food around here. I suggest you try the church. The Archbishop is a hard man, you'll get little from him. Nor from Father Abbot, I'm sorry to say. But there's a deacon, Ruthric by name, who would help you. He speaks both English and Norse, and is loved by both people. One of the few you can say that about. He is a kindly old man, and can often be found puttering around the church and the abbey grounds. He has hardly any hair and looks like a strong wind would blow him away, but he's tougher than he looks at first. I am sure that he would spare you a morsel or two."

I recalled seeing the church the last time I had been here, and after asking some brief directions, I set off to go there. I threaded my way among the crowded streets, and near the north end of the city found a tall, ornate wooden church large enough, I thought, to accommodate most of the population of the city. I opened the door and walked from the noise and chaos into the dark, silent peace within.

There was no one within. I saw rows of empty benches, and upon a raised platform in the front was the simple altar. My footsteps echoed as I walked down the aisle, and I suddenly felt I was in the presence of something holy. It was frightening in a way I had never been frightened before, and the knowledge of the sins I had committed in pursuit of my oath came down upon me. It brought me to a halt. On impulse, I went up to the altar, genuflected in front of it and crossed myself, then knelt down, head bowed before it. I do not know what I hoped—that God would speak to me and release me from what I had sworn, or that He would whisper forgiveness in my ear, or that He would spur me on to finish my vengeance. In any case, nothing happened. The church remained dark and still, but no peace came to me, and the Lord spoke no word in my ear.

Had God abandoned me, then? In the years since I had accepted Christianity, I had always thought that I followed God's law as well as any. I fully expected to reach heaven after I died, and the thought that my actions could possibly damn me never crossed my mind. Now, suddenly, I felt rejection from every part of the dark interior of the church. I said, in a small voice, "God, forgive me for what I have done..." and I heard only my own voice, echoing back at me, mocking, and no other response came.

I bowed my head. Was that the answer, then? Had I finally crossed the line from salvation to damnation, with the killing of Arni Kolsson before his own wife and child? Or had it been even sooner? Perhaps I had damned myself long ago. Who could tell?

A swell of defiant, despairing anger swept me. Well enough. If I was damned, then I would at least complete my oath. If it was too late for my salvation, too late to stand on the side of the good men of the earth, then why should I strive to be good myself any more? Evil men had taken much from me, and in swearing the oath, I had given up everything else I had but the oath itself. Were I to give up the oath, would I not be left with nothing at all?

Finally, in some despair I stood, then turned and went out through a little side door into the churchyard. I could see the gate of the abbey in front of me, and the sweep of the street curving before it. There were many people about—men in the robes of the church and men in ordinary street clothes, women carrying baskets, well-mannered children with their parents and wild children scampering about and laughing despite the proximity to the forbidding bulk of the church.

In a quiet corner on the other side of the churchyard lay a little house, and crossing from it toward me was a tiny, bent old man with wispy white hair, dressed in a black robe that seemed too big for him. I knew that this must be the man I sought, and I went up to him, and he squinted shortsightedly up at me.

"Are you the Deacon Ruthric of Jorvík?"

"I am." His voice creaked like two branches rubbing against each other.

"My name is Kári Solmundarson. I have come from far away to Jorvík, and I have no food nor money, and no place to stay. I wish to know if you might have somewhere that I could shelter. As for food, I can work for my food..."

He interrupted me. "You are a fighting man.

It was not a question.

I looked down at him, and felt my cheeks suddenly burning, as if in shame. Yet what shame was there in being a warrior? There seemed no use in denying it. "Yes,"

"I knew it. Every word you speak is like a sword blow. You do not have to fight your way into here. This is God's place, and all of God's creatures are here welcome. There is a house within the precincts of the abbey where travelers stay, and where we lodge men who claim sanctuary within the church, and they can feed you there as well. You need give no thought to that."

"I have no need to receive alms...."

He looked up, with a glance of surprising keenness in his watery eyes. "Do you not? You come into the city with no food, no money, no place to stay. If you are not in need, who is? It is only your pride which is stung."

I said nothing. He was right.

"Now, come along, and I will show you where the lodging house is, and I will introduce you to the cellarer. He will get you food enough."

I thanked him profusely.

As we walked, he looked up at me curiously. "Where have you come from? And what brings you to Jorvík?"

"I am from the Hebrides, but I came through Wales to here. I have come to look for a man named Kol Thorsteinsson, whom I am told lives here."

Ruthric nodded, and smiled a little. "Yes, Kol. He has made quite a name for himself in his four years here. He once was a warrior, I think, like you are now, but he has a good heart."

I looked down at the little deacon, trying not to show my surprise at how he had described my foe. "You know him, then?"

"Oh, yes. I know nearly everyone here in Jorvík, I think, except the new folk, the Danes, who come and go so quickly that I never have a chance to meet them. But Kol I know well enough, for he gives well to the church and is known to be a holy and God-fearing man."

"Where does he live?"

"There is a fine house on the west end of the city, that he purchased when he arrived here four summers ago. He lives there with only a few servants." He looked up at me, a little suspiciously, I thought. "How do you know him?"

"I knew him when I lived in Iceland." I did not explain further. Ruthric did not press me and we walked on toward the abbey.

"Brother deacon," I said, after a moment of silence between us, "you said that men ask for sanctuary here. What sort of men?"

He shrugged. "Any who have committed crimes. If they come to the church door and hold to the ring that is there, they can claim sanctuary. Then they are given a month to leave the country. If they stay after that, or if they return here at some later time, their lives are forfeit. Until they leave they are given lodging within the abbey walls, and the law may not touch them until the month is up."

I thought of the crime I was planning to commit, and wondered if I might soon be relying upon sanctuary myself. Trying to keep my voice light, I said to Ruthric, "They have a similar way in Iceland, where men may be outlawed for various offenses, although it is the law of the state and not of the church which governs it."

"Here, it is both."

I was shown where my lodging would be—a simple cot in a house within the abbey walls—and I was given food, plain but filling. Then Ruthric took his leave of me and returned to his duties, leaving me alone with my misgivings.

In the church I had decided I would indeed fulfill my oath, but now it seemed impossible. How could Kol Thorsteinsson, whom I knew to be arrogant and a man of quick temper, have become a respected and holy man, a well-known citizen of the community of Jorvík? I was dismayed. I felt more and more that fortune was turning against me. The first of my enemies I had killed in Iceland, where my plight was well known to all, and there my actions would at least be understood, if not condoned, by all. Glum I had caught up with in a Norse settlement where he had established himself as a swaggering lout, and his employer had been neither surprised nor upset when my vengeance had caught up with him. Arni had gone to Wales, and there I had been on more tenuous footing. I would probably have been killed if I had been caught, but by luck I had escaped without harm.

But here, in a big city in a strange land? Were I, an unknown wanderer, to go into the house of a wealthy and well-liked man and slay him, what would happen? I hardly had to ask myself for an answer. It was obvious.

I finished eating. Suddenly the turmoil and uncertainty resolved itself. Why had I come to Jorvík, then, if not to strike down Kol Thorsteinsson? I told myself that I had no choice, that I had sworn to do this, and then had affirmed my oath that morning in the church. The consequences were un-important. If I was caught and executed, then that would simply be my fate, unpleasant as the prospect sounded. I had never worried about my own like-lihood of surviving, and I could not start doing so now.

With that decision made I stood, and thanked the brother cellarer for the food. I took my leave first of the refectory and then of the abbey grounds.

The streets of Jorvík are meandering and narrow, and it was only after I had asked for help several times—and twice simply been given a glare by peo-ple who either did not speak my language or did not wish to admit that they did—that I found myself standing before the house of Kol Thorsteinsson.

It was indeed a fine house, ornate and well-built. I wondered how he had been able to afford such a structure. I knew he had much wealth in Iceland, but he must have brought considerable money with him into his exile. He seemed to have established himself here with some permanence, and I won-dered if he planned on returning at all. Kol, alone of the older members of the band I was pursuing, was unmarried. Perhaps he had decided to start a life here in a new place, where none knew what he had done.

Almost none. Here I was, to bring justice out of his past. Setting my teeth, I strode to his door, and rapped on it sharply.

A servant boy answered the door, and looked up at me questioningly.

"Is your master, Kol Thorsteinsson here?" I said in a grim voice.

The boy nodded. "Yes, he is."

"Then get him for me, please."

He turned and jogged back into the house. A moment later, Kol came to the door, wearing a broad smile, as if he expected to see a friend waiting for him at his doorstep. To my surprise, I saw little of the arrogance in his face that I had seen there before, and I wondered at the change in him.

Even so, the smile crumbled into disbelief when he saw that it was me, and he stood for a moment in silence.

"Kári Solmundarson," he finally said, his voice quiet. "I never expected to see you again."

"I am certain that you did not. Nevertheless, I have found you."

Kol nodded. "It was inevitable, I suppose, that you would catch up with me. I should not have run, but should have gone to face you after the Assembly. I was a different man then."

"You look the same to me," I snarled.

The smile returned. A faint one, but still, he smiled. I had seen men smile in the face of death before, but it had always been from defiance. This looked different. He looked tranquil, accepting, almost glad. I did not understand it, and it disturbed me.

"Very well, Kári," he said calmly. "You have found me. I suppose you have found all the others, too?"

"No," I said. "Flosi, Grani, and Gunnar remain alive. The rest are all dead at my sword."

He nodded. "You have done very well, I suppose, in taking God's vengeance into your own hands. I will be the next, I suppose, to feel your blade. Very well, I am ready. I have faith that God sees what happens, and I hope He will take from my accounts a little of the suffering for which I am destined in purgatory, because I am soon to suffer at your hands, I think."

I was completely unnerved by his words. "Take out your sword, Kol Thorsteinsson," I demanded. "I know you to be a keen fighter, and I would not strike down an unarmed man."

He laughed—he actually *laughed!*—and said, "My sword? I sold it soon after my arrival here. As for striking down an unarmed man, I fear you will have to do so, as I will not fight you."

Kol's words stung me, pointing out as they did my own arrogance and wickedness. I could not stand the thought of this man, who had killed my wife and child, standing there in judgment of me. I wished only to stop his words, to stop his tranquil smile, which burned me like fire.

I cut him down upon his own doorstep.

I looked down at him as he lay dying, and I saw that he was still smiling.

I glanced up, and saw the little servant boy peering around the door, eyes wide. As I turned to flee, I heard him cry out, *"Murder!* Stop him! He has slain my master!"

My feet pounded down the muddy street, and behind me I heard the sound of pursuit. I ran faster, flying and dodging among the carts, merchants, children, dogs, women carrying baskets, men leading cattle and goats. Still the pursuit grew. I could hear it, although I did not turn to look. I knew what the outcome would be if I was caught, and remembered the villainous Thorodd's handling at the hands of men in Jorvík. Then the thought crossed my mind—was I now in the leagues of men such as Thorodd?

I continued to run until my legs felt as if they were aflame. The streets twisted and turned before me. I feared I would get lost or trapped. But then I saw the massive, peaked roof of the church before me, and I ran up to it, and grasped the heavy brass ring on the door. Only then did I turn to look at the crowd that pursued me.

Most were armed with something—sword, pike, pitchfork. It looked as if there were thirty or so men, shouting angrily at me. I held on to the ring with an unbreakable grip, and in a quiet voice which nevertheless seemed to fly out over the heads of the crowd and still their furious voices, I said a single word.

"Sanctuary."

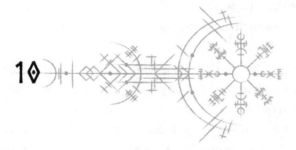

10

TWO THINGS HAPPENED. FIRST, THE CHURCH door swung open, dragging me with it. I would not let go of the ring, which I felt was the only thing between me and death at the hands of the mob. Behind the door stood an imposing figure of a man, very tall, dressed in black robes, flanked by several other clerics.

Secondly, a well-dressed man came pushing his way through the crowd, an angry expression on his face, and the two men faced each other across me.

"My Lord Archbishop," said the man from the crowd, "this man has killed Kol Thorsteinsson."

"He has claimed sanctuary," responded the robed man behind me, in a deep, rich, musical voice. "You know as well as I do, Thorulf, that you cannot touch him."

The man scowled, but did not respond.

The Archbishop looked at him down the length of his aristocratic nose, and his eyes glittered dangerously. "Now, do your job as Sheriff, and disperse this mob from in front of the Lord's house."

The Sheriff looked at me and said, through clenched teeth, "One month. Then the rope goes around your neck and you'll find yourself dancing in midair." But at a further glare from the Archbishop he backed down, and walked back into the crowd, saying, "Go on, go on home. You can't do anything here." Muttering among themselves, the crowd dispersed, with many dark backward glances at me, and a few surreptitious ones at the Archbishop.

The Archbishop now turned his gaze upon me, and said, "Follow me." With some reluctance, I followed him into and then through the church, and back outside through the door on the side. The other churchmen followed as well. Then we went around the back of the church to another building, a wooden house even more ornate than Kol's house was. All the time neither the Archbishop nor the other churchmen uttered a word.

He went into the house, and at a word, dismissed the other clerics. Then he led me back into a little, dimly lit room where there was a large desk. The Archbishop sat down behind it, and motioned me to sit as well, and he tented his long, pale fingers and looked at me.

"Now, tell me, and do not lie to me and compound what you have done. Did you kill Kol Thorsteinsson?"

"I did."

He nodded. "Why did you do so? Were you trying to rob his house?"

"No. I killed him because Kol was one of a band of twelve men who killed my wife and child and my wife's whole family."

His eyes narrowed. I suddenly thought he looked a dangerous man. "I have already told you not to lie to me. There is no point in it. You have claimed sanctuary, and admitted what you have done. You will be given a month to leave, or your life will be forfeit. Now, I know Kol Thorsteinsson well, and I know that he cannot have done the thing you tell me he did. Therefore, you are lying. I ask you once again—tell me truthfully why you have killed him."

I met his eyes steadily. "I have told you honestly. I cannot change my story, because what I said was the truth."

There was a pause. "You are expecting me to believe that Kol Thorsteinsson, who has been a fine and honest merchant here for four years and has given much to the church, is a murderer of women and children? With no one's word but yours for support?"

"I have none here to support me, but that does not change the fact that I speak the truth. Many men know the truth of what I say, and were they here they would tell you so."

He frowned at me. "You are a stubborn man, and my heart tells me that

you are lying. However, you have claimed sanctuary and your wicked false-
ness does not change that. Should you wish to confess your sins, the Father
Abbot will hear your confession. I suggest you look to the health of your
own soul."

"My Lord Archbishop," I said softly, "I think that it is too late to give
thought of that."

At that, he looked at me some moments, his lips tight and his eyes glittering with disapproval. Then he called one of his servants to accompany me
back to the lodging in the monastery.

Sitting on my cot, I gave some thought to my position. Very soon I decided that I should leave as soon as possible, and only take advantage of another free meal and a night's sleep before I went. There seemed no need to
remain here in a place where I could accomplish nothing but to put my life
at further risk.

By this time it was evening. I stood and went to the refectory, where a
number of churchmen and a few travelers were eating. The brother cellarer was as friendly as ever, and once again I ate well. He cheerfully gave me
enough to stock my bag for the next day's journey and more.

As I was eating, Deacon Ruthric came up to my table, shaking his head
dolefully. He seated himself on the bench near me. "My son, my son. Why
have you done such a thing as what they say you did? I regret my ever telling
you where Kol lived. Had I known you to be a common murderer, I would
not have done so. To think that I told you about sanctuary as well! You have
played me false, very false, and now I have the weight of Kol Thorsteinsson's
murder on my soul."

I leaned forward. "Do I strike you as a dishonest man?"

Ruthric seemed caught off guard by the question, but nonetheless he looked
at me appraisingly, his mouth open a little and his watery eyes narrowed. "Had
you asked me that this morning, I would have said no. Now, a man who would
murder such a one as Kol? Of him I would believe any sort of evil thing."

"Brother deacon, I swear to you that what I am about to tell you is true. I
believe myself to be already damned myself by my actions, but if I am not, let
me be damned now if I am lying."

Ruthric looked scandalized by the oath I had spoken, and drew away a
little. "Go on."

I spoke in a low voice, so that none else could hear me. "Kol Thorsteins-son and eleven other men deliberately burned the house in which I lived, five years ago. In the flames died my wife and young son, my wife's three brothers, and my wife's parents, and their old servant-woman."

Ruthric looked at me in silence.. "You told the Archbishop this?"

"I did."

"And he did not believe you?"

"No."

Again, there was a pause. "I would certainly not, either, wandering stranger that you are. Easier to believe that you are a common murderer or robber. Except...." He stopped.

"Except what?"

He looked up at me, and I saw the quick flash of understanding in his expression. "Except what I heard Kol say, shortly after he had arrived. Kol's confessor is the Father Abbot, and what has gone between them is solely their business and the Lord's." He swallowed, a little nervously, but then went on. "When Kol first arrived, he did everything he could to establish himself as a holy and respectable man, and gave a great gift to the church. But he came here one day, and asked me who might be his confessor, that he had a great sin to confess and wished it taken from his shoulders. When I told him that the Father Abbot was away for a day, he became very agitated, and said his fear was increasing daily that he might die unshriven. I told him that the Lord heard him, and not to worry, that the Father Abbot would be back the next morning. Then, God forgive me, my curiosity was too great to forebear, and I said, 'It is difficult to imagine a fine, God-fearing man as yourself committing such a great sin.' Kol looked at me, deep shame in his eyes, and said, 'Brother deacon, it is something which will haunt me until the day I die.' But he did not say what it was."

"I know what it was," I said. "And now you do, as well."

Ruthric looked thoughtful. "Yes. Perhaps I do." Then he looked up at me. "I am glad to hear that you are not a common murderer. Somehow, you didn't seem the type. Nevertheless, young man, remember that the Lord has said, *'Vengeance is mine.'* You are taking the Lord's place, and no good can come of that, to you or to anyone."

I looked at him long, and said, "That may be. The weight of that sin be on my soul, along with the weight of many others. Such a weight as will break my back before I can leave it behind, I think. Nevertheless, I have sworn to bring to the sword all twelve of the men responsible for that hideous deed, and there remain only three."

"If you know it is wrong, then perhaps you should consider letting the remaining three go free."

"I cannot do so. I have given up all I have for the oath. Now the oath is all I have."

Ruthric shook his head. "May God forgive you."

"I think it is too late for that." I stood. "But I thank you for believing me."

He too stood, and wordlessly left the refectory. I left as well, and went to the lodging house, and dropped onto my cot. Would you expect me, in such a state of despair, to have spent a restless night dreaming of hellfire? Strange creatures humans are. That night I fell asleep quickly and easily, and any dreams I had were gentle and unremarkable.

In my travels I had become accustomed to waking early, and light was barely beginning to show in the eastern sky when I awoke. I thought it better to leave quickly. Although I had been guaranteed sanctuary, I had no idea whether the townspeople would honor it if I showed myself outside the abbey walls. I had nothing to gather together. I simply dressed, strapped on my sword, shouldered my food bag and my water flask, and walked out.

Few people were about, and I was fortunate not to encounter any of those who had pursued me the day before, or perhaps I was simply unrecognized as I walked down the streets and out of the town in the half-light before sunrise. It was a cool morning. The year was already turning toward fall, and I knew if I wished to go to Scotland, that I would have to leave soon before the winter storms started.

I walked down the road from the town, heading east simply because that was the way I had been walking before. When I had walked well out of Jorvík, I asked a farmer, who was out early gathering hay into bundles, where the nearest seacoast settlement was.

He looked up at me, his eyes narrowed. "Why?" he asked. He spoke with an accent and I knew then that he was English, but at least he had understood my question and was willing to speak to me.

"I need to leave here. I have been outlawed."

He nodded. "Get you hence, then, and take the rest of your countrymen with you. Whitby is the nearest place you will find any ship to bear you. It is fifty miles that way." He pointed off toward the northeast.

I wished to ask him more, about what sort of ships put in there and whether I might find one to take me to Scotland, but he had turned his broad back to me and I did not persist.

I set off over the hills in the direction he had pointed. The cool day gave way to rain, and as the hills rolled higher and higher before me into bracken-covered moors, the wind picked up until I was walking into a stinging gale. I clutched my cloak about me, but it helped little. It was not nearly as cold as it had been in Wales, and I was now well-fed and well-rested rather than hungry and exhausted, as I had been then, but nevertheless I felt I was trying to walk as a huge, cold, weighted hand continually pushed me backwards. I was nearly crawling by the time I stopped for the evening. There was still at least an hour's light before me, but I could go no farther. I was weak as a child, and I sat on a rock outcropping to eat my cold and cheerless meal before trying to compose myself to sleep as best I could in that inhospitable place.

Then, I turned around to survey the path I had trodden, and I realized that I had the entire vale of Jorvík at my feet, and had been sitting with my back to one of the most beautiful spectacles I have ever seen. I stood, silent with awe.

Despite the drizzle, I could see for miles. I knew I had been progressively getting higher and higher—my aching calves would have told me that had I not known. The last climb had been sheer agony, seeming nearly vertical, but it brought me up onto the top of the highest moor in the area. From that vista I could see the veils of rain swirling downward like curtains of gauze, shifting and parting in the wind. As I faced west, looking out over the valley, the sun broke through the lowest edges of cloud just before setting, and the veils of rain became shot through with gold and scarlet, and the undersides of the gray clouds suddenly lit up as if afire. It lasted but a moment, then dimness fell about me again, and the wind caught at my cloak and made it snap about my legs.

I sat down, feeling breathless and exultant, reveling in the beauty of the world. Then I remembered the rejection I had felt in the church in Jorvík, and I realized that such beauty was not made for me. In the oath I had sunk my heart, and the oath was all there was. If there was beauty and love and joy left in the world at all, I had chosen not to embrace those things but to cling to blood, pain, misery, and death.

I had done it. I had chosen. Uncle Magnus had been right, but it had taken me over a year to realize it. It was I, in my arrogance, who had made the choice, and now, what did I have left but what I had chosen?

I lay down on my face in the wet bracken, shivering and alone, and I wept for all that I had given up of my own free will.

It took me three days to reach Whitby. It was the hardest walking I had done since leaving Wales, all up and down steep-sided moors and glens, and the weather was uniformly gloomy and damp. It was only in the last five miles that the hills began to slope downward, imperceptibly at first, but finally in a great sweep toward the sea. And I heard the cry of sea-birds, which brought my heart into my throat with the loneliness of their cries.

The hills ended in a line of cliffs, upon which sits the great Abbey of Whitby. I went past it without stopping. I went down to the little settlement that huddled along the edges of the harbor.

Like most such settlements, it was a babel of voices of many sorts—harsh and kind, high-pitched and deep, shouted and quiet, English and Norse and others besides. I wandered among the people there for a while, and finally found a tall, red-haired man who was shouting in Norse to some workers busy shaping a timber for a mast.

"Is there a ship here which could take me to Scotland?"

He rounded on me, scowling. "Do I look like I have time to answer stupid questions?" he snarled at me.

I shrugged. "I suppose not. But I ask only for a yes or a no. Do you know of a ship here which might take me to Scotland?"

His scowl became even fiercer. Then he gestured angrily up toward another man, stout and fair-haired, who was supervising the unloading of a bunch of casks from a large skiff. "Olvir over there could tell you. He's just in from Scotland. Now, away with you. If you have no work with which to occupy yourself, I do."

I made my way over to Olvir, and coming up, I called his name. Olvir whirled about quickly, as if he was being attacked, and I instinctively put my hand to my sword-hilt myself. Then he stopped, looked me up and down as if he could not quite believe his eyes. "What do you want?"

"I am looking for transportation to Scotland."

"I don't take passengers."

"I can work for you. I have served on board ship before."

"Oh?" He grinned, a little unpleasantly. "What sort of work?"

"I was a warrior with Jarl Sigurd Hlodvisson of Orkney."

"Oh?" he jeered. "A warrior with his honor the Jarl of Orkney. A pleasure to meet you, warrior. Do you have a name?"

"Kári Solmundarson."

"Now then, Kári Solmundarson, tell me why I should take a man who has simply walked up to me out of nowhere, claiming to want transportation? How do I know you're not a villain planning on slaying me and my crew and taking our cargo?" Here he sneered a little bit, and I knew he was mocking me.

"I am no villain, and I can work for you as well as any other. I wish only transportation as far as Dyrness in the north of Scotland. If you cannot give me that, then I will find another."

He looked at me appraisingly once again, and then his lip curled a little. "Very well. I think I can use you. To Dyrness, you say? We are going that way, around the north of Scotland and then to the northern Hebrides. We leave tomorrow morning, and if you are here on the shore by sunrise, you can come along."

I felt once again the push of fate at so easily having found transportation to the place I wished to go. I did not question it further. I thanked Olvir, and said that I would be there. He laughed, and turned back to his work, and I thought that he seemed a harsh, sneering fellow. I wondered how it would be on board ship with such a man.

We left shortly after sunrise the next morning, after loading up a number of empty casks and wooden crates, which I presumed were for cargo to be obtained on the way to Scotland. I was immediately struck at how demoralized a crew Olvir had. They were, almost to a man, silent and unfriendly, and had no life in them. Three of them had evidently escaped in the night, and Olvir himself only shrugged and laughed it off, saying that the three who had left must have had too much spirit. Only Olvir, and his second-in-command, a scar-faced man named Herulf, and one or two others seemed to find any cheer or comradeship on board ship.

I soon found out why. Thorodd, the chieftain by whose orders I had nearly been killed in Wales, had been but a petty villain, but Olvir was a black-hearted devil of a man, the likes of which I had never met before and never wish to meet again. He kept his crew in line not by encouragement and praise, but with the lash.

We were only two days out when one of the crew, a somber man named Hrapp, was clumsy in tying down one end of the sail and it came loose, billowing out and flapping until two others caught it and tied it securely. While this would have been a cause for a mere reprimand on most ships, here the entire crew froze into silence, watching Hrapp standing, swallowing convulsively, white in the face. Olvir looked at him, and his grin flashed out.

"Hrapp!" he shouted. "You idiot. You should be thrown overboard for that. But because I am such a good-hearted man, I will not do that." He turned. "Herulf! Come here." Herulf, his evil looking second-in-command, came up, and I found to my amazement that he was grinning, too. I realized that these two men were enjoying the effect they were having. They were feeding on this man's fear.

"Herulf, I think that Hrapp here needs to be taught a lesson. You know what to do, I think."

Herulf nodded, then went to a wooden box that stood in the prow of the ship, and from it he took a many-thonged whip. Then he walked in a leisurely fashion to stand before Hrapp, and said, "Strip off."

Not a sound could be heard but the splashing of the waves, and the creaking of the boat timbers. Every crew member had his eyes fixed on the two men. Olvir had stepped aside, and was standing with his arms folded, watching with satisfaction.

In a single convulsive gesture, Hrapp pulled his shirt off, and then stepped over to the mast. Herulf tied his hands securely to the timber. Hrapp was shaking uncontrollably, and I saw with some horror that there were already lines of knotted scars along the skin of his back. This was not his first time beneath the lash. Hrapp's breath was coming in harsh whines of terror now, and he had his head bowed, his eyes closed. Herulf looked at Olvir questioningly, dangling the whip in his hand as if testing its weight.

"Twenty," Olvir said.

Then I could not stop myself. "Twenty?" I cried. "Twenty lashes for such a thing? You villain, you should be flogged to death yourself for treating your fellow men so."

There was a collective gasp from all the men aboard, and Hrapp himself turned his head to look at me in astonishment. Olvir looked over at me, black amusement dancing in his eyes.

"You wish to have me mend my ways, young noble warrior? Perhaps you should be the next one under the lash."

"I would slay you first."

"Oh?" Olvir looked out at his crew, and shouted suddenly to them, "Which of you will capture me this young man, and protect my life, so that I may teach him a lesson?" To my amazement, I found that whole, demoralized crew swarming about me, and my arms were pinioned before I could draw my sword. My sword itself taken and given to Olvir. None I suppose, wished to be thought unwilling to support Olvir, and to be the next to feel the lash.

"Now, Herulf, finish with Hrapp." I stood there, held securely, while the lash whistled and sang over poor Hrapp's back, and he shrieked and struggled to escape his bonds. Finally it was over, and Hrapp was untied, and stumbled away to collapse upon the deck facing away from us. Then Herulf came over to me, shaking the droplets of blood from the whip, and he grinned at me. "Since we cannot trust you to submit properly, someone will help you strip."

My shirt was pulled roughly over my head, and naked to the waist I was driven over to the mast. My hands were tied above my head, and I braced myself for the first stroke.

Then I heard Olvir behind me shouting with hilarious mockery, "Look, crew, at that lovely smooth back! It will be the last time in his life he has such a back." Then he snarled, "Give the noble warrior forty. It will teach him to keep his mouth shut."

And I stood for my forty lashes, determined to remain motionless and to make no sound as the whip cut bloody crisscrosses on my skin. The pain of the flogging was far less than the pain of my shame, knowing that I had taken up with villains—and I thought it unlikely that I would ever reach Dyrness alive.

11

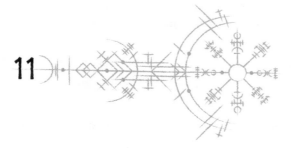

IT IS WITH SHAME ENOUGH TO hang my head, shame enough that it is more than half my wish to stop my story here, that I admit I stayed with those evil men for nearly a year. It was one of the blackest times of my life, during which I felt that I had indeed been damned to hell, but here on earth. I had never known what evil there was among men until that time. I thought that I had plumbed the depths of evil in the death of my wife and child, but Olvir and his men were worse still, for they loved to cause pain and death. They lived for it, fed on it. To this day, it sickens me to think about it.

After I was whipped it seemed that I was more accepted by the crew, and some of their stony-faced hostility relaxed. I am not sure why. Perhaps this was an ordeal that they had all gone through, and only afterwards was one considered truly one of them.

For a week after the flogging I had to go shirtless, until my lacerated back had healed sufficiently that my shirt did not rub me raw. The cuts pained me considerably, although not as much as one might think. I stored up every bit of that pain in my heart, in determination to one day pay back Olvir and his cronies.

In the year I was with them, I never again went under Herulf's lash, although I saw many of my comrades do so, for offenses ranging from serious to insignificant. After that day I did what Olvir told me to do without question, more out of a wish to bide my time for escape than out of fear of a second flogging. Still, he did not trust me. One day he was in a black mood, and came to where I was seated silently pulling an oar, and he stood in front of me for a moment, glowering. Then he reached down and pulled me under the chin and raised my face to him. I did my best to mask my defiant anger, but I think he sensed it nonetheless.

"Pretty boy," he snarled in an ugly tone. "I could have your handsome head lopped off if I so chose."

I looked down and did not respond.

"I could whip you bloody again. I could have you flogged to death."

"Please, don't," I said, in as meek a voice as I could manage. This seemed to satisfy him, for the moment at least. He pushed my face to the side with his hand, spat at my feet, and then strode off, cursing and muttering.

I added that to the list of deeds for which I intended to pay the villain back.

Olvir's mistrust of me provided an unexpected benefit, however. He would not let me off the ship to participate in his evil ventures. In that autumn I learned the terrible means by which he obtained his cargo, to sell at Whitby and other places. He spent the summer and fall roving along the coast of Scotland, and every few days he and a few trusted crewmen went ashore on a skiff, and raided any homes and farms they found. Thus they obtained great quantities of wool, meat, dried fish, skins, and various other goods, as much as they could haul, by robbing honest farmers and house-holders. I also heard that Olvir and his men slew many of these poor folk for sport, but not before raping the women, often before the eyes of their husbands and children. The more I found out about Olvir and his men, the more hideous I found them. Yet, trapped aboard ship, with none other I could trust, there was little I could do to attempt escape, much less to destroy them and stop their career of pillage.

Only during the winter did we all put ashore. It was in a remote cove in Scotland, so far from any settlements that I thought I would die in the frozen wastes if I tried to flee. So I and the others were told—perhaps it was a lie to keep us from running away, I do not know. After my narrow escape from freezing to death in the mountains of Wales, my heart failed me at trying to cross those icy moors alone. So I stayed with them, although it pains my heart to say it.

When spring came, we took to the ship again, and began to sail northward. I knew that we must be approaching Dyrness, although I did not
know exactly where that settlement was. Glum had only told me that it was
along the coast in northern Scotland. My heart rose a little, and I gave more
thought to escape. But still, no way seemed to be open to me.

One clear spring evening, after one of the first sunny days we had had in
weeks, Olvir and his trusted accomplices returned from a raid with the skiff
laden almost to sinking. We were anchored a little way off shore, and instead
of the usual grunts and groans of hard work, there were exuberant whoops
and yells coming up from the skiff. The rest of us looked at each other, wondering at their cheerful mood. When we hauled the cargo on board ship, we
found out why.

As he came on deck, one of Olvir's companions on the raid grinned
broadly, and pulling out a dagger, he pried the cover off one of the casks
they had brought aboard. All of us nearby looked in curiously, and found
that it was filled with a strong, dark brown liquor, whose sharp smell filled
the salty air.

"There'll be cheer tonight, men," the fellow said, and tossed the dagger to
the deck. "There are three more just like it still on the skiff."

Olvir, overcome with his good fortune, invited all of the crew—trusted and
untrusted alike—to drink deeply of the stuff, as soon as the rest of the cargo
was brought on board and the skiff taken up. With some enthusiasm, they all
pitched in to finish the work at hand, and then all joined in the drinking.

My wits suddenly became alert. I quickly decided not to drink any myself,
and to wait and see if an opportunity might present itself to escape while the
crew were drunk, as they all seemed likely to be soon. I pretended to drink
a little, and watched from a quiet corner as more and more of the stuff was
consumed, and a second barrel was hauled out and pried open.

It was a strong drink. Several of the crew passed out, to the amusement
of the others. All were staggering about within a half-hour after the first
lid had been opened. One of the men fell overboard, and none went to help
him—even I did not do so, as I did not want any of the others to realize that I
had not drunk any of the liquor. Olvir himself had collapsed in a heap on the
deck. Herulf was slumped nearby, and by the time night fell, virtually every
man on board was unconscious.

When I felt sure that none were left awake, I stood silently, and surveyed the men around me. I was certain this would be my only opportunity to escape. If I did not take advantage of it, such a chance might never come again. However, I could not simply leave the boat. I felt I had an account to settle, both on my part and on the parts of all of the men who had to bare their backs to Herulf's whip.

A half-moon hung in the sky, lighting the ship and the nearby coastline with a ghostly white light. Close at hand, an object glittered on the deck—the dagger dropped by the man who had pried open the lid of the cask. I went and picked it up. Then I went over to where Olvir lay, his ugly mouth open in a snore.

I took a handful of his hair, and his eyes opened a little, but not enough to really see me. He was still deep in his drunkenness. "This is for all the men whose lives you have destroyed, both on this ship and elsewhere," I whispered fiercely. Then with one quick motion I slit his throat. He did not make a sound.

I then went and did likewise to all of the other men who had been in Olvir's group of trusted cronies. Walking silently among the living and dead men, I counted the ones I had slain, wishing to make sure that all of the most evil ones were dead. When I came back to where Olvir lay, eyes half open staring unseeingly at the starry sky, I realized with a sudden shock that I had not seen Herulf either alive or dead.

At that moment, I heard a noise behind me. I turned slowly, the hair on the back of my neck and arms standing up, and I saw what I had feared. Herulf was standing there, an evil grin on his ugly face. He held an axe.

"So, handsome boy," he said, his voice still slurred with the drink he had consumed. "You thought to find me asleep, and slit my throat like you did the rest. Now you'll be the one to die." He raised the axe, and brought it down. But he was still more than half drunk, and missed me completely. I backed up warily, however. Even a misguided stroke could sever an arm, and I was without any weapon except the short dagger I held.

I bumped into the skiff, lying overturned on the deck, just as Herulf swung at me again, and again he missed, but to my dismay he stove in the hull of the skiff. My retreat was now cut off. My heart sank at the thought that even if I escaped Herulf, I might still be trapped on board this hideous ship.

He came at me again, and this time I ducked beneath his wild swing and gave him a great push. He had brought up the axe again when I charged at him, and the weight of it over his head, combined with my shove, overbalanced him. He fell backward, and went over the gunwale, and struck the sea with a loud splash.

I leaned over the side to see if he had gone under. He frantically flailed in the water. His axe was gone, but he still lived. As I watched, by chance his right hand caught at the side of the ship, and held firm. He pulled himself up before my astonished eyes, until he was holding the gunwale with one hand, and I heard his feet scrabbling for a toehold. He looked up at me, and there was murder in his eyes.

I returned his stare, and fury leapt up in my heart. I lashed out with my dagger. It pierced his right hand, and pinned it to the side of the ship. He did not scream, but his face froze in a silent rictus of agony, and he pivoted on the point of the knife, trapped.

"That," I snarled at him, "is for the lashes which that hand has inflicted upon my back and upon the backs of many innocent men. Die now, let the sea take you if you are not too vile even for her taste." I jerked the dagger out. He dropped back into the sea, and the black water closed over his head. I never saw him come up again.

I stood on the boat, breathing hard, and looking around me. The skiff was useless. A black hole had been broken in its side. It is strange, however, what a desperate man will do. It only took me a moment to decide. There was nothing else for it.

I would have to try to swim to shore.

I knew myself to be a strong enough swimmer, having grown up as I did near the sea. But to swim in the dark to an unknown coast? Still, I did not hesitate long. To drown seemed less fearful than to spend another night on this ship, not knowing what that strange and unhappy crew would do when they woke to find that I had slaughtered their leaders.

I searched until I had found a leather bag among the oddments in the hold. Then I quickly stripped off all of my clothes, and stuffed them into the bag, and cinched it tight. I went to the side, and looked into the dark water. My heart gave a shudder within me, but I steeled myself.

I was about to dive over when a voice behind me said, "Wait."

I whirled around, my terror suddenly doubled, and wondered who I would be facing, stark naked and weaponless—I had foolishly discarded the dagger. It was Hrapp, the man whose whipping I had protested, at the expense of my own back.

My fear, however, was unfounded. He said, "Don't go yet." Then he turned and disappeared, and I heard him rummaging around in the hold. Within a moment he came back, and handed me a long slender object, wrapped in cloth.

"It's your sword. Olvir hid it after you were flogged. I thought you would want to take it."

I looked at him in amazement and gratitude. "But I cannot swim while holding it."

"Strap it to your back. Then it won't hinder you."

He helped me to tie a leather strap around my upper chest, but under my arms, and he secured my sword to it so that it hung down behind me, still in its cloth wrapping.

"Kári, thank you for what you did. They deserved to die."

I nodded. "Thank you for returning my sword."

"God keep you." He reached out and clasped my arm. It was the first time I had done that in a year. It is a sign between honest men, and among such villains I had had little reason to use it.

"And you, as well," I said, and then turned back toward the black sea. I looped the strap of my clothes bag over my shoulder, and without looking back, I jumped in.

The water was icy, and the shock of it nearly took my breath away. I came up spluttering and coughing, and already chilled to the bone. Even so, I could see the coastline in the distance, and hear the breakers on the shore, and I swam toward it.

The sword was, as Hrapp had predicted, little hindrance. The bag, however, was a problem, pulling clumsily at my shoulder and upper arm as I tried to swim. Still, I did not wish to abandon it and reach the shore naked and with no hope of clothing myself. I began to tire, and the swells were increasing as I came closer to shore. I pulled my head up a little, treading water, and it seemed that I was not too far away from land, but my feet still touched only more frigid water.

Then a wave rushed over me, and I caught a mouthful of salt water, and choked. The tow of the backside of the wave pulled me down, and the water closed over my head. I held my breath, but I had already breathed in water. I gagged, and the black world around me went blacker still as my consciousness faded.

———————

THE MOON WAS HIGH ABOVE ME when I felt my life returning. I opened my eyes a little, then retched and vomited up seawater. I lay on my belly, my lower half still being dragged at by the clutching waves. My clothes bag lay a little way away from me on the rocks, and my sword was still tied tight to my chest.

I vomited again, and lay on the rocks for a moment, then I struggled to my feet. My armpit and shoulder had been chafed raw by the leather strap of the bag, and the strap of my sword had likewise rubbed a red stripe across my upper chest. It had tightened up from being soaked with salt water, and it was with some difficulty that I loosened its hold on me.

I looked back out to sea. Olvir's ship still stood at anchor. It would undoubtedly stay there until the sun woke up the crew from their drunken sleep, and they discovered the carnage around them. Perhaps Hrapp would tell them what had happened, but perhaps not. He was a strange man, and his sudden assistance of me at the end was the strangest of all. I have never seen him since that night, and I often wonder what happened to him.

I was shivering uncontrollably, and thought again of my near death in the Welsh mountains. The memory spurred me on despite my exhaustion. I pulled open the knots of the leather bag. Again, they too had grown tight with water and my pulling on the straps holding them fast as I swam. My icy fingers ached by the time I loosened them. The bag had held fairly water-tight, and my clothes were damp but not soaked as I had feared they might be. I hastily dressed, and after that felt more comfortable. I sat down to wait for morning.

As soon as the sky lightened sufficiently that I could see my way, I began walking. I did not wish to be visible from the ship should any look that way. I did not really believe that the remaining crewmen would wish to pursue me, and the skiff in any case was unusable. But I hated the very sight of the ship and wished to put as much distance between it and me as I could.

I walked for miles that day, enjoying the feeling of being my own man again, able to walk if I wished and fearing no man's whip. I saw no one the first day, and the weather remained pleasantly cool and sunny but quite windy. I would have been hungry as well as lonely then, had I not been fortunate enough to happen upon a thicket of juicy black berries growing along the side of a little river as it wound down to the sea. I ate enough to take the edge off my hunger, and put several more handfuls into my leather sack. Then I drank well from the stream before I forded it and went on.

I walked that day until exhaustion and evening forced me to stop, and I rested comfortably enough in a small thicket of stunted trees that cut the wind a little.

Around midday of the following day, I came upon a little settlement that I recognized at once as being Norse. A handsome fishing ship, clearly of Norse build, stood at anchor in the little harbor. I knew that my people had many settlements in northern Scotland, but the Scots of course do as well. It raised my spirits to come first upon people who spoke my language.

I called out to the first person I saw. He was a man of about fifty years, hale and strong but gray-haired, who was walking up toward one of the houses.

When he heard my call, he looked over at me in some surprise, and then came up to me.

"You look like debris that the sea has cast up." He smiled warmly as he said it.

I laughed. The feeling was overwhelmingly pleasant, to laugh again after a year without laughter, to find out that I indeed still could laugh. "You have a keen eye. For I have indeed been cast up on the beach, nearly drowned."

He clapped my shoulder, and it stung the raw spot that the strap of the bag had left on my shoulder, and I winced a little. He frowned and apologized. "Are you wounded?"

"I feel like a well man for the first time in a year. But I am famished and thirsty, and beg of you a little food and a place to rest for a day or so. I have no way to pay you—"

He cut me off. "Don't even mention such a thing. I would take no payment if you had it. Come with me, and we will see to it that you are fed, and you shall tell us your story."

The man's name was Leif, and his wife was Hild. They gave me good food and drink, and listened while I told them of what had happened to me in Whitby and afterwards. When I told them of being flogged, Hild said, her kind voice shocked and dismayed, "You must show us what they did to you!"

I pulled off my shirt, and turned my back to them. Hild cried out in horror at my scars, and I felt her fingers running lightly over my back. Leif said, his lips tight, "What villains, to treat a good man in such a way."

Then I told them of how I had killed the leaders in their drunken sleep, and of the fight with Herulf, and how I had recovered my sword because of Hrapp.

"I hope he is not made to suffer for it by the rest of the crew," Leif said.

"I doubt he will be. He is a closed-mouthed man, and none were awake to see what he did but him and me. None will know if he does not tell."

Then I told them of diving naked into the sea, and how I almost drowned but was washed up on the shore.

"Luck must smile upon you," Hild said. "Few men whom the sea takes ever find their way back out of it again."

"I have been told that I am lucky." My smile dimmed a little. Memory suddenly flooded me. Kári the Lucky. I realized that I had not thought of my oath for months, but suddenly there it was, like a demon riding my shoulder, and I knew that it would not be denied for long.

Leif looked at me narrowly. "I see that there is more story behind you than what you have told us. But the rest can wait for another time."

And we spoke of other things then, but the joy of my escape was suddenly dashed to pieces, like a ship foundering upon hidden shoals.

———————

DURING THE DAYS THAT FOLLOWED, I helped them with their chores, and they fed me and gave me a place to sleep. Leif was a fisherman, and I assisted him as best as I could, although I do not know the trade and probably was more hindrance than help. Still, he was gracious about it, in that and in everything else.

One evening, I decided to clean my sword. I had left it in its cloth wrapping—the sheath was long gone. When I took it out, it was tarnished but otherwise undamaged, for which I was glad. Olvir must have given it no thought after tossing it in the hold. This puzzled me, as it was a fine weapon. Olvir always carried a heavy axe, and perhaps preferred that over even a well-made sword. I do not know.

"You have been a warrior," Leif said, seeing me carefully sharpening and polishing my sword.

"I have." I did not look up. I did not wish to meet his eyes.

"Yet, I think, you take no joy in it."

"I did when I was young. Now, I use my sword only when I must."

He looked at me curiously, and finally I raised my eyes to him, feeling strangely ashamed. "Yet you prepare it for use when you are here, among friends. You are thinking you will use it again soon?" He ended the last statement as a question, and sat looking at me.

For a moment, I simply returned his gaze. "Is Dyrness very near here?"

He shrugged. "Not near, not far. About fifty miles further along." He raised one eyebrow. "It is in Dyrness that you plan to use your sword."

I nodded. "And still I take no joy in it, but look upon it only as a job to be done. I am glad to be alive, yes. But my life itself has been only a burden to me, and a source of pain and death to others. Perhaps it was fated that way, I do not know. I have a job to finish. The next part of it is in Dyrness, and afterwards only one part remains."

"I smell vengeance," Leif said simply.

"You have a keen sense of smell," I said wryly, and would say no more.

I stayed a few more days, and Hild helped me to fashion a rough leather sheath for my sword, so that I could again hang it at my side. I paid them with hard work, as much as I could do. Then I took my leave of them.

The day I left, Hild saw to it that my bag was filled with food and that I had a new water flask at my shoulder before I left, and after thanks and farewells I began once again to walk up the coast.

Mist rolled in and rolled out, rain fell, the sun shined, the wind never stopped beating upon me, and three days I walked. Never another soul did I see on that rough, unforgiving Scottish coast. It was the evening of the third day that I rounded a little headland, and saw a settlement ahead of me, much like the one in which Leif and Hild lived. I knew it was Dyrness without being told.

I met a young man on the shore as I walked into the settlement. He was tall and well-muscled, with sandy hair to his shoulders. His face was already bronzed and weathered by the sun and wind. He was standing close to the nearest house, shaping an oar with a heavy, broad-bladed knife as I came up to him.

"Greetings," I said.

"Greetings, stranger," he returned, and then stopped his work, looking at me curiously.

"Tell me, are there any Icelanders in your settlement?"

He set down the knife, and his curious look deepened. "Strange you should ask, for a ship put in two weeks ago from Iceland. They are on their way to Norway, I think, and will be leaving in a few days."

I shook my head. "No, you misunderstand. I mean folk living here, who have come from Iceland."

He frowned for a moment. "I think that there are a few men here who have lived in Iceland. There has been shipping between here, Iceland, and Orkney for years. I think old Grímbold lived there for a time, and there are Grani and Gunnar—"

I interrupted him, feeling my face flushing and hoping that he would not notice. "This Grani and Gunnar, where do they live?"

He pointed off down the shore toward a little house apart from the others. "They came here four years ago, and moved in with old Geir, a fisherman whose sons had died in a shipwreck, and who needed extra hands to help him. They worked in exchange for food and a roof over their heads. Geir died two years ago, and there they still live. Strange they are, those two. They have few friends but each other, and no one here really knows them." He brightened. "The captain of the ship which put in two weeks ago, though, he is a different sort. Strong and brave, but kind, and quick enough with a story or a song. Young, too. Only a few years older than I am. You should meet him."

"Perhaps. But my business concerns the other two."

"Oh." The curiosity in the young man's eyes indicated that he wanted to hear more, but I turned away and strode off toward the house he had indicated.

I had no further fear or misgivings. By this time, I felt that I was irretrievably damned, and in the previous year had dwelt in the very mouth of hell. Though I had escaped, the oath still held me tight. As long as I lived, the oath, the oath, always the oath.

I came up to the door, and without knocking I threw it open. Grani was sitting inside, alone, a torn net draped across his lap. He had only a moment of horror-struck recognition before I slew him.

Gunnar evidently heard the commotion, and came running from outside. As he entered, and saw his friend slain, he gave a cry of dismay and fell to his knees beside the body, lifting it to him as one would with a lover. I brought up my sword to kill him, as well. He looked up at me, bitter hatred in his eyes.

"Go ahead. Kill me. You have slain the only one whom I have ever loved, and I have no desire to live now that he is dead. I have nothing left. And I see in your eyes, Kári Solmundarson, that you do not, either. Let us both be damned together."

Then I brought down my sword with a cry, and struck off his head before he could say more, for his words cut me like a whip.

I wiped my sword clean and went back outside. A few others had heard the outcry and looked upon me, not knowing what had happened. They seemed unsure of whether to stop me, and unsure whether they should fear my blade, which I still held in my hand.

A man peered in the door of the little house, which still stood wide open. "Stop him! He has killed Gunnar and Grani!"

Several of them approached me, but warily, not knowing if I would strike out at them. They were simple fisherman, not warriors or fighting men, and weaponless as well. I simply stood, waiting for them to come at me. I did not intend to resist, but of course they did not know that.

Then I heard a warm, familiar voice calling out from the other direction, "Kári Solmundarson!" I turned to find myself facing a young man with handsome, even features, clear gray eyes, and long, curling chestnut-brown hair. Before I knew what was happening, he had thrown his arms around me in a warm embrace, and with a sudden flood of recognition I knew who it was.

It was Thorfinn Karlsefni, the young man who had told me where to find my enemies after I fled the Great Assembly, and whose father, Thórd Hesta, had given me passage to the Hebrides.

He drew back, smiling gladly. "How have you come here, my friend?"

To answer that would have taken hours. In the end, I fell to my knees and wept, as the men of Dyrness watched me in silent astonishment.

12

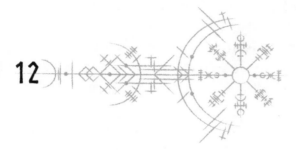

THORFINN STARED AT ME IN AMAZEMENT for some time, as did the others. Finally, he put his arm around my shoulders and led me away. None tried to stop him. He said nothing to me, probably not wishing to make me even more distraught than I already was, but finally he brought me in to the house of the chieftain of Dyrness.

The chieftain's house was small and simple. Thorfinn walked in without knocking, leaving me standing just inside the door, and went forward with the confidence of a trusted friend. The chieftain was old, I could see that even in the shadows, and I wondered how Thorfinn had become so highly favored in such a short time. They spoke together in whispers for a moment, and then the chieftain motioned for me to approach.

I went up to him, every motion of my legs seeming labored, as if they were made of stone. My head was bowed, and I neither knew nor cared whether I would soon be put to the sword for what I had done to Grani and Gunnar.

I looked up at the chieftain of Dyrness, and saw that he was not just old, but ancient. He was bent nearly double, but his broad shoulders stood as testament to a once vigorous man. He stared at me in silence for a moment.

"Thorfinn has told me a little of your plight, and why you have killed Grani Gunnarson and Gunnar Lambason. I had the greatest respect for Thorfinn's father, Thórd Hesta, and I have equal respect for Thorfinn himself. He has pledged his own life to yours, that you did what you did out of desire for proper justice, and that you are a good man and true, and no common murderer."

I looked up at him with eyes that felt dull and empty. "I do not truly know whether I am as good as he has said. But I too hold Thorfinn Karlsefni in high regard, and I would not break such a trust with him. I will not disturb the peace in Dyrness again. I only did so this once from an old issue of vengeance." I frowned at him. "But you speak of Thórd Hesta as if his tale is ended. The last time I saw him, he was hale and strong, and prickly as ever, when he carried me to the Hebrides. It was only five years ago, even if to me it seems a lifetime."

Thorfinn turned toward me. "My father is indeed dead, my friend. He was lost at sea three years ago, along with his whole crew, on the way back from the Orkneys."

I remembered then the voyage I had taken with him, and it seemed like I had been a mere fledgling, hardly aware of the evils in the world, when I fled Iceland. The thought that Thórd and his men were all drowned added to the already insupportable weight on my shoulders, and I felt on the verge of collapse. I again bowed my head, but this time could not raise it.

"My friend is near exhaustion with his grief," said Thorfinn to the chieftain. "I ask you to excuse him and me. I will bring him to my lodging, where I will find him food and a place to rest."

"Go with my good will," said the chieftain.

Thorfinn led me to a small house nearby, and I was given food to eat and mead to drink, and I was offered a place to lie down. Everything that came to me seemed to come through a dark fog, like a pall of death that hung about me. Even Thorfinn's kindness hardly cut through it, and when I slept, it was like the sleep of an evil man who is soon to die, full of dreams of slaughter and blood and damnation.

———————

I KNEW THAT THORFINN WOULD BE leaving soon. In the days that followed I thought much of it, even though at first I did not speak to him about it. For even sunk in despair as I was, one thought was still uppermost—the completion of my quest. I finally asked him about it one evening, as he sat for his evening meal with myself and a few of his men.

"Thorfinn." Everyone turned toward me in surprise. Since coming to Dyrness I hardly ever spoke unless spoken to, and some of the men there had never heard my voice. "Have you heard word of Flosi Thórdarson?"

Thorfinn regarded me for some time before answering. "He is the last, is he not?"

I nodded.

"No. I have heard little that would help you in your quest. After the Assembly, Flosi had arranged to leave with the Sigfussons from Hornafjord, but you stopped all four brothers before they could get that far. I heard they had intended to sail east, to Norway or Denmark, but I don't know exactly where, nor whether Flosi himself ever got there. Perhaps when he realized the Sigfússons were all dead, he left without them and went somewhere else."

"Perhaps. But you are going to Norway, are you not?"

"I am." His expression became more serious. "Kári, is it not perhaps time to give up this revenge? You would take now a long and probably fruitless voyage, just to—"

I slammed my fist down on the table. Several of those present looked at me in alarm. *"No!* I have given my life for this vengeance. I cannot stop now. I only ask if you will take me to Norway. If the answer is no, then I will find another way."

Thorfinn's expression became pitying, and his pity cut me worse than any anger would have. "Kári," he said, his voice gentle, "I owe at least that much to Thorleif Crow, who has been my friend as long as I can remember. But I would take you regardless, because all men speak of your courage and your desire for justice, and I believe you to be a good man who is worthy of whatever help I can give. When we leave, you may come with us."

I looked up at him in confusion. "Who is it that speaks of me in such a way?"

"Many in Iceland, who thought justice was not done at the Assembly in the matter of the death of your wife and child. It is widely said that there has never been a man born to rival your courage and your heart."

I stared at him in astonishment, and when I spoke, my words tasted bitter in my mouth. "My *heart?* My heart is gone. It died in the fire with Ingrid and Thórd, and what has replaced it is made of ice and rock, all frozen, all hard edges. Sigurd Lambason begged for his life. He would have wept had I not struck off his head first. I ended Ketil Sigfússon's life as he stood, wounded and unable to defend himself. He stripped off his shirt so that I might strike him to the heart, and I drove my sword into his naked chest. He asked only that I make his end quick, and at least I gave him that much." I laughed, and it was a harsh, ugly sound. "Arni Kolsson I killed before the eyes of his wife and son. Kol Thorsteinsson had become a wealthy and honored citizen of Jorvík, and I slew him upon his own doorstep. Even Gunnar I slew as he wept over the body of his lover and only friend, whom I had killed as well." I looked around me. "So, Thorfinn—am I a man of heart, or not? What do you say now?"

His men glanced at one another, disturbed by my words. As for Thorfinn, he simply looked long at me. "I say that you are a man whose life was destroyed by ugly circumstance, and that you have been driven harshly by a terrible oath. I pity you with my whole heart. Yet I cannot find it in myself to condemn you for what you have done, for who can say what any man might have done in your place?"

I bowed my head in shame at my own words, and in shame at being the object of Thorfinn's pity. "I thank you," I said quietly, without looking up. "I will go with you, if you will have me." But the knowledge of how I must appear in his eyes hurt me worse than the blows of Herulf's whip.

WHAT MORE SHALL I SAY OF myself? We left for Norway about a week afterward, and my spirits lightened a little simply at being at sea, but still I felt in darkness even during the day. Nothing remains in my memory of that voyage but a continual sailing in shadows that none could see but me.

It took almost three months to reach Norway, partly because we made several stops on the way. We stayed a few days in the Shetland Islands, and at a seaport in Denmark, where Thorfinn knew some merchants and fishermen with whom he wished to renew old acquaintance. I was impressed with my young friend's prowess in sailing. It seemed that he had not been idle during the five years since I had left Iceland, but had made several long ship voyages, and had been twice to Norway and Denmark. He had also gone once in the other direction, to the settlements in Greenland, although he had found the climate there uncongenial at best.

"Cold and harsh," he told me one evening, as we stood in the stern of the ship watching the sun set. "Yet they say that there is a land beyond Greenland, even further to the west, which some have visited. They call it Vinland. It is rich and fertile, and not barren and rocky like Greenland. My father had a friend, Eirík Thorvaldsson, who has been there, and Eirík has a son, Leif, who wishes to go there too. Leif is a good man. He and I will go there together one day, maybe."

"Maybe," I said.

His kind eyes turned toward me, and I saw again the pity in them that I deserved, and also despised. "Perhaps you should give up your quest, and come with me on a different one."

I shook my head. "Thank you, my friend, but I cannot. If I am successful, then after this voyage I plan on taking only one other—the voyage that all men must take, and from which there is no returning."

———————

WE CAME TO ANCHOR IN OSLO, and there Thorfinn Karlsefni and I parted ways. He had business to do, and I had my quest, driving me ever onward.

"I will not ask you again to abandon your quest," said Thorfinn as we stood together on the shore of the harbor. "But I will tell you that I believe you to be a good man, and I believe also you will discover that for yourself before all is over."

"Perhaps. I truly do not know."

He clasped my forearm. "God watch over you, Kári."

"And you, Thorfinn. I thank you for your help."

Then he went back along the shoreline, and I went up into the city, thinking of nothing but the seeking my last quarry, Flosi Thórdarson, who had seemingly disappeared into the wide world.

For a year I wandered in Oslo and the country round about, feeling like a lost child who is sure that just around every corner he turns there will be the face he seeks, yet it was never there. In my travels I relied much on the goodwill of priests and abbots, and everywhere I asked for word of Flosi, but none had heard of him. My clothes became rags and I had no money to purchase others. I was now no better than a beggar. Or, perhaps, I was worse still, for a beggar knows his station in life and may count on finding a place in heaven in the end, whereas I felt lost and homeless, and that my damnation was assured, a thing as solid as the ground upon which my feet trod.

I was pitied by a fisherman of Oslo, to whom I told a little of my story, and he gave me free passage to Denmark. I wandered in that country, too, taking alms where I could get them, and avoiding kicks and blows from any who might seek to drive away a ragged and dirty pauper. Some looked in wonder at the sword that still hung by my side, and no doubt asked themselves if I had acquired it by thievery. I certainly no longer looked like much of a warrior.

Everywhere I went, there was no word, not the slightest trace, of Flosi. I spent two years in Denmark, until I could find a way back to Norway. Then I went up the coast, working a little for food and a place to stay, usually in a barn with the animals. I was given shelter over winter by a farmer north of Oslo, in exchange for hard labor, but I was thankful for it and did not complain.

The months slipped by, until finally I lost track of how much time had passed. Another winter came, and I found my way to an abbey near Trondheim, along the western coast. The abbot, Everardus, was a kind old man, and in exchange for helping the brothers of the abbey care for their animals I was given a warm place to sleep and food to eat. By this time I had given up asking about Flosi, and had decided that it would be my fate to die here in Norway, far from anyone I knew, ragged and penniless and forgotten. It seemed somehow fitting.

Then one day early in spring, Abbot Everardus sent one of the brothers to call me in to speak with him. I was in one of the small outbuildings where the tools were stored, sharpening the hoes and other tools with a whetstone.

"What is it about, Mattheus?".

"I do not know." He gave me a reassuring smile, and patted my shoulder. "But I am certain that it is nothing serious. Father Abbot holds you in high regard, never fear."

I thanked Brother Mattheus for delivering the message, set down my whetstone, and walked outside and across the courtyard to the abbot's dwelling.

Snow lay all about, and it seemed still winter, but the birds called and buds were flushed with green and rose upon the tree branches. I knew that warmer weather was not far off. The abbot's dwelling was set a little apart, and there was a small garden near the door. He liked flowers, I was told, and allowed himself this one small luxury.

I went up to the door. Everything was silent, and I felt hesitant about disturbing the tranquility. I knocked as gently as I could on the door, and a moment later heard the abbot's voice say, "Come."

I opened the door and walked in. He was seated at his simple wooden desk, and smiled at me as I entered.

"Please sit down."

I did so, and looked at him questioningly.

"Kári, you have been a good and faithful helper to us all winter, asking nothing more than food and shelter. Yet, you have never made confession to any here, although several of our brothers are priests and could hear you should you desire it. Brother Thomas, who assists you with the animals, says that you will not speak of your past to any, but seem always downcast, and wonders if you might have a great matter on your mind."

I looked up at him with some reluctance, and when I spoke it was in a quiet, hopeless voice. "Brother Thomas is correct. But I cannot make confession, Father Abbot, for I have done great evil and have not repented of it, nor sought to stop its completion. I have no doubt that I am damned beyond help."

I expected him to rail at me, or become stern, as the Archbishop of Jorvík had, but he only smiled. "God's ability to forgive is unending. You have only to renounce your sin and confess it, and forgiveness can be yours. None is beyond redemption."

"If any man is, then I am."

His expression became serious. "What have you done which is so terrible? I think that you are weighed down by it, and speaking your thoughts to me might relieve your burden a little, even if it is not the same as the confessional."

Great weariness fell upon me. How many times had I told this story? "Father Abbot, since you have asked me, I will tell you, but I must ask you something first. I had given up asking, but it seems that my grandmother was right—that a sworn oath will not let a man rest, wherever he goes. Since

I arrived in Norway, I have always asked this one question before I would tell any man about my past. Therefore I ask you—do you know anything of an Icelander, a man named Flosi Thórdarson?"

To my astonishment, his face brightened, and he smiled at me. "Flosi? Of course I know him. I know him well, he stayed three years with us, and only last fall left for Iceland, as his time of outlawry was done. It was only a few weeks before you came here." He looked at me with frank surprise. "It is strange you should speak of him, for he is also a man who thought himself beyond redemption, but who found it."

I stared at him for some moments in blank amazement, and then I felt once again the talons of the oath sink into me, and this time they pierced to my heart, so that I almost cried out with the agony of it.

"Father Abbot," I said, my voice stretched thin, "do you know what sin it was that Flosi committed, which he felt might place him outside of God's salvation?"

"I do, but it was told to me in the confessional, and must remain unspoken."

My eyes met his steadily. "Then you should also know that I know what he did, for I am the man whose wife and child he killed in the fire."

The Abbot's eyes grew wide. "He said that one man survived...."

"It was me. I have hunted down and slain eleven of the twelve men who were there that night. Flosi is the last."

The Abbot looked alarmed. "You intend to slay him as well?"

I nodded. "It has been my intent for ten years, to kill them all."

"Then praise God that Flosi was already gone when you arrived. I beg you, my son, do not pursue him. He has repented his sin, as you should yours, and he is now a good and staunch Christian. I plead with you, abandon this evil quest."

I stood. "Many have asked me to do that, and still I have gone forward. I have given up everything, and now there is nothing left to me but the quest. Do not ask me to give that up as well."

"You would cling to this evil—"

I interrupted him. "You should know that I, too, am outlawed in Iceland, and that outlawry is lifelong. If I return there, like as not I will be struck down as soon as I set foot on shore. But I must follow him there, to kill him if I can, and be done with this terrible oath."

The Abbot's kind face seemed stricken with guilt and horror. "God forgive you, Kári."

"Father Abbot, I thank you for all the kindness you have shown me, and I ask you to forgive me for placing you in the position of betraying a man you obviously hold in high regard. But as for God, I have betrayed him far more, and I do not think his forgiveness can extend so far downward."

I left him, and without a backward glance I walked from the abbot's house, and across the courtyard. Only minutes later, I was striding out through the abbey gate, still dressed in my ragged clothes, with my sword strapped to my side.

IV

THE BALANCING
OF ACCOUNTS

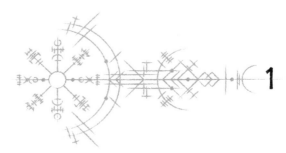

1

IS IT TRUE THAT MEN ARE fated to walk certain paths? Perhaps there are men who know better than I. All I can say is that every time I tried to give up my oath I was confronted with it again, and every time I needed transportation to reach my goal, it was provided. Yet who provided it? Surely it was not God who did such a thing. Was I fated, or did I choose, to do the deeds that I have done? My Uncle Magnus thought he knew, and maintained that I have chosen this path. I wonder to this day if he was right. The day I stood on the top of the moorland above Whitby I felt I had chosen every step of the way. The day I left the abbey in Trondheim, I felt dragged along by a fate that would not let me rest. Which is the truth, I cannot say. As I sit here now, I am certain only of two choices that I have made since the day I spoke the oath—the speaking of the oath itself, and one other, which I shall describe presently. Whether the rest of my actions were fated or chosen, I truly do not know.

I walked through Trondheim and down to the waterfront. It is a busy place, and I was reminded of Myley, and also of Whitby. The latter memory pained me, as I recalled my captivity with Olvir and his strange crew.

I began to ask if any knew whether there was a ship on which I could work as crew in return for my transportation to Iceland. Some men just shrugged and turned away to their business. Others said they did not know.

But finally, I met a tough, work-hardened sailor who told me that there was an Icelandic ship captain, Runolf by name, who had put in the day before, and who might be able to help me.

"He comes here often. He is a good man, Runolf. I don't know if he would have need of you, but he might know if there was anyone else to ask. I saw him up near the merchants' dwellings, in the town, this morning. He has many friends there."

I thanked him, and made my way back up into the town, toward the Merchants' Row, a line of small shops and dwellings which lay parallel to the shore. I questioned some of the men who were there, and finally a tall, broad man with flaming red hair was pointed out to me. As I turned to look at him, he burst into ringing laughter at some story he was being told, and clutched his belt as if to control his own mirth. I smiled a little. He looked better than Olvir, at any rate.

I walked over to where he stood. At first, he seemed not to notice me, but finally he glanced my way, and his eyes passed over me from head to foot. "I'm sorry, fellow, but I have no alms for you today," he said, not unkindly, but the man who had been talking to him snickered.

"I am not an alms-seeker," I said, "but a man who seeks work and passage to Iceland. I have served aboard ship and know the tasks well. I am strong and will serve you honestly and faithfully."

He did not answer for a moment, but his smile faded a little, and he looked thoughtful. "I must admit that you don't talk like a beggar, and that sword is not an adornment which beggars usually wear. But otherwise, a beggar you seem. If you are not truly one, how do you come to be dressed in rags?"

"I have wandered for five years, in Norway and Denmark, working where I could find work, sleeping where I could find rest, often outside in all weather. I have no money to buy clothes, and have had to wear what was on my back. This sword was my father's, and I have worn it now nearly thirty years, and it has been tried in my hand in battle."

His smile returned. "Well enough. I'm sure you are a pinnacle of courage, as well, and have killed many a valiant foe." He gave a glance at his friend, who smiled a little. "Why do you wish transportation to Iceland?"

How I had changed since my youth! Thirty years earlier I would have been goaded by what he said, and driven to defend my honor, first with words and then with the edge of my blade. As it was, I felt a little stung by his mockery, but I also sensed that he was a good man. I knew that in my present state, I could not expect better than ridicule. What concerned me more was how to answer his question. I considered for a moment, wondering what to say.

I have never had it in me to lie, and in the end I simply spoke the truth. "I have sought for ten years the man who killed my wife and child. He was in Trondheim for three years, but left shortly before I arrived here, and returned to Iceland. I wish to follow him to Iceland, to complete my revenge."

Runolf's eyebrows went up a little, and again he exchanged a glance with the man he had been speaking with. "And what is your name?"

"Kári Solmundarson."

There was a moment's silence, and Runolf's smile vanished. In a stern voice, he said, "What you say is impossible. Kári Solmundarson is dead."

I gaped at him. "I tell you that I am he."

Runolf looked at me appraisingly. "Strange that you should say so, beggar or warrior or whatever you are. I have been told much about this Kári, and you certainly do not seem to be him. He was like a god to look at, they say, tall and fine-featured. I have heard recounted how a hundred men slew his family. They say that he brought revenge upon twenty of them before leaving Iceland, and in fact killed three with one blow. He was the best sword fighter that Iceland ever saw. Yet they say that he went off after the other men, who had fled his rage, and he was lost at sea and has not been heard from since."

Runolf's friend laughed. "And now you will tell us you are this hero?"

I smiled a little despite myself. "Whether I am a hero or not, I do not truly know. And whether you believe it or not, Kári Solmundarson is my name, the son of Solmund Thorgrímsson and Hallbera Ketilsdottír of Kolnsey in the Hebrides. I might also add that your version of the story is not quite correct. It was not a hundred men, but twelve, who slew my family. Six I killed before leaving Iceland, and the other six I have pursued to far lands, and all have perished at my sword except for the last, Flosi Thórdarson, whom I still seek. I have wandered for five years in Norway and Denmark looking for him, and who would not seem a beggar after such homeless wandering? I have only found out today that he has returned to Iceland, and therefore it is to Iceland I must go. This that I tell you is simple truth. It is up to you if you will believe me, or believe some wild tale which has grown with each telling."

He looked at me again, long and steadily. "The truth, the simple truth?" He looked over at his friend, who was staring at me with an unreadable expression. "What think you, Ulf? I may be a fool, but I believe him."

"I know not," said Ulf. "I have heard stranger tales that have been true."

"As have I." Runolf turned back to me. "I suppose that if I believe part of your story, then the part about your being an accomplished sailor is true as well? Well, whatever the truth is about that, we shall see. I will take you as a crewman. But first"—he reached into a small sack hanging at his belt—"go buy some new clothes." He dropped a silver coin into my hand. "We will not be leaving for several days, as I have much business to attend to here. But meet me on the waterfront tomorrow morning, and you will go out to the ship and assist my crew in unloading." He clapped me on the shoulder, and left me there, once again amazed at—dare I say it?—my good luck.

The following morning, dressed in clean, new clothes for the first time in five years, I met Runolf at the shore, and was rowed out to the ship by one of his men. For the next five days I worked at unloading cargo, and reloading both empty casks and casks full of merchandise to be taken back to Iceland. I found Runolf's men to be a friendly lot, as far opposite to Olvir's strange and somber crew as could be imagined. I was fed well, and felt welcomed.

The night before we were to sail, some of the crewmen were swapping stories, and someone asked me for mine. I felt reluctant to tell the whole story, so I simply said that I had traveled widely, and had crossed Wales and England on foot, and of my nightmare experience sailing up the coast of Scotland. They demanded to see the white scars that still crisscrossed my back, and several of them cheered when I told them that I had slit Olvir's throat.

"A villain like him deserved it," said one man.

"Why do you wish to go to Iceland?" asked another.

I hesitated. "Because I have kin there, and I wish to find them again."

This satisfied them, and they asked no further questions. The whole story seemed to have impressed them, and my high standing among them was assured.

We sailed the next morning, and met with fair weather, for the most part. Only a few days of rain troubled us, but no storms, and we were never becalmed as we had been on my voyage from Iceland to the Hebrides. Runolf was a hearty, warm-hearted man, who laughed easily, and his men served him out of devotion and loyalty rather than any sense of command. I found myself wishing that I could stay with them, for after only a few days I felt I was already part of the crew. It had been long since I had known such camaraderie. But I knew that even if Flosi was not in Iceland when I arrived, even if he had already fled elsewhere, my oath would not allow me respite. I was nearing the end, and it was driving me cruelly.

Two and a half months later, the lookout saw the dark line of Iceland's south coast in the distance, running along the horizon like a smudge of charcoal. Only a few hours later we could see the white tips of mountains, and the cliffs had grown and had gained a definite shape. My heart pounded within my ribs as if it were trying to escape, to fly away toward that land from which I had fled ten years earlier, where my wife and child slept their long sleep in a little churchyard, and where my best friends had lived and died. It is not my home, and yet when had any man been gladder to see his destination in the distance?

It was late the next afternoon when Runolf's ship anchored off Hornafjord. I worked with the crew to unload cargo onto the two skiffs, while other men were tying up the sails. Runolf was overseeing the unloading. After the first load had been taken off to shore, I walked up to him, feeling in my heart a strange reluctance.

"Runolf, I thank you for agreeing to take a ragged wanderer on board your ship, and I can never repay you for what you have done. But when the cargo is unloaded, I must stay in Iceland. I tell you truly, were I not bound to stay here, I would ask you to allow me to become one of your permanent crew, as I have seldom been among men whom I liked better, nor served a captain who is more deserving of respect."

He looked at me, and a smile flitted across his face. "I knew from the first that you weren't a beggar. You prove it yet again. No beggar could thank me so eloquently. You have served me well, and have paid your transport with your own muscles. When the work here is done, go and God be with you."

So it was that the following morning, I said farewell to my fellow crew members, and was rowed ashore at Hornafjord. My first steps onto the shore felt like some strange dream, where time runs backward, like I was slipping back into my past life. That feeling persisted as I walked away from the little settlement at Hornafjord, and up toward Flosi's dwelling at Svinafell, which only lay a few miles away.

It had hardly even been spring when I had left, but only two and a half months later, the meadows were already beginning to turn russet and bronze. The short Icelandic summer was drawing to an end. I walked steadily, the seabirds calling above me, the wind rustling in the grass, my mind tumbling with thoughts.

It was the end. The very end of everything. Flosi had surely returned to his home at Svinafell, to his wife and his servants and his fine house. What would he do when I walked through the door? Would he beg, as Sigurd Lambason had done, or swagger, like Thorkel Sigfússon? Would he fight nobly like Ketil Sigfússon, or try a cowardly trick such as the one Glum Hildisson had attempted? He was a changed man, Abbot Everardus had said. Would he try to stop me with pious words, like Kol Thorsteinsson had done?

It did not matter. It was truly the end. I would walk into his house, and if he was there alone, I would kill him. If he was surrounded by his men, they would kill me. Even if I slew him, I was certain to be killed myself, once men found out that I had returned to Iceland despite my outlawry, and had already slain a man. So, truly, my story was nearly done regardless of how it turned out.

I topped a little hill, and saw Svinafell in the distance. My heart began to beat hard, and my hand went to my sword hilt. My steps quickened, and when I reached the door, I was almost running. No one seemed to be about. The farm was quiet except for the sounds of sheep and goats, and the ever-present searching rustle of the wind.

I flung the door open, and strode in. For a moment, my eyes were confounded by the darkness within, but I soon saw that there were only two people inside. One was Flosi's wife, Steinvor. The other was Flosi himself.

The first thing that I noticed was how old they both looked. Steinvor's face became deathly pale when she saw me, and she started to speak, but the words caught in her throat. Flosi simply stared, and I thought he looked relieved. Relieved? I had pictured many times what his face would show when I finally saw him, but relief had never been part of the picture. I stopped, caught in my own confusion.

"Kári. Kári Solmundarson. I have been waiting for you. I knew you would come sooner or later." He came toward me, and before I could respond, before I could strike him down, he had thrown his arms around me in a warm embrace.

"I... I have come here to slay you," I stammered.

"I know that." He released me, and when he stepped back a pace, I saw that his eyes were wet with tears. "I will not stop you from doing so, if that is what you choose. But I ask you, let us talk together first. Steinvor, get us food and drink, please, my love."

Steinvor seemed as astonished as I was, but she went to get meat and drink, and Flosi motioned for me to sit. Feeling more than half in a dream, I resheathed my sword and did so.

"I left Norway almost a year ago," he said. "It was a terrible crossing, we left too late. We hit storms that nearly sunk the ship. I feared that we should be lost at sea."

"When I crossed, we had fair weather nearly the whole way." I felt dizzy with astonishment to hear myself respond to him so. Such a conversation, like a meeting between two old friends—it was hardly to be believed!

He laughed, a warm, cheering sound. "Your luck has never failed you."

"Only once." Even then, I could not summon up my old, fierce anger. "The night my wife and child died."

Flosi stopped, his cup held frozen in his hand, and looked at me. I saw the grief well up in his eyes. "Kári, I tell you, that I have done penance for that day ever since it happened, and more every passing day. I know you will never forgive me for what I did, and perhaps you should not. I know as well that you will slay me when this meal is finished. But I tell you truly now, that I would gladly give my life if your wife and son could be given back theirs."

I bowed my head. The grief suddenly seemed insupportable, although I knew then that the anger at Flosi was gone.

The fire was dead in my heart.

"So much could have been avoided," Flosi said, "so many deaths, had your action at the Assembly gone well. At the time, I feared what might happen, and I rejoiced when I knew you would lose, but now I wish that it had gone against us then. It might have been so, had Mord Valgardsson not attempted to betray us."

I looked up at him, and frowned. "Betray *you?* How do you mean? He owed no allegiance to you. He simply wished for my cause to succeed, and overreached himself when he tried to bribe Eyjolf."

Now it was Flosi's turn to frown in confusion. "Why would Mord have wished for you to succeed? He came to tell us when he found out you alone still lived, and asked us what he should do about it. He asked us if we wanted him to kill you as you lay wounded, but Ketil and I would not have that, feeling that we had already done a heinous enough deed in burning Bergthorshváll. In the end, we decided that he should simply watch you carefully, and report to the Sigfússons whatever action you were planning. He said he could do so most easily if you lived in with him and his wife. So he invited you to do so."

"But he assisted me in my planning, at every step!"

Flosi shook his head. "So it seemed. It pains me to have used such a deceit, but Mord insisted it was the only way. Mord had all along been one of our staunchest allies. In fact, Mord was here at Svinafell more often than he was home with his wife, in the time before Hoskuld Thrainsson was killed. Hoskuld accounted Mord one of his closest comrades. It was Mord who first warned Hoskuld that you and the Njálssons were jealous of him and wished him dead, even before Hoskuld's wedding. Each time Mord overheard you and the Njálssons plotting Hoskuld's death, Mord came in secret to warn him, and thus Hoskuld escaped again and again."

The ashes in my heart began to rekindle, but the anger was no longer directed toward Flosi. I had no doubt that he was telling the truth. But had we truly been so stupid, not to see this?

I kept my voice calm with an effort. "Flosi, there were no attempts on Hoskuld's life. The Njálssons and I had no wish to kill Hoskuld, and his death only came when his insolence had grown intolerable, and even then he himself drew sword first. And afterwards, I think Skarp-Hedin was more grieved at it than were many of Hoskuld's own kin."

There was silence for some moments. Flosi leaned back in his chair. "Kári," he said quietly, "swear unto God that you speak the truth."

"I swear before the holy throne that none of us plotted to kill Hoskuld Thrainsson nor attempted to do so. The day he was killed, we had been going to him to speak with him only, for Mord had told us that Hoskuld was plotting an ambush, and we wanted to confront him about it."

"Mord told you that?"

"He did. At every step, Mord told us what Hoskuld was planning, and who he was conspiring with."

"Dear God," Flosi said weakly. "We have both been played for fools."

I stood up suddenly. Steinvor gave a little gasp, and grasped his arm, as if to shield him. Flosi said, a little breathlessly, "Kári, if you are going to kill me, well enough. God knows I deserve it for what I have done to your family. But I ask you, seek out Mord Valgardsson afterwards. He lives still, I hear, and should be made to pay for what he has done."

I looked down upon him, and as I did, something in my heart seemed to untwist. I reached out my arm to him, and after a moment, he reached out and clasped it, his eyes wide with amazement.

"Flosi, oath or no, I renounce my claim upon your life. Let my broken oath be lain upon my soul, along with the countless other sins I have committed. But now, I shall go to wrest the truth from Mord. Then, if I still live, I shall come back here, and we will speak further about it."

Flosi lent me his horse, and I rode off across the meadow where Hoskuld Thrainsson had died so many years ago, toward the skirts of the mountain where the little farm of Hof lay.

On horseback, the journey only took the better part of a day, but I had started late, and was forced to camp when the light finally failed. I could not sleep for the heat within me. It was the first time I had felt that in years, and I wondered at it.

I arose early and continued to ride. I came to Hof by mid-morning, and tethered my horse at a railing in the front of the house. It looked much the same as I remembered, but in some disrepair. I remembered that Mord had never cared much for work about his own house, leaving that to his strange, silent wife, Thorkatla.

"Too busy twisting others' lives into ruins to mind his own house," I muttered as I came up to the door, and threw it open.

Mord was sitting inside, drinking from a large wooden cup, and he looked up at me as I entered. His face registered no surprise, but his dark eyes flitted about in an amused fashion.

"Kári, my friend,. You've returned, despite the sword of outlawry hanging over your head. You always were brave. I saw you coming from a distance. I knew it was you, there is none other like you. I thought I'd wait for you in here. Have some mead, I pray you."

I advanced upon him, and drew my sword. "Mord Valgardsson. I swore to kill twelve men, and I have spent ten years, traveling the world over, and have slain eleven of them. Flosi's life I spared yesterday, and if what he has said is true, then your life I shall take in his place."

He looked completely unconcerned, and took a sip from his cup. "Oh? And what did Flosi tell you?"

"He said that you fed lies to both the Njálssons and to the Sigfússons, and set them upon each other. That you stood back and watched them slay each other, and did not speak a word to stop it."

"Fed you all lies?" He grinned. "I did that. Give each animal food unto its kind, isn't that the way? What better did you deserve?" He stood, and his face was twisted with a bitter hatred I had never seen before on any man. "What did you little lordlings deserve, but what I gave you? You were easy enough to dupe. Who was it that arranged for you to kill Thrain Sigfússon? I did. I was also the one who warned him that you and the Njálssons would be coming to seek compensation, and I advised him to refuse it. It was I who brought you news of his bragging and swaggering, and it was I who told you to take action against it. Then I went and warned Thrain that you were coming, and told him to get his friends together to defend him. And all of you did as you were told, like the obedient children you were." He paused, bitter triumph flickering in his eyes. "I thought I had failed then, because I did not count on Njál and Ketil being able to reach a settlement. But later, I found that Hoskuld Thrainsson was as gullible as his father had been. To Hoskuld I said, 'Take care, for the Njálssons wish you dead,' and then I said the opposite to you and the Njálssons. And all of you believed it! Fools! Never have there been any fools such as Skarp-Hedin and his idiot brothers. Even I did not expect them to believe so readily that such a weak-kneed young colt as Hoskuld Thrainsson would try to ambush them, but they swallowed the lie whole. And Grani Gunnarson and Gunnar Lambason came along just in time to provide a story of an aborted ambush." He laughed. "Those two? They had no skill, nor any interest except indulging in their unnatural passion for each other. Inept young fools. They would have more likely cut their own horses' heads off by mistake than succeed at ambushing anyone. Yet even so, I have succeeded." He gestured out of the open door behind me. "And with all of them gone, Sigfússon and Njálsson alike, I have taken the money I have hoarded for years, and I have bought up the land left behind. Yes, the land on which Bergthorshváll once stood is mine now."

I felt the waves of arrogant evil beating upon my face, like the waves of heat coming from a fire, and I wondered that I had never felt it from him before. Had I been blind, or had he simply been so practiced at evil that I could not have seen it even if I had tried? I came up to him, sword pointing at his chest. His eyes, still restless, flickered back and forth across my face.

"So, you will slay me now, Kári, Lucky Kári?" He laughed again, a spiteful and hideous sound. "What will that gain you? Your wife is dead, and your son. Your friends the Njálssons are dead, too. You have wasted your life chasing around the world for the twelve men who happened to be there the night Bergthorshváll burned, while the one who caused it all was living here in comfort." His grin flashed out, white in the half-light. "If you kill me now, what will that avail? My wife is dead. I am an old man, and can have only a few more years left even if the fates are kind to me. I have spent the last ten years in ease here in Hof, and where have you been? What ease have you known?" He tore open his shirt, and bared his chest to me, like an obscene parody of the noble gesture with which Ketil Sigfússon had ended his life. "So strike me here, Kári the Lucky. Strike me to the heart. The men about here who know me, and who know you are outlawed, will cut you down like the villain and murderer you are. Let you bleed out your life in the dirt. It is better than you deserve."

I stood for a moment, looking with astonished eyes at him. Every time in my life that I had thought I had plumbed the depths of evil, I found that there were men in whom it went deeper. The Sigfússons now seemed honorable men to me. Thorodd, the petty chieftain who had tried to have me killed in Wales, seemed as a bothersome fly, hardly worth my attention. Even Olvir had only been a study in evil, a pale reflection, compared to this man.

Mord's smile widened, and for the first time his eyes rested upon mine and stayed there. "I thought so," he sneered. "You dare not. Now get you hence, before I tell my servant to go spread the word that you have returned, and you are forced to flee again like the cringing dog that you are."

I gave a great cry, and struck him with my sword so hard that the point pierced all the way through his chest. Just before his eyes slid into the blankness of death, a flash of astonishment flickered in them, and then was gone. As he fell, my sword hilt was wrenched from my hand and fell with him, and with a clatter he collapsed to the floor.

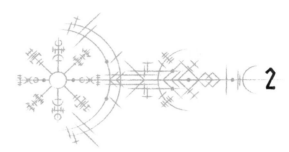

2

IT IS NOW TWO WEEKS SINCE I slew Mord Valgardsson. I keep asking—is God just? If so, Mord must be burning in hell at this moment. For myself, I am no longer so certain that God is indeed just. So often the wicked live and the innocent die. I cannot comprehend it.

I left my father's sword where it was, piercing Mord's body. It seemed a fitting place for it to find rest. As for me, I shall not bear a sword again. Kol Thorsteinsson, you were right—to put down one's sword is truly to relinquish a burden. Kol smiled when I slew him, on his doorstep in his new home in Jorvík. Now I understand why.

Flosi has gone to the men of the District Assembly, and told them of my return and of our reconciliation. He has told them of the treachery of Mord Valgardsson and the reason for which I slew him. Among these men was a sandy-haired twenty-five year old named Tjorvi Gudmundsson—the same one who as a youth had seen me coming out of the marshes of Kringlumire after killing Ketil Sigfusson, and who had predicted that I would one day return to Iceland. He smiled when he saw me, as if he had been expecting me. Strange, for no man could have reasonably expected me to return, and in fact I did not expect it myself. But the fates are strange, and Tjorvi is a lucky man to be able to read them so closely. I often wish that I had that ability.

Based upon Flosi's words on my behalf, the men of the Assembly have granted me permission to stay in Iceland until the next Great Assembly, at midsummer next year. All seem certain that when the Great Assembly meets again, my outlawry will be rescinded and I shall be allowed to remain here indefinitely.

It has taken me the better part of two days to tell this story to the lad who writes this for me, and his patience and his pen have been tried sorely. I shall not impose upon them much longer. My story, or at least what I have lived of it thus far, is told. Flosi tells me that he has delayed as long as he will, and will leave tomorrow morning for Rome with me or without me. I will be on board that ship.

Will I ever return here? It is a question which none can answer. Not even my friend Thorfinn Karlsefni can say for certain. Karlsefni is now back in Iceland after a two years' voyage to Vinland with his friend Leif Eiríksson. That story is worth another manuscript all of its own, and perhaps he will one day find his own eager young lad to record the adventures he had there. But if Karlsefni, who is the finest sailor I have ever known, cannot predict if I will return from this voyage, then none can.

I must ask—do I truly deserve to return to Iceland? Probably not. But little will that affect the outcome, I would guess. When I was young, I thought that men always received their just rewards, that there was justice to be had on this earth. Now I wonder if there is even justice to be had at the hands of God, who let my wife and child die and allowed the man who willed their deaths to prosper for ten years further.

And what should be my fate? Do I deserve to find rest here, after all of my troubles? Am I an evil man, or a good one who has been driven to evil deeds by circumstance? Once again, I doubt any can answer. Probably the question is meaningless in any case. A man is what he does. His intentions mean nothing, accomplish nothing, are nothing.

Runolf, the Icelandic ship's captain who brought me here, told me that I had become a legend here in Iceland, like the heroes of old. I have found that it is true. However, I have noticed a strange thing. Men are happier to believe in their image of Kári Solmundarson, the golden-haired impeccable sword fighter, than to know the real Kári, whose hair is beginning to gray, whose hands are rough from pulling oars, and whose back bears the scars not of valiant battles but of the ignoble blows of a whip. I find that I am not really welcome here, not because of the deeds I have committed, but because men sometimes love their dreams more than they do reality.

So perhaps it is best that I go with Flosi, and vanish from this place again, and leave men to their glittering images and visions of heroism and valor. What harm will it do them? Perhaps it will give them a little hope that there is truth and courage and goodness in this poor, wicked world.

So Flosi and I will go to Rome for absolution, for the sins we have committed during our long and sorrowful lives. I do not know if I have any hope that it will be granted to me.

Flosi is certain of forgiveness. *I* am not.

Yet, I still have hope that it has not all been in vain. Perhaps I will return one day, back to these shores that I first touched over thirty years ago, in the company of Skarp-Hedin, Grím, and Helgi Njálsson, who still remain of all the friends I have ever had the best and truest. Ingrid and Thórd lie here in the land where they were born, and when I come to die I would rest easier next to them—my only child, and the only woman I have ever loved, or ever will.

If God truly keeps men and women in the palm of his hand, as the churchmen have told us, perhaps he will see to it that I may live long enough to return. Let my last words written here be that I still do not truly know if a man is driven by fate, or makes every choice himself. I still do not know if I am good or evil. I know only that I am one weak and foolish man, and whether God has a plan for my salvation, I cannot say.

At this moment, I have no such high-flown hopes. I wish for nothing now but to see the mountains of Iceland once more rising from the sea, with the light of the rising sun shining red-gold on the glaciers. If I may one more time in my life see that sight, and arrive safely upon these shores, I will ask for nothing more.